MIMOSA ROAD

Also by Ruth Linnea Whitney

Slim: A Novel of Africa

Mimosa Road

A novel

by

RUTH LINNEA WHITNEY

2022

MIMOSA ROAD
A novel
By Ruth Linnea Whitney

For Judith Marie, my brave-hearted big sis

Contents

PART THREE

PART ONE

"While gorgeous to look at, the beauty of the mimosa tree is only skin deep. The blossoms, feathery and fluffy, look like cotton candy and have an intoxicating scent. However, its seedpods are poisonous to pets as they interfere with the neuro-transmitters which send signals between nerve cells. Consuming mimosa seeds can result in muscle tremors, spasms, and convulsions."

Jake Emanuel, Certified Arborist

Prologue

Nothing in the look of her foretold the dark path her life would follow. Not the jam of light-brown curls, the face softened by thick bangs but longer than she liked and slightly off-kilter, as if the two sides didn't quite match. Calling her pretty would be a stretch. Appealing would be more on the mark. But she liked the green tint of her eyes, their bright, inquisitive gaze, and the nimble grace of her hands with their long fingers.

Her first week in college, she lost ten pounds, started wearing Henry Miller-style wire-rimmed glasses, and straight hair in a shoulder-length blunt cut. These touches did nothing to soften her image. Still, she won the attention of Will, who had no inkling of his own extraordinary good looks. He could have had anyone and he'd chosen her.

Hindsight offers clues to the acts she carries out as a grown-up person, hindsight being a lot keener than foresight. Consider her name, for instance. It was her father's brave choice, her mother having named her big sister Lucy. Though it was his turn, she resisted his choice. "Cassandra. A Greek name. It's pagan."

But he prevailed. "It's not pagan. Do you know what it means, Cassandra? One who has the gift of prophecy. That's Biblical."

"She's no prophet."

"You don't know that."

"She's an infant."

"Give her time."

Time revealed that the name suited her, though the match delayed its coming-out to the world. Her modest bearing and native reserve masked her prophetic gift to those who assumed a prophet must have a big presence and a big voice. Cassandra had neither. She ducked the limelight. Yet she had a prophet's gift. Not the kind that predicted the future, but one that perceived injustice and joined an effort to upend it.

Her sensitivity to oppression was her father's legacy. Carl Frederickson had a fire in him for justice. Family lore had him joining the Communist Party in the Thirties, though when she asked him about that association, he winked and shook his fire-red hair. "Cassie, Cassie, I left all that when I met your mama." Cassie could never fathom why he married Mabel. What drew him to her? People said she was pretty in those days, but he wasn't one to be blindsided by surface beauty. Sometime after their marriage, Mabel began attending an evangelical church and adopted a fire-and-brimstone fervor.

As a small child, Cassie sat with her mother in the pews. Once, the preacher told his sermon with a felt board. He moved the felt pieces around the board to show the story of the man blind from birth. One felt picture showed the man begging by the road. The second showed Jesus putting mud and saliva on his eyes. The third showed him washing in the Pool of Siloam. The last one showed him opening his eyes and realizing he could see. Cassandra loved the felt board story, and the miracle stayed with her. But when he didn't use the felt board, his voice turned into a rant, often about sin, and she shut him out. Finally, when she turned twelve, she refused to go. Her mother's ardor felt toxic, like an infatuation with a man too fond of the booze.

She stayed home with her father, who didn't go near the church, but kept his fire for justice. She caught that fire, his yearning to make the world better. The yearning sometimes came to her in dreams, in inklings, in waking images that floated up from a rose bush in full bloom or from the shadow of a stone. It came as a hum deep in her belly, the sense that something was not right, she must say something, do something. It was a hum felt rather than heard, a subliminal nudge, like the sense you get when you feel someone unseen watching you.

The fire stayed with her as she grew, in embers but still warm.

In 1974, she left home for a distant country. She'd married Will by then, and they had two small sons. Together, the four of them left their comforts and ordinary new beginnings, waved their good-byes to bewildered parents and friends, and traveled 9000 miles, give or take, to a country about which they knew nothing, except what it no longer was, the Belgian Congo. Joseph Conrad called the country The Heart of Darkness.

If she'd not left home for such strangeness, Cassandra might have remained innocent of such darkness. But she made the journey to a place stranger than any foretelling. There she learned the deep truth of Conrad's words. And there she became an unlikely assassin.

One

Cassandra is Cass now to those who know her. She sits ruminating in the living room of the house assigned them for committing to this place. Two years. Can she make two years? Maybe. If she can get through this present hour until Will gets home. She spent the morning in what passes for a shopping district here and missed her chance for a jog while the boys were in kindergarten and pre-school. Afterwards, against the white sound of their whining, she does stuff around the house that Leon, their house man, would be doing, were he not at the funeral of an uncle, the second uncle-funeral in three months.

Now she's watching her two adorable boys and ruing the moods she inflicts on them. Is she taking pleasure in her sons' company? She is not. She is like that moth shimmying up the glass sliding door dividing the living room from their large front deck. Tiny tendrils draw the creature sideways across the transparent surface, wings open and still. Bound to glass, the moth is seeking an opening, a way out.

"My picture's a barn. Barns have to be red," Matheo says imperiously.

"But mine's Rudolph," Corey cries.

"I thought you were sharing boys," she says.

"I'm a sharing boy. He's a stingy rotten warthog."

Corey's small face caves from the horrors of the depiction. His wail sweeps over the pile of crayons, drawing paper, Cass' armchair, and the grey moth making minor tracks across the sliding glass door.

She propels herself to her knees, snatches the crayon from Matheo's fist, snaps it in two, and lays the halves between the boys, whose faces register astonishment and sorrow. "That was mean, Mommy."

She quite agrees with Matheo. Guilty as charged. At times, she's a dreadful mother. Mean as parrot poop. She stands abruptly to vacate the scene before she does something even meaner to her fair-haired boys. She goes to the phone on a table near the kitchen and dials. "Susan?" She and Cass moved here within days of each other. They have children of similar ages and husbands who head off to the 1800-bed hospital each morning, leaving the two good women to cope with supplying a household from shops in the city whose offerings include, say, toilet paper and canned strawberry jam flown in from Cape Town. They fall into friendship out of despair at the strangeness and at hunger for adult companionship, and, early on, get used to covering each other for childcare. "I'm fine. Not at my best here is all. Any chance you could pop in while I take a quick jog? Fantastic. You're a peach."

Will never liked her jogging after dark in Seattle, and when they moved here, made her promise to give up jogging after sunset. '*This is Africa, for God's sake, there are hyenas prowling after dark, and who knows what-all, there are locals who believe the hyena can inhabit a human soul.*'

She gives him her promise, if a nominal one, braided with the common-sense God has given her. She's never seen a hyena, day or night, knows nothing of the soul or its inhabitants, and, besides, takes that hyena story for an urban legend, Kinshasa-style. Well, it isn't sunset yet. She has time, though not much, before the sun perches its red ball on the sky's crest, before darkness dethrones the ball, and before Will returns from his day at the hospital. She thinks of the lapse in her promise not as dissembling, but as protecting a jewel they have in common, the tranquility and lightness of the marriage. This is where she lives now, in thrall to a desire to keep the jewel whole, not cause it to implode over something as inconsequential as a jog around the neighborhood. Moreover, it's her jog, not his, her day to arrange as she sees fit. Then, why not tell him? Because she doesn't believe she can persuade him to see it her way. Better to let it lie.

Locals have been predicting rain for days now as they move away from the dry season, which they call winter. There's that and the heat and humidity rising in confirmation. But despite all the talk and the foretellings, she never gives much thought to rain. She told Matheo's kindergarten teacher at the American school in Kinshasa, she's lived her entire life in Seattle, after all, and rain doesn't much worry her. Ms. Barder, seasoned expat, regards her for a moment, brows lifted, amusement held in check and says something to the effect that *this is not your Seattle drizzle. Rain here is as far from Seattle drizzle as the bullet train from The Little Engine that Could.*

Touché, she thinks, recalling the exchange. *Whatever. Well, the rain can just hold off until I squeeze in my run.*

She kicks into a slow jog through the neighborhood named Mimosa Village for the tall mimosa trees towering over the front yards. Their foliage of deep rose strands springs outward from a yellow core, strands resembling the crown of a crested crane. She moves on down the street, peopled mostly with other families who traveled the same high-wire route to a far country. Here is Susan's house on her left, immediately next-door to their own. Her friend, mother of two, has paused her nursing career for now, as Cass has her teaching. She's a pretty blonde who moves on the voluptuous side of plump, in stark contrast with Cass, who lives a half-size above too skinny. Susan wears a perennial band-aid on her left great toe for reasons she won't discuss, though they talk about everything else, such as her husband Logan's ho-hum approach to their sex life and a corresponding interest in the only female resident in his program. His other prevailing enthusiasms include diagnosing rare infections and lobbing a winning serve in tennis. He has a particular way of talking, in a series of rushes, often dropping the ends of phrases, as if he's lost the trail of his idea. His sentences sometimes trail off before she can catch their meaning. His problem is not dementia, as he's only thirty, but she supposes some loss of emotional heft for the idea.

Susan and Logan Shaw are the only couple she knows who have been in therapy, a recent phenomenon related to his dalliance with the female Internal Medicine resident. Cass is fascinated by this admission from a woman who won't unveil a blight on her great toe. When she passes on this intimate detail of her marriage, Cass has a hint of gratitude, a blip, really, that Will isn't a dallying kind of guy. Or, is it hubris to assume her marriage is uniquely immune? Okay, maybe. Still, honesty, what he calls straight-shooting, is so essential to Will's makeup that she'll go to the mat with anyone who suggests he could ever lie to her. He has this duty to be honest, just as she has a duty to ferret out injustice and make things right.

But she's honored to be Susan's confessor and can't think what her life here would be like without her. No question she's eased her through a bizarre and challenging environment. More than that, she's grateful to Susan for being her friend at all. Cass' native reserve inhibits the kind of self-revelation that encourages friendships. She's a bit of a hoarder in this regard. She takes her time, months, maybe, even years, to reach a level of comfort and ease with another woman that rises to friendship. But Susan has an exuberant openness, and, with Cass, at least, has skipped the foreplay and picked up as if they've been intimates forever. Of course, being here, so far from home, may have loosened her normal hold on being Cass.

It strikes her now that this gratitude to Susan for being her friend is the same indebtedness she once felt to Will for choosing her above all the others. Not that she'll say as much, ever, to either of them. No. She'll hold onto that secret for dear life.

Next to Susan and Logan, across a bright fuchsia bougain-villea hedge, are Cliff and Marybell Barnes, a mildly religious couple whose three teenaged sons have persuaded a python to inhabit their basement. Not that the python had a say in the matter. Cass doesn't know the details of capture, but they managed it and found, also, a family of white mice to shut in with the python. A few weeks after their arrival Cass and Will accept an invitation to observe the monthly feeding. They stand on the far wall to witness the ritual, snake semi-coiled in-wait, mouse quivering, darting, weaving here and there on the con-crete center, helpless to evade the predator's stealth. In perhaps fifteen minutes, moving hardly at all, the python corners its prey, drops its jaw, opens its mouth and snatches the creature crosswise. For a time, the pink tail keeps up its sweep over the concrete, though eventually it, too, ceases. The python gnaws the plump body until only the tail remains visible then disap-pears inside the maw. From here, the python walks the mouse down its throat, muscling on alternating sides. Ultimately, the python coils its long body into concentric circles and forces the mouse into its stomach. Cassandra watches the violent death with a full-on gaze until the meal is consumed, the ritual ended. She thanks the oldest Barnes boy, who tells her with a wink, "Anytime." She has no plans to return, though her own reaction surprises her, more fascination than revulsion for what she's witnessed. There's also a temptation to sneak in one night and release the mouse, one she resists.

She jogs on along the perimeter of Mimosa Village, which isn't a real village as Zairois know them. More a suburb of Kinshasa's urban sprawl, a gated compound for physician staff and families of the 1800-bed hospital President Mobutu named after his mother, Mama Yemo. In consultation with an American surgeon, Bill Close, he has the houses designed to suit the sensibilities of Western expatriates from North America and Europe who will comprise most of the community: three-bedrooms, two Western-style baths, and kitchens equipped with modern electric appliances. Outside the gate to Mimosa Village and across Mimosa Road, a real African village has just celebrated the installation of a single water tap, its first, for its one hundred or so inhabitants.

She jogs on, waving to the sentinel standing at the entrance gate and tries to imagine his off-duty circumstances. She doesn't know where he lives, but she can estimate the paltry sum he makes as a sentinel. She can discern behind his casual wave and placid expression a resentment and perhaps anger toward the strangers who live in the lavish estates he guards.

Sweat streams down her forehead and neck while her lean body settles into its stride. Her lips form a smile as she reaches the tennis courts on the far opposite corner from her house, then thunder sounds and clips her buoyancy. Seconds later, lightning veins the dark air over the courts and rain pummels her bare head. There's your beloved air-natural, she thinks as she gauges her options and spots a mango tree nudged up to the tennis court. Bending, she tucks herself far under its branches and the thick growth providing some shelter for her bare skin from the pummeling. She wears only shorts and shirt sleeves and begins to shiver, knees on the grass parking strip as sweat turns watery on her neck. Folding her arms to her chest, she squeezes her eyes shut against the liquid blur and the gaze of Matheo's kindergarten teacher with her wry observation about tropical rain and The Little Engine that Could.

Inside the leaves, green and thick, and the smear of pounding rain accented by the odd slap to the tennis court, she imagines chunks of pavement floating up from the red earth, the mango tree unbinding its roots, the world rearranging itself, and her shivering self being carried into the afterlife. Assuming there is one. She's no longer so certain of this coda to history. Her history, in particular. Daylight is closing on her now and letting in night in that sudden way of the tropics. Maybe this truly is the moment she meets her comeuppance and comes face-to-face with the careless disregard for common sense that lives under her skin like an influenza that erupts when her resistance is down. Here is the evidence, deep and telling, circling inside. She's absolutely the sort of ridiculous woman who heads out under a threatening sky for a run that could have waited until morning. Now she's caught out in darkness.

Under the mango tree near the tennis courts in Mimosa Village, the deluge takes a breath, the rain lessens and ceases altogether. But there's wind now and darkness. Fruit bats fly out from wherever they were hiding and sweep long and high over the tennis court, the same fruit bats that appear during late afternoon tennis matches she and Will have and usually lose, thanks to her, with a few other couples, including Susan and Logan. She's always enjoyed seeing the fruit bats swoop overhead, but now those winged rodents brushing the sky, dark upon dark, might be birds of prey.

She ducks out from under her mango refuge, towels her face and neck with a handkerchief snagged from Will's drawer and sets into the remnant of her jog and her return home where Will is waiting, and she steels herself against the fallout.

But there is no fallout, no outburst from Will when she returns home a bit after his return from the hospital. He's wet, too, having been caught by the tail of the downpour. He stands before the open refrigerator, assessing his chances of a hot supper any time soon. Thankfully, all of her earlier domestic doings include a casserole that lacks only a twenty-minute warm-up. "Just needs heating," she tells him, turning to face him and stepping into his lean muscled arms, kissing the warm niche behind his ear, as a wordless peace offering for her sin that remains unmentioned for the moment.

Two

The rains begin. Sofia feels the air thickening and humidity rising and crawling on her skin, in her nerves, in breasts tender as if with child. She knows the big rain her body foretells may mean danger to the house where she lives with her three children, a short walk from the Zaire River. There is a man, too, Gabriel, her husband for seven years. But he keeps the hours of a man without cares. He goes to his job in daytime, but too often the morning light wakes her and she finds him already gone from their sleeping mat, or perhaps he never slept here at all. If she asks him where he goes at night without her, he says, I had a bit of business to do. What is it to you, woman?

Woman, he calls her. Maybe he has forgotten her name.

But after his son was born, he removed the woven bamboo roof from their house and laid a tin roof with wide eaves to protect the walls made of sticks woven like a basket and daubed all over with mud. Is stronger, he said. It will withstand the rains and it will last until my son grows into a man. Maybe he did it only for his son, Elombe, and not for the wife he forgets. Elombe means brave one in their language, Lingala. Sofia does not care. The image of Elombe growing tall and strong pleases her. It was a fine thing that man did. One day, she will ask him to make a strong door out of wood for the entrance. For now, she will enjoy the new roof. The first rain pelted the bare-earthed hut with its new tin roof, but let the dwelling stand firm and dry and never touched his son.

Such a rain was new to Madame Cassandra, and she came to her house to see how they fared. 'Just making sure you're OK,' she said.

Sofia pointed to the tin roof. 'Gabriel, he made it. We are OK because of that.'

'That is a good roof," Madame said. Such pride Sofia felt in those words and, for that moment, in her husband, too.

Madame was not long in Africa when first she walked through the small village across the two-lane from Mimosa, the village-that-is-not-a-village, named for a flowering tree. It is no more than a kilometer from her house, but to Sofia, that place called Mimosa is a dream, like pictures in magazines sold at kiosks near the Okapi Hotel. She met Madame early one day as she squatted over her mortar and pestle, pounding cassava flour for the fufu that is their mother food. Gabriel had slept on their mat the night before, and he stepped outside to find the strange White woman beside his hut. Madame had a few Lingala words, and she spoke them to Gabriel. "Mbote, Sango nini?" Good morning. How are you? Gabriel frowned at Madame and barely said, "Tikala malamu," good-bye. He touched a finger to his nose, as he took himself off to catch his fula fula to his job.

Sofia wanted to tell Madame there is no help for some men, but she could not say this in words Madame would know, and she said only, I am sorry. And Madame shook her head and said, 'Nayebi." I know.

After that day, Madame invited her to her house. Sofia stopped first before the sentinel, who sent her a rude look from his high station at the rich people's gate. She knows that look from the one Gabriel gives when she asks where he goes at night. 'I come to see Madame Cassandra. She invited me,' she tells the sentinel. 'Yo. It is so?' he speaks with a lip of scorn, but he lifts the iron bar, and she walks through and up the paved street, counting the houses. So few, each big like a hotel. Plots big enough for many houses and green grass growing even in the dry season, and touching the houses. At her hut, Sofia must sweep the dirt clean and pluck each blade near the house. Snakes must not find a place to hide. Mimosa people don't worry about snakes. Sofia even hears of one house whose people invite a snake to live inside.

Snakes are not for friendship. Sofia knows this. She cannot imagine what they must be thinking.

In her village, there is no iron gate, no paved street, no tennis court, no house grand as a hotel. Still, Sofia does not want to live inside the high gate, for such wanting cannot live inside the life she knows. What is the point?

Sofia may be a stranger to her husband, but she is no fool. She knows another rain is coming and she must take care to prepare. She re-fastens the cloth doorway and places new red bricks at the entrance to make a small wall against the water. When evening comes and supper is finished, she instructs her two girls to wake her if rain wakens them. When night falls, she tucks the mat of Elombe close to hers. They sleep.

They sleep too well. In the thicket of a night storm, Sofia wakes, not to the noise of the rain but to the sudden stillness of the rain ceasing. And not only to stillness but to the absence of the small round boy tucked on the mat beside her. The two girls cling to sleep. She does not know how. She bounds upright and snatches the cloth she fixed with such care. Elombe is a strong boy. Maybe he tore the cloth and made a tunnel to crawl through. She snatches aside the cloth and roars out through the darkness to scan the hardpack for the small boy. She stands tall in the robe of night and makes stepping circles on the sodden mass. Wide, frantic circles all along the earth surrounding her hut, always with a mewing sound in her throat, and a plea rising to the night. *Where is my sweet one, where? Where are you?* She prays to Nzambe, Creator God. *Bring him back to me.* She goes on in this way stretching her circles long and far.

Time and hope have no boundaries until her circles take her to a flame tree not far from her hut, and her bare foot prods a slip of roundness slapped up against a clump of bamboo. His fat hand rests on a round stem of a fallen bamboo. Her hand reaches out and meets the tiny thumb, the bare arm, the silent chest. She lifts him from the bamboo into her arms, still mewing, praying, and keening, too. He is cold. He has no more breath. She returns to the hut and lies with him on the mat, her hand cupping the cold, round face with wide dark eyes that call to you and invite you into his world. What world now? She wants to go wherever he has gone. She remembers when her belly delivered him to Mama Yemo Hospital and the nurse wrapped him in the blanket she brought, and Sofia took him to her breasts. So strongly he drank. She tries to remember if he is two years nearly three or three years nearly four, but she cannot. She only knows his name means brave one, and facing down the storm is his last brave act.

The sun shines hot on the fine tin roof of the small hut. Again, there is no Gabriel on the mat when Sofia stirs. Sleep came late, late in the night, and when her first-born, Kamina, calls, "Mama, what is wrong with Elombe?" Sofia moans, remembering, first pushing away the night horrors, then pushing hard against the new day. But like her mother, Kamina is a clever girl who must find her own knowing, and she moves in close and lies her head on the shoulder that will not rise. "Kufa, Mama?" she says.

"Anh, kufa." Dead.

They lie together with Fimi, the younger sister, past the hour of dressing for school until Gabriel returns from his bit of business, smelling of old whisky and sour fish. His eyes turn wild as he reads the story on the mat. A cry bellows from his deep pit inside, filling the small hut. Together the girls cry "Tata, Tata," but his bellow drowns their cries until he soaks up breath enough to bend down and yank Sofia to standing. He pulls back an arm and lands a hand to her face. Another. The sound of striking flesh fills the hut and moves Kamina to grab her father's leg with her small hands. He shakes her off with a quiver used for mosquitos and other pesky bugs.

"What is this? What have you done to my son?"

"The big rain. He is drowned. I could not save him."

"Zoba," idiot, he says, and "Zabului," devil.

"Molangi." She spits the word, drunkard.

The striking hand pushes her back to the mat, where his boy lies, too. There is no sound from Elombe when she lands.

At the entrance, that man turns and faces her again. "Woman, you are dead to me, too." He backs outside, tearing the cloth from the doorway.

There are hours when no one stirs. Only sounds leave the hut and weave outward circling and entering the doorways of huts close-by. The three under the fine roof cannot stop their keening, for the sound holds Elombe in their hearts. In the hours of high sun, no one comes to see the source of the sorrow, though talk rises abroad in the small village.

At last, in the golden time before darkness, the Old One of the village stands where the cloth screen once hung. She bows, not speaking, until, at last, Fimi sees her and says, "Mama, Ndoki is here."

A witch, the child says. Most in the village know her as Mama Kundi, a name that came late to her, after death came for her man, Stephane, and her two sons found a new place to be home and she found this small river village, and here she stayed. The name first found her when a child heard her playing her kundi in a patch of light. And the name made sense to the child, for it means light in her language, and he felt the kundi soften the edge of a hard sorrow. She and the name have never parted.

But this small one calls her a witch. If she is a witch, what spells does she cast? None but a spell on death. For death has stayed far from her. So long is her life. No one else in her village is close to her in years. What more can life ask of her? She has given her man her own two babies. She has carved her heart into pieces of sorrow she must carry forever. She cannot let them go.

Now her smile plays strangely in a field of wrinkles as Fimi burrows into her mother's side. The old mouth lets go a laugh, a dry braying sound. Fimi covers her ears.

Sofia sees her and sends the name, ndoki, off with a tired shake of her matted hair. "Mama Kundi." For this is who she is.

"What brings sorrow to this house?" Mama Kundi wraps her voice in a low tone to ease the child's fright.

"My son, my son, my son." Sofia plies the words over and over, as if she cannot bear their ending.

Mama Kundi presses together hands that are worn and creased like firewood ripe for burning.

Fimi scrambles to stand in the doorway before her. 'Tata says Mama is dead, too. He is so angry."

Mama Kundi turns a hand into a fist and slams it into her open palm. She makes a low sound of half coughing, half mooing.

"Mama is not dead. See?" Fimi says.

"Anh-hnh. I see," Mama Kundi says. "And where does Tata Gabriel take himself?"

Sofia dry-spits on the mat, where she has risen to sit.

Mama Kundi's arms open wide, "We must make a fine grave for this sweet boy."

"A fine, big one. Big enough for me, I must go where he goes," Sofia says.

"NO, Mama," the two girls cry together,

"Do you not hear your children? You are not dead, too."

The mother of Elombe places a large mortar upside down just outside the doorway. Now all the village will know there is a death in her house. Soon drums in the village take up the story of Elombe to weave out for broadcast along Mimosa Road. By the next new day, Sofia has left the mat. She has carried water from the village spigot and washed the body of her son. She has gone to the riverbank and washed herself. She has warmed the chicken mwambe the Old One brings. Kamina says, "Mama, we must find a shovel. For Elombe."

"Anh hnh," yes, so we must, Sofia says. She cannot think if Gabriel has one. Or, if the shovel went with him. It must be so. That devil! Let him use that shovel for his own grave, then. She must find another before the moon rises.

A voice lifts behind her, drawing her thoughts from moons and shovels and digging. "Sister, I know of your sorrow. I hear of it."

She turns and seizes on the face of Daniel, Gabriel's brother. Gabriel is the fist-born of this family, Daniel is the younger, with a roundness that Gabriel lacks and eyes that rest on hers without asking or judging. "Which sorrow do you speak of? The drowning boy or the leaving man?"

"Leaving? What is this?"

"Gabriel cannot stay with a woman who lets her boy drown."

"Ezali bosoto." It is rubbish. The words blasts from the kind, plump face that is unused to yelling.

She laughs at the outburst that must have surprised even himself, and she tells him, "He is a devil but I must find a shovel."

"I come with a shovel. You must show me where his grave will be. From this day on my way from work I shall stop here to see you and your children. I must know how you get along."

"But you have already your own wife and children. Three children. You have worries enough."

"My brother is one who brings shame to my family. What kind of man does this? I can't bear to let his actions be our whole story. I cannot walk away, too. Do you see? What kind of man does that, my sister?"

The week following the deadly rain, the boy is laid in the earth. Daniel brings a tall man to pray for Elombe, and this man prays to Nzambe and Jesu Christo and he reads for her boy in a sing-song way. Daniel speaks of the boy and his bravery and how he is with the ancestors now. The village women stand with their pestles in hand. They make a circle around the large mortar. Each, in turn, strikes her pestle to the rim of the mortar and so they make a pattern sound to mark the boy's footsteps into the country of the ancestors. Mama Kundi plays her kundi, this harp of her childhood in the far country of the North. The harp has a small carved head, a quite wide carved belly, and eight fishing strings stretched taut between the two bodies. Mama Kundi holds the harp against her chest and the fingers of both hands pluck-brush the strings over and over in a rhythm that marks the sadness of the hour. There is no escaping that sadness. But she believes the kundi is the house where the goddess lives, and the voice of that goddess singing through her fingers also brings a consoling spirit to this place.

While Elombe's body lowers into the hole that Daniel dug with the other men, the women keen for a long time. The cries, ragged and high, send sorrow into the air above the clumps of earth layered over the small wooden box. Sofia keens, too, that she will not be going where Elombe goes. The women bring chicken *mwambe, fufu,* and *saka saka,* and they feast in Elombe's honor. And nobody says Gabriel's name.

The weeks after Elombe's burial bring Daniel to her hut. All the village knows of his coming, for he leaves his Mazda car near the village spigot, and he, alone among the visitors, drives a car. He walks the clear bumpy path to Sofia and her girls. He comes straight from his office in the Ministry of Communication wearing leather shoes made in London, trousers, and a tunic, called an abacast, the color of sand. He wears no necktie. For this is the way of authenticite. It is for authenticite that their children have African names. What kind of country sends you to prison for naming your son Peter or your daughter Mary? But so it is in this place since authenticite. Names of this kind are forbidden now. Mobutu Sese Seko himself wears an abacast and he, alone, wears a cap like the skin of a leopard. He despises weakness and he wants to be a wild creature himself, free to devour as he will. He despises all things Western.

Now Daniel comes without fail. Instead of a shovel, he brings an envelope stuffed with Zaire-dollars and places it in

Sofia's hand. "What is this? I cannot accept." She pushes it toward his hand.

This displeases him. He tucks it firmly against the back of her hand. She surveys his face, the heat raising droplets under his chin and his jaw as the air gathers itself for another rain. Daniel is the brother who stays true to his duty. She feels his effort of kindness toward her. What kind of man does this? he is asking. Always asking. She cannot refuse. He will not allow it. She studies the abacast he wears, made of fine fabric that tells her he is rich enough to give her Zaires for food.

How can he be a brother to a man who leaves without seeing his own boy placed in the grave?

He is not hers. He has his wife, Alicia. Sofia knows this, of course. But he is more hers than Gabriel ever was. She never knew where that man might go or how much he might drink, when he might strike her, or when he might enter the hut bearing the kind face she barely remembers from the early marriage bed. Sometimes she could not stop herself from yelling at him, especially when he was too filled with beer to properly aim his fist. The girls could forget the mean, drunken times, so happy were they to have their real Tata home. Now they smile when Daniel calls from outside the hut. "How are my beautiful nieces today? And school? You must make your mama proud." How then can Sofia refuse the Zaire-dollars Daniel offers for her girls? She cannot.

As the weeks carry her forth from the night of Elombe's big rain, Sofia finds she can bear each new daylight and each moon rising. She can think less of the small wooden box lowered into the earth. For now she is thinking, *Daniel will come today.*

Three

A knock breaks into Cass' musings. About air-conditioning, of all things. She wears a sweater against the chill inside, while the boys play on the deck in shorts, shirtless and barefoot. To Cass, air conditioning is the felt-equivalent of elevator music. Of course you can't bear the bruising heat for long but you can give yourself a brief reprieve from hours of canned chill. What a waste of space and energy. She steps on a dining room chair, stretches up to the control box and clicks the button to off. She steps down, removes her sweater, and lets her bare skin absorb the warmth. She goes through the kitchen to the door to find Sofia from the River Village.

"Sofia! What are you doing? Come in. Come in."

The young woman steps into the kitchen. Cass stares through the blanket-silence and finds herself wondering how Sofia must see this house after her own hut, and what she must make of the people who live here. Though an easy walk apart, the two villages inhabit different time zones, even different centuries. Cass hasn't been there for some weeks. But whenever she does enter the community she knows as the River Village, she feels as if she's stepped inside the seventeen hundreds. Then she wonders if such thoughts are condescending.

Cass shows her to a dining room chair and puts the teapot on to boil. Sofia stands before the table and refastens the waist of her pagne, the colorful wrap skirt Zairois women took up after authenticite. When Cass sets the two steaming teacups before them, Sofia finally sits on the front chair edge, sips her tea, and brings out the story she's come to tell. "I come for asking, Madame Cassandra. I wish to work for you."

Cass' laugh sounds jarring to her own ears. "You want me to hire you? Doing what?"

"I am nanny. You have need. Is possible?"

"I see," Cass says, vying for time while she remembers the sort of expatriate she meant to be as they prepared their move to sub-Saharan Africa. Not a colonialist who hires a nanny or a houseboy, she knows that much. In fact, once she comprehended the complexities of shopping here and cooking, she acquiesced to a houseboy, Leon. She calls him their cook. She has to make life livable, after all. But nix on the nanny, which would surely be too much for her prophetic sensibilities. She spoons grains of sugar into her cup and stirs, gathering an appropriate response to the petition before her, in muted tones, as a token of her activist scruples. "Thank you, Sofia. I'm so sorry. I have no need. But do let's remain friends."

Sofia stands and walks to the kitchen, turns, slanting her face away from Cassandra. "Of course Madame, you have need."

Irritation at the woman's failure to drop the matter nicks Cass. But she plies an even tone into her response as she stands. "I'm sorry you had to come for nothing. I know it's stifling out there. Shall I drive you home?"

Sofia stares at the linoleum between her plastic Bata shoes and Cassandra's sandals, silence full between them.

"Is there something else, Sofia?" Cass speaks rapidly to press ahead of her advancing annoyance.

"Daniel. He came to us, you know, after Gabriel left."

"Gabriel. Is he . . . your husband?"

"Annh. Husband no more. He leaves after the big rain."

"He left you and your three children? That's awful. What's rain got to do with it?"

"That rain, the one that took my son. Must you not know this?"

Sofia's affect has a flatness that belies the chaos of a life undone and infuriates Cass whose voice takes its own course now, words colliding, shrieking. "Took? What do you mean took your son? How . . . How would I know this? I've heard nothing of this."

Sofia gives her a fleet smile. "The rain comes. Elombe goes out. My too-brave son."

Cass can't stem the tears or speak for a moment then gathers herself as Sofia tells the last of her story. Daniel, the brother of Gabriel. He help us very much."

"Your brother-in-law. That's good. I'm so glad."

"Daniel is not like his brother. So much help he gave us."

A warning ticks inside Cass. *So much help he gave us.* The tense is wrong. "So you said."

Sofia's voice drops to barely-audible range until Cassandra has to lean in to hear the news. The day she waited until the moon rose and still no Daniel. Another day, still he did not come. Three days more when she traveled by fula-fula to his house and his wife, Alicia. Always before she had the look of a stylish madame with her hair in tender braids and her fine new pagne tight around her waist. Always before she served her tea and biscuits on a silver tray. But on the day of Sofia's last visit she serves nothing. Her hair is in shambles, her face streaked with tears, and she can barely make a straight sentence. At last, her news. It is a week now that Daniel does not come home. After three nights, she went to see what was what. At the Ministry, his friend met her there. 'Where is Daniel?' she asked. He was gruff, told her to shush, which was not his usual way.

'Let me walk you out,' he said to her. And they walked out of the building onto the street, many steps from the door and the ears of the men inside. 'Daniel was taken by the guards of the president,' he told her. She took to screaming, and he placed his hand over her mouth to stop the sound. 'Listen. You must be so careful,' he told her.

The Ministry men spoke of a cadre. Against the President. They suspect not only Daniel but two others in the Ministry, taken together. They believe Daniel and the others make a coup against the President.

Alicia asked this man, Daniel's friend, what coup. For she did not know of any coup, ever. She told him, 'No. That is not possible. Daniel is not that kind of man.' This friend of Daniel said he believed her. But the president, he said, must take great precaution, for he knows there are many who wish, out of jealousy to banish him from office. 'He must take such care,' he told her.

She wanted to smack that man's mouth for saying such words. But she did not. Alicia is not that kind of woman to smack a man, even now. She is a woman who carries her tea fixings on a silver platter. And what she did next was ask this man, 'Where is my Daniel?' He told her he was taken to Kinshasa Prison and there he stays. She asked what plans they had for her Daniel, and this man he did not know.

Cass hears the long story about Daniel and why he stays away. At last, she lets out a loud exclamation of frustration, half-growled, and five-year-old Matteo bolts into the dining room. "Mommy, what's wrong?"

Cass kneels to the gray carpet and surrounds him with her bare arms and soft murmurs. "No no, Mattie, don't worry. Could you do Mommy a favor and go show your brother how big boys pick up their toys?"

He stiffens his plump torso, frowning. "He knows how already. He just doesn't like it."

"Well, you're the big brother, aren't you? You can set an example. Go on."

Matteo's frown deepens and he stomps from the room.

Cass takes Sofia's hands in her own. "Oh, Sofia. Are you planning on visiting him?"

"Anh. It is far. But I must go with Alicia. We can bring him food."

"Maybe I can help. Let me figure this out. Come in, sit down again. You'll have more tea? Or something to eat?"

"I must go to my children."

She nods and releases Sofia's hands. Sadness, disbelief, or some blend of the two flatten Sofia's affect and raise a corresponding rage in Cass. This is the work of the Ministry. But they are Mobutu's henchmen. They don't act without his permission. He's the one behind this. Her breath quickens. She wants to vomit on the air he breathes. Instead, she covers her face with her hands for a moment to collect herself and figure a way out of these sorrows for this young woman who lives alone now in the River Village with her two girls, and no way to feed them.

"Au revoir, Madame Cassandra," Sofia says at last.

Cass watches the plastic Bata shoes slip down the stairs, around the corner of the house, and disappear into a life she cannot know. She knows the hut and the mats where they sleep with an open fire in the dirt center where Sofia cooks their meals. She knows the two small girls who wait for their supper, perhaps at this moment. She does not know if the derelict husband has left money for food or tuition for the school they love, and, if not, how, then, they must live.

As if waking from a stupor, she pushes down the steps and around to the front walk, calling after her. "Sofia. Wait. Tomorrow, then. You can start tomorrow."

Sofia nods, and Cass sees her through the gate just as Will exits his car. When he joins her on the walk, she sends him her news on a laugh. "I hired a nanny."

"You've gone over to the dark side."

"So it seems." They step from the hedge of purple and rose bougainvillea blossoms along the walk framed by coleus plants. They move through the light tinting gold and the heat seizing her shoulders as she tells the key elements of Sofia's story. "Can you believe it?"

"Mobutu? His so-called Ministry? I find it entirely credible that he'd detain somebody like Daniel who must see right through him."

"We have to do something."

"Let me ask around. I agree it's inexcusable. But keep in mind that we're outsiders here. We don't want to make it worse for this guy, Daniel. I've heard stories about Kinshasa Prison. There have been people. . ." He ceases mid-sentence and raises a hand to his throat, mimicking a throat-slicing. "Don't try anything funny."

"What do you mean?"

"What I mean is, I know you, Cass. You see this stand-up guy, Daniel, brutalized by the thug who thinks he's God Almighty's emissary. You want to get in there and do something, somehow. Guess what? This is the Grand Canyon. You're in a tiny rubber raft. You can navigate some rapids. But you can't change the canyon. You can't tame it. You're an outsider. An incomer. Okay?"

"Okay," she says, looking into his eyes, stark blue and earnest, and the modest nose with the small thatch of freckles that have never faded. In high school, he had a bigger crop of freckles that, somehow, couldn't obliterate his good looks. Still, he has this tiny remnant that he can't lose. It's who he is. Like the woman keen to jump in and do something about some abuse, some breach of kindness, much of her passion has faded, but a trace remains. He knows it's true. Or, he suspects it. "Okay," she says again, with as much conviction as she can muster.

Four

The invitation comes from the office of the President himself: "The honour of your presence is requested by President Mobutu Sese Seko in reception at the Palais de la Nation, Gombe District." The invited, physicians at Mama Yemo Hospital along with spouses, will be greeted by Mobutu himself. Still burning from Sofia's revelations, Cass doesn't know if she can bear standing in the same room as that man, let alone touching his hot flesh. She considers declining. Spouses are add-ons, after all, included as a gesture of politesse. The polite assassin, how quaint, she thinks. In the end she goes along, out of curiosity and from a low-grade hope of making her disapproval felt. "Nothing funny," of course.

Early the Friday evening of the reception, she and Will mount the steps of the presidential palace, situated near the Zaire River in the Gombe District of Kinshasa. Months before on the trip over, they stopped in France and drove the fifteen miles from Paris to Versailles. This Zairois rendering of the French homage to its royalty tells volumes about Mobutu's hubris and narcissism, with its surround sculptured gardens and grand front facing while his subjects go hungry. From her reading, she understands that this palace pales next to his real palace, Gbadalite, in his village birthplace. That's the true Versailles of the Jungle, featuring swimming pools, night club, four-star hotel, and runway that accommodates a Concorde he often charters, probably for visits to his other domains, vineyard in Portugal, 16th century castle in Spain, and 32-room mansion in Switzerland, all supposedly paid for from public money. It's widely reported that Mobutu makes no distinction between the public and the private purse.

They near the top step and move toward the domed center. Cass takes Will's arm. She alternates her focus between the glowing opulence and her own rage, though since that first eruption in the kitchen, she's worked to keep her choler in check. After all, she can't be a constant slave to uproar. She has her two sweet boys to think of, her life to tend. Anyway, as Will reminds her, they are outsiders. There's nothing they can do.

They enter the cavernous room and eye a line of well-wishers snaking around the perimeter. They fall into line and begin their approach with the others. She weighs her resolve. Since the invitation arrived, she's been toying with possibilities: Ask him to his face if he remembers the moment he went from promising student of Winston Churchill's writing to assassin of political enemies. Make her handshake noticeably limp. Lift her hand above his own and refuse to lower it, while holding eye contact.

Ever at ease in social gatherings, Will strikes up a banter with the guy ahead of him, a doctor originally from Dubrovnik. A tall blonde whose reddened complexion and powerful physique suggests he's only recently left the rugby field. She often sees him in bikini swim trunks lounging by the pool at the Okapi Hotel. He's known in the wider surgical community as the general surgeon whose only cases are hernias. This raises the narrative that a hernia-repair is the only operative procedure he mastered in his Dubrovnik medical school, and, perhaps, explains why he's at Mama Yemo Hospital to stay.

Cass glances at the centerpiece of the long snake: the man known to Zairois as Papa Marshall Mobutu. Black horn-rimmed glasses, leopard-skin toque, and puckish mug with a half-grin that won't deign to clue you in on his amusement. Although his photograph is mounted in every public place, even the last roundabout on Boulevard 30 Juin, the main thoroughfare in Kinshasa, this is Cass's first actual sighting of the man who joined Patrice Lumumba's Mouvement National Congolais, took part in his killing and installed himself, in 1965, as head of state. In 1971, he changed the country's name from Congo to Zaire, and his own name, in 1972, from Joseph-Desire-Mobutu to Mobutu Sese Seko. He makes frequent radio broadcasts to his subjects, whom he addresses as *Ba Mama, Ba Papa, Citoyen, Citoyenne*, always tacking on *President et Fondateur de la Revolution.*

Cass edges closer to the sweat-stained hand, pressing her own palms together. In a prayer pose, she realizes, never mind that she left the habit of praying on the pillow of her small childhood bedroom. Maybe she ought to try it again: *Help. Quick. Help me decide my next move.*

About six persons back from Leopard Man, her heartbeat takes an uptick and she feels short of breath, as if she's been running. Another step. Moisture at her temples, at the base of her scalp. *Should get a haircut. Short hair works better in this heat. Susan can give me a trim. If Susan were here, I might have the spunk to refuse to shake that hand.*

The Yugoslav takes the hand held out and shakes with vigor. Leopard Man returns his own vague smile. Will steps forward, shakes the hand with less vigor and gives Leopard Man his enigmatic half-smile. A voice rises over her left shoulder, that high, raucous laugh. Susan. Startled from her languor, Cass moves in step to face the President straight on. His hand stretches toward her. She lifts her hand away and touches Will's shoulder. "See you shortly," she tells him and withdraws from the line. *No, I won't check for his reaction,* she thinks. *Let Mobutu Sese Seko evict me from the room, if he likes, or from the country, for that matter. I'm not touching that flesh. It's not happening. He has a roomful of subjects falling in line after all. I'm nobody.*

Movement eases her breathing and gives her courage, and instead of meeting up with Susan and Logan Shaw, who've joined the snake, she crosses to the hors d'oeuvre and drink table quite far from the receiving line. A Zairois tending the table wears a boubou shirt of black, yellow, and green fabric imprinted with the image of Leopard Man himself. Zairois storekeepers tend toward a surly stiffness when serving expatriates. A remnant of colonialism, she suspects, a holdover from Belgian disdain for its African subjects. This Zairois, too, holds himself with gravity, but no trace of surliness. "Qu'est-ce que vous desirez, Madame?" He gives a slight bow, a dignity he deems fitting in the presence of Marshall Mobutu.

She brings out her best college French, learned from a professor who picked his up from a mistress in the French countryside during World War II. Hers may be inelegant, but good enough. "Un verre de vin blanc, s'il-vous plait."

The solemn young Zairois hands her a glass half-filled with white wine. Cass sips and turns to watch the snake gain upon Mobutu and survey the remaining crowd for a friendly face. Finding herself among strangers, apart from her three mainstays, she steps into the center of the room, closes her eyes and lets the music backdrop surround her head and cushion her discomfort. Rich strains of choral music that she rather likes, if a touch military like the Marseillaise. The Zairois national anthem? Surely not at a festive gathering. But who knows?

Cass' hand, tanned and lightly freckled, touches the top three buttons of her fuschia silk blouse. She sips again, opens her eyes. From here, she can observe the receiving line. So far as she can tell, no one else has resisted the handshake. She contemplates joining Will, already caught up in a circle of hilarity across the room, beyond the snake, with an expat couple who live down the street, the Agassis. He's Persian, she, American, both followers of the Baha'i faith. Will occasionally plays tennis with the husband, and enjoys it though he's a bit keen on winning, he tells Cass, and has to be watched for cheating.

"You're not a fan?" She turns in the direction of the voice. A young Zairois, not exactly handsome but with a smile wide enough to melt a room. Trained on her. He must have seen her refuse the president's hand. She feels like a child caught at some minor delinquency. A flush sweeps over her face and suddenly she wants nothing more than to escape that gaze and make her way down those wide front steps to the Mazda. But that would only arouse more interest. She fingers the top buttons of her blouse. "Moi-meme?" You talking to me?

"Oui, Mademoiselle. Human behavior. It is a hobby of mine."

"A hobby, is it? Anyway, your English is excellent. You must have a good ear."

"Two years at the London School of Economics will do that for a person. Even me. An employment perk for agreeing to be in the government employ."

"I thought bureaucrats were supposed to be fat and drive a Mercedes." Teasing now, a lilt of flirtation in her voice. *Don't be ridiculous, Cass. What are you doing?* But she can allow herself to admire his physique, lean and taut like a serious runner. No harm there.

"Ministry of Finance. Advisor of Something-or-Other to Marshall Mobutu." His big laugh circles overhead, as if Something-or-Others are not worth a piffle of his trouble. She loves his dismissive riff on the system. "Xavier," he tells her.

"Cassandra." She shakes the hand he offers. "And how do you come to advise the President?"

"I knew him first in Katanga."

Katanga. The breakaway province. In the months before moving here, she read about that mineral-rich province seceding from Congo. About Patrice Lumumba, Congo's Prime Minister at the time, opposing the break and meeting his reward by firing squad. About Belgium, the United States, and Mobutu all playing a part in the murder. Cass studies the lean face that wears a sheen of teasing. She can't imagine such a face siding with Mobutu, but why else would he be Minister of Something or Other? She wants to ask about his loyalties in Katanga, but says simply, "The breakaway province."

"So it was."

"Isn't that where Patrice . . ."

"It was. And he was a prince among men." He clips the surname and slips in a velvet add-on that takes her by surprise: "In fact, I was one of the students protesting on that day.".

"In 1961, wasn't it?' she says.

"Some moments in time live on in us, do they not."

"One of our American writers says something to that effect. "The past is never dead. It's not even past."

"William Faulkner," he says.

"I'm impressed."

He shrugs off the accolade and says in a voice fleshed with mirth, "Of course, I knew Marshall Mobutu, but Marshall Mobutu did not know me. back then." With that, he says,

"Well, I'm off then. I must, how do you say? circulate. A pleasure, Mademoiselle Cassandra. Perhaps we'll see each other again."

"Sure. Why not?" she says. Knowing it's only a pleasantry, she feels a pang of loss as he turns away.

Five

The sign looms high above Sofia and Alicia, standing at the gates.
PRISON CENTRALE
DE
KINSHASA.

Though silent on their wooden base, the words sound inside Sofia's head, like a radio turned to full blast. Like static when she cannot find the slot for tuning and the dial remains in-between. What kind of day is this? What kind of family are Alicia and Sofia becoming, that they should stand beneath such words? This is not a family for such a place. They are a family who knows kindness and would never steal a grain of rice from another. Once, in a long-ago summer of hunger, Sofia saw her father catch a runaway chicken that had trespassed into her mother's kitchen garden. Sofia wanted to capture it, and take it inside to her mother's pot and have a feast.

But there would be no chicken mwambe that night. Her father grew so angry, he nearly squeezed the life from the chicken. "No child of mine will ever be a thief. We are not that kind of family. You'll have dried fish and rice, and be grateful, too."

Sofia made a pouting face for her father. He lifted the writhing chicken from his own arms to hers and made her carry it across a wide field to the neighbor's plot, where it belonged. He watched until the woman of the house stepped into the yard and took her chicken from Sofia with a single nod of her head. There was no sound from any creature but the chicken.

If Sofia is not at home here, so much less so is Alicia. Her father teaches at University. Her mother is a nurse at Mama Yemo Hospital. Her brother studies in Brussels to become a surgeon. No, hers is not a family at home in Prison Centrale de Kinshasa.

Yet here they stand and wait with dried fish and cooked rice, saka saka, fou fou, mangos, and some bottles of boiled water. The plan is that this food will last Daniel a week, since they know the prison provides little food, and only prisoners lucky enough to have families who visit have enough to eat.

Still, the women wait, and no one responds to their knock. Are they invisible? Fimi stays with Mama Kundi, and Kamina stays in school, and the three children of Alicia and Daniel stay there, too, for Alicia wants to know what is what at the prison before the children see Daniel. Only by seeing for herself can she know if it is a place for children to enter. Madame has parked the car alongside the outer wall of the prison yard. Madame believes she must stay close, for some reason of escape. Sofia fears it is too close, and Fimi sends her away with an angry cry. Alicia is the one who leans in close and tells her, "Tokenda mosika te, mwa Fimi," We do not go far, little Fimi.

At last, a strand of metal keys jangles, the thick gate opens inward, and a surly boy-guard asks what is their business in this place. Alicia says they come to see one called Daniel Sakombi. who was taken prisoner a week ago. She tells him she is his wife and Sofia is his sister-in-law. He takes a long while to frown and check them for guns, and at last hands each a visitor's token and a head-twitching sign to enter and he points to the next gate. They step across a dirt enclosed yard to a second entrance, where a guard opens the metal gate and asks for their visitors' tokens and, satisfied, ushers them to the next. And so it goes twice more until they step into a hallway where smells of urine, dried fish, and old burnings line the walls and the concrete floor. A dim bulb gives poor illumination of the reception window, where a woman with a short neck and tired eyes asks their names and their business, Alicia first. Sofia feels a keen wish to be gone from here back to Madame's Mazda car and Fimi. Alicia takes the arm of Sofia, and tells the woman, "Semeki na ngai," my sister-in-law.

The tired woman calls to a man in prison khakis. He is young with a baby-moonface, he should be in lycee studying his maths, not wearing a long gun on his shoulder like a flag. Then Sofia remembers that he attends no school at all. It is like that with the guards. He unlocks a grimy white door and walks Alicia and Sofia into a long hallway of cells on either side holding thirty or forty men squeezed on benches behind iron bars, as if waiting their turn at the bank. The cells are made for four or five men, not ten times that number. Some make sounds, low infernal keenings. A memory swatch sews itself to her seeing eyes. Her lost Elombe, her night search, the bamboo branches that took his last minutes, his strong legs, kicking no more. Holding him, silent and still, against her beating heart.

Sofia hears Alicia's breath trying to break free of some fear that constricts her. Sofia steps just behind Alicia, trains her gaze a few steps ahead on the concrete, and keeps at bay the face of Fimi in the Mazda by the outside wall. The moon-faced guard strides alongside them. His face and his swagger tell how proud he is of this place that locks up good men and honors thieves who steal from innocents to build a runway for the Concorde that flies him far from any who would know his thieving. Or, maybe that man Marshall Mobutu has never seen the Prison Centrale de Kinshasa. Because he has no need, not with this child of poverty, who holds grown men at gun point and thinks only of the money coming soon to buy him rice and dried fish and beer.

At the end of the long hall of cells, the moon guard stops, tells them, "Ici. Unanh." He cries loudly to another close by. This one, a grown man in guard clothing, steps to a cell that is nearest. Sofia see only four men inside. She thinks this must be the wrong cell. There is no Daniel before them. Alicia starts up a whimper. The older guard issues a command sound bearing his name. "Yaka awa, Sakombi." Come here.

Then the far-left corner releases a tall man from the concrete. He has the shape of Daniel, but not his vigor or his neatness. This man wears a rumpled gray prison suit and a face startled, as if trying to remember his own name. But he catches the presence of Alicia, and Daniel returns to the face in a flicker of hope and relief.

Alicia's breath rushes forth followed by her laughter. "Iyo, mobali na ngai, ngai oyo. Sofia mpe." Yes, my husband, I am here. And Sofia, too.

Daniel nods lightly to Sofia. Then he gives up the old Daniel laugh and touches his belly. Alicia catches his meaning and switches the conversation from Lingala, the language of the guards, to the basic English he and Alicia and also Sofia learned in school, but the guards did not. "When do you last eat?"

"Yesterday. A bit of boiled beans and corn. But no oil or salt. On such a diet, a prisoner grows weak. When they become too weak or ill, they are taken from here to a larger cell. They are called 'the dying.' And you know what is their fate."

"We have food for you. But not enough for all," Alicia says, eyeing the others who share his enclosure.

"We are not so many in this cell. That young one has no visitors to bring him food. He will have a share in what you bring." He lowers his voice and aims his word, still in soft English, at the concrete floor and a cockroach loitering along the smudged surface between them. Sofia contains her urge to crunch it to death with her Bata shoe. "It is not the guards who control this place. No matter the guns they carry." He lazily eyes the moon-guard and his long rifle with a wisp of smile." "No. The two standing back are with the Control Committee. They keep me under permanent watch. They have power over me and the others. I live in fear of displeasing them. I must keep them happy. Or, they make my life an even darker hell than I already know. There are stories of such men going as far as killing a prisoner. One day a man I know came to be absent from his cell. I asked another prisoner where have they taken him. This man, all he said was 'Dead.' Nothing more. Sure, they help themselves to the food you bring and give me the leftovers. Money is the engine of this place. If I have money to give them, my life takes an upturn."

Sofia flicks a quick survey of the two Control Committee men, to see what watch they keep over Daniel, what dark purpose they find in him, what excuse they might make for beating him to death. One is a fat man who sits on the concrete with legs straight ahead and eyes closed as if in sleep. Still, she believes he watches Daniel through closed eyelids. He wears no shirt, and no matter the roundness of his belly or the woman-breasts he bares without shame, his shoulders are tensed, in readiness. She feels this. Now she turns her back on the cell and says her warning to the opposite wall, in whispered English. "Be careful of the fat one." Daniel gives no sign of hearing, only a small head twitch. She turns for a look at the other inside the cell. Standing taller than anyone she knows, on the opposite wall. He wears a khaki shirt and a fixed gaze on a long face of little flesh. A face for a weapon, she thinks. If that head butted you,

you'd collapse from the impact. Again she turns away and says, "The tall one, too."

She studies the moon face for signs that he takes meaning from Daniel's English. Or, the two Control Committee men. What if any of them knows the meaning of Daniel's harsh words? If they steal his food, what else will they do? Her heart thrums in her chest with the weight of these questions. But their faces tell her not to worry. They take nothing from his English. Or, they take everything worth knowing inside until the moment is ripe for striking.

Alicia says nothing for a minute. Sofia believes she must be having the same thoughts. Then, she stretches tall and stiffens her upper back, and turns to the moon face. "Fungola, palado." Open, please. She speaks as a queen to a servant worker.

Daniel raises his voice and both hands. "You must keep rein on your voice. That is how it must go in this place. Give him the bag. He will deliver."

"Ahnhn," Alicia says. With that single outburst, she must leave her frustration, and she turns to the moon-faced guard and holds out the raffia bag of provisions for Daniel's week to come.

"Pesa ngai," give me. He receives the bag with a head bob of indifference and a ray of insolence.

Alicia turns once more to Daniel and crosses her arms in a meaning that Sofia understands from her early season with Gabriel when he wanted her and she, him, before beer claimed his thirst and rain stole his son. Sofia shuts her eyes against the ache of watching this gesture pass between them. She would send her own heart gesture to Daniel if she could. If he were free. If he were hers. Of course, she keeps this sign hidden in her own heart. Daniel is not hers. He is not free. She must not betray Alicia, her sister and her friend.

Six

Everything is different here. As Cass moves further into the strangeness of this place, as she tries to navigate the strangeness, she begins to see chances for inventing a new self, or freeing a self she's been harboring all her life, one yearning to be free. She's had a subliminal awareness of this self, but apparently awareness is not enough to achieve freedom. The universe must also kick in a spot of luck. So it is, whether by that spot or by misfortune is anyone's guess, that a striking opportunity presents itself in a boxing match, of all things, imported from the States, a contest between Mohammed Ali and George Foreman.

Cass has never seen a boxing match, not even one of those brawls shown on television just for show. Nor is Will inclined to follow these orchestrated blood-lettings. At first, she means to avoid the fight, especially since it will take place at 4:00 in the morning, Kinshasa time, to suit a sensible hour for closed-circuit streaming in the US, Eastern Time. American promoters and fans must be humored. But as the American hype of this phenomenon they're calling the Rumble in the Jungle reaches into the expat community, their interest escalates. A training camp is set up for each fighter, open to the public. She and Will take the boys to visit George Foreman's camp. They're leaning toward Foreman in this match, maybe because Archie Moore is his trainer. There he is some 50 feet away, former light-heavyweight champion working his magic with the 19-year-old heavy-weight champion.

For former-English major Cass, the kicker comes in the form of rumors that writer Norman Mailer has arrived to record the event in his brawny, self-conscious literary style. Then, one of the surgical nurses Will knows from Mama Yemo says he can get him two tickets. So their brief phase as boxing fans begins.

Cass engages Sofia to spend Fight Night at their Mimosa home, with her two girls, of course. Just days into Sofia's tenure as nanny, the benefits of the arrangement are apparent to both women. Sofia has income, modest but sufficient. Cass' two boys play well with Sofia's girls, laughing and scrapping over favorite games, quite like siblings. Often when she returns from her various tasks in the afternoon, she sees her boys' delight over a toy constructed of found-objects, such as bottle caps, wood scraps, lengths of sisal, cobbled into a toy similar to or, at least as interesting as one she might have purchased at Toys-R-US, but at zero cost. For $30 US each month, she gains a nanny she trusts and also a larger worldview for her boys simply by playing with two girls from the River Village.

Sofia and the girls arrive that Wednesday at an hour of bedtime for Cass' boys. No matter when Will and Cass roll in from the fight, there will be school tomorrow. Sofia will stay to manage their morning preparations while Cass and Will sleep in.

In the hours before the fight, Cass reviews with Sofia the night's sleeping arrangements and the morning prep. Which bedroom will she and her girls take, what's for breakfast, what time the boys must leave to catch their carpool. "Oui, Madame," Sofia says several times throughout the recital. Cass catches a touch of mirth in Sofia's response to her coaching. And she hears the strident thread of her own voice, in this rather officious laying out of plans. Who is she kidding, to claim a self that champions justice? She who assumes Sofia requires her coaching, being, after all, incapable of figuring all this stuff out on her own. Apparently, her confidence in this poor African inhabitant of the River Village stretches only so far.

After a round of exclamations over the wonder of new friends sleeping in their very house, Matheo and Corey consent to Cass tucking them into their shared bedroom. Sofia does the same with her girls, shuts the door and takes Cass aside for "a bit of news."

While Will takes an hour in the study he's devised of a fourth bedroom, the two women seat themselves in the living room. Cass feels Sofia's tightened posture, perched on the edge of the couch, and then turns to broach the news. "What news?"

"Daniel," Sofia says, and again. "Daniel. We saw him. He is without food, except a bit of boiled beans. Alicia and me, we bring food. This Kinshasa Prison has many gates. It is dark. They rule Daniel by fear. Not only of beatings. For some, it is a place of killing."

The familiar hum, the brooding sense that she must do something, nudges Cass. Suddenly she stands and paces across the area rug and the linoleum, back and forth, and tries to digest the story curdling in her gut. She doesn't doubt the truth of Sofia's words, only wonders what to make of such a dark and violent world, and how from this world of strangeness to respond. "What can I do?" she says finally.

"They say he make a coup, you know," Sofia says. "Against Mobutu. Daniel. No. He is not that kind of man."

"Let me think about this. I have to see what can be done. Maybe there's someone . . ." She abandons the thought to the empty air, where it belongs. For what possible help can an expat such as herself bring to this madness?

"Oui, Madame," Sofia says in a voice faint with aspiration.

Will and Cass nap for several hours, then reluctantly waken to their alarm and head in the Mazda for the boxing match in the 20th of May Stadium at the ungodly hour of 2:30 A.M. Shivering, despite the 80-degrees-F evening, Cass wishes only to return to bed. But they've bought the hype promoters disseminated from thousands of miles distant, and there's no backing out now. They tunnel in silence through the dark streets, winding along Mimosa Road, then on toward the Lingwala district of Kinshasa, where the stadium stands open and ready to fill its 125,000 seats for the Event of the Century. One fula fula passes them heading from town. A military jeep weaves crazily around them. She's heard stories of military thugs aiming long rifles at the windows of incomers from a strange country, such as her own. Surely not now, she thinks and shuts her eyes, letting herself float along the river of darkness surrounding their small metallic refuge.

Inevitably, Sofia's words enter the darkness and trace the edges of her silence. Daniel. *We saw him, Many gates. Beatings. A Place of killing. He is not that kind of man.* She holds the words inside, keeping them from Will, but feels queasy about her deception, as if she's depriving him of secrets that belong to him alone.

"I'm sure Mobutu will be there," she says, finally.

"You kidding? Of course. This is his big moment, when the world sees the glories of the country he's pillaging for his pocket. Think how proud he must be."

Right then she nearly upends her vigil by spilling Sofia's prison report into the silence. Instead, she catches herself and pivots to ask Will about his studies. They moved here immediately after he completed his residency, and he must wait a year before taking his Orthopaedic Boards. In eight months he flies to Chicago, to face the reckoning.

"Taylor says if we review all the American and British JBJS journals from the past ten years until now, we'll pass. I think I've covered a year. So far."

"Not too bad. You always seem to pull it off."

"Hah. We'll see," he says. "Don't remind me. Fight's a good distraction."

Inside the colossal arena, they press up through the interior artery between two banks of benches. The colossal interior is nearly full. A sea of Zairois. Except herself and Will. None of their friends from Mimosa decided to brave the hour. An odd feeling, this awareness of being the sole White spectators in a sea of color. A voice from another pocket of her brain pipes up. Uh, hello, this is Africa, Bimbo. What do you expect? True, but she lives in Mimosa, a buffer that allows her to forget race altogether. She turns toward the front of the arena. Norman Mailer will be sitting somewhere up there in the celebrity seats close to the ring. David Frost, who will lead the narration for TV. And others. But she can't manage a sighting across the vastness.

She and Will pause at the top of the ramp to discover any empty spot on the backless benches to their right. A black trail of strangers sighting them. Cass feels a blush at her neck taking an upsweep. "Let's sit here," she says. Squeeze in just here, anywhere, and be done with it.

Luck waves at them then in the person of a Zairois two rows ahead, off right. A man standing, smiling big, calls Doctor Ramsey. "Il y a deux place ici."

Will lifts his head as if rousing to an alarm and tugs her arm. "Oh, hey. It's Alberto, one of my scrub nurses. He's got two seats for us."

They step mindfully over the crowds of Zairois to seat themselves on the bench beside Alberto, their savior. So, Cass finds a home place inside the massive arena.

Ali steps first into the ring in a silky white robe and sets up a stream of bouncing in place, a flesh version of the phrase they heard from Ali's lips at his training camp. "Float like a butterfly, sting like a bee." Bouncing and shadow punching, keep it moving, avoid stasis. He believes a moving target has a better shot.

The mostly pro-Ali crowd sends up another phrase. "Ali Boma Ye." Kill him, Ali.

Will and Cass find themselves at odds with the pro-Ali crowd. While visiting the training camps, they can't miss the contrast between the African blacks and the American blacks. There's a difference in affect, an artlessness in the Zairois blacks. Whether imagined or real, this perception endears them to Cass. Especially in Ali's camp, as he carries on his unrelenting self-pro-motion at the microphone. In English. A typical Zairois might well speak French, along with Lingala and a tribal language, but probably not English. He might well miss the arrogance that mutes her affection for Ali. If Foreman has similar feelings of superiority, he holds them close to the bone. Both she and Will find themselves rooting for Foreman, phoenix from a hard scrabble world of prison to champion of the world.

Foreman keeps Ali waiting alone in the ring, Prerogative of a reigning champion, perhaps, tactic of intimidation against an opponent he knows is no slouch—and, clearly, has the crowd's heart. At last a roar rises outside the ring and Foreman enters with an entourage. He wears a satin red robe and a grave expression.

Even from a far distance, Cass can see the two men of the hour stare each other down. Ali's mouth is open and working.

Foreman's is shut-in behind that grave expression. He's the younger, the heavier, the champion. Always, he knocks them out in two rounds.

Before the first bell, the trainers and the referee surround the two fighters, giving water and who-knows-what instruction. Ali delivers to Foreman his non-stop palaver; Foreman returns with silence and a grave stare. The support players fan away to their posts outside the ring.

Ali wearing white trunks, bounces in place, defying stasis. Foreman wearing red trunks, shadow punches while stepping small, holding his ground. The "Star Spangled Banner," in brass, fills the air. The Zairois national anthem follows. To Cass' ear, it sounds more Marseilles-French than African. A vast shout reverberates. Ali leads the crowd in his anthem, "Ali, Boma Ye," Ali, kill him. The two men stare each other down. The bell sounds.

Ali dances, takes the first punch. Foreman head-butts Ali's mid-section.

Ali backs into the ropes. Foreman whales on Ali's body.

Ambient temperature in the stadium: eighty degrees Fahrenheit.

A round ends: even on points.

Cass charades fascination for what's unfolding far off in the ring: Foreman backing Ali into the corner ropes; Ali leaning on the ropes, taunting Foreman, "That's all you got, George?" Foreman taking the bait, punching Ali's torso, throwing a punch and almost himself from the ring; Ali bouncing to the middle, all speed and grace; a cry rising from the crowd of 60,000, "Ali, Boma Ye;" Foreman punching hard to Ali's jaw.

The fight wears on.

About Round Five, movement on her left diverts her attention. Someone squeezes in beside her on the bench. She turns to see. Here is the man who knew Mobutu from Katanga, the lean face, intense and familiar. Xavier. "Mademoiselle Cassandra." He greets her with the wide grin she remembers. "It was you who refused a certain handshake. I hoped we might meet once more."

"Ah, it's Minister Xavier?" Something in his tone tells her that the charming insider is not all-in for Mobutu Sese Seko, though he's quite cagey about it. "It's Madame, actually." She gives a head bob toward Will, having his own distraction with the scrub nurse, though their conversation is punctuated with silent scrutiny of the ring.

"Un medicin, non?" A doctor, right? Xavier leans into her, his words barely registering in the cavernous noise-factory. She wonders how he could possibly have this information. Has he been checking up on her? She finds the prospect more intriguing than upsetting. She feels interest from him, but no threat. Because what threat could he bring?

There is a roar around her, a sea of voices crying, "Ali, Boma Ye." Xavier joins the cries that flood her head, even as he drops something small on the concrete between their feet. She bends down to retrieve it, a business card, and scans the bold print: *Mouvement Pour le Justice au Zaire. MJZ.* Movement for Justice in Zaire. She turns to give Xavier her back, avoiding his arm stretching to snag the card. Moving here and there out of his reach, she feels herself using the same silly, flirty gesture she used in junior high years with a boy she "liked." Not that she means to flirt with this man. Surely not. But intrigued, she reads on: "Les mercredis de midi a l'hotel Intercontinental." Noon on Wednesdays at Intercontinental Hotel. Some meeting. In R467, inked in below the name. A hotel room number, she suspects, though what will occur in that room, she has no idea. Xavier's lean face flashes annoyance at her toying antics. He's not amused. But she's strangely exhilarated at the idea of a meeting he wants to keep secret, and she considers tucking the card into her purse. But there's no need. She's already committed the time and place to memory. "Interesting."

"Some few friends doing a bit of business is all."

"A bit of business, is it?" She says extending the card and a half grin.

"Oui." He accepts it with due finesse and not a trace of mirth.

She nearly asks if it's possible for an outsider to join this reunion in Room 467, herself, for instance, but she resists the impulse. Such a question would tip her hand.

Maybe there's no plot to de-throne Mobutu, and she's over-reacting. It wouldn't be the first time.

She turns to see Will from the side, the edge of the grin she loves, the muscled forearms and those three stray freckles at the elbow. Could she eavesdrop on some secret meeting at Hotel Intercontinental on a Wednesday noon? An image of herself playing sleuth in a strange hotel quickens her pulse. No reason for Will to find out. He'll be at the hospital. And it might be nothing. But what if it turns out to be a gathering like those old meetings back at the UW, a Zairois version of the SDS? Even though Will hated that war, she's never told him about her work with the SDS. She has no doubt he'd be horrified. He'd never approve of the Zairois version, never in a million years. Far worse than jogging after dark where hyena's lurk. She nudges his shoulder. "What round is it?"

"Round eight starting. George is looking wrecked."

In the ring, Foreman is slogging more than bouncing. He's younger than Ali, and heavier, but he can't find his classic killer punch. Ali's fists cover his face against the stray jabs that keep coming. George may be wrecked, but to her, both fighters look sluggish.

Score is still even on points. For a moment more. Then Ali punches, taunts, and delivers a blow that decks the world-champion. The referee counts. The floor holds dominion over the massive young body, though he keeps his head up. Come on, rise, George, she thinks. George does not rise before the count ends. Ali has done it.

Pandemonium. Thousands in the stadium leap to standing. Cass and Will join the leapers, though not the bellowing cheerers. They bid farewell to their respective seatmates and move toward the aisle. Cass recites the room number and the time of a reunion that beckons her as they join the stream of strangers toward the exit. She skates her gaze about for another glance at Xavier, author of this strange streak of joy rising inside her, but he has slipped away.

Seven

Sofia wakes to morning light different from her normal waking with sun streaming through the doorway of her hut. This light is sent from the ceiling lamp throughout a room that is not her own. She rubs her eyes and tries to think of this room and why she has come here before yesterday returns. How she agreed to stay the night at Madame Cassandra's, how she washed Fimi and Kamina in a shower of water she didn't have to carry or heat on the fire in her hut, but warm and running full over their small bodies as they laughed and shouted over this wonder.

The fight, she thinks. The two boxing men from a far country come to beat on each other. Madame Cassandra told her that each man earned five million dollars for this fight. That is more money than she can count. What a strange game boxing is. To receive pay for letting a man work his fists on your body and bruise your face into a shape your mama would not know. Imagine if she could earn money for all the fists Gabriel has landed on her head, her arms, and her belly only a month after Elombe was born. She would be so rich, she could fly away on the big planes she sees in the skies over River Village and she could make a home with Fimi and Kamina, and they would all keep safe from Gabriel's fists.

She shakes her head and lets the strangeness of such a world bring to her face a smile, her hips hugging the high bed on which she sleeps, with Fimi and Kamina on either side. This bed, too, is a strangeness. In her years of being a mother, and in all her years of being Sofia, she has never slept on a bed so far from the floor. When they wake, will Fimi and Kamina find it strange, too? She wonders.

She is first in the house to wake. Such a grand house. There are many sleeping rooms. All rooms are far from this high bed and no sounds reach her through the wooden door. Each boy sleeps apart from the others in his own room. Sofia finds it a strange way to be family, with each person a tribe unto himself. Only Madame Cassandra and the doctor sleep together in a room, lying together as one tribe. She would be so with Daniel, if only such sweetness could be true.

She draws herself around Kamina's roundness and away from an image forbidden her, one she must not keep. Alicia, if you knew, you would despise me, too.

It is early, the sun barely edging out darkness, but she must come awake and see the children dress for school. She steps into the bathroom with water that comes from a small turn of a handle, warm for washing. Of course she knows of this water from her job as nanny, but today, alone, she will have her own shower, her first, and this, too, is a wonder.

A coil of worry forms in her belly as she hurries out of her pagne and into the tub. She pulls the curtain, and the small hand of Elombe tugging the cloth floats before her sight. My brave one, she thinks, letting the image pass, turning the knob, letting the magic of heated water rain on her skin, her hair, sending her odd guilt for stealing Madame Cassandra's hot water into the drain.

Later, when she reaches the village water tap, the new memory of her shower floods her, and muddies her pride in their own tap where water runs free for one hundred people.

Still, it is a fine tap that serves them, all in the village, not a single family only. And she brushes the wonder of her shower from her mind.

She rounds the tap and lets the sight of her sister-in-law settle before her in her doorway. A notion flickers, an imagining that Alicia has read the story of her forbidden desire and comes to strike her and send her away. But this silliness fades as Alicia waves her forward and the two sisters-in-law embrace, as always, for she loves Alicia, too. She does.

"It's time to see Daniel again," Alicia tells her. "But my mama has taken sick. I don't know when I can return. I worry for Daniel, sister. If I go too long between visits, what will he eat. He may grow weak. Can you go . . . ?"

"Without you? I will, of course. No worry. When Madame Cassandra can take me, I go."

Madame Cassandra has an opening on Saturday afternoon to drive them to the prison. On this day Matheo and Corey stay with their tata, but Sofia's girls come, and it is decided that all will enter the prison together. They must make a strong showing before the authorities, Madame Cassandra says. They must give weight to their petition of his innocence. They must go in numbers. She tells her idea and Alicia agrees.

Sofia doubts their weight will mean anything in this place. Standing together before the gaping words, she knows how small she is and how large the guns the men carry inside the walls.

PRISON CENTRALE

DE

KINSHASA

Fimi drops back her head and stares up at the gaping words she cannot read. Frowning, she points to the massive sign. "Nini boye, Mama? Wapi tozali?" What's this, Mama? Nini ezali ndako?" What is this big house?

Prison, her sister tells her. For she listens to the grown-ups and she knows what is what. "Uncle Daniel is here."

"But Daniel doesn't steal, Mama. He is our friend."

"Anh-nh. Daniel is our friend. He does not belong here," Sofia says, lightly touching the top of her head.

"Yet here we find ourselves," Madame Cassandra says, her voice barely brushing the surface.

Each member of the small delegation carries water and food to Daniel for the coming days: cooked rice, dried fish, saka saka, fou fou. They wait, as before. They wait until the girls' patience drains into whimpers, and Madame Cassandra sings a song to lift the girls from their weakness. First a song from her own country. "The wheels on the bus go round and round, round and round, round and round. The wheels on the bus go round and round all through the day." The girls learn the song quickly, and finish off laughing together. Next she sings a song from France: "Frere Jacque, Frere Jacque." The girls look over at their mama, for they don't understand French.

"Ndeko. Ndeko Jacque," Sofia says in Lingala. It means brother.

This, they do understand. "The big rain drowned my brother. I saw his mat in the morning, but he was not there. Mama said he's dead now." Fimi says in Lingala, telling it to Madame Cassandra, who knows this, but Fimi has a story of her brother and she cannot stop herself from telling it.

Madame nods her head. "Yes, the rain was too big for Elombe. He couldn't run fast enough." Madame says this in French, words she has said many times before. Sofia feels her own heartbeat quicken and her tears gather.

Fimi breaks in with a song to the "Frere Jacque" tune, "Ndeko Elombe, Ndeko Elombe." She jumps as she sings, as if her brother gives her happy feelings, and no cares of how he lies in the deep hole Daniel dug for him and will never come home to them and no one will ever touch him again.

"Non, Fimi. Tema!" Stop. Sofia's words snap from her like a coupe coupe to crop Fimi's dance steps mid-air. The child begins to wail from her belly.

"Fimi Fimi, we must be so quiet if we want to see Uncle Daniel in this place," Sofia tells her.

"Shh-h," Madame Cassandra says, drawing the child toward her.

Kamina comes to stand beside Fimi, and her wailing softens, and ceases. The four visitors grow still as they stand through a long, slow wait, until, finally, the keys jangle, the metal gate opens, the questions of their business come, their answers follow, and they are led into the corridor of smells, old burnings and new urine, and prisoners growing more gaunt and sorrowful each week. Moon Face is there, the young one who should be studying his maths, but no Daniel among the prisoners in the corner cell.

Sofia exhales her surprise to see his absence there. A black worry clamps hard on her skin and her neck, sucking what calm she had, stealing her breath.

Madame Cassandra turns to her. "Do you see him? Daniel. Is he here?"

She shuts her eyes to slow her pulse and only shakes her head. The words will not come. Only his absence preys on her like a crocodile circling her pirogue in the depths where she cannot see it. She remembers such a time when her tata carried her in the pirogue he carved of a Tola tree on a small river near their village in the North country. And a crocodile found their pirogue and tormented them by tracking their course from the deep understory of the river. At last, they pushed onto sand stretching to safety, and her tata tied the pirogue to a post on the small dock. He lifted the white fish he caught, handed Sofia a small box of gear, and they scurried from the crocodile and his river to home ground.

"*Ezali awa te.*" He is not here. Her voice carries the words heavily, against her wishes, for they mix with words she remembers from Daniel, of prisoners too ill taken to a larger cell, and of the name they are called, the dying.

"Not here? Well, where is he?" Madame Cassandra turns cross and steps toward Moon Face leading with her chin. He cares nothing for her complaint, but only for the long gun he hefts and his bellyful of power over life and death. Her complaint matters even less since he has no English, only Lingala and the language of some small tribe different from Sofia's own, and Madame has no Lingala, only a bit of French, which she tries then, pushing him to tell where Daniel has gone and where they can leave his food and if he even needs food anymore.

"Avec moi," Moon Face swallows the smile that waits inside him. Leave it with him. Sure, he will take Daniel's food, since no one in this hole has enough to eat.

"Te," Sofia says. No.

The girls release their questions, too, but Sofia sees from their faces that they know what is what. Some part of them feels the danger of annoying Moon Face. He and his long gun do not care if they are children. They know they must keep guard on how loud they are, for their own voices are prisoners of this place, too.

"Te," Sofia says again. "We go now." She turns from Moon Face reaching for the bag of rice and beans she holds. The Control Committee prisoners watch her as Daniel says they watch him, like a hyena on hunt, and he fears those two more than he fears Moon Face. But Sofia feels only anger at the fat one who still wears no shirt. The big folds in his belly tell her he has food enough for six men. He must be stealing Daniel's food. Her anger has no nowhere to go except to her two feet that thrust her from the corner cell. The girls scurry beside her.

Madame Cassandra stays behind them, and stops to ask the woman at the reception window about Daniel and where he sits this day. The woman stares at Madame before answering in sullen French that must taste sour on her tongue. "*Alle dans une autre cellule.*"

"*Alle? Pourquoi?*" Gone? Why?

"*Transfere.*" Transferred. The word beats out of her like a hollow drum.

"*Nous devons le voir.*" We must see him.

"*Pas possible.*" Not possible. Madame's drumbeat is strong but Madame cannot make that woman hear her in this place.

Eight

Cass takes the stairs to the fourth floor of Hotel Intercontinental and lingers near Room 467 to catch her breath and let the AC dust the heat from her shoulders and her temples, clinging to the chill before it becomes too much. Breasts on high alert, tingling, her gaze finds the room number beside the door. She paces lightly toward it on the thick carpet, only a couple years old, like the hotel, a lavish contrast with the unspeakable dregs of Prison Central de Kinshasa. The image of the long rifle hefted over Moon Face's shoulder unnerves her, alone and unprotected in the long hallway. *What am I doing here?*

She paces her breathing to hear sounds drift out from Room 467. Nothing. Gradually, her breath resumes its normal gait. Still only voices in other rooms, a child sighing Mama Mama, the exhalation of the AC, her own stomach churning hunger. She should have eaten lunch first. Such urgency, she felt, and for what? Tonight she'll be laughing to herself about this goose chase. Alone. The escapade will be her version of Susan's great toe band-aid. She can't risk speaking of it to anyone.

A voice stirs behind the door to Room 467. A male voice. Muted. Clipped. Xavier? Might be. Her father had no hearing out of one ear; a farm accident in youth had blasted it away. He always aimed his good ear to the speaker in any group. "Now see here," he'd preface many of his statements. She'd give up one of her own ears forever to be with him again right here, for one day. She has her mother's excellent hearing, and the woman herself lives on, in Missoula. No one asked Cass which parent should be given the longer Life Line. She presses her excellent ear against the door. There's a cough. A shush. Another male voice saying what sounds like *louer une piece.* She mentally surveys her French vocabulary. *Louer* means to rent. Rent a room. Someone else pipes up, "Trop cher." Too expensive.

She makes out a chair scraping and, without forethought, darts down the hall toward the stairs, turns left into an alcove and tucks in hard beside an icemaker, thick enough to hide her, she hopes. A door opens. She faces the wall. They won't see her, surely not, if she's lucky. If they do, so what if they happen to be on the same floor of some hotel? It's a free country. And it's not as if she's plotting a break-in. She wants to help, is all. She wants to join their cause. But who is she to them? A *mondele* from a rich country who has nothing to do. They might have guns. They could shoot her and walk away. Fear ripples inside her as someone clears his throat. Someone starts a humming. Footsteps move past the alcove. And the long hallway holds a silence so taut her own skin feels distended and she can barely breathe.

She moves forward in the alcove for a stolen glimpse of five men dressed in slacks and short-sleeved shirts, probably traditional boubou shirts. Young Zairois professionals short of cash. *Rent a room,* they said. *Too expensive.*

That's something I could do. Another thought surfaces. She finds a paper scrap in her handbag and writes a note in English, which she knows Xavier can read, but most others cannot: You need rent money. I can help. Call me. She scrawls her Mimosa phone number scrawled at the bottom beside her signature, Madame Cassandra. She slips the scrap under the door to Room 467.

Xavier's call comes a week later in the evening, a time of great inconvenience. They have one phone. It sits on the desk where Will hangs out each evening re-reading old *Journals of Bone and Joint Surgery* for the Orthopaedic Boards he'll take in Chicago, next summer, to become fully-qualified for what he's already doing each day at Mama Yemo: Orthopaedics. Each night he's pinned in place, the old med-school discipline at the ready. Cass minds the discipline, his frequent declines of her suggestions to go to Aerwa, the American Embassy Recreation & Welfare Association, where they can enjoy Stateside burgers, fries, and first-run movies. But she recognizes how small-minded and petty this 'minding' is, and she tries to limit her whining to joking complaints. More than his schedule, she minds him hoarding their only phone. He's not hoarding it, of course, a ridiculous claim since she agreed to place the phone there. But her fierce desire for the occasional private conversation animates her charge of hoarding.

Will answers on the third ring. She pauses in the hallway to hear his end. "Oui. Madame est ici," he says in his American-soused French. "Cass," he calls.

"Just a sec." She lets the hot blush making its vast sweep upward from her neck to her right-sided part run out of heat and subside. She steps into his study, wondering, as she reaches for the phone, why she agreed to install their only phone in his study. For that matter, why she allowed him to claim custody of their sole non-bedroom room. After all, she's a woman who read and embraced Virginia Woolf's long essay, "A Room of One's Own," in her Modern British Lit class, though, admittedly, coming here has sidelined that embrace, for now. She takes the outstretched phone and leans against his desk to still the minor dizziness her body is hosting. "Allo," she says.

"Madame, c'est moi, Xavier." He goes to English then. "Can you speak, is now OK?"

"Yes, of course."

"I found your small paper."

"Ah, that." She gives a light laugh, feeling Will awaiting her next word.

"We must make a meeting."

She laughs again. "Yes, I can do that. Shall we meet somewhere for lunch and have a lesson, then?"

"A lesson, is it? I understand. You are not alone." He laughs. "Café de la Paix? Noon. Wednesday next."

"Of course. Sounds good. See you." She re-seats the phone and flicks Will a wave.

"What was all that?" he asks absently.

What, indeed. Think, think what to say. She turns toward him frowning at the dense print on his journal page. "Oh, just that social worker. At the hospital. I may have told you," she finds herself saying. "Maybe I didn't tell you. Anyhow, I met him at Mobutu's grand celebration while you were waiting to press the palm of His Nibs. He noticed that I opted out of shaking the hand of our dear leader. That seemed to amuse him and we started talking." Here she catches herself veering off into treacherous terrain. But no treachery, no worries. Will merely gives that half-grin she loves.

"Seems like a good guy. I said I'd give him a few English lessons. His English is already pretty good. But he realizes it's the lingua franca of our time. He's ambitious, you know?" She shrugs ending her monologue on a rising inflection. Sounding so plausible, she half-believes her own story.

She steps away from Will already sinking back into his Ortho journals. Leaving him to his amazing concentration, his deep study, though not leaving the lie she's just told. A small lie meant to serve a greater purpose. In this case, protecting a jewel that is their intimacy and the marriage itself. Still the lie remains tethered to the crook of her solar plexus, the place where her yearning for justice smolders. What's she supposed to do? Turn a blind eye to Mobutu's brutality? Abandon his victims? 'Call me if you change your mind,' she told Xavier. Here he is, calling, and she is ready.

Turning, she thinks of another continent, another desk, and Will seated behind it on a spring afternoon toward the end of his residency year in General Surgery. Images drift up. Will lifting a bulky manila envelope from the US Department of Defense. Will sliding a paper knife under the seal, his gaze fixed hard-steady as if the knife is cutting into flesh. Will removing a pamphlet and waving it for her to read: "Vietnamese Language and Customs."

After their spate of laughter ebbed, he gave her his deadpan look. "There's the military for you. Why waste words, right?"

Later on, he would reveal that since he was married and the father of a small son, he could have avoided Vietnam but agreed to go because, well, it was happening and he was a guy who stepped up. He'd joined the Navy Reserve, and received a deferment for active duty until he finished medical school. He'd forgotten that the Navy provides the medical care to the Marines who don't have their own medical corp. This was payback time. He flew off to Tan Son Nhut Air Base to begin his year as a Battalion Surgeon while he still believed in the War, before he read Bernard Fall's *Street Without Joy*, before he saw the body bags collecting on the tarmac for shipment back home.

On a cloud-thick Seattle September afternoon, she mounted the steps to the Suzallo Library and turned for a look at the spectacle of students on the quad holding up signs. There was much written and broadcast in those days about the War, but she shunned news of its progress or failures. She enrolled in classes at the U to distract her from Will's absence and the War itself. She couldn't deny any of it, but she didn't have to wallow in the dangers he faced in that Marine outpost called An Hoa.

But on that day, she stood before the grand double doors of the Suzallo Library and read the posters spouting disdain and outrage: "Resist the Draft," "Hell No We Won't Go," "Make Love Not War." Though she had only sketchy notions then of what the War was and was not, her gut began to stir with its hum. She swept longish bangs from her wide forehead and thought of Will. Gone. He was so gone. Thousands of miles gone from her and the so-called real world where these signs waved. What might he make of them? What if they were right? What if no one went and the War collapsed for lack of interest?

That moment of new seeing tweaked the knowing inside her: Something was not right. It sparked her interest in a place where War had landed without the consent of that green and lovely country. She began to buy Newsweek, the journal her mother called "a liberal rag." She checked out a copy of Bernard Fall's account of the French failed experiment in Indochina and tucked into it with a fever. She felt him then, in the center of that frayed and violent place.

Days into her immersion, after lunch in the Student Union Building, the HUB, she absently picked up a flier about a meeting: UW SDS Meeting. DISTURBED BY AN ILLEGAL WAR? Come stand with us. Friday, Sept. 26. Outside the HUB.

On that Friday, she stepped toward the HUB with a hitch in her side, asking the question feathering the edge of her brain, her belly, What are you doing? The group coalescing before her in the near-distance might be members of a hapless squad rooting for some little-known field hockey team. Laughing, giving each other high-fives. They were buddies, all of them, revving up for a Friday night keg-party. But there were the black power grips, the signs sweeping the overcast sky, signaling passion and outrage, shouts bursting from the group of around thirty. "Hell No, We Won't Go."

No, not a keg-party. These were not even the liberals her mother hated. These were radicals proclaiming beliefs, precepts to live by, charges to commit and damn the consequences. She wondered if any of them had a husband who'd traveled to that distant war. Did any in that crowd even believe in marriage anymore? They were a tribe.

She had no one to stand with, no tribe at all.

Even the baby-guru, Dr. Benjamin Spock, had come out against the War. He'd addressed an SDS meeting right on this campus. Did he have a tribe?

Martin Luther King, Jr. had spoken out against the War. Back in early college, a year before they killed him, she'd driven miles to another campus to hear the deep baritone eloquence tell her how small her life was, how limited, and prod her to wonder if another self could find room in there, one that did more than pine for justice.

Dr. King was gone. But maybe, in some new realm, she could become part of his tribe.

She moved toward the group, louder now and more raucous, stepped into the back of the clump of passion-mongers, and listened for a chant to join. "Hell No, We won't Go." Not that one, since there was less than zero chance of her going to the jungle outpost, An Hoa, where Will was mucking through rice paddies. Her voice had to channel words of her own. How about "Whose War is It?" That was it. Those were her words, words to shout, words to live by. She released them at full volume. She exchanged a smile with a woman beside her, who took up Cassandra's words. And so she found herself part of the

SDS tribe, eventually writing and taking photos for *The Daily*, working fiercely, rabidly, happily, against a war she'd only just discovered. How easy it was.

She said nothing to her parents about these activities, which amounted to her adopting another kind of religion, since she'd long ago given up her mother's. If she told her father, he'd be proud, but he might spill the news to her mother and wreak havoc on himself. She couldn't chance hurting her dear father, who could take on the world but couldn't take on Mabel Frederickson. So it was a private affair that she would later mark as her conversion from ignoring the sufferings of the world. This was where she recognized a different world. She would embrace it. She knew where she wanted to belong.

In all the letters she wrote to Will that year spent in the bush of An Hoa and in Hootch 8 at the Naval Hospital outside of Danang, she never mentioned SDS.

Cass has never known an expat to ride a city minivan here in Kinshasa, the preferred means of transport about the city and environs. But she elects to do so on the appointed day. She slides onto the bench seat, pressed from her right by a lavish woman with a large basket, from her left by a skinny man, wheezing and muttering words she can't make out, and from behind by a steady thumping of feet. Don't forget bodies on the peripheries hanging out of windows. She can barely breathe, though smells breathe through her, people sweat, street grime, fruit past eating prime. A long-legged man straddles the open doorway of the minivan and sends constant bellows into the air as the van careens around jams, potholes, corners, and hails all comers so he can push them into the big squeeze inside. She shuts her eyes and prays a fervent self-serving prayer that this trip will end well.

Her escape comes when the van pulls onto a parking strip and stops, at last. She scooches herself over the lap of the skinny muttering man and out onto terra firma, blessed pavement, and hands the pusher her coins and takes a moment to get her bearings and a few deep breaths before pressing on to Café de la Paix. She assumes a modest pace to accommodate the current of anticipation alive within her. Not sexual but a kissing cousin, as it were, of erotic anticipation that precedes an assignation. It's not the prospect of meeting Xavier again that's generating the current. Rather, it's the purpose behind the meeting, the sense that she's entering a forbidden realm with eyes wide open, in full consent.

She turns a corner and Café de la Paix emerges, an apparition of affluence after the grime traced in the fula fula. She finds the name Café of Peace curious and poignant in a city where guns and beheadings form a backdrop to the everyday. In four months here, she's had more encounters with guns than in her previous thirty years. Not only Moon Face and his long rifle, but the twin soldiers that stopped them last week on Mimosa Road and dunned them for "documents d'identite" as they headed out to some Embassy dinner that Susan finagled for the four of them.

There was a curious incident involving guns at Ndjili Airport several months after they arrived. Later, she wondered if the incident were a kind of omen. She and Will had come to claim stuff they sent ahead by cargo ship for separate arrival: kitchen supplies, bedding, towels, books, and sundry other stuff for their two-year stay, including Corey's favorite stuffed dog, which Cass had insisted he allow them to ship with the rest of their cargo. A cruel ask, Cass realized when she saw Corey's grief over his doggie's absence. Whatever was she thinking? Additionally, Will shipped a smaller box of shot gun shells, in case he got an offer to go bird hunting somewhere in that strange African plain where they were headed. Might happen. Who knew? He was one who liked to be prepared. An expat who knew the lay of Zaire claimed that a hunting club would have a shotgun he could borrow, but that shells would be rare finds, indeed. On that morning at Ndjli, they came to retrieve their stuff at Customs: seven large unmarked boxes and an eighth small one bearing images of shotgun shells with bold letters reading SUPER-SPEED SHOTGUN SHELLS, all addressed to William Ramsey, M.D., Mimosa Village, Kinshasa, Zaire, Africa.

"Bonjour," Will told the Customs officer, young, lean, fer-rel-faced.

He gazed soberly at the eight boxes on the Customs trolley. He pointed to the small one, the sole incriminating one. "Qu'est-ce que c'est?" What is it?

Cass watched Will eyeing the container in question, an am-munition box whose indelible images marked them as importers of contraband. A stillness claimed Will's handsome features, his neck, and hands that were small for his six-foot height. He ducked his head, licked his lips, and prepared to answer. She tried to predict what he would say when the unveiling laid bare shotgun and shells, and what the ferrel one would do to them, what security goons he would call in, and where he would in-terrogate them. Could they make a run for it? "Pour le sportif, vous savez," Will said with a lilt and grinned at the officer, who lifted the box in both hands, frowning, and cocked his head to read words that were upside down. She knew then that the Customs officer could not read English, likely could not read, at all. He set the box on the trolley, swung an arm indicating the exit, and gave a dismissive grunt.

No order to open please. No unveiling of forbidden effects. No call for security bruisers, no interrogation. They made their escape in excessive calm, apart from Cass having to stop and catch up to her heartbeat to prevent a collapse. Outside, they broke into hysterics, laughing and hugging before loading their cargo into the Mazda, and heading home to safety in Mimosa Village.

Café de la Paix is a sidewalk café with a dozen sets of white wrought-iron tables and deck chairs spaced across a granite-tiled piazza. Each table hosts a sun umbrella trimmed in gold and white striped fabric edged with the letters SKOL STAR and center-mounted against the 95 degree Fahrenheit sun. The café would look at home in any restaurant en plein air on the Cote d'Azur. Xavier has taken a table in the far back edge of the square, away from the street. He wears a fedora-style sunhat and sits with his back to the other patrons, head down as if in deep study. She approaches him wordlessly and eases herself into a chair, also facing her back to the street. He greets her with a quick look-up. "Madame." He has the look of a nervous cat about to dart away.

"Xavier." Her voice sounds faint inside her head. Maybe he hasn't heard her. She clears her throat and says with more heft, "Xavier. Been waiting long?"

He looks up, does not speak, merely shakes his head.

She finds his silence strange and feels a pinprick of unease in her belly, a feeling of being trapped, a blush starting. What's she doing here? "So. I overheard someone say rentals were expensive. I'm prepared to help," she says, answering her own question. "Shall we order lunch first? I'm buying." And she hears how she must come across, expat dishing out largesse to a poor native.

"No need for that, Madame," he says without a trace of the carefree, ironic Xavier she met first at Mobutu's reception. Where oh where has Xavier gone? Where, oh where can he be?

A waitress appears with notepad. "Que voulez-vous?" What do you want? She has dark hair with a complex network of braids riding high on her head, large eyes, and a gold and black pagne. Quite a beautiful young woman, severe and unsmiling, with no use for social nicities.

"Les crevettes, s'il vous plait." she says. The shrimp is their specialty. Never a fan of drinking alcohol at lunch time, she adds, "'Et un coca cola,"

"Les crevettes aussi, et une bierre," Xavier says. Shrimp and a beer.

Cass waits until the waitress leaves hearing range to say, "Look. I don't know any rentals here. I can help with the money. To a certain point."

A remnant of their earlier silence returns. His voice turns soft, gentle. "I know a place. An apartment. This." He leans in and produces a photo of a nondescript building front.

"How much?"

He glances over his left shoulder as if blunting a blow he feels coming. "Is cher. Expensive. One hundred zaires each month."

Officially, two hundred dollars American, at the Al Pettibone rate. Unofficially, on the black market, fifty dollars American. When they arrived, Al Pettibone, a straight arrow missionary who worked in the Mama Yemo business office, sent them to a bank to buy zaires at the official rate. Cass revealed the exchange to Susan, who gave an explosive laugh and levelled a surprising tirade of abuse on the absent missionary. 'Al Pettibone. What a unit. What a dick. I don't know anybody who buys zaires at the bank. Except Al." And she gave Will a two-word roadmap to the dark cadre of illegal money changers: Tommy Hendricks. They knew Tommy, an immensely fat neighbor who grew up in Zaire with missionary parents and knew how to navigate the shady underbelly of Zairois life.

"Not so cher. It's about what I figured. If you make the arrangements, I'll handle the payment part. Here's November's rent." She places a small envelope on the table between them, with its wad of zaires inside.

Since their entry into Tommy's shadow world of money changing, Will and Cass have kept their stashes of zaire bills on the book shelf inside *World Poetry*, a fat volume of verse, "from antiquity to our time." They tucked it next to William Butler Yeats' "Second Coming." It was her idea to cache their cash alongside one of her favorite poems. Always the same page, or they might forget where they left their stash. At times, she worries she may have jinxed herself by her choice of poetic lines: "Turning and turning in the widening gyre, the falcon cannot hear the falconer. Things fall apart; the center cannot hold." What if Yeats' words are a harbinger of some horrid dissolution in her own life? But that's absurd, she thinks, just as absurd as Will's worries about a hyena coming for her after dark.

Or, is it absurd? Her body answers straightaway, stirring a dollop of dread in her chest and tripping her pulse to rac-ing-speed. She places a hand over the region of her solar plexus. Okay. But ever since those heady SDS days, she's been waiting for the moment to do something significant, she realizes now, something more than a demonstration of youthful exuberance, something that could change a country. She'd be flirting with real danger, make no mistake, to herself, to Xavier and those five young professional idealists, maybe even, God forbid, to Will and her babes. But isn't that always the case with those who stand for justice? Here she's given the chance of her life, to fight a true and palpable evil in this man Mobutu. She can't let this chance escape her.

And so it was that after Will headed out in the Mazda that morning and she escorted the boys to the Mimosa gate where the school bus stopped, she opened the poetry to Yeats, opened the white envelope and withdrew bills equaling fifty zaires. She counted the remaining cash: one thousand four hundred zaires in lumps of tens and twenties. Good. Could Will possibly notice the missing fifty? Surely not. If he does, she'll tell him he should visit the markets. Five zaires for a roll of toilet paper, seven for a box of cereal, expired. Welcome to shopping in downtown Kinshasa, Dear One.

As Xavier takes the envelope and quickly counts the contents, she says, "So, if we're in this . . . " She pauses not knowing what to call it, ". . . business together, we need to exchange contact info. You have my number but . . ."

"But you do not also have mine." His eyes take on a half sleepy look, worlds away from his deer-in-the-headlights panic-watch of her. Until now, he has never believed she'll come through with the money. She understands that now. But he knows he can count on her, conscientious Cass. She is a spoiled rich American woman who does not have to work for her food, but she will do as she says. She will come through. She eyes the envelope he folds into his inside jacket pocket, and he pulls out a card with his name and work information. He scrawls a telephone number on the back. "My private number," he says.

"Perfect. Thanks." Reading the number, she can see the risk he's taking in trying to unseat the leopard-hatted killer he knew in Katanga, if that's what he's about. He hasn't stated their precise aim in so many words. She can only assume this is so. She does assume. She will assume the funds she gives him are to remove Mobutu from power, for the betterment of Zaire.

Thankfully, she's heard nothing about guns. For herself, she'll not go near any guns or do anything incriminating. She'll pitch in her fifty bucks each month and live her life. She believes that success will see Mobutu escorted from office, maybe taken out on some male memsahib chair and set adrift on the Zaire River, go over the Stanley Rapids near Mimosa, and meet a natural death. Nobody is talking about killing him. But whatever happens, whatever end he meets, he'll deserve it.

If anybody gets wind of Xavier's clandestine meetings, he could end up like Patrice Lumumba. Another horrific miscarriage of justice. As for herself, based on conversations she's had with old expat hands here, she feels she's not at risk of being shot. Worst they'll do is ship her out of the country, send her home. Still, she must take care to keep a lid on her small role in this *justice project*. She can live with that. She's no stranger to keeping secrets.

Nine

It is evening. Sofia hears the girls outside the hut playing the hopscotch game Sofia herself remembers playing as a child in the North Country. She called it *tumatu,* but Kamina calls it hopscotch, a name she learned from Madame Cassandra's children. Kamina has drawn a hopscotch court with the handle of a pestle Sofia knows she snatched from her cooker supplies, but it is her second best, and she has no energy to spoil their game, for her worry over Daniel takes energy she normally uses in scolding. And the laughter of her girls is a balm to her sorrow. Let them play while they can, she tells herself.

Other sounds seep into her hut where she squats over the fire, heating rice and a generous slab of dried fish on the cooking grate. Somewhere in a far hut, a baby cries, and Sofia tells herself she must see why this sweet boy is feeding so little he must cry with all his might. Not now. Too tired. Tomorrow, then.

And now there is the low pluck-brushing from Mama Kundi's hut. Sofia takes in this sound like honey and also a touch of sadness, for it returns her to the day Mama Kundi played over her brave son's new grave. The grave is not so new now, but still she smells the dirt Daniel shoveled over him and always she smells Elombe's sweet breath.

She lifts her weight onto her heavy legs and stands to move away from memories. There is no point in drowning herself in that swamp. She pulls aside the new cloth she hung from the doorway and steps out into the new evening. She calls her daughters to supper. "Kota na kati." Come inside. She calls again, and they race toward her and throw themselves inside the hut.

After they are all three inside, Mama Kundi pulls the doorway cloth aside. She holds her kundi in both hands and gives a slight head bob.

Sofia greets her and asks if she is hungry.

She eyes the cooking grate and lifts a ribbed hand to ask if they have enough for all.

"Tozali na ekoki." We have enough, Sofia tells her, and it is so tonight. Plenty of fish, and many leeks Madame Cassandra gave her, also a papaya from her tree, and biscuits Sofia made yesterday.

"Anh-hnh," Mama Kundi says, accepting. Sofia is glad for she must speak with Mama about Daniel before Alicia returns. Soon, she knows. Maybe tomorrow. If there is help for Daniel, Mama Kundi will know of it.

Sofia piles the food on their plates. The four of them eat sitting straight-legged on the floor of the hut. They eat with fingers that know how to manage the food with ease. Sofia has seen the family of Madame Cassandra eat with forks and spoons, but her girls spill less food on the floor than Matheo and Corey, and this gives Sofia a secret pleasure. They eat slowly and without saying much, and when they have eaten their fill, she sends the girls outside for more play before she talks to Mama Kundi of Daniel.

"Speak to me of Daniel," Mama Kundi says.

Daniel. The name presses hard on Sofia's throat. She thinks of little else these days. Yes, she has eaten her usual, but food cannot fill the hollow in her belly. She gazes at Mama closely and sees from the dark flecks in her eyes that she already knows what she will hear. How, she cannot say. Even so, she tells the story. Though it will not fill the hollow, the telling is like a rope she holds to keep herself from drowning. "I went to Kinshasa Prison. Madame Cassandra drove me in her Mazda and also my two girls." She pauses.

Mama waits for her to go forth with her story.

She tells of the locks they meet and open, the food they carry, the long gun of Moon Face who should be studying his maths, and when she reaches the empty place where Daniel is no more, she stops to fill her lungs and regain breath to go on. "He is not there. He is in some other place." She stops before telling the name she remembers: Those who go to that place are called The Dying.

Mama Kundi listens with her eyes shut. Finally, she tells her she knows of that place and this other wing. She does not say what Sofia already knows. They are starved. They are skeletons. Visitors will not see them there.

Sofia squeezes her hands together and touches them to her chin, quivering as she tries to stay from weeping.

"A na bomoi," Mama says. He is alive. I feel him. His heart still beats.

"Azali? Anh-hnh." Sofia's voice falls in relief before faltering as she asks herself how they can take him from a place she does not know. And if they do find him, how can they fight the others who have all the guns?

"*Matabisi,*" Mama says. A bribe.

Surprised to hear her own laugh, Sofia shakes off the word matabisi, like brushing small ants that circle the mat where she dries her fish. Who can pay this matabisi? She barely has money for rice. Even if she finds it, who can say if Moon Face will use the money to take her to Daniel or if he will give the smile to hide his greed and take the money to the bar. Before she can think of such things, she must think of Alicia, who returns soon from her mother's house. She must think how to tell Alicia that Daniel has gone where she cannot go.

After their talk, Sofia calls Kamina and Fimi in from playing and tells them it is time to wash the pots and the plates. Mama Kundi says she will do the wash-up and let the girls have rest. No, Kamina says. Mama Kundi must not do the wash-up. She must tell us a story. This one time, Mama.

Sofia thinks her first-born is learning bad ways from Madame Cassandra's boys. But maybe it is not so bad to let the girls listen to stories, for it will not be long before the Old One goes to the ancestors. She herself can do the wash-up. This one time. "Anh-hnh," she tells them and bends down to fill the bucket with pots and plates and takes them to the village tap. As she leaves the hut, she hears Mama Kundi telling how she played hopscotch in the North Country when she was their age, and she hears her girls laugh. You don't believe I was your age? Mama breaks out a laugh and tells of living on the banks of the Ubangi River. She learned to play her kundi there. Then she starts the pluck-brush of strings that fills the hut with gentle harmony.

At the village tap, Sofia waits as a small boy squats before the faucet. His hands press together and form a shallow cup. But his hands are a sorry cup and hold too little water to quench his thirst. When the faucet has no more water, the boy races to the pump handle. He is a small boy, no bigger than Elombe when he crawled out to meet the rain. It is a hard push for him to manage.

Sofia stretches one of her cups toward the boy. He takes it and holds it under the faucet while she stands at the pump handle and pushes hard several times. When the water begins to flow and fill his cup, he drinks, fills it again and drinks, laughing. Sofia laughs, too, and tells him "Ekokki." Enough. You don't want to burst. He nods and holds out the cup. She tells him it is his cup now. He nods again, clasps the cup, and runs off toward the far opposite edge of the village where his hut sits. She cannot remember his name but knows his hut. She knows his mother, who has only this boy and no other, and knows that he and Elombe were supposed to become friends.

After the plates are washed, Sofia takes the bucket and returns to find her girls sleeping on their mats in the corner away from the doorway. She smiles at Mama Kundi standing in the center. But Mama folds her ridged hands to her chest. Her face is sharp like a scythe to give force to her words. Be not afraid, she says. Don't fear of the prison. Don't fear of the men who carry long guns. We will find Daniel. I remember an uncle who saved me on the Ubangi River. I waded through tall grass into the river to cool myself. I was a foolish girl. I couldn't swim, but it was terrible hot and I could touch the bottom. I splashed around in the shallows and saw a hippo rise from the underwater. So close, I knew he could take me into his wide jaw. And he would, too. I stood still and waited for my own death. But this man, my uncle, saw the hippo and the foolish girl who couldn't swim from his pirogue. He watched the hippo watch me and prepare to strike. Uncle cried out, 'Yaka awa!' Come here. I cried back what he already knew, that I could not swim, and Uncle began to splash with his paddle to draw the hippo away from me, and the hippo turned from me to Uncle and prepared to charge him. Uncle knew that Hippo loved water but could not swim. Uncle paddled like thunder out into the deep of the river, and lost himself from Hippo. And I climbed, splashing, from the river to the grasses and ran and ran to my father's hut.

My father was a fishmonger. My mother grew maize. But there was an uncle who outran a hippo. I remember him. He saved me. He was family, too. We will find Daniel.

Ten

Cass' secret nestles into the rhythm of her days as the calendar turns over and spills into mid-November and the Saturday before Thanksgiving. She counts the wad of zaire bills clumped inside the fat volume of *World Poetry* and those haunting lines, "The center cannot hold." She hopes the poet is wrong about the center; she hopes Will is not keeping count of the bills.

The boys talk about Turkey Day. "But where are the turkeys?" Corey asks.

"There are no turkeys in Zaire," Matheo tells him with such an officious tone that Cassandra has to laugh.

"There are turkeys, sweetie, just not in the shops we know. We're doing something new for Thanksgiving."

"What?"

"It's a surprise."

Corey jumps up and down while Matheo's lower lip protrudes. "What kind of surprise?"

"Silly. If I told you, it wouldn't be a surprise, would it."

"I don't like surprises." Matheo sounds, for all the world, like Eeyore from Winnie the Pooh. He frowns at his mother, who hugs him.

Here, then, is the contrast between her two boys: To Corey, all of life is a surprise and that's fine with him. He's ready for any surprise. He will fling his small body toward it and climb on for a ride. To Matheo, a surprise is a hyena lurking under his bed waiting to strike. As the disparity between them returns to Cassandra's current memory bank, she wonders what kind of mother forgets something so fundamental to a son's essence. Don't answer that, she thinks. Don't go there.

"Here's a hint: Leon knows where we can find a goat."

"Do we get a pet goat?" Corey's wondrous exclamation bounds around and through them, and even tamps down Matheo's wariness.

Cass feels a distressing pang over Corey's naïve wonder, knowing what lies ahead for this soon-to-be-purchased-billy goat: a large cooking pot for their Thanksgiving dinner. But they're committed now. She can hardly turn around. She'll prepare the boys for the goat story, in due course.

She considers asking Tommy Hendricks along on this outing to purchase a goat, because she's invited Tommy and his family for Thanksgiving, and because of his long experience with Zairois and his savvy gift of gab. There are many unknowns in this landscape she's yet to fully embrace. She's getting there, though. In a funny way, this business with Xavier is helping ease her toward feeling more at home in this strange landscape because her ties to him give reign to that essential part of her that loves facing truth, even if the path to truth-telling takes circuitous routes of secrecy. In the end, Tommy's heft deters her. She worries about having space in the car for Tommy, Leon, the boys, and the goat, and decides that Leon will be support enough to get them there and home, safely.

And so they head East in the Mazda, leaving the familiar Kinshasa of tall buildings and pavement and passing a series of storefronts, of single level and gaudy siding, with odd pairings, one offering cement, another canned goods, a third vending beer. Out front, small round patio tables with bright umbrellas and chairs tipped in toward the tables, as if anticipating rain. A giant sign marks their identity: Centre de Chirurgerie Medicale. A line of patients snakes from roadway to doorway.

The paved two-lane recedes to dirt track, and, before long, further deterioration sets in. Small pits become deep ruts. She slows to weave around the potholes and give the Mazda its best shot at navigating the sorry state of the roadway. Each time the car takes a hard jounce, Corey says a phrase learned in pre-school, "C'est tres dangereux." It is very dangerous. Soon Cass, Matheo, and Leon join in, and their laughter trails the pronouncement while Corey's affect remains earnest, and Cass gives his hair an affectionate tousle. "Not to worry, sweetie, we're getting close." Cass plans for the outing to take only the morning, a Saturday, but has brought a snack of banana chips, peanut butter sandwiches, cucumber, and orange Fanta. Just in case.

They press on, passing an open area of savannah and fields of plowed dirt backed by stands of timber called okoumwes, tall trees of many uses. She pulls to the muddy lip of what passes for a road and pauses to watch three women in the center of a vast field of dirt. Leaning on their hoes, they catch sight of their audience. Two wear infants on their backs.

Corey rolls down his window and calls, "Mbote, Mamas."

The women wave and holler back, "Mbote mwa moboli." Hello, little boy.

They drive on. The women disappear from the rear window, the road worsens, and a series of wide muddy patches emerges from a recent rainstorm that she swerves to avoid. A few kilometers further on, a makeshift farm stand emerges on the right. A small wooden kiosk, tin roofed and open-air, displays banana, papaya, mango, avocado, and saka saka. "Ici, Madame," Here, Leon says. Cass noses the Mazda into the clearing near the farm stand and stops.

A boy sits astride a bicycle with rusted fenders and fat tires. He wears a shirt with a diagonal tear exposing a taut belly, and meets them with a bewildered frown. A young woman behind the trolley gives a spirited smile. She wears baseball cap at a jaunty angle, loop earrings, bright peach top with circular mandala design covering her slender front, and holds a bunch of carrots by the green tops. She is like a Life Magazine photo of the quintessential carefree farm girl in the States. Leon exits the car and approaches the kiosk, reaches across the counter and surrounds the girl's hands with his own. Corey bounds to the kiosk and begins shouting, "Mango mango mango."

A woman of middle age steps toward them. Barefoot, wearing navy and red striped man shirt over her yellow and red pagne, she leads a goat by a rope, a stocky fellow with bright white fur, white tail in a tight erect curl, and brown head accented by a wide white stripe from horns to chin. Leon meets the woman with a handshake and they exchange three alternating kisses to their cheeks. The goat regards the strangers straight-on, those widely-spaced eyes wanting to assure the visitors, I come in peace. Leon introduces his niece, nephew, and sister.

Acknowledgments pass more or less in unison, "Enchante,"

Whereupon Corey rushes the goat, brushes his nose to the animal's, and says, "Enchante."

Laughter all around, then the sister says something in rapid Lingala. Leon translates. 'Sa chevre prefere. Alingi nguba." Her favorite goat. He likes peanuts.

Her favorite? Cass regards the goat's sturdy bearing. Maybe. Or maybe not. Still, she places in the outstretched hand the one hundred zaire notes Leon quoted. Elena gives her a pointed look. "Ma prefere," she says and Cass pulls another ten from her handbag. Elena nods. Together, the two women accompany the favorite to the Mazda. Cass opens the trunk. Leon bends

toward the goat, somehow hefts him, belly-up, and singlehand-
edly tucks him into the trunk, and shuts the hatch.

At first, the return trip is seamless for the humans, if not
for the goat, who starts up his commentary with the first pot
hole, and, thereafter, tenders his steady "Ba-a ba-a." Matheo
and Corey find this amusing, their hilarity fills the car, though
as giggles diminish over kilometers logged, their conversation
turns to naming the goat.

"Peanut," Corey says.

"No. Snow Shoe," Matheo says.

They sling names back and forth until Leon offers a third
alternative. "Taba."

"It means goat, in Lingala, boys. Seems fitting. Okay?"

"Taba, Taba." Each boy plays the name softly on his tongue,
and with indifferent shrugs, they acquiesce. Cass feels a pinch of
sadness for the short life the goat called Taba will enjoy, or tol-
erate. She expresses regret to Leon for taking his sister's favorite
goat. He slides her an ironic smile, as if to say, Maybe he was her
favorite, maybe not. And she gets, with a twist of admiration,
the ruse his sister employed to up the asking price, and, for a
moment, catches an image of the poor creature smashed inside
the space where, in American crime movies, dead victims ride.
In the moment of sorry distraction, she misjudges a pot hole
large enough to entrap the Mazda. The car pitches as if to roll,
and lurches to a stop.

"Oh-oh. What happened?" Corey says.

"Don't you see we got stuck," Matheo says.

"I know. But are we, Mommy?"

"Stuck. For now," Cass says, hoping it's short-lived. "We
don't need to worry yet."

The goat brays.

"Shut up," she says with a fretful growl, pushes her door open and steps outside.

Leon tries to do likewise, finds the passenger door stuck, and crawls across to the driver's door.

Cass stands frozen on the mud-glommed ground. Goat for Thanksgiving. What an inane idea. She should never have listened to . . . who was it? Susan? Leon? What's wrong with roast chicken? What an idiot to fall for such a sketchy notion.

Leon moves to the rear of the car and leans his heft into the bumper with a steady Umph-2-3-umph. Matheo runs to join him, pushing with all his five-year-old might. The car jiggles lightly. Cass feels small, too, like her own seven-year-old self with falling arches, made to wear ugly high-top shoes instead of patent leather mary janes like the other girls. Her jogging shoes are pink, a bright almost-neon fuschia alongside the ragged brown hole in the earth. She hadn't wanted the pink; it was the only color in her shoe size.

The road stretches long and empty as far as she can see. She wishes the three women with hoes would come help push, though, of course, the two infants would preclude their helping. A remembered-story surfaces, a mother lifting a Volkswagen that was crushing her child, thanks to some miraculous wave of maternal heft. No way could it happen, yet it had. Supposedly. Not here, she thinks. Not happening.

Movement now on the roadway East where they've not gone, shadow shapes on the mud-soaked earth approaching the foursome standing outside the Mazda. Stuck. Waiting for the shadows to congeal into friend or threat. She withdraws a clean handkerchief from her handbag, wipes the sweat from her forehead, and squints into the blur of khaki and camouflage advancing toward them.

Within moments, a jeep, khaki green with open backbed, rolls into full view, pulls alongside the tilting Mazda, and stops. Four guys wearing all-camouflage shirts and trousers and green hard hats sit on the rim of the back bed. Long rifles ride their shoulders. The Army has landed, she thinks.

The camouflage-troop jumps down. Still shouldering rifles, they surround the Mazda and flood the air with Lingala chatter and new energy. Leon tells Cass, "Mettre au point mort. La voiture." Put it in neutral. Of course.

"They're giving us a push, boys." Slipping into the driver's seat, she sings her relief, and adjusts the gears accordingly. The four Army men plus the driver assume their positions around a car that is diminished in size, she swears, her hands on the wheel steering as the push, rock, push-push, rock-rock goes forth until a last push rolls the Mazda from the muddy crater up to the dry flat. Cheers erupt. The boys shriek and jump into the empty cavity.

"Natondi yo, merci beaucoup," Thank you, a grinning Cass tells them in Lingala and in French. Thank you.

The driver, taller than Will's six foot, presses in close enough to Cass for her to see sweat veins on his cheeks, a brown streak on a front tooth. "Matabisi," he says,

"Matabisi?" A tip. Of course. She has two more ten-zaire notes in her handbag. She withdraws one and extends it. He fixes lazy eyes on her, holds her gaze, turns aside, and spits. Quiet falls on the other Army guys who watch the tall soldier. Both groups watch him as he pours out words, strands of Lingala, she assumes, though maybe it's a tribal language, his mother tongue: Does someone like him even have a mother? Whatever tongue, the words from his mouth sound chewed, gutteral. Leon comes to her side and tells her in soft French that the soldiers are not paid in many months. They are so hungry.

Cass shrugs and opens wide the mouth of her purse to show its contents: the scorned ten, a second ten and five one-zaire notes. The tall driver is unmoved. Another soldier slips into the mudhole and raises his fist to Cass, nearly touching, just inches away. Corey jumps before the soldier nearest him, stomps and aims his foot for the soldier's leg. He tilts his round face upward. "Mister Baba, I'm gonna kick your butt."

As if waking from a nap, a different soldier, squat and mus-cled, moves in from behind and puts a camouflaged arm around Corey, who tries to wriggle away. The soldier tightens his grip. Corey yelps and sends up a wobbly plea to Cass. She stretches toward Corey, out of reach now, and the soldier tilts the barrel of the rifle toward him. Her cry towers over the pair, stocky Army thug and round-cheeked three-year-old: "Let him go."

Corey twists his head round to see his mother's face. He eyes the gun, quits his cry, squeezes his small fists, causing his cheeks to bulge. His eyes grow large and round. He's three years old and swallowing his fear. He shouldn't have to do that. Not a three-year-old. But Corey knows what is what in this moment: This is not Mommy mad at him and Matheo over the red crayon. This is a bad man with a long gun, a real one that could kill him dead.

Cass covers her mouth to keep from screaming. Mustn't provoke the bad man with the real gun. Matheo runs to her side. She grips his shoulder and leans to whisper, "Don't move. Don't speak. We must not provoke him anymore." Small whimpers roil in his throat. Her own breath grows shallow, she flexes her jaw, bites her back molars. The goat is quiet.

Leon steps between her and the driver. His voice, low and slow, carries his message in Lingala, like a record played at the wrong speed. She gets only one word: *Monganga*. Doctor. He must be telling about Will being a doctor. More words from the soldiers, gazes flicking, a shout of disgust from the driver.

The goat brays. A modest bray that, nevertheless, reaches the soldiers stationed behind the Mazda and the one holding Corey against his rifle. "Nini boye?" What's this?

"Taba," Leon tells him. Goat.

"Wapi?" Where?

"Non," Cass cries as Leon readies his answer, and she pleads, in tortured French: Don't tell where the goat is. He may know but don't tell him. And whatever else you do, don't open the trunk. An escape route is taking shape inside her. Tell them if they release the boy, we will give them a grand matabisi. But first the boy. Let him go.

Leon squints at her in confusion, then as the idea takes hold in him, too, a half-smile previews the message he delivers rapidly this time, but in low range. More blather among the camouflaged five concludes with the stocky one slipping his arm from Corey and shifting the gun further back on his shoulder. Corey darts to Cass, who lifts him into a massive hug. His cheeks burn crimson as he releases his cry on a cascade of hiccups to her shoulder.

She backs with her boys away from the soldiers and nods to Leon, who steps behind the Mazda and opens the trunk. He lifts the goat and wrestles him to the dirt, grabs the rope, and leads him to the tall driver, who spreads his arms and gazes in slow wonder at the white creature with the wide brown head.

The animal gives the driver pause, that's clear. But to what end? What's his next move? She catches her breath to see what she faces, whether pleasure or anger.

"Ntalo mingi," Expensive, Leon tells him. "Mingi."

The wind starts up, making a deep sweep of the stillness, the sky tilting from yellow to gray light, the soldiers giving in to laughter.

"Il va pleuvoir," Leon says. Cass doesn't know about rain, but some current in his pronouncement, some urgency, jumpstarts her to tighten Corey in her arms and grip Matheo's sweaty hand and sweep them into the car. Corey pours into the seat behind her own. Matheo crawls in beside his brother, Leon rides shotgun. She starts the engine and presses the accelerator, feels the car gain blessed traction on the washboard surface. In the review mirror, she watches the driver and another soldier lift the goat and drop it onto the metal surface of the backbed. Ouch, she thinks. The other soldiers take up their posts on the narrow rim.

The road ahead curves and the jeep bearing the goat named Taba disappears from sight. The moment they achieve forward motion, Corey says, "Mommy, it was all my fault."

"Your fault? Of course it wasn't your fault, you silly goose."

"But I said I was gonna kick his butt. I shouldn't a said it.' His words of regret slide into a whimper and he throws his body into a full-on wail. She sends him soft sounds of comfort to no effect, and his wail continues along many kilometers. It's as if he's been holding his breath through the time of danger, and only now permits himself the relief of exhalation. The fear, the anger, the torment he felt in the grip of the bad man are released in the wail nearly until Kinshasa, when it ceases and he falls instantly into sleep.

The secret she's carried, the plan she's joined, the hope born of a desire to bring justice to a poor country fall from favor. Damn her activist scruples, damn the infernal hum seducing her sound judgment and mother wit. Damn Xavier. Endangering her own neck is one thing. Putting her babies in peril is quite another. Nothing is worth that risk. Nothing.

PART TWO

Eleven

Sofia's hands hold back the cloth barrier to usher Alicia inside, and afterward her hands form fists she keeps hidden. The silence is thick so as to fill the small hut. Sofia has a fear that her forbidden desire for Daniel will find words to bring to this silence, and she will lose Alicia, too. But it is a foolish fear that vanishes, for the eyes watching her face flicker with a different fear as she takes in the silence. Sofia cannot look at her sister-in-law as she pours each of them tea she heated ahead of her coming. She must first collect herself and her words to make the best sound. All the time she prepares their tea and biscuits and collects herself, she holds firm to Mama Kundi's words. *He saved me. He was family, too. We will find Daniel.* But when the tea is poured and the two women sit straight legged on the hard dirt floor under the fine tin roof Sofia cannot anymore delay speaking.

First, she asks about Alicia's mother.

Alicia says nothing. The news of her mother can wait as she watches, and, finally, says his name. Daniel. How is my Daniel?

Sofia nods. She starts slowly. "It was as before. At first. Only this time, with Kamina and Fimi."

"Iyo-iyo" yes-yes, Alicia says and gives a half-nod that has no appetite for more waiting.

Sofia reaches the moment of the absent prison cell and Daniel in the place where they cannot go, the place of the dying.

She lets the words run free from her and now she looks at Alicia whose face melts as she takes in the meaning of the story. Her cool elegance crumbles with the pain, but her beauty remains. Seeing this beauty, Sofia feels a sorrowful truth that she has known but Alicia's absence has let her forget. This truth strikes her like punches to her belly that Gabriel gave when he stayed here under the fine roof: Even if they find Daniel and free him, he will go to Alicia, not to herself. Never to herself. Alicia will always be first in his heart. He is kind to herself, but, truly, his kindness is born of pity for a woman alone.

She slips to her knees and leans into Alicia, hugging her hard. She tells her that Madame Cassandra is going to help with Daniel. Sofia says this thing, not knowing if it so, or only a way to separate Alicia from her pain.

And do what? Alicia says, biting her lower lip. What can she do?

She wants to help. She has a husband. He knows the president. Sometimes he will listen more to the White Man Doctor than to his own people.

At this, Alicia startles her by making a sound with her lips as if to spit. What good is that to Daniel? Marshall Mobutu is the one who sent him there. He stole Daniel from me and sent him to that place because he knows the things people are saying about him. That he is a cockroach who steals money from his people. He knows he has reason to fear a cadre of guerillas. But Daniel is not one of them. He is not that kind of man.

"Nayebi," I know, Sofia says. She does know the kind of man he is.

This Madame Cassandra, Alicia says. She may have a good heart. She may want very much to help. But he is not her people. If that man Mobutu decides to bring him to the stadium and take a coupe coupe to his neck, she has no power to stop him.

"Nayebi," Sofia says again. There is truth in Alicia's words, and her own words bear only a thin slice of truth that can be overcome by lies. But she must try for Daniel. She must see how she can turn her words into truth. She will start with Madame Cassandra and exchange her words of hope and promise with true plans to free Daniel from Mobutu's prison.

At the start of the next week, Sofia walks Kamina and Fimi to the hut of Mama Kundi, who takes them, these days, to their school and meets them afterward until her work at Madame Cassandra's is finished. From Mama Kundi's, Sofia walks to Mimosa Village and arrives early at Madame Cassandra's house. Doctor Will meets her at the door. "Sofia, how are you?" He looks fine and tall and busy, but saves for her a quick smile and invites her inside.

"Malamu," Fine, she says, though the word means nothing on this day, and she can't help thinking she may never again be fine. Or, as with the roof that Gabriel built, she will be fine, but there will still be drownings. A fierce impulse moves her to tell him about Daniel and what is what. "Doctor?" she says suddenly.

"Oui?" He has eyes only for his keys now and steps for the door, but he turns. He must go but he has a moment for her. What is it?

She loses courage. He has a moment, but no real time for her or her Daniel. No, not hers. Alicia's Daniel. Doctor Will must go quickly to the hospital named for Mobutu Sese Seko's mother. "Kenda malamu," Go well, she tells him. He nods and hurries down the steps.

Madame Cassandra enters the kitchen, where Sofia prepares the breakfast of oats, toast, papaya, and coffee for Madame, who chooses it before tea. Matheo hurries through the door to the table, but Corey rushes to Sofia and squeezes her around her belly and begins a story that cannot wait. The words are in English, with now and then a French word. "Tres dangereux" and "mauvais homme." Sofia has more French than Corey, and enough for this sketch. Madame has so-so French and a little Lingala. Together, they may make a fuller understanding of his story.

"Nini boye?" What is this? she says. What is Corey telling me?

We went to buy a goat, she begins. You remember I told you I wanted to cook a goat for Thanksgiving?

Sofia remembers. She thinks of the goat with pleasure. She's hoping to eat some goat on Melesi Mingi. the Day of Much Thanks, a holiday in the country of Madame Cassandra. To Sofia, such a day is curious, for in her country, there is 30 Juin, the day of independence, a day for francophones, a day for the birthday of Mobutu Sese Seko, and a day for the birthday of Yeshua. But there is no day of thanks. Once she said thanks for her brave Elombe, but he was too brave and left for some world she cannot know. And she said thanks for Daniel and his kindness to her, but he has left, too, for some room beyond seeing. Now she spends her days in a village-that-is-not-a-village in a house of many rooms, a house her people did not build.

Madame's story continues. Leon came, too, to show the way. He won't come here today, I told him to go to market and buy three chickens, and tomorrow he will prepare them for Thanksgiving. And in a mix of French and Lingala and hand motions, she tells about the Army men, the guns, and the man who grabbed Corey. When she finishes the story, she shuts her eyes. lifts her hands and squeezes them into fists, as if she still can't believe the wonder of their escape. She says she was a fool to travel so far for a goat, only to give it to those men. Even the one who took Corey and made him so afraid.

Sofia nods. Madame throws out an arm as if to slap someone, but there is no one within reach. She speaks with such carved quiet. I have no desire to spend 110 zaires on a goat for Mobutu's Army.

"Nayebi," I know, Sofia says. Those Army men, you know, I hear in my village that they are not paid for many fortnights. The goat will help them very much.

"Mbele," Maybe, Madame says. They're starving. But that's no excuse for scaring a small child to death. She squeezes one hand into a fist and slaps it into the palm of the other, a hard slap of anger that pleases Sofia, and gives her hope that when she pleads for Daniel again, Madame will be ready to help. And if help truly does come, Sofia will be ready to say thanks to Madame and to Creator God and the ancestors who stand ready to make her world whole.

"Daniel." His name leaks softly from her lips, and reaches only her ears. She looks down at her plastic Bata sandals, peeking out from her long pagne.

Giggles drift through the open doorway to the kitchen. Sofia wanders in to see what is what. The small boys are having a laugh at breakfast. A good laugh. "Mister Baba, I'm gonna kick your butt." Sofia can't keep herself from smiling. She cannot know the meaning of all the words the boys trade back and forth. But she knows who Mister Baba is and knows he is far far away.

Twelve

Cass won't lie. She's relieved that the goat her boys christened Taba hasn't made it to the table for Thanksgiving dinner. By now, he may have turned up on a spit over a fire built by the Army. Certainly, on that dark day, he wasn't long for this world. But she last saw him standing in the open back bed of the jeep, ba-aaing his heart out, and this is the image she chooses to hold.

In fact, the soldier thugs may have saved her from having dinner at home, as the Hendricks learned of their dilemma and invited them for the feast, along with the Shaws and a solo guy, Vernoy Benson. In lieu of goat, Cass and Will are contributing two loaves of bread and three pies, all baked the day before. Tommy and Lindy have roasted seven chickens, two for each family present, plus one for the solo guest. Susan and Logan bring green beans and canned cranberry sauce that crossed the ocean with them. Vernoy bears two liters of Portuguese wine, decanted from a five-gallon jug and a gallon of apple cider, an unlikely find from months past.

The celebrants arrive ensemble, in late afternoon, the hour between daylight and darkness when the dying sun burnishes the landscape and penetrates the picture window to glance off a framed collage of butterfly wings hanging behind a living room couch. The women wear African wraps of brilliant tropical design. The men wear bou-bou shirts, the Zairois man's dress staple, short-sleeved pullover shirts of somewhat more muted fabric with jeans or shorts.

Despite a propitious welcome and coming together, an incident almost sabotages the celebration. It occurs almost immediately with a comment Matheo makes to one of the Hendricks girls, his age-mate at five. All six of the children, three, four, and five-year-olds, have gathered in the older Hendrick girl's bedroom and helped themselves to her drawing materials, pushing the girl, Camille Hendrick to stake her claim: "I'm the real artist, anyway."

"Unh-unh." Matheo holds up a paper offering his own drawing as evidence to the contrary. It's yet another rendering of the soldier standing behind a green truck, holding a long rifle.

Camille sends a brooding gaze over the image. "You're not supposed to draw guns."

"You can so. Just ask Miss Overholzer."

"I don't care. Everybody in my class knows I'm the best artist."

Matheo goes off-script then. "Well, everybody says your daddy is fat. And he is, too."

Camille chokes out her indignation. "Nu-unh nu-unh nu-unh."

Her younger sister, Angie, says, "Daddy is, too."

Whereupon Camille dashes from the room to the kitchen and floods her mother with her indignation. Lindy takes a seat with Camille in her lap and soaks up the words. "Matheo says Daddy's fat."

"Okay-okay, that's not the end of the world, is it?" Lindy croons.

Tommy picks up the gist, and strides down the hallway into the doorway of Camille's room. Arms folded over his abundant belly, he addresses Matheo. "So. You think I'm fat?"

Having overheard the children's exchange, Cass pauses her breath to catch Matheo's response. She feels for her l'annee, as the French call the first-born. Even at his tender age, he has a strong sense of morality. He knows it's wrong to lie and she doubts if he'll see his way clear to do so now. But it's even worse to insult your friend's father who is their host, and she wants to throttle that boy. What has she done or not done, that he can allow himself to say such things? What kind of mother is she? She fists and unfists her hands and vows to tutor him on guarding his mouth in the future. But Matheo faces a more immediate question: Does he tell the truth and risk Mister Hendricks' anger? Or, does he go against his own principles and lie? At last, a single word, soft and distinct, surfaces. "Yes."

That's my Mattie. Cass steps toward the children's room and waits for the indignation Tommy is capable of unleashing. Once in the hospital, she heard him laying into another nurse anesthetist asleep under the operating table. As head of the department, Tommy was making rounds to see if the staff was observing protocol. When he saw his colleague snoring under the table, he lost it. She remembers him saying "Zoba," idiot. Over and over. But now laughter drifts from his daughter's room out into the rest of the house, and his soft joke nudges her son. "There's only one correct answer, my boy. We can't be kidding ourselves, now can we."

Mattie sends wary glances about him, and shakes his head. Nearly felled by relief, Cass smiles and steps lightly for the table, where dinner is served.

They are seven at the adult table in the alcove between kitchen and living room, an identical layout to their own, and six at the makeshift card table serving the underage crowd. Seven chickens, roasted and sliced, cover the larger table, along with lavish side dishes, mashed potatoes, sweet potatoes, green beans, celery sticks, fresh buns, and tropical fruits. Tommy lifts a carving knife over one of the chickens and prepares to slice the roasted flesh.

Vernoy clears his throat. "What say you, friends, before we tuck into this lavish feast, we bless the food? Seeing as how it is Thanksgiving."

"That's your assignment, should you choose to accept it,' Tommy puts in.

"Whyever not?" he says and delivers a prayer wholly unlike the sort Cass' mother ever spread over her childhood dinner table. "We give you thanks, Mother and Father of us all, for these plates and for the creatures who offer themselves for our nourishment. Keep our eyes and our hearts open for the ways we should step forth in light and in shadow. Look upon us with kindness in this terra incognita, and use us as instruments of your justice, truth, and healing. Amen and Amen."

His Amens usher in a full minute of silence, even at the children's table. Then Susan says, "That was . . . lovely."

"You're my kind of missionary." Will serves up his half-grin.

"I'll drink to that." Logan lifts his glass for Vernoy to fill it with the Portuguese wine he decanted.

Cass catches herself measuring Vernoy's words alongside the remembered prayers of childhood, her mother's fervid pleas for someone's health that her father dubbed "gall bladder prayers," prayers that utterly put Cass off the practice of petitioning the Almighty for any notice. This is a different brand of talk with the Holy One, a different tribe of pray-er.

Lindy Hendricks slays the silence with a query. "Tell us more about your going-for-a-goat adventure. Will you?"

"Well, as I told you, we bought it from Leon's sister. Not cheap, I might add," Cass says before laying out a fuller version of the events of last Saturday. She plays down the pointed gun.

Afterward, Lindy says quietly, 'That Corey. He's a brave little guy."

Cass catches Corey listening, and traversing back to the rifle pointed at his belly plumpness, shoulders lifting in bracing mode, face slipping into a pre-crying phase. Vernoy Benson catches the shift in his expression and tells him, "Thank goodness Mister Baba lives far away, right, Corey?"

"Right. I told him, Mister Baba, I'm gonna kick your butt." And he peels out giggles again.

"Next time, we'll bring you along, Tommy," Cass says. "To be fair, though, Leon was heroic. He kept his cool."

Tommy Hendricks lifts his glass of orange Fanta to acknowledge her. A teetotaler who grew up the child of missionaries in the Ubangi region of northern Zaire, abstaining from alcohol may be his primary nod to discipline.

Eating takes over, and silence, a kind of reverential nod to all that is real and true in the world, even a world inhabited by Mobutu and men with rifles. Will, a man of fat appetite and lean frame, tucks into his second helping of chicken and mashed potatoes. Tommy often boasts about his one-helping diet, even a plate requiring sidecars. He shoots a rueful frown at Will's plate and turns to Lindy. "See there, Babe. Look at how much he eats."

Lindy rolls her eyes at Cass, who winces as an anecdote about Tommy and Lindy in bed replays in her memory, an exchange Susan overheard on a late-night walk around Mimosa:

Lindy: I'm on top. I do all the work.

Tommy: What do you mean? I play with your tits and everything.

A sliver of shame streaks through Cass' breasts. She sips her wine and trips the topic away from the bedtime story. "You grew up in Zaire?"

"Up North. The Ubangi region. I'm a PK. Covenant Church. My old man wanted to save the world for Jesus," Tommy says.

"How's that working out for him?" Logan barely breaks audible.

"Paul Carlson was up there," Vernoy says. 'Did you know him?"

"I was a kid finishing high school when the Simba soldiers stormed the village. Doctor Carlson got caught up in the trouble. He could see this was no cake walk and he better get out of range of the bullets. Eventually. But he and another guy decide to climb a wall. Paul lets the other guy go first. Gets shot for his kindness."

"Who's Paul Carlson?" Cass says.

"The Zaiorois loved the guy. Monganga Paul, they called him. Doctor Paul. He and my dad were buddies. Dad used to say he and Paul split up the job. Paul took care of their bodies; he took care of their souls."

"They shot him? A Western-trained doc taking care of Zairois." Cass takes long swallow of her wine.

"They said he was a spy against the government. That's what I read in the New York Times," Vernoy says.

"That day was ten years ago, you know?" Tommy says. "I remember us sitting at the table on Thanksgiving a couple days later. We always went around and said what we were thankful for, you know? I couldn't say what I was thinking, 'I'm thankful it wasn't you, Dad. Or me.' Finally, my mom said she was thankful Monganga Paul's soul had gone to heaven." A half-gargled laugh squeezes from Tommy's throat and his fist thumps the table. Cass' right arm jerks, and the wine in her glass swishes wildly. "That's when the whole religion thing took a nose dive."

"Tommy." Lindy sparks out his name in full complaint.

"Just talking about me, Babe."

"So you've lost your faith, then?" Cass presses.

"You could say."

"Lost? It's not like faith is a bucket of coins somebody loses or a wallet that gets snatched. Faith is how we see. It's our window on the universe," Vernoy says.

A field of silence descends around the table. Tommy turns to Vernoy with wonder for this offering. "You're some kind of philosopher, then, are you."

As Vernoy shakes his head, she catches the dark lines wearing his fifty-plus years and giving weight to Tommy's charge. She can see the philosopher in him taking the measure of the universe. She's heard Vernoy's story from Lindy, how he did all the course work for law school, then dropped out and never took the bar exam. He made scads of money in insurance, best salesman in the known universe, etcetera. On his fiftieth birthday, he decided it was time for a change. He wanted his life to be about more than preserving the portfolios of prosperous Americans. Let's venture overseas to a Third World country, he says to his wife of thirty years. Their oldest son has just had a child. His wife can't bear to leave the continent with her grandchild alive and kicking on it. But Vernoy is with this new dream of a bigger life. He goes; she stays. They're still married. She comes over once a year; he flies home once a year. That's how they work it out.

Now he's not having any of Tommy's philosopher nonsense. "I'm an insurance broker-cum-Ministry of Finance occupant. Don't tell that lot about my philosophizing. They'll have me shot."

Gusts of laughter around the table skip Cass, who waits out the hilarity, unsettling though it is. At last the quiet resumes. "You're in the Ministry of Finance. Do you know a guy named Xavier?"

"Xavier. Of course. He's one of the principles in Mobutu's cadre. How do you know him?"

She feels Will taking her in with that half squint, his hand holding his wine glass suspended, awaiting her answer. "Yes. How do you know him?" he says drily.

"Hey, a girl has to have a few secrets." The lightness of her tone backfires, wobbles a bit, and trails off. "The fight. Ali-Foreman. Remember that guy who sat down beside me that night? We exchanged names, a few pleasantries that's all. No biggee." She feels the lie clogging the small geography of her short waist, pinching her air space, and she sends up a wor-ry-wish that is her present version of a prayer, the hope that Will won't be counting the stash of zaire bills, catching the shortfall, and connecting them to this talk of Xavier. Even if she still prays in the normal way, she can hardly ask the Almighty to save her from the consequences of her lie, even a lie of omission. Even one she'll no longer require, with her new resolve to abandon Xavier's project.

Despite Vernoy's refusal to embrace the philosopher mantel, Cass finds herself attracted to the guy. Not that kind of attrac-tion, mind. She's not vulnerable to extramarital trespassing, and if she were, it would not be occasioned by this fifty-something guy with a lantern-jaw and a gut paunch. She recalls Susan's revelation about Logan's dalliance with a spritz of relief that Will isn't the dallying kind. That's old news for her new friends, anyway, therapy having put those horrors to bed, so to speak.

No, it's the cool prayer Vernoy said at the table that draws her, the desire to know a man who speaks of going forth "in light and in shadow," one who talks of being "an instrument of justice," and being treated with kindness. Surely, here's a man who can understand her and the pulse inside to free the world of oppressors like Mobutu. Cass tries for an air of nonchalance as the gathering disperses itself willy nilly around the living room and she follows him and his pie and coffee, shamelessly, to a corner seat near the wall-sized view window to a poinsettia tree blooming red over the outsized deck and the lavish green lawn beyond. She takes a facing chair. And here they are seated apart from the others at the edge of the room, for a spot of privacy, Cass hopes, though she doubts he has any such thought. She sips her coffee and forks her mango pie. "Who do you suppose the rebels thought Paul Carlson was spying for? Mobutu?"

Vernoy takes a slow bite of his mango pie. A chuckle goes down with his swallowing. "In '64 when Carlson was killed, Mobutu was only a sergeant, leading the armed forces. He didn't become president until '65. They weren't a thinking lot, those Simba rebels. They were young. Followers of Patrice Lumumba, the guy from Katanga. A straight-up leader, by all accounts, which doesn't mean his followers were as clear-eyed. Of course, the rebels would know Mobutu arranged for Lumumba's killing. With a hand from the US, by all accounts. They picked Mobutu for what he wasn't: a Communist. Not the first time we've backed the wrong fellow." His baritone eases the prickly subject matter through her, like cacti wrapped in satin.

"No kidding. Look at Ho Chi Minh." She feels a ping of sorrow for Lumumba, the man who would be leader of Zaire, if not for Mobutu.

Vernoy nods absently. "As I said, the rebels were not a thinking lot. A guy like Paul Carlson? From what I've read, not the sort of colonialist-intruder-missionary James Michener writes about in Hawaii. Not at all. The rebels had no understanding of a White fellow from a rich country traveling across the world to help the poor of Zaire. A simple man of faith who offered his hands to the people. I hear he even fixed their outboard motor, and they pegged him as their enemy." His baritone turns husky and low. "He was out of their imaginal range. And they had this weird belief that dawa, which was water applied by a medicine man, would make them impervious to bullets."

She takes her last bite of pie and weighs the wisdom of confessing the instinct for justice still chasing her, to someone who would understand. Who could deny what her gut tells her, that something is not right, she must do something? Surely not this Vernoy person before her, he of the beautiful prayer. A quickening of her pulse and the words are out in the world, rising between them, all timbre and meaning. "Interesting that this band of rebels had a better grasp of the situation than the US government. Surprised they haven't sent old leopard skin packing. In retrospect, the rebels were right. He's turned out . . ."

"Worse than they or anyone feared." He slides his long frame back in the soft chair, appears to fix on the ceiling fan, and says softly, "Ah, the retrospectoscope."

Cass takes heart from his relaxed posture. "What if Carlson had lived? Maybe he'd participate in a scheme to dethrone Mobutu."

"Dethrone?" He straightens in the armchair and sharpens his gaze on her. "Why are you so interested in Carlson, the spy that wasn't?"

"Just wondering. A man with his moral compass. It might occur to him, is all." Cass shrugs. "I've always been fascinated by people who stand up, and speak out for justice, no matter the cost to them personally. It's this . . . thing about me."

Silence, like a knockout blow to their tete a tete, then his fretful response: "This line of inquiry, you must know, is fraught with peril."

"What do you mean?" She knows precisely what he means.

"Terra incognita," he says drily.

"As in, 'Beyond here be dragons,' like those Old-World maps."

"Exactly so. I don't know you at all well, Madame Ramsey." His tone takes on an uber-formality that unsettles her. Her jaw stiffens, protruding a touch. She looks away, as if the blush moving upward from her neck will be unseen by Vernoy. I've overstepped, she thinks. But Vernoy continues. "Mobutu holds sway over a kleptocracy. He's a thief of the public purse and an assassin. It's true. I'm sure you've heard about the four ex-cabinet members arrested on charges of treason."

"Recently?"

"Early on after his coup. They were tried before a military tribunal. Heads covered, they were hanged in the stadium while 50,000 citoyens looked on. But you, you're nothing here. Nothing. Or, no more than a thing. If Mobutu or any of his ilk get wind of your notions, you may be convicted of an offence abhorrent to the Minister of Communication."

"Daniel." The name startles from her lips. "That's where Daniel works. Or worked."

"Daniel?" he says mildly.

"Do you know him?" she presses.

"So you think there's only one."

Maybe she does. In such a strange place as this, you never know. Two months after they arrived here, a letter reached Will from Roger, his best Vietnam buddy. The envelope read "Doctor Will Knee-Man Ramsey, Hospital, Africa." He keeps it on his desk, as a reminder to laugh on hard days at the absurdity of this world where they find themselves. So, yes, maybe she believes this Vernoy Benson knows Sofia's Daniel from a neighboring Ministry.

The earnest gaze meeting her own morphs into amusement. "Big fellow, Daniel, good heft on him, never met a stranger?"

"Yes. Yes. Yes." She's nodding, trying to check the optimism rising inside, for knowing a person means nothing if he's lost. You have to know where to find him, how to rescue him, and how to return him safely to his family.

"Come to think, I haven't seen him around these past weeks."

"No you haven't. Because he's in Kinshasa Prison."

He whistles softly. "That hell hole. Whatever for?"

"Some memo he wrote intercepted by the wrong people. Now they say he makes a coup, against Mobutu. Quoting his sister-in-law here, my nanny."

"What did I tell you? That ilk will do anything,"

"You know him, Daniel. He hasn't done squat about a coup. It's not in him."

"So has this nanny visited him?"

"Once. The second time he was somewhere else. They wouldn't let her see him."

"That doesn't sound good." He makes a poof with his lips, as if exhaling smoke.

"Oh no." She shuts her eyes and she's back with Sofia and the girls standing under the massive words rising like meteors overhead:

Prison - Centrale

de

Kinshasa

And the young round-faced guard hoisting a long gun over scant shoulders. And Sofia's voice tolling those heavy words, Ezali awa te. He is not here.

"But we have to try. Will you help?" Cassandra presses.

"You think I'm some kind of magician?" His slow grin eases her a touch. "We're on treacherous ground here. Any one of us incomers may be deemed undesirable, a threat to the prevailing order. They have a phrase for that here, you know. You become an Immigrant Interdit. Or worse. This in particular is what we need to keep in mind. Mobutu would as soon herd a person blindfolded into the stadium to face a firing squad as take a piss."

His piss hisses between them, lingering, and moving her to protest. "Look. On the matter of dethroning the leopard-skin-emperor, I'm not stupid. I was just letting my mind run a bit. My real hope now is to somehow spring Daniel from that hellhole."

"Good to know. Because Leopard Man doesn't care what color you are, how many children you have and what ages, or where you are from. He cares only that you stay clear of him and his territory, which is everywhere you look. You can't beat the guy on his own turf. And remember, Mobutu Sese Seko, Fondateur de la Revolution, Assassin in Chief, is a friend to your country and mine."

His words move into a place of sunken dreams within her. "Whatever," she says flicking a backhand his direction. She feels not only the weight of truth in his words, but the irony of herself arguing for the very position she so recently abandoned. And, true enough, she has abandoned Xavier's project. A fool's errand, if ever there was one. She knows it now. "But you could help Daniel. *Nothing wrong with that, is there?* You could do it with finesse. I know you could."

"Wait," he says abruptly. "Tommy Hendricks. He's your man."

"Tommy?" She skates a look across the room, where Tommy is downing yet another orange crush, and playing Rock-Paper-Scissors with all the children.

"Ezali malamu," Tommy says to all six.

She smiles. "He speaks Lingala. There is that."

"Indeed." Vernoy leans into his professorial mode. "And he has heft. Here, being fat means you have enough to eat. For some Zairois, being fat also goes with having wealth, and wealth means power."

"Really?"

"Look around you. Haven't you noticed that driving a Mercedes often goes with being fat?"

"Maybe." There was that time driving on Boulevard 30 Juin, when a Mercedes started backing up. She honked repeatedly and the driver bolted from his black Mercedes and strode toward her. She locked the doors of the Mazda, rolled up the windows, and shook her head as he vulturized her from alongside the driver's door. She shook and shook her head. He shook a fist at her and stalked away. Recalling that hulking figure, she thought, Yes, he was crazy-fat. "Okay. Tommy and you. You'd make a great team."

"I can't see it." He adds, "You know he has a plane."

"A private plane? You've got to be kidding."

"An Aero-Commander twin engine. Not precisely his own. But he's tight with a pilot. Calls him Captain Alongi. Has him on retainer. Claims it's his escape hatch. You never know. He has it by virtue of the matabisi. That's his modus-operandi here."

"Ah. That's . . ." She flares an arm toward him as if to grasp the word she seeks. "Will you talk to Tommy?"

"Let me think about it." He pushes himself to standing and gives her a parting nod.

She turns back to Tommy, still entertaining the troop of children. It's Corey's turn. He jumps with his whole slight body after each palm pump and lets out a giggled hoot. Another image returns, Corey brushing his nose to the goat's while telling him 'Enchante,' and, in its wake, another image, that same goat, christened Taba, turning on a spit over an open fire. In the image, he's quiet, no more ba-a-ing, no sound at all.

Cass' tete-a-tete with Vernoy follows her into December and the weeks leading up to Christmas in a land of no snow. Portions of his baritone lament toll in her head for days afterward: *You're nothing here . . . no-thing . . . Can't beat the guy on his own turf . . . herd you blindfolded into the stadium . . . . face a firing squad as take a piss . . . a friend to your country and mine.* She holds his words in that belly-cache that is her home address for truth. But onto that cache, his words of solace come to rest: *Let me think on it. We'll talk.* Yes, think on it. And see what will be.

One of her SDS cohorts used to say, "Think globally, act locally." The phrase comes home to her now as a way out of this present dilemma, and as a balm for her nerves. The Xavier project is global, freeing Daniel is local. Forget Xavier. She was an idiot to think she could join a coup plot with impunity, even at a low level. Beyond here be dragons, dragons that could tear them apart, even a spoiled rich American woman who does not have to work for her food.

Go with freeing Daniel. That's a local enterprise, one that would feed her yearning for justice and not involve a firing squad. A decided plus. And a distinctly do-able enterprise, especially if Tommy Hendricks takes the lead.

There's one distasteful task before she can embrace the new scheme. She must rescind her promise to fund the apartment, disengage from Xavier, and let him know of her decision before the January rent comes due.

Late on a weekday afternoon, but before Will's re-entry from the hospital, she shuts the door to Will's study and makes the call. Xavier is caught off guard, maybe a touch curious but pleased. She keeps her message brief. "Can we meet? Same place? Good. See you. Ca va?"

"Ca va, Madame Ramsey. Bien sur." His voice comes lightly across the line, with his assumption that another check is forthcoming, for January's rent. Then the switch to English sinks the voice a touch. "Is there a problem?" But his English would carry the earnest tone of the second language effort. And she can't suppress a lilt of regret for her part in the rise and fall of Xavier's hopes.

"See you then." She can't afford to linger, for she must tell him to his face. She owes him that.

The next week takes her for another wild trip in a *fula fula*. She closes her eyes and imagines that a trip in an automatic washer would not be so very different. Once freed from the shimmying squeeze-box conveyance, she steps hard onto pavement, pauses to breathe through a hint of dizziness and get her bearings. She wipes sweat from her neck and the line where her bangs stick to her forehead, and, at last, she crosses the granite-tiled piazza to the same far-back table where they last met. "This must be our local. Good to see you," she says, a moment of camaraderie to savor before everything changes.

"C'est-ca." He sweeps out a hand to her appointed chair. Relaxed now, he opens the conversation she's dreading. She's lost sleep these last nights since her chat with Vernoy, attempting to wrestle her regrets to silence. "We have an apartment. A studio. Not big. But enough. And not easy to find. Is good."

So hopeful. So sorry. "Sounds good." Her echo bears her reluctance to turn the charming Minister of Finance into an immobile mannequin version of himself.

"I am glad you called, Madame."

"Cassandra. Call me Cass. Unless you want me to call you Minister." She tilts her head in a way that might be seen as flirtatious but it's only an effort to delay the distress.

He nods. "Is early. I appreciate you come early for January rent."

"Early, yes. I wanted to give you lead time."

"Lead time." A flat gaze across the table.

She catches her hands, clammy palms sliding every which way. Stills them. "Thing is, Xavier."

Only the stillness of his body telegraphs his concern. "Oui? Tell me."

"Thing is." She pauses her announcement amid the audible confetti of Lingala-French-and-what-all tongues tossing round and round the piazza in a metallic swirl, and laughter weighted with strangeness. "I have a problem. The Army, Mobutu's goons, nearly shot my three-year-old."

"What do you say? Where was this?" His response is hoarse and brusque, as if his throat is seizing.

She tells in brisk shorthand strokes how a journey to buy a goat for Thanksgiving came to the brink of violence. How her guardian angel or a stroke of luck or a quick-thinking Leon pulled them from the brink. How risking herself is one choice, but leading her babes to danger is a risk she is unprepared to take. "You have to understand."

Xavier bobs his lean, nearly handsome head to confirm he's heard, he understands. "Oh, I understand, Madame Cassandra." Yes, he keeps the Madame for this exchange. Because there's no point in dropping it since they are colleagues no more. That pairing and any future friendship is fractured, like a gourd cracked beyond repair, and it can no longer hold the contents.

As he shoves himself to stand, the chair teeters and lands on its back, sending a metallic clang over the piazza. He bolts. There's no other word and no stopping him from his swift, skating removal from her world of richness and lies to his own band of incorrupt resisters for justice. Her own pleas to wait, *try to understand*, fall short and wend back to the table on the edge of the piazza, their local no more.

She presses to her feet and bends over the upturned chair, heavy, metallic, and sets it upright, glancing around for any reaction from nearby customers. No trace of anyone observing the minor upset, a relief. *Isn't it just perfect that I'm unseen,* she thinks, feeling small and absurdly foolish over the incident, the fuss she's brought to poor Xavier's life, the hash she's visited on his hopes. *What a dope I am*, she thinks, as he strides off and out of sight of the woman who traveled 9000 miles to betray him.

She steps away, too, before the waitress returns to take her order.

"Where were you?" Will's question startles her as she opens the screen door and steps through the kitchen to the study where he ever keeps himself when not at Mama Yemo. A friend back home, Suzette, once remarked that if Will were not a doctor, he'd be a monk. 'You've nailed it,' she told Suzette. Now, as then, she sees the truth of those words in the purity of his purpose, the singularity of his focus. At the moment: his Ortho Board prep.

"In town. Tutoring that guy, remember I told you?"

"Oh, right." He's noncommittal. "He paying you?"

"Just lunch. Should he be? I didn't figure I should charge him, given the way the government stiffs its employees. Remember

those soldiers on the goat trip, they hadn't been paid in months."
There's truth in her words, but the lie inside spins effortlessly
from lips suddenly dry with unease for delivering her falseness.

"I guess not." His voice sags with some letdown, not grave,
but not forgettable either. He holds the volume of *World Poetry*
whose lines share lodging with zaire bills. Anxiety feathers up
from her gut and she licks her lips. *Is he doing a count?*

"Is the stash still tucked in with Yeats' "Second Coming?""

"Apparently the poem is infecting the stash."

"What does that mean?"

"Things are falling apart. The center is not holding. Isn't
that how the lines go? The stash isn't holding either. The stash
is shrinking."

"Shrinking? By how much?"

"Maybe two hundred since I last checked."

"'Think someone's stealing?" The words come of their own
accord, freely but weighted by her shame for what she's become.
Someone so keen to save her own skin, she'd sacrifice Leon
and Sofia, who barely survive on what she pays them and still
wouldn't dream of stealing.

"Do you?"

"Think someone's stealing?" She meets his query straight-on
and the gaze she can only describe as surgical. "I do not. Thing
is, I guess I'm the culprit. Food here is ridiculous. You do know
that a roll of toilet paper costs $5.00."

"Yeah? It's obscene. Not that we're hurting. But it kind of
feels like play money, especially when Tommy doles it out of
that gunny sack he hauls around like Father Christmas. It's easy
to let it run out like water. I think I'm channeling my dad. But
just . . . be vigilant, that's all, can you do that?"

A quick nod that skirts the emotional undertones, because if she honors this parent-child exchange, where he's the

bread-winning-benevolent father and she's the child who needs reigning in, she'll lose it. She'll lash out and maybe even spill the shameful truth about where the money went. *Well, if you must know, I've been helping a rebel group prepare to unseat the so-called President. There. Now you know. Divorce me, why don't you.*

Instead, she says, "Tommy," and lifts up a quick laugh at the name she's been harboring, all afternoon, in the front of her mind. She comes a breath close to mentioning her talk with Vernoy. If she tells him about the scheme to rescue that they're trying to set in motion, will he force them to abandon it? Or will he get behind it? Timing is key. *There's a time for everything under the sun and there will be a time for revealing the plan to Will. A perfect time.* Just not now. "I'll try to keep a closer count. I'm not tutoring that guy for free anymore. Maybe I can enlist some paying clients, what do you think?"

He slides the poetry volume back into its vacant slot on the shelf, turns with a nod and lays a fifty-zaire note in her hand. "Sure. If you want to."

She gazes down at the large bill in her open palm. "What's this?"

"I don't want you to feel strapped."

"Thanks, Honey." She leans into him with a long hug and a silent promise to herself and the Creator God of Vernoy's prayer to stop excusing these lapses of truth as serving the marriage, when they're nothing but lies. She knows Will is a monk and a straight-shooter who will never lie to her. *You deserve better,* she tells him mutely and closes her hand around the bill.

Thirteen

Sofia waits through long days for the time when she dares pain Madame Cassandra with worries over Daniel. Madame has already much worry for her boy, Corey. One more worry from Sofia might bring word of no more nanny. If this word comes, Sofia and her girls will have a life with no food. The pay she receives each week is not big, but enough.

At last, there is a morning when Sofia's two girls and Madame's two boys are each at their separate schools and the tight veins of worry are faint under Madame's eyes. If there will be a time, can it be now? Maybe. So it is that she asks Madame if she would like to know Mama Kundi in the River Village.

"And who is Mama Kundi?" Madame smiles with eyes at their half-lidded place.

"She is not a witch, though some say so. She is a woman from the north country. She is a wise friend, older even than she knows. She plays a harp from that place, a kundi. That is why her name came to be Mama Kundi. You would like to know her?"

"Of course, I would like this very much. When do we go?"

"We must go before our children return."

In the village, they find Mama Kundi bending full over the hard ground of her own hut sweeping the dirt. Her broom has a short handle. Sofia sees the puzzle in Madame's face and she smiles. "We must keep the dirt free of everything. There must be no green growing plants for snakes to hide in, no wood for breeding termites. Nothing alive must come inside, except us. It is very different from the houses of your village."

"Mimosa?" She makes a high, full laugh and says again, "Mimosa. It is not a real village, now is it?"

"Ezali te," It is not, Sofia says with a small laugh.

Mama Kundi pries herself to stand tall and sends her broom into a firm shake. Madame Cassandra cannot stop looking at Mama. "Tell her I have seen her walking on Mimosa Road," Madame says, at last. And Sofia repeats her words.

Mama Kundi says to Sofia, "Tell Madame I have seen her driving on Mimosa Road. Her car goes very fast."

Madame smiles and stretches her hand to Mama Kundi. "Enchante."

"Kota, Mama." Come in. Mama Kundi says.

Mama Kundi bends again, this time toward the doorway of her hut, and leads them inside, waving a hand as if directing a flock of sheep. They follow into the house Sofia knows, like her own, but with only a single room and a single mat. The fire in the center burns with low flames and a grate for heating the teapot, ready for guests. Sofia has a flicker of surprise to see three chairs circling the fire. She wonders how these chairs came to be here, for they were not here the last time, and the visit is a surprise. Or, maybe it is not. She watches Mama Kundi's face for a sign of knowing. She is not a witch, but she has knowings that others do not have.

The two guest mamas seat themselves around the fire they do not need for warmth. Mama Kundi pours tea into their cups and presses a warm cup into each hand with such care as to make Madame smile again. Sofia drinks her tea and there is a sweetness to the taste already, and Sofia cannot help but wonder how she comes to have sugar, for the cost is more than Sofia can spend. But Mama Kundi has other surprises, more wondrous than this. It is why they have come.

Sofia stares into the cup at some tea leaves still floating there. What meaning do they hold, those leaves? She looks at Mama Kundi, and at Madame, and tries to think how she will bring the story of Daniel into this place. She sees Mama Kundi nodding her bone-thin head. Today she has a long braid down her spine. There is something soothing about her braid that Sofia loves. But before she can speak to Mama Kundi in rapid Lingala and ask her to speak of Daniel's sorrows, Madame Cassandra asks Mama Kundi about the place where she was born. Sofia breathes easily as she translates.

Mama Kundi tells of her years in the Ubangi region of the North Country. Sofia puts Mama's words into French for Madame's ears. Mama Kundi's face slips into a frown. "Nayebi mondele kuna. Moto monene." she says. I knew a White man there. A fat man.

Suddenly, Madame says, "Tommy Hendricks? It is possible? Of course, he is from there, too. Tommy!" Madame is so happy to say this name Tommy, her laugh spreading to the ceiling of the hut and all around. When the laughter ends, she stares at Mama Kundi, then at Sofia. "Does she know Tommy, the one who lives in Mimosa now?"

Sofia delivers the French words into Lingala. Mama Kundi nods and Sofia tells Madame, yes, she knows that fat bwana in your village. Big smiles touch the three mamas.

Madame takes a long time for her next words. Hearing her, it is Sofia's turn to be happy. "It is possible that this Tommy will help us find Daniel. Is possible. I am not sure, but we hope. We hope he will help us."

"More than Doctor Will," Madame says. "Doctor Will has too much work. And he has no Lingala and his French is poor. But Tommy Hendricks has Lingala and he knows the Zairois. He can do business with Mobutu's men. That cadre. He will know what they mean and what they do not mean. He will know how to make them listen."

It is Mama Kundi's turn to laugh. She tells a memory of the North Country, for Sofia to translate. 'This Tommy. I was still with my Stephane in that place when this Tommy began to be so fat. His mother told and told him he must stop eating so much rice and fufu. Each year from his twelfth, he grew fatter and always I saw him sorrowing, and alone. The few mondeles laughed at him and no girls would lie with him. But I saw the Zairois come to think his fat gave him power. That is the way in the villages in Africa. He is a smart mondele. He was still a boy when he began to do a bit of business with the men. He learned Lingala and Swahili quickly. He became rich and would go to Nairobi on a train and there he bought a Nikkon camera.'

'One day, he left the Nikkon camera outside his house, and went away for a time. When he returned, the camera was not there. This Tommy knew which ones would steal in that village. And he went to each hut saying he must have his camera returned. And for whichever person returned it, he would give a matabisi. At the last hut, an older boy came to the door. Tommy saw the camera inside, against a wall. Tommy knew him. And, sure, he was one who would steal a camera. In that village, and even at the Grand Marche in Kinshasa, if a thief is caught, the Zairois who see it will fall upon him with their anger and their fists. I have seen such a beating many times. I have feared for the thief.'

'But Tommy did nothing with his fists. He did know the boy's name, and he said it. And he thanked him with many grand words for keeping his Nikkon camera safe from thieves. He took the boy's hand and kept shaking it and thanking him with such strength until the boy said, You are welcome, Bwana Tommy. You are welcome. Here you see where I keep it for you. It ended so. After that day, Tommy took pictures of many in the village. Many believed he kept a copy of their soul inside the big Nikkon. They must always respect this man. When I see him now, I see him still carry this respect."

Sofia hears this story with surprise, though she does believe it. And she feels an opening inside where hope can grow.

Fourteen

The sensation of strangeness comes roaring back at Christmas. Cass has always loved Christmas, even after she ditched her fealty to the doctrines her mother held up as the barrier to fire and brimstone and the exit plan from hell. She loves the smell of pine boughs, the glimmer of candles in the dark, the chill and the chance to bundle up in sweaters and wool scarves, and, yes, even the kick she feels guessing the contents of a gift just before tearing open the package. Will likes teasing her about her fondness for opening presents and gently kids her that this part of her has never left childhood.

Now she must open her mind to Christmas in a place where temperatures average around 87 degrees, daytime. Not the hottest month, according to Leon. That would be March, when thermometers can reach 105 degrees. But humidity in December knocks it out of the park. Beyond merely oppressive, it can hover at 100 percent.

Cass tries to resist the urge to shower more than twice a day.

She tries to open her mind to Christmas beyond the 47th parallel. The boys are less rigid about the geographies of Christmas, though the week before the 25th, she comes upon them on the patio, both with flushed cheeks, from the humidity or from disquiet about Santa. Mattie stands on a deck chair and calls out an imperious demand. "Where's the chimney on this house?"

"No chimney. There's no fireplace. Why would it need a chimney?" she says.

Mattie jumps down, knocking over the deck chair, and runs inside to his room. Cass rights the chair and follows, watching him flop weeping onto his bed. "Mattie, sweetie, what is it?"

"Baba's right. Santa's not coming here." Baba is a Zairois school mate of Mattie, a boy half again Mattie's size. Each morning when the school bus drops him off at the private Belgian school where he attends kindergarten, the same scenario ensues. At the metal gate, and not yet in sight of the teachers, Baba steps up to Mattie, tells him in French that he's going to beat him up, and pops him. With some coaching from Will, Mattie has learned to hold up his small fists to defend himself but still gets a whack on his chin or an ear before trudging to the big classroom. Each evening Will returns from the hospital, he asks Mattie about Baba. Has Mattie stopped Baba from hitting him? "No, Daddy. He hit me again."

As she hears Will's telling, she recalls the Ali-Foreman fight weeks ago now, the part where Ali's fists covered his own face to fend off Foreman's blows. She tries to swap two five-year-olds into the scene, but can't hold the image. Mattie has a history of avoiding, even dreading combat. Already, at five, he's asserted the pacifist nature she suspects will be his M.O. going forward. So different from Corey, who jumped up to the soldier and told him he was going to kick his butt. Two brothers: how can they be so different? She and Will need to talk to his teacher. This isn't right.

Now she sits on the edge of his bed and turns her attention to the matter of Santa. She leans down and hugs his heaving shoulders, straightens up. "That's because Santa has a different name here, silly goose. Santa is called Father Christmas, only they say it in French and call him Pere Noel. You know lots of things are different here. He doesn't use reindeer to pull his sleigh. That's only in the North where it's cold. I've heard he uses giraffes in Africa. Sometimes even elephants, in places where the vegetation is super thick. Here, because we're in a city, I'm thinking giraffes would be the thing." Mattie's shoulders have stopped heaving.

She continues. "Of course, he doesn't need a chimney. Not here. He can come in by a door. There are stories about him having a magic key that can open a door anywhere. Also, we can leave a window open and he can squeeze through to leave the presents. Okay?"

She sees from the side view looking down, that his eyes are open. He's listening hard. She feels this, and feels a tightening in her chest over the lengths she's going, the passion she's investing, in assuring this small boy that a lie is true. Santa in Zaire. A sleigh pulled by giraffes. A magic key. What a crock of lies she's pitching that he'll outgrow. Oh, he will. In two years when he's seven. Or, maybe, given his guileless nature, he'll hold out till he's eight or nine. Then will he blame her for defrauding his innocence? She has a friend back home who remembers being so traumatized when she learned the truth about Santa that she avoided the whole Santa business with her toddler and stuck with the manger story. She was a bit of a missionary on the topic and swore to Cass that it was the moral high ground, to avoid the trauma of revelation that his parents lied to him all along.

Mattie twists onto his back and takes her in with wide eyes. "Santa's fat," he says finally, frowning.

"Like Tommy," Corey says, popping onto the other side of his brother's bed and setting up a steady bounce.

"Yeah. He couldn't squeeze through a window."

"But Santa has his magic key, too," she says.

Mattie's frown morphs into a reflective gaze, and he nods. "I'm telling Baba next time."

"Good boy," she says.

But she's looking at Corey who has said Tommy's name, and, for a moment, her breath stalls as her talk with Vernoy kicks in. He hasn't called, and she's been waiting, all this tine since Thanksgiving. Or, wait. Was she supposed to call him? He gave her his card. Yes, all this time she's had it wrong. It's her move. She'll have her chance at Christmas dinner, at Logan and Susan's, this time. Susan has said she's inviting him. Good.

But she and Susan have a more urgent plan to work out, bringing Pere Noel to Mimosa. On the Saturday before the Wednesday where Christmas lands, they plan a day in town to procure surprises for the children, and some for the adults, too. Normally, the schools observe the Belgian work schedule, which means class Saturday mornings. But both schools declare this day to be a *conge,* a no-work day, a holiday, and throw off the mothers' plans, until Sofia agrees to watch both sets of children. "Likambo te," No problem, she says softly.

"Bless you." Susan leans in with a hug when she brings her girls to Cass that morning, and tells Sofia she's paying her extra for her services. It's Logan's day to ride with Will, giving Susan the Mazda for the day. And so the two women head off on Mimosa Road into town. They wind past the River Village, the small shops and cloth factories, fula fula wreckage yards and Mercedes dealerships, the turn-off to consulate row, and ease through the roundabout where she feels a blend of low-grade queasiness and high hilarity at the obligatory photo of Mobutu Sese Seko in horn-rimmed glasses and leopardskin toque holding virtual court over the madness of Boulevard 30 Juin.

First stop is the Grande Marche, a concrete conglomerate of all things useful, desirable, surprising, and strange. They park the Mazda and engage a slight young man in plastic Bata shoes and torn t-shirt to guard the car, an unwritten contract both Cass and Susan feel is a bit of a scam, but one they always observe as a precautionary measure, and they enter the covered portion of the acreage on the hunt for toys to please small expats from a rich country. They pass bins of produce, beautifully-arranged local fruits--papaya, pineapple, plantains, guava, avocado, stalls of dried fish, a favorite staple of most Zairois families, and a stall featuring a dozen varieties of dried insects, even what looks like cockroaches. Further along the concrete maze, they pass various sized kilo bags of rice, flour, sugar. A hardware section offering several sizes of mortar and pestles, the standard appliance for a village kitchen, dish pans, wooden stools, plastic buckets, hoses, stiff brooms, hammers, saws, and nails, etcetera. A display of multi-colored cloths, some sewn into pagnes and boubou shirts. A kiosk with school supplies, small cahiers, notebooks, and worn textbooks, such volumes as Algeria I, American history, and a crude English-Lingala dictionary, assembled and printed by Christian missionaries.

At last, in what feels like the heart of a concrete jungle, a children's department appears. A pile of sad-looking stuffed dogs, a tangle of plastic buckets and shovels, and a selection of matchbox cars, all donated she suspects by Western missionaries. Cass lifts a red car and asks the price. The vendor answers with a grunt. "Un zaire."

"Un zaire pour un matchbox?" Cass says and wonders if the vendor makes it up as she goes.

"Mondele." The name she expels mimics her insolent expression that shows with clarity what she means to say, *You're lucky I sell you anything,* White Girl. Resentment now welling in Cass' throat, like bile. Then, some kind of internal stop light rising: *Come now, Cass, really? After all the uber-colonialist Belgians put her through before independence. Of course, she's bitter. You would be, too. Surely, you're not going to blame the poor woman.*

The poor, rude woman, who will not make me a fool. "No merci," Cass tells her airily and moves on.

Just beyond her table and the array of mini-toys, tucked in a back corner beyond the main route, Susan stops at a table displaying a small hand drum, an ancient wooden board game called Bao, an import from Arab traders, and four small wooden cars. A diminutive older man sits behind the table. He has a rumpled dignity that would suit a professor of philosophy at the UW or head librarian, say, at the Suzzallo Library. He lifts a wooden hammer and a genuine soft smile beneath his gray mustache. "Bonjour Mesdames," he says.

"Bonjour, Monsieur," Cass says and asks if they're all hand-made.

All made by himself and his son, he assures them. In her mind, he hails from India. Perhaps he's one of the foreigners banished at the start of Mobutu's authenticite campaign. The President sent an official to the business owner's door with a slip of paper declaring that the business they'd started and run forever was now owned by a Zairois. Handed off to a local who had no more expertise with markets than Mattie or Corey. No clue how to run a business. He sent them all packing, Greeks, Italians, Portuguese, Belgians, East Indians. The economy stalled, slid, tanked. Many months later, Mobutu rescinded his ban and invited the foreigners to return. Many did. Perhaps including this distinguished maker of wooden toys.

"Perfect," Cass tells Susan, who lifts the drum to examine stitching along the side and taps the leather head.

"How do you say, Do you have more than one?" Susan asks, lifting the drum higher.

"Y a-t-il d'autres?" Cass turns to the vendor.

"Oui. J'ai trois autres."

"Parfait," Cass says with a rush of brightness.

"Uh, let's not be too effusive. We should bargain," Susan says softly.

"Combien pour toutes les petites voitures. Les bois?" How much for all the little wooden cars? Cass says and turns to Susan. "Who needs matchbook cars when we can buy hand-crafted beauties?"

But the vendor slips deftly into a clipped English. Of course. The language the British brought to India. "Each car costs two zaires. Each drum costs five."

"We'll take four of each," Susan says.

Cass nods. "And two Bao boards."

"One will do. We can share." Susan tells her with a wink, raising a minor disturbance in Cass that vanishes as quickly as it came.

After the morning in town, the two friends decide to hold off collecting their children. Wrap the gifts at Susan's, maybe have a bite of lunch before re-entering the friendly madhouse of young children. No luck finding Christmas wrapping paper, but they have bought several editions of the local news rag, The Salango. The government mouthpiece will serve better as wrapping paper for children's toys than as a purveyor of current events. Susan had the foresight to bring Scotch tape and a few rolls of red ribbon. As they set about wrapping their purchases, Cass observes Susan's artistry with smoothing the newsprint around odd corners, resulting in a wrapped package of classic elegance. Cass' own misshapen orphans suffer by comparison. She can't help wondering who would want hers.

She lifts the Bao board they mean to share, intending to solicit Susan's take on where it will land, under whose tree. Susan holds up an index finger. "I have an idea. But nature calls." Moments after the bathroom door shuts, the phone rings. Not in Logan's study behind a closed door, but out here in the great room where everyone has easy access. 'Susan is indisposed," Cass will say when she picks up.

The speaker on the other end is Belgian. Or not. He may be a French-speaker, but she detects a familiar, stilted taint to his French. Not so different from Will's somewhat tortured French.

When they were packing to move here, Cass discovered in a desk drawer a scrawled note from the head of Will's Orthopaedic residency program: "Has exceptionally high I.Q."

Not that Cass was surprised. She's always known how smart he is, never doubted what a quick study she'd married, and always marveled at how he not only read as much as she, but more widely.

She read him the note from his teacher and asked if he remembered it. "Yeah, he'd had a few drinks," he said, laughing. Unimpressed, as always, with any laurels thrown his way. But he freely acknowledges his tin ear for language.

"Voulez-vous laisser un message pour Madame?" She's secretly proud of her own accent, which is quite good, she's been told, better than the caller's. If only she had a decent vocabulary.

"Non merci," he says, flattening the R-sound.

Sounds a lot like Will, no kidding. How odd, she thinks.

Christmas Day arrives, geography aside. They have their Santa ceremony beside a jerry-rigged clutch of palm branches Cass painstakingly wired together and covered with cotton balls and paper chains, meaning to approximate a Christmas tree but looking more like a hedgehog, very large but without a face. Not her best effort. Corey has a giggle fit and Mattie, frowning, asks, "What's it for, Mommy?"

But the presents hit the mark. Mattie opens the box with the hand-carved car, lifts it and pets the smooth wood sides and hugs the car to his chest. Corey seizes the hand drum, leaps up and begins beating the taut head with small chubby hands and dancing around the room. A gift from her mother back home is an instant hit, a small playroom tent. Cass gives her mother thumbs up for a surprisingly spot-on choice and for sending it on time. Will's gift takes their breath away. It's saved till after the other gifts are opened, including Will's gift of a cool necklace of colorful beads and earrings for Cass, and her gift of a set of malachite cufflinks and a T-shirt inscribed "Mondele," meaning White Man, for Will, who immediately puts it on over his plain white T-shirt. He announces that Santa left one more present. "Straight from Pere Noel's sleigh," he proclaims. "Be right back." He threads through the kitchen door, outside, and, in a lo-ong ten minutes, returns carting two small cages. Each contains a bunny rabbit, one black, one white.

"Wow, are they real?" Corey says.

"Of course, they're real, doofus," Mattie says, as if he played a major role in capturing them.

"Now. Big decision. Who gets which one?" Will says.

No pondering for Corey. "The black one's mine."

"I don't care. The white one looks so soft," Mattie says.

Cass leans in behind Will and squeezes his muscled arms. He turns and pulls her down to him, and for a long moment, the children are far from their minds.

In late daylight, two hours before darkness swallows the sun, the Thanksgiving group gathers again for Christmas dinner. Susan and Logan host this time and offer a swathe of elegance absent at Thanksgiving, Cass can't help noticing. There's a tablecloth of white linen, candles in two silver candelabras, and red cloth napkins. Even the children's table is set to perfection with a red tablecloth, green candles, and several small pine cones that must have crossed the ocean, too. More astonishing is the artificial fir tree, decorated with bright red and green balls, tinsel, and delicate strands of electric silver lights. Cass gazes on the scene. "Your tree is so lovely." she says, trying to skim her voice of envy for her friend's aesthetically sophisticated choice, compared with her own hedgehog on steroids. A tiny part of her admires the foresight to pack these items from home, even as she clings to her aggressive indifference toward such domestic fussing. Who can be bothered with such petty details? She has higher matters to occupy her, after all, such as her moral obligation to help proliferate justice throughout the developing world. Oh, wait. The Xavier project is on hold. Kaput. And where is Vernoy?

"Vernoy's not coming? I thought you said you were inviting him," Will says. He must have caught her forlorn glance around the table. And she's told him how much she enjoys Vernoy.

"I did invite him. He'd already accepted another invite. Secretly, I suspect it's the Capitaine. He doesn't like it," Susan says.

"You must be kidding. Unless he doesn't eat fish, at all," Cass says.

"No, I talked to him before. He studies these things. Claims it's an invasive species. Doesn't approve," Tommy puts in.

His statement releases a slurry of laughter, perhaps as much for the timing as the sentiment itself. For just then, Susan is making a slow circuit around the table with the main course, grilled slices of El Capitaine, a Nile perch.

Every few months, a fisherman brings the aquatic giant to the main gate of Mimosa. A month ago, Leon met a fisherman at the gate and hauled its forty-five-kilos up to Cass' doorstep. Could he have custody of the head and gills, Madame? Of course, he could. And he cut the silvery flesh into serving sizes and packed them into Madame's refrigerator.

"To heck with naysayers," Cass says, raising her glass. "Here's to El Capitaine, my new favorite fish. Which is saying a lot for a girl from Seattle."

But she regrets the absence of the naysayer who was supposed to be her conduit to Daniel. Unless, there's another. She turns back to Tommy, lifting his own glass of Orange Fanta, and feels the weight of another route. Not only does she miss Vernoy the go-between, she misses his prayer from Thanksgiving, which still seems pretty funny to a seasoned backslider. But his words have stayed with her. The evening they talked, she asked him to write them down for her. He just laughed. She remembers her favorite line, *'Keep our eyes and hearts open for the ways we should step forth in light and in shadow.'* In lieu of Vernoy, Lindy asks their six-year-old daughter to say a prayer, and she races through *'God-is-great-God-us-good-and-we-thank-you-for-this-food-and for Christmas, Jesus. Amen.'*

"Whew," Tommy says, and a low whistle. "Thanks, Peanut."

Camille makes a mugging face to her dad and plants a dollop of butter onto her mashed potatoes.

The Capitaine is as yummy as her tongue remembers, a savory cross between halibut and Dover sole, sautéed in lemon butter and served with lime wedges and capers. Where'd she find capers? she wonders.

Evening now, after sunset, the time of day when hyenas love to prowl, according to Will. But they're twelve together taking a shakedown walk after dinner, not a woman jogging alone. There's safety in numbers. After all, if a hyena meets a dozen humans, he'll have to decide which soul to invade. The walk is Tommy's idea, which she finds odd, since he can't take two steps without breathing hard. But he says he's trying to "shed some blubber." He's tired of being known as "that fat mondele."

Somehow, between clearing the dishes and heading out, Susan makes a quick change from willowy caftan over slacks to jeans and an aqua short-sleeved blouse, a stitch low-cut for the occasion, Cass feels, though no one else seems to mind, certainly not Will, serious lover of breasts, even her own, petite as they are. She catches herself with that film of envy again, and shame for her pettiness.

The group sets a brisk pace down the paved slope from Susan and Logan's. Cassandra starts with the fast group before it devolves into Will and Susan pairing the kids into buddy groups to insure no one is forgotten and Logan and Lindy becoming a walking pair. She catches Logan going on about meeting up with a present or former member of the KGB, she's unclear which, and Linda giving a predictable startled gasp. Then Tommy surprises her again by tugging on her shoulder and urging her to fall back and "keep a fat mondele company."

Well now, she thinks. Maybe this is my moment for Daniel.

She slows to let the first group push ahead and joins Tommy, sweat gathering on the edges of his face, his chins. He grins at her. Just then, Corey calls, "Daddy, let's go to the River. I want to." They've reached the main gate and the sentinel, apparently already snoozing at his post. "Bonsoir, Monsieur Sentinel. Open, please," Corey says and jumps toward him.

The sentinel blinks open his eyes, jerks his lean body upright in his chair beside the pavement, and grins widely at Corey, a grin she has never seen. Nobody can resist Corey, it seems. Or, maybe all small children are exempt from the rancor he may feel toward mondeles. Laughing, he stands. "Pour toi, j'ouvre." For you I open. Corey jumps and claps his hands.

Will shakes his head at the sentinel. "Merci, Monsieur. Pas ce soir." He reaches for Corey and lifts him. "Not happening tonight buddy," and swings him high overhead. Corey kicks and squeals his frustration, then as the swooping grows, his delight. Cass sees Mattie wanting his turn at Daddy's swinging. She's tempted to say, 'Come on, Will, stop playing favorites.' But she can't bring herself to expose this gap in their marital tranquility to these still quite new friends,

They leave the gate and regain the perimeter, and, again, she and Tommy take up the rear. He stops walking for a moment and delivers a new surprise. "Vernoy stopped me yesterday. He says you have a job for me." A pause for breathing, a small grin. "Undercover," he says with a faux-dramatic rise in his tenor voice.

"So Vernoy did talk to you." She grins, feeling more pleased than the moment deserves. After all, this connection may not lead anywhere at all. Still.

"He didn't give me details. What's up? And what makes you think I can fix anything?"

"Someone in the River Village had this idea that you might . . ."

"I know a few families over there."

"There's a woman there from the North Country. You knew her up there. Quite old. A bit stooped. A widow. She calls you Bwana Tommy." She searches his face to see if she's jogged any memories.

"Mama Kundi!" He slaps out a big laugh that draws the others to turn and look. He tosses them a windshield wiper wave.

"She says you have your ways. She says this Bwana Tommy carries much respect. And so can help us find Daniel. She feels this." Her voice lightly approximates Mama Kundi's.

"Daniel. Do I know him?"

"Maybe. Don't know. I doubt it. He's my nanny's brother-in-law. A good guy in one of the government ministries. He's languishing somewhere in Kinshasa Prison."

He whistles. "Which ministry. Do we know?"

"Communications. Somehow he must have gotten in the crosshairs of Sese Seko."

He whistles again. "Okay. So give me broad strokes, how it happened."

She gives a brief account of Sofia's history and Daniel's abduction from his office, visits to the prison up to the last visit and his vanishing into the seedy reaches of Kinshasa Prison.

"Ministry of Communications. Do you know what his job is?"

"Hm. Not really."

"Me either. But I can guess. His job is to keep an eye on journalists who put out The Salongo, the daily. You seen it?"

"I buy it now and then. Out of curiosity. To get the pulse of this world where I find myself."

"Right. So you know anybody putting out that rag isn't a journalist as we think of them. Every paper must be approved by guess what? the Ministry of Communications. Here's where our boy Daniel comes in. You say he got caught in the cross hairs. I'm making a wild guess that he failed to follow decrees from on high."

Of course, this scenario ought to have occurred to her, but had not. She can be a bit slow on the up-take, no doubt about that. She covers her face. "Oh my god, Tommy. Makes perfect sense. From what I understand, he trained as a journalist, even spent time in London. What are the chances he's still alive?" She clenches her fists and waits.

Tommy says nothing. The others are far ahead of them. At last, he says, "I won't lie. Plenty of stories out there about people getting hauled into the stadium under a black cloth and shot by firing squad. And that prison. You wouldn't wish it on the Barnes' python. But." He hesitates, clicking his tongue to the roof of his mouth. "I'll see what I can find out."

"Okay. Great. You want to talk to the family first?"

He nods.

"Ask Vernoy to pray for you," she says, only half kidding.

"Sure. What can it hurt?"

"Let me know what you find," she says, thanks him and presses her pace to catch the others. The children are a single, small cluster moving in sync with Camille Hendricks and Corey leading the troop, hand-in-hand. She thinks of a tiny frog perched on a cluster of lily pads, the swiftly-moving river heading downstream. They look happy. As do the four adults. She thinks to move up and join Will and take his hand, but has a bout of shyness. He looks perfectly happy without her. Susan is on his right; they're laughing uproariously at something. He feels far away, like a stranger to her, his wife, his boys' mother. *What's wrong with you? You're being ridiculous. It's not the first time.* When he was in Vietnam, she felt the miles between them, thousands, and had to close her eyes to bring him home, to remember. Everything she did that year felt small and petty, compared to The War he lived every day where the dead fell around him. The sounds of incoming that sent his heart racing double time. Those body bags, the injured Marines, the triage he administered, measuring out their lives in minutes, seconds. This one won't make it anyway. Leave him here. To die. This one has wounds too bad to heal in time for useful service. Send him home. This one goes straight to the O.R. where we'll fix him up to go back out to face the Enemy.

But he came home. To her and Mattie. And now Corey. He's here in the flesh. She tightens her jaw, pushes herself forward, and moves in between him and Susan where, after all, she does belong. She takes his arm; he kisses the top of her head. What was so funny? she wants to ask, but does not.

They walk on, leaving the laughter behind them. The street is quiet of people sounds, except for breathing. The air, too, is alive and breathing. Tiny bird cries overhead in trees on either side, some slithering creature wrestles in the tall grass outside the high wire fence. Crickets sweep the air between the saw grass and the flowering mimosa trees. She closes her eyes and feels the river out there, too, the Congo, riding the low darkness toward the sea.

Fifteen

It is Christmas no more when the others come to Sofia's tiny house and squeeze under the fine tin roof. Sofia has never seen Gabriel since he left that day of sorrow. She does not know if he thinks of them at all. She knows that he loved his son, but she cannot know if he also loves Fimi and Kamina. She knows, sure, he does not love her. Is he dead, too? Maybe. Or, no. She does not miss him. She tries not to twist her belly into a knot against the girl she was who let herself lie with a devil like him. In that day before they wed, Mama Kundi said she had a bad dream that was a sign of displeasure. The dream was of a Zairois with dark skin everywhere but his face, which was white. He smiled wide so she could see all his teeth, and, as she watched, a shadow crossed his face now covered with fur like a hyena. His mouth opened wider and his teeth glistened, still smiling, and the hyena man snapped his jaws. Mama Kundi said she knew this dream was a warning from the ancestors that she must tell young Sofia. You must leave this man Gabriel, Mama Kundi told Sofia. But Sofia laughed. This man Gabriel was clever and handsome. He was hers. She could not leave.

Does she wish him dead? Hm maybe. She wishes more that she could go back and kill the girl who would not believe Mama Kundi. She was a fool, a twit. Still, she is glad of the tin roof she does not forget he made. And she tries to let her sorrow over Elombe be less now, just as the rains are less.

All of these things fill her mind as the others fill her hut: Mama Kundi, Alicia and her two girls, and, of course, Sofia and her two girls. Madame Cassandra does not come but she sends Bwana Tommy. Sofia tells the others that Bwana Tommy will talk of Daniel, but she makes no promise that he will find him in Kinshasa Prison and see him walk out the front gates. She tells them only to come together and talk of Daniel and see what is what.

Mama Kundi brings her kundi, for in her language it means light. And the problem of Daniel requires much light.

Sofia heats her kettle on the open fire. When the others come, she pours it in the cups Madame Cassandra gave her. Bwana Tommy has walked from Mimosa across Mimosa Road, carrying his orange crush, one for himself and two for the children to share. Because he walked, he enters the hut breathless, sweat pooling at his neck and alongside his nose. He spreads a white handkerchief over his face to wipe the sweat. It is a hard job to be so fat in this place.

When he comes, Bwana Tommy stands in the doorway and tells everyone hello. "Mbote nyonso." He stands before the children and gives each hand a shake. He greets Sofia and Alicia with a kiss to each cheek. He sees the chair Sofia sets before him, a chair strong and wide enough for such as this Bwana, and he sits down with a breath loud enough to fill the room. He smiles and takes a long drink of Orange Fanta. Mama Kundi bows before him, and he stretches his hand to hers. It is hard not to laugh, hearing the sound Mama Kundi makes, like a big chicken clucking, and he does. Then he says her name and shakes his head.

Quiet comes to the small hut, and grave faces. Alicia stands but cannot be still. Her face has stretched into all shapes of sorrow, and the beauty Sofia once envied is in hiding. "Do you think . . . he can . . . still be alive?" she says, in soft hoarse rushes. He cannot have the answer. Still, she must ask and be fearful of the answer.

"You speak English," he says, his mouth wide with pleasure and surprise. "How come?"

"From Daniel. He wanted so much to be a real journalist. Not to learn from the kind of worm that speaks only for the government. A worm. This is how he speaks. And he must leave Zaire for a time. Not Belgium. He hates the Belge for their ways against the Zairois. He said the British are better to teach real journalism. He must go to London and study there, and so he did, and we went with him."

"Your English is very good."

"Yes. So, too, Daniel. We came back speaking English, and you see where it takes us." The cut of her voice is sharp with anger and pain, and she wants to go back to the life she had before London and English and this nightmare of prison. "He took his good English and his fine ideals to the Ministry where he got hired. There was one journalist at The Salongo who was not a worm, and this one wrote an article that said true things Mobutu did, and words against that man and his government, how they do not pay the soldiers or the prison guards and people go hungry while Mobutu Sese Seko has a private plane and houses in many countries. Daniel agreed to the job of checking the piece for its grammar, and to make sure nothing critical of Mobutu and his government comes to print. But inside, he despises that devil Mobutu, and, like a fool, he let that article with its hard words go into the Salongo pages. How could he not know what that devil would do to him? But now he is there. Somewhere in that hole. We must find him. If he is not already . . ." The cutting voice stops short of the word she dreads. She cannot say this deepest fear for her Daniel. Here she changes her words into Lingala, the language of her comfort. "Salisa ngai, palado." Please help me.

All eyes look to Tommy, who sits as a boulder sits and makes no sound. Sofia holds her breath and waits with the others. Mama Kundi shuts her eyes and rests her head at a tilt on her backbone. Stillness has come even to the children. Fimi squeezes her small hands in her lap to stay strong.

At last, Tommy makes his chest long and reaches his giant arms behind his head and clasps them. "I know that prison. It's dark and filled with men who are hungry and will do anything for a bit of food and a few coins. We must go there when the New Year comes."

"Matabisi," Alicia says. "That must be the way, is it not?"

"Of course," Tommy says, for he knows matabisi is the path toward all things in this Mobutu world. Alicia has a coin purse inside her pagne and she reaches for it and holds it out to Tommy. He flips a hand in telling her to leave off her nonsense. And Alicia gives a quick thank you bob of her head.

Now his eyes find Mama Kundi with her harp. "Namoni." I see you, he says and tells her she must come to find Daniel.

"I come," Mama Kundi says.

He says to her, to bring her kundi, for he has an idea.

"I bring," she says.

"Ezali malamu." It is good, he says, and tells her she must bring her magic to that dark place.

Sixteen

The last Monday of the old year, Sofia comes to Cass' kitchen. "Ca va, Sofia?" Are you okay? she says, already seeing she is not. The change in her face, her posture, the worry that weighs on her lightness and deepens the lines between her wide eyes, these clues tell her of Sofia's true state of mind.

In the States, Cass would take Sofia into a tight embrace, but this is Zaire, and it's not their practice to hug expats. But she reaches for Sofia's hands and squeezes them to her torso and tells her she talked with Bwana Tommy. "Noki,," soon, she tells her.

"I fear very much for Daniel. Each day, each minute, he is nearer to death." Sofia's voice is flat. Her bowed head is the picture of sorrow.

Each minute, Cass thinks. Her belly knows the truth of this urgency. Daniel may be already dead in some hell-hole.

Behind her in a distant room, the phone rings. "Oh!" Her startle-reflex pings her torso. She jumps toward Will's study, opens the door, and snatches the receiver from mounds of JBJS journals and legal note pads with his indecipherable scrawl. "Hello?"

It's Susan. She has news. "I wanted to let you know. You remember that I just hired a nanny? I'm a qualified O.R. nurse. I've never stayed at home like this. Except right after the babies.

I'm going to the hospital. Now. This morning. See if I can get on. Part-time, anyway."

A Pause. Silence. "Cass? You okay?"

"How will you get there? Logan drove the carpool this morning."

"What are you doing this morning?"

What am I doing? On her last fula fula ride into town, Cass overheard two Zairois men discussing a *mondele mwasi,* a White woman. "That woman, you see her? What is she for?" one of the men asked the other. "She has a man to cook, she has a man to garden, she has a man to work for money. Her children are already more than six. What is she for?" The other man gave a snort and the two laughed together. Cass knew they must be talking about her. Or not. The two looked directly her way, though they appeared not to see her. She knew Zairois men viewed expat-women as a different species, really. So, maybe they truly didn't see her. Even so, she turned her head and torso away, toward the opposite window to keep them from catching the blush sweeping her face, that took her straight back to the twelve-year-old Cassie who couldn't talk to a boy without turning red.

The reddening eventually subsided, though the question did not. What am I for? It followed her into the privacy of reflection, and now with Susan.

"Cass? You okay?" Susan says again.

"Yeah. Sorry. Actually, I have the car. I can take you."

Under a covered walkway leading to the hospital entrance, the two expat women pass a line of Zairoise, stoic and silent, in colorful pagnes. Each totes a box or a lump of something high on her head and wears a tiny child tied to her back. "Look at those women," Cass says.

Susan leans into her. "The Mother's March. They all just gave birth, maybe twelve hours ago. They do this march every morning. The new ones healthy enough to walk. The complications stay in bed. There's 130 give birth each day. More than 3500 a month. Wrap your mind around that one, Sunshine," she says with jaunty amusement.

"I can't imagine," Cass says, recalling her own wobbling movements after several days postpartum.

Inside the hospital, they part. Susan heads left to Administration. "Knock-em dead," Cass calls after her, aware of a tightening in her belly, some resistance to a wholehearted send-off. She can't be jealous of her good friend for being more like Will than she herself is. It's what she's always known, her being a nurse, after all. Besides, she doesn't want to be like Will. She isn't worried that he'll be drawn to someone who shares his tribe. That's absurd. He's always said he's happy they have different fields of interest, more things to talk about. Besides, he had his chances with all those nurses back at the UW, and he had chosen her, English major.

More likely, she's jealous of the bounce in Susan's step toward her newly-minted life, while she, Cass, remains inert in a strange hallway, the last woman standing to face the question asked in the fula: *What am I doing? What am I for?*

Okay, then, move. Cass takes a right leading her to Pavilion One, Will's orthopaedic ward. God willing, she won't bump into him, since she never told him she'd be coming here today. What do you care, Cassie? Have a little sense of self. She doesn't want him to hear about her impulses, that's all.

She recalls that Will's in surgery today anyway and moves into the wide eighty-bed room, all orthopaedic patients. Actually, one-hundred forty are ortho patients, in many cases one on the bed, one underneath. On her left, a bone-thin woman bends over a bucket, inserts a mop, lifts and squeezes it, and rights herself. She pushes and swipes the string mop across the concrete floor. She works the long-handled mop around the wrought-iron bed frames, between and around belongings stored alongside, taking care to avoid patients lying beneath. Every so often, she retrieves the bucket and re-immerses the mop. The patients pay her no mind. Some lie in a fetal side-crouch, inert and silent. Some sit against a wrought-iron headboard, gazing straight-on, seeming lost in their thoughts or simply lost. Several lie in a form of traction, plastered leg suspended by a wire to an overhead bar.

She turns to the far-right quarter, and Will's words return to her. *'I have twenty paraplegics, or quads'* She takes them in, mostly refugees from the chaos of Kinshasa's roadways. *'In many cases, this is permanent. This is where they live,'* he tells here. The first patient by the door stops her. It's the eyes. Intelligent and old, though he himself is young, in his twenties, maybe. Younger than she is, gazing up from his propped seated position. "Bonjour, Monsieur."

"Bonjour, Madame."

She tells him her name, and he gets her connection to the doctor. He nods his head, angular, a chiseled shape above soft blankets, a remarkable head, really. He extends a hand with its long, graceful fingers, that sits inert in hers.

He nods again, and she sits on the chair beside his bed. She takes the chair to be a sign he must have visitors, as not all patients have such a chair. "Alors, parlez-mois de vous," she says. Tell me about yourself.

The nudge is all he needs. He talks with the tongue of a sophisticate. She asks him to please slow his speech for her sorry-command of French. He smiles. She asks where he learned his French. At University, he says. First here at the National

University of Zaire. He studied in the Faculty of Arts and Science. Eventually, he came to focus on Journalism. It was his heart-work. Do you see? The professors gave him high marks. He was brighter and more ambitious even than most bright young men. They had high hopes for him. They recommended him to University of Paris Sorbonne. He stayed there eighteen months. By the time he was 24, he'd established himself as a leading journalist in the new country. He had appeared on radio and television. He traveled with President Mobutu Sese Seko.

You traveled with Mobutu? she says, quickly banishing her frown, trying for a neutral tone.

But he misses nothing and tells her that, in that day, the President was young to the job. He had hope. He did not yet rule by fear. He called the young companion his Number One journalist. Invited him to his table. Called him on the telephone and asked his counsel on matters of state. Counted him among his inner circle. Truly. Ilinga tries to cross his middle finger over the index finger but cannot, and tells her, "Comment dites-on 'Nous etions serres.'" How do you say, We were tight.

Now Mobutu lives only by fear and his bank account. He does anything to keep his office. Anything at all. It is often so with such men of power. But the young journalist was eager and ambitious, and he made those trips with one he did not truly know. He did not know what he was doing. He did not foresee the kind of man he would become. You see? He could not know.

She nods and feels this sorrow of his not-knowing enmeshed with other sorrows he can't express.

He makes an explosive half-cough, half-laugh and says it was in Paris that he met his wife. She also studied journalism. He learned the ways of the new Western man. He was prepared for a wife who had her own room. You know Virginia Woolf? Of course, you do.

Cass smiles at the reference she knows nearly by heart, Woolf's long essay, "A Room of One's Own." She's also delighted at the news of his wife and asks if she still practices journalism here.

"Je ne sais rien d'elle," I know nothing of her, he says. His expression shifts and follows his words into a bleak story of a bus crashing his motorcycle and severing his spinal cord, his wife delivering their babies to his father up country and herself to the big city and the anonymity of a new life. "My wife. She is a woman. I could not take care of her needs. Women, they are the restless ones."

Cass shuts her eyes and waits for the wisdom to find words not smothered in pity, which she senses this man of chiseled face and elegant French would resist. Aware suddenly that, although she told him her name, she hasn't asked his. She does so now.

"Je m'apelle Ilinga," he says.

"Enchante, Ilinga," she says. The moment of Corey telling the goat 'Enchante' surfaces and, inevitably, the horror of the squat-bodied Army thug aiming a rifle at her three-year-old.

Her full-on shiver elicits a puzzled look. Cold? he asks.

Not cold. Just a frightening memory. She smiles to move her thoughts away from the Army thug with the rifle.

He tells her about the cold he found in Paris. "Un froid effrayant." A frightening cold, he says, though his lean face reflects a fondness for the memory. In that winter, he took up smoking.

In the Paris winter?

To get warm, he says with a throaty laugh.

She asks if it worked.

Of course. He smiles and she sees a handsome man on top of his game. For a brief time. He loved running around that big park in the center of Paris, Luxembourg Garden. And in those ways, he made it through those eighteen months. He returned home. If he had stayed . . . He shrugs. If only. Who knows? "Peut-etre que je serais entier." Maybe I would be whole.

Maybe. It's possible. Only God knows, she says. Her own words flummox her, since she's given God no more than passing mention since she left the little church with the felt story board. Except for the odd prayer when Will was mucking about in rice paddies in the death zone. And when Vernoy prayed at Thanksgiving to the Mother and Father of us all.

God, he says now, and rolls his gaze at the ceiling where it rests for a time, as if seeking the face of the divine who might only be in hiding. "Je connais moins Dieu que les femmes." I know less of God than of women, he says. If there's bitterness in his words, she misses it, and senses only a grand fatigue that tells the story of the hours of the life left him, lying untended since his accident.

Tell me more about the accident, she says, knowing it is his life now. There it is between them, his accident story, told with a reporter's efficiency. An old story to him. As he moves through it, he picks up speed. August, 1969. An afternoon. Not long after Paris. He had a motorcycle. He loved that machine. Perfect for his work, chasing down stories. This time he was investigating some state houses. He would write articles about their doings, perfunctory, perhaps, but he truly believed they were a roadway to the kind of journalism he still hoped to bring, the journalism he studied in Paris with such blind yearning.

He turned off Boulevard 30 Juin. An Army green bus chock-a-block with passengers moved into his lane and, literally, physically, cut him off, severing his spinal cord at the level of C-5 or C-6.

He has not seen the motorcycle since. And he has no memory of the immediate aftermath. It has all disappeared into dreams with the life he left seven years ago, the life that turned into a saga of hospital beds and days without treatment. For his condition, quadriplegia, there is no real treatment.

Cass keeps her gaze squarely on his, tucking into the barest of nods.

He presses on. There is only nursing care to keep the body that remains intact, free of pressure sores and infection. He spent the first two years of his new so-called life at the University Hospital, then was moved to the large city's mass treatment center, Mama Yemo. To Pavillion One. *"Juste ici devant vous."* Right here before you. *"Comme vous voyez, je suis ici depuis."* I am here, as you see, ever since. A quick intake of breath. If only he could go abroad, to the States, he could get better physical therapy. He could improve, he says.

"If only." She nods a too-quick nod while holding tight to words disputing his vision of the U. S. of A, his savior. Let him have his fantasy. What harm can it do him now?

He comes forth now with words that clamp her breath from its source. "Une figure de cire, c'est moi." A wax figure, that's me, he says. A person in history, he goes on, famous, quite beautiful, and carved in wax. Like Madame Tussauds. The figure has no movement and no real life, but the facsimile, see how beautiful. Squinting hard at her, he breathes his question. "Que suis-je pour l'instant? Quoi que je sois pour?" What am I for now? Whatever am I for?

"Ah-h Ilinga." She's unable to hold back the intake of breath, the soft exclamation. Her thoughts vault back to her own moment in the fula fula and the two Zairois laughing and asking,

What is she for? Meaning herself, she believes. Carrying the question now, she adjusts the pronoun: *What am I for?* Her gaze surveys this end of Pavillion One, where the paralyzed live. A tragically-young woman lies near the room's far edge, a pixie of a girl meeting the air before her with a stunned and puzzled gaze. In an adjacent bed nearer Ilinga, there's a boy she can't quite place in age. Ilinga follows her gaze. That one? he says. He is one from a village in the Bandundu region of Upper Zaire. He is a man of twenty-four, but still a boy, do you know? "Le petit Loti" the Little Loti, the others here call him.

He was a hunter of rabbits and small birds. Once, during a hunt, his hunting partner shot him accidentally, and he became a paraplegic. In Loti's family, they follow the way of tradition, which says there are no accidents in Africa. There must be a spiritual dimension to all of life. The one who knows of such things is the local witch doctor. He is the interpreter of the spirits. The traditional belief is that every pain, misfortune, or suffering is blamed on somebody in the village. So, the family of Little Loti asked their village witch doctor to discern the reason for his illness. And he divined that to rid him of the evil they must first put him nude on the ground, cover him with dirt, and leave him for a time to repair. In good faith, the family followed his instructions exactly.

As you see, the ceremonial cure did not take. His legs remained immobile. His bed sores became infected. He became for them a lost cause, a useless being, his spirit grown too feeble for living. They brought him here to wait for his body to follow.

Ilinga does not hide his tears. He cannot know how long le petite Loti will stay among the living.

She nods and draws her gaze fully over the paralyzed ones around her. Poor souls, everyone. How do they come to a place so different from her own with two feet to walk freely upon the

Earth, and arms to spread wide on a sunlit morning, or lift a four-year-old. How do they deserve this circumstance? Where is fairness? A wedge of queasiness inside her: No fairness in this place. She focuses again on the elegant, former journalist before her, and, on impulse, asks a question she might better leave unspoken. Did you ever hear from Mobutu after the accident?

"Une fois-une fois," one time-one time. He draws out his answer as slow liquid. The president came to his bed in hospital, came with his henchmen. He saw the man you see. He took off his leopard skin hat and held it to his breast, the way you do when death is passing by. He turned and left the bedside. That was the end of it.

To remove his leopard skin hat, at least that's something to remember, she says. And you must know that he remembers you.

No, not at all. It was one time. After that day, he is a cipher, drifting away like refuse on the river.

"Je suis vraiment desole." I'm so sorry, she says.

"NON." His No is explosive and fierce, like a hot wind. He sweeps away her sorrow, wanting none of it and resorts to a flat affect to review their so-called friendship. He rode in his private plane. He went to Mobutu's home. Each morning before the sun grew high, you could find him walking in his garden. A habit you could count on. He visited famous gardens in France. For one who makes a cult out of authenticite, he works hard to mimic the gardens of Europe. Even now, Ilinga imagines it is so. Those hours they spent gave Mobutu time enough to ink Ilin-ga's face in memory. He makes a half-fist with the hand resting on his belly, scowls at the air between them, and explodes his whip-speed rant at full volume. "De quoi me soucier?" What do I care? He wears a leopard-skin hat and steals money from the poor. He is nothing to me. Zero. A devil who kills his enemy with a smile on his face.

"Right. All right, then," she says in English, thinking, Wow, she thinks barely able to absorb the strength of his criticism. She places a hand over her mouth to hide the smile of pleasure at his daring. She's never heard a Zairois trash the president like this in plain words. But here is a man willing to spell out his truth to her, a stranger. Here is a man with nothing left to lose.

She checks her watch. Nearly time to meet Susan. She's spent so long with Ilinga, she'll have to forgo visits with the other patients for now. She touches his long fingers and assures him she'll see him again. Maybe he believes her, she can't tell. But he nods, moving the one body part that will do his bidding, the elegant, angled head with razor-sharp intellect intact.

As she turns from his bedside toward the door of Pavilion One, Ilinga calls after her. *"Madame. Attendez."*

She stops and steps toward him. He is as close to sitting up as he can be. A wild sheen to his eyes. "Do not believe my words."

"You mean you never met the president?"

"Bien sur je le connassais," of course I knew him, he says. They dined together. They talked of his world. But he caved to his power. He could feel inside himself the evil heart hiding behind the thick spectacles, the fat smile. Ilinga knew this. He felt this, but thought more of his wallet than of his heart. His own deeds are like the Earth piling upon Le Petit Loti. "Main-tenant il est trop tard." Now it is too late. He can do nothing.

His anger is such that she half-wonders if his elegant head will melt the elegant brain still intact. No one around him in the other beds appears to hear anything unusual. Maybe this is not his first venting. Likely not. She crosses her arms over her chest and bids him Au revoir.

When she reaches the car and Susan is not there, she leans back in the driver's seat and hears again that singular phrase about Mobutu: *A habit you could count on.* She tries to picture the leopard-hatted devil savoring the tropical lushness she loves, and she cannot, but a voice inside offers a new story, a notion unformed, involving Ilinga in a plan for justice, if only there were a plan. But that plan is no more.

Seventeen

A big rain comes to the night before the day they will find Daniel and free him. It must be so. Hope will not leave her. The rain breaks into a down roll like barrels on a steep hill. A rain big enough to drown all chance of sleep for Sofia, lying on her mat, listening to the battering on the fine tin roof. A rain almost as big as the one that changed her life. There is thunder riding the waves of rain. Again, as before, Sofia feels tiny, like a stick-body waiting to be carried from this place. Still, she holds hope captive and will not let go.

At last, quiet overcomes the thunder and the battering, and Sofia sleeps enough to be strong for the morning when Mama Kundi will come and together with Alicia and Bwana Tommy, they will go to find Daniel.

In the early hours, she takes the girls to stay with Madame Cassandra. Afterward, she waits with Mama Kundi in her own hut. Mama Kundi talks of Mobutu. Sofia is curious to hear her stories of a man who is not like other men, a man who came to be feared by all in her country, and also herself.

Mama Kundi knew him long before now, when he was born Joseph Desire Mobutu in her very village called Lisala. Sofia listens to Mama Kundi telling of that time in Mongala province in the far north country, when the mondele peoples, called Belge, took Zaire for its own. His were the Ngbandi people. A small tribe. His father was a cook. Marie Madeleine was the second wife of a Mbongo chief. With that man, she had four children. She took herself away and met another man, who would be father to Joseph. That father died when Joseph was eight, and his mother placed him with the clan of an uncle. Joseph took the uncle's name, Sese Seko Nkuku wa za Banga. It means warrior who conquers.

Mama Yemo knew Joseph was a smart boy, and she saved her money and sent him to Catholic boarding school. Joseph could not accept those Catholic brothers and their rules. They kicked him out of school and made him to be a soldier. He took his soldier ways far and came to be the man everyone knows, President Mobutu Sese Seko.

Sofia asks Mama Kundi if she saw in those days of the North country the man who is chief of all Zaire.

There was a devil in that boy Joseph, Mama Kundi says. He was a sorry boy of strong brain and greedy appetite. He liked no one to tell him a rule. He wanted everyone to bow at his feet. Some say he was the favorite of Marie-Madeleine Yemo. She was the only one he heard. While she lived, he listened to her voice. He stayed with the rules that make a village safe. You know, we have such rules here, to help when one is lost, to bring food when one has none, to send kindness where sorrow comes. Marie-Madeleine Yemo, she knew such things. She spoke of them. When she died, Joseph forgot her voice and made his own rules to follow and became half man/half beast that cares only for his belly and his skin. Why do you think he wears the skin of a beast?

He is like them. Because of that, Sofia says.

Yes, Mama Kundi says. When Joseph Mobutu made Congo his own country and even called it by a new name, Mama Yemo could make him listen. He could keep the beast from entering.

When she went to the ancestors, he let out the beast who lives inside him, and you see what comes to this place. You hear how he treats the ones who will not bow to him, how he slices through their necks like saw grass.

Sofia lets out a cry. Daniel! The one who saved her from following the path of her brave Elombe. She sees the face of Daniel, broad and proud, with softness, too, like a candle flickering against the darkness. She sees the candles Alicia burned in her kitchen on a day long before her world tumbled to trouble. The name of Daniel sends back the horror of Mama Kundi's words, he slices through necks like saw grass. She scrunches shut her eyes and tries to keep the slicing coupe coupe at bay.

Here, then, is that face, riding into memory from the prison, a face startled and gray like the earth waiting for rain. Daniel! Do you breathe still? Can you stay strong until we find you?

Mama Kundi knows what occupies her mind. She makes a humming sound and takes Sofia's hands into the bone yard of her own. "Naino te." Not yet. I feel him among us. We who still stand tall.

Bwana Tommy enters, then, his big breath first, his feet and belly next, and he fills the hut. In spite of his lion presence, Sofia opens her heart and greets him with laughter to have him inside. The hut is lighter now. We go? he says.

Two white Mazdas with red hospital markings park outside the gates of Kinshasa prison. Bwana Tommy tucks in close behind the other Mazda, and the group of three steps out into this bright day with a dark purpose. To see Daniel among the living. This is the first thought for Sofia, and, she knows, for Alicia, too. Here is Alicia alone and leaving the second Mazda. On another day, in another place, she would lean into her sister-in-law with a laugh. Sofia would say, Look at you, driving woman. What a fine business this is. And Alicia would say, It is, isn't it! Today she bounces her look from one to the other, like a person seeking a place to park her anger. But she is smaller than the last time and her face has a child's sadness written strong across her features. "Tokende na kati?" We go inside? she says.

As they make quick steps toward the first gate, Sofia says, How is it, this driving of yours? How do you know this?

I must teach myself many things now. This is one.

Before Sofia can ask about a license, they reach the first gate Maybe she has no license. What is a paper license for anyway?

As before, they unlock the many gates visitors must enter to find the ones taken from them. The visitors bear food for Daniel, along with their hope that Mama Kundi speaks the truth. They come again to the hallway of fish smells and urine and smoke from families cooking outside. And here is the reception woman with short neck and tired eyes. She calls for the moon-face guard who should be in lycee with a cahier and not with a long gun over his narrow shoulder. There is knowing in his eyes when he sees the family pressing to see the tall Daniel. And he says some words to the reception woman, then turns to the family and says "Ekoki te," not possible.

"Nini boye? Ezali wapi mobali na ngai?" What's this? Where is my husband? Alicia says. Her voice demands, but the guard and the woman do not bend.

Bwana Tommy presses his belly toward Moon-face, who is more boy than guard, for Bwana Tommy can mash him like a cockroach against the concrete wall and walk away. Bwana Tommy steps back and says a word close to Moon Face, "Matabisi," tip. He stretches out a hand with some folded bills. Before Moon Face can snatch the bills, Tommy squeezes them back into a fist and tells him, Take us first to Daniel Sakombi.

They enter a long hallway. There is only this one guard. Tommy touches the shooting end of the long gun, meaning the boy guard must lower his gun. Tommy nods to Mama Kundi. She is ready with her harp and begins her plucking. Not the soothing brush notes that send a boy softly to the ancestors, but a sharp cawing sound that brings shivers to Sofia in the hot, close hallway. Sofia sees the fright in Moon Face. He lowers his long gun to his belly. He frowns and aims his thumb at the hallway end. They follow. There is a door to a dark alley and a barred room with two men enclosed in the cell. Here is the smell of sweat and the foul scent of animals on the hunt. Wooden coffin boxes line two walls. Sofia knows these boxes from giving Elunga to the earth. The sorrow from that time erupts from her as she sees two men lying on mats, each belly facing a different wall. The tall man is nearer the bars where the family stands watch. His wall wears a looping design like the Congo River, and in the middle, a heart, and the name Alicia. A splotch of black chalk follows the name. Odd markings that show a mind gone to mud. Three cockroaches crawl along the hard dirt floor beneath the chalk drawings. But the rough drawings also tell of his heart. There is only one name, Alicia, and no Sofia written in chalk beside his mat. She can believe he writes her name in his heart, but what kind of woman believes such a lie?

"Awa," here, Moon Face says.

Alicia takes herself between Bwana Tommy and Sofia. She stares at the wall. Maybe she reads her name. Maybe seeing her name in this place is like poison, for she starts a cry in her low throat. It rides upward and falls from the cliff of her sorrow. The cry becomes "Ezali kufa kufa, Daniel na nagi,' he is dead, dead, my Daniel. The outpouring fells her to the concrete soaked in footsteps and the leavings of others before her.

"Zila!" Wait! Mama Kundi's voice lifts high and strong over Alicia's death cry. No. Not dead. Her fingers begin to pluck-brush the strings of her kundi and weave the consoling voice of the spirit alive inside the small house of the harp. So sharp a difference from the earlier cawing twang that earned them fear from the boy guard. No, this is another voice, a different kind of magic. You see the tall man-figure lying before them. He moves. He quivers. He moans. "Alicia." He turns on his belly, pries himself to his knees, and sees her, his face, swollen and gray.

A quick breath from Alicia, a cry pours forth. Yes yes, my Daniel. I am here. I wait for you. I am here.

Moon Face follows the lead of his long gun and steps back from Tommy. He means by his leaving to send Daniel to the dead ones before him. But Tommy is too fat, too fast. He blocks the boy guard, and pushes him, belly-on, toward the cell.

Sofia gives her joy a squeeze, inside, where it must stay hidden but strong. Moon Face will unlock the cell and Daniel will come free. She watches to see this become so. But Tommy changes the plan she waits for. Her joy turns thin. He tells each one to give the food to Moon Face, cooked rice, saka saka, fufu, papaya. Also, the gourd with fresh water.

No no. I cannot, Alicia says.

You must, Bwana Tommy says. He will deliver to Daniel. That's how it has to be.

Mama Kundi goes forth with her gentle plucking.

Bwana Tommy holds a fist to Moon Face, then opens the fist to show what it holds. "Matabisi. Olingi oyo? Fungola sikawa," tip. Do you want this? he says.

Moon Face frowns and nods.

"Fungola sikawa." Open the door now.

"Mposo ekoya." Next week.

Their leaving steps are slow and heavy, for a second guard escorts them away from Daniel, and Tommy can do nothing except raise his fist with the matabisi and say to Moon Face, "Kokundola motema." Remember, he says and waves the zaires until Moon Face sees them no more.

Eighteen

A habit you can count on. Ilinga's phrase plays on inside the parked white Mazda. Something about the phrase fascinates Cass, and she almost says it aloud as Susan joins her, before she catches herself. The phrase would raise questions she's not prepared to face. By happy convenience, Susan's news from her interview fills the enclosed space for the drive home. She's nailed a part-time posting. Three mornings a week in the Operating Room. "I couldn't have designed it better."

Still, Ilinga occupies the silences between breathless outpourings, the limp-thin limbs of his young body where sinew and strength ought to be, the ironic tone parrying the elegance of the head and the grace of the hands. She navigates the chaos of Boulevard 30 Juin, the familiar twists and jams on the industrial sections, on to the relative calm of the Mimosa Road. All the while, she's balancing her attention between Susan's good-luck-victory and the young man's bad-luck-mauling by a city bus and by the injustice life brews. Willy nilly.

Somehow, Cass rouses herself to this moment with Susan. "Hey, congrats. We'll celebrate with you tomorrow night."

Nightfall. The tight group of expats gathers for a valiant effort to usher in the New Year over a fashionable supper and a new game. In fact, they've tasted and digested the pork loin and sweet potato/mango dinner at Susan and Logan's table. Again.

Susan insisted on hosting, wanting to show off a stunning new tablecloth her mother sent from Aix-en-Provence, where she ensconced herself all fall, with her *significant other*, having long since divorced Susan's father on the grounds of "terminal boredom." During their sundry heart-to-hearts, Susan has passed on the details without tipping her hand about her Mom's behavior that Cass herself finds both disturbing and titillating. Susan seems to vacillate between embarrassment and embrace, with a twist of envy.

The children, all six, are sleeping over at Cass and Will's, again, under Sofia's watch. Sofia's girls are asleep at Mama Kundi's. Cass has felt a change in Sofia's affect, a darkening in the last few days, but in the chaos of settling her in with the boisterous six, she postpones her questions, vowing to find out tomorrow.

Enter: Group Therapy game.

"You guys ready?" Susan says, with a slow wink.

"Susan's mom sent this for Christmas. Happiness is having a hip mother-in-law." Logan's comment lands with an ironic bump.

Mom of the terminal boredom, Cass thinks, picturing Will's mom, tall and elegant, who would never leave his father.

"She says her friends are a tad stodgy, that maybe the younger set will give it a whirl."

"Full disclosure: I'm a tad stodgy myself," Vernoy says.

Logan tags on his own mumble of solidarity with their older and, perhaps, wiser, friend.

Susan's well-appointed living room bends to the latest hippy-chic, with oversized pillows arranged in a large semi-circle on the living room floor, alternating boy-girl-boy-girl. Cass sits between Vernoy and Logan and across from Will, seated between Susan and Lindy, and Tommy between Susan and

Vernoy. The arrangement doesn't strike Cass until later, after everything has played out. For now, Susan starts them off. She opens the plain black box, clears her throat, and says, "Group Therapy. Is it really a game?" Leveling her baby blues at each player around the circle, she asks, "What say you all?" Without waiting for their replies, she reads on: "Yes, Group Therapy is a game. But Group Therapy is for people who want to do more than just play games. For people who want to open up. Get in touch. Let go. Be free."

Vernoy casts a scowl at the plain box and crosses both hands over his middle. "Hold the phone, kids, I feel like Rip Van Winkle here. I just woke up in the wrong decade."

"Not to worry, Pops. Think of it as a stretching exercise," Susan tells him, teasing, and reads off the rules of the game, simple rules. Select a token and move it counter-clockwise along the game board, starting at the space labeled "Hung Up" and arriving at the space labeled "Free." To reach Free, a player draws from three decks of cards and does as the card instructs. First card is Tommy's. "Ask someone to hold you and rock you. Give yourself to the experience," Tommy reads and makes a fist bump in the air. "Yes!" He turns, laughing, to Vernoy and says, "Rock me, Pops."

Laughter erupts around the circle, from all but Vernoy, who frowns intently. "Rip to you, Big Boy." More laughter swirls over them.

Tommy turns face front to Vernoy, who extends his lean arms toward Tommy's massive shoulders and belly, and at arms' length side-tilts him, up-down, marionette-style.

Susan casts a dubious grin on the "hug" and solicits the group's judgment. "Which is it kids, 'Cop Out' or 'With it?'" Each lifts a card reading Cop Out or With it. The group is split, half and half. "All right. I'll be the tie-breaker. Give him a pass," Susan says. "Next pigeon."

She turns to Lindy whose card from the yellow deck reads, "Stand facing the group member who threatens you most. Pushing your hands against his, tell him why he frightens you." She makes a sour face and jumps up before Tommy, who lounges back against the couch cushion and slow-eyes his wife of a decade. Still standing, she leans in pushing her hands against his belly front."

"Moi?" Tommy says in mock horror.

"Oui. Every night I have nightmares of your heart attack."

"My heart attack?" He erupts in a spate of coughs. "Sheez, Babe, Happy New Year to you, too."

"I'm not kidding. I live in fear." She pulls herself into an erect posture, mirrored by an expression of severity she rarely shows.

Bewilderment stuns the five players looking on. Reading their faces, Cass suspects they're all thinking, What have I stepped into? Susan lifts a 'Pass" card. "I think that deserves a pass, don't you?" The others follow suit whereupon Susan draws a new card and reads silently. Landing her gaze on Logan, she reads aloud. "Turn to the person in the group you know best and tell them something he or she doesn't know about you." She leaves her seat between Will and Lindy, crosses over to Logan, and, hesitating, squeezes her fists, as Cass has seen Corey do in the heat of a temper.

"I've never told you this. But here goes. In all our years together. Where are we at now? Ten? I've never had an orgasm. I've tried everything." She continues to make her case, laying before them her many efforts at arousal: positions, clothing and no-clothing, lighting, ice cubes. But the witnesses cannot eclipse her cardinal utterance I've never had an orgasm.

Sparks of disbelief erupt from the silence. Cass feels them inside her, and in the others, too. She holds her folded hands in that slip of time between horror and wonder. Vernoy speaks first. "Okay, then, Susan. Tell us how you really feel, why don't you."

Susan shrugs, lifts her chin, and spreads her gaze with a hint of challenge about the circle. She reveals no regret that Cass can detect. Logan's face is a cipher, absent any squint of mirth. Sweat bubbles at his temples as he rises and steps from the room. So much for midnight, Cass thinks. She tries to catch Will's eye, but he's looking toward the bay window with a gentle grin, as if remembering some sweet moment from long ago.

Logan steps now across the threshold from the hallway into the living room, pauses, then launches himself into a handstand Cass never dreamed he could manage. Yes, he has a mean serve on the tennis court, and heft in those shoulders. But she never imagined they could wrestle him from the pull of gravity. She detects trembling in his hands as he lowers himself to kneeling. A red scarf covers his head, shoulders, face, and his right hand holds a dark slipper raised before them. A voice notches above and edgier than Logan's, rising. "I'm Buster Brown. I live in a shoe. This is my dog Tige. He lives there, too."

First silence reigns, then laughter released from incredulity. But Logan isn't finished. "I hear she's caught in a flood, Tige. There's sludge out there. Toxic sludge. Shall we rescue her?"

"Do you wanna rescue her?" It's Tige speaking, low and slow.

"Not really."

"Are you sure, Buster?"

"Why not? Let's see if she can swim."

The laughter sinks into murmurs. Logan stands, exits the room with his props, and returns as himself, bare head and blonde hair grazing his left eye. Susan leaves the circle for the kitchen, and returns bearing a plump green bottle of Portuguese red wine inside a wicker sleeve. As well as Cass knows Susan, she can't read her expression, but she holds the bottle by the wicker handle and appears ready to speak, whereupon Vernoy stands with his own proclamation. "Friends. The game appears to be inflicted with that bit of toxic sludge. What do you say we declare a Cop Out and move on?"

"Hear-hear." Will's cry nudges the others into raising the Cop Out card.

Nonplussed by the spate of Cop-Out cards, Susan pours wine from the wicker bottle into the juice glasses she's arranged on the coffee table, from cupboards outfitted by teetotaling missionaries before them. Not even Susan has managed to fill her cupboards with stemmed wine glasses. She lifts a glass and carries it across to Logan. "To my best friend," she says.

Logan lifts his left hand, clears his throat, and says, "What do you say, Tige? Do we make her sleep in the shoe box tonight? You guess not? But you watch her close, okay?" He stretches a big hand behind her blonde head and gives it a squeeze. He drops his hand, takes the glass, swallows the wine in a single gulp, and extends it Susan for a refill.

"I believe I'm sticking with Rip," Vernoy says and sips his own.

Cass and Will walk home in the still-humid, not-quite midnight air when the temperature sinks to perfection for walking. She smiles in the darkness and wraps her arms around her middle, in a swell of appreciation for Will, their marriage, and their chemistry. On an impulse, she takes his arm and says, "Love is never having to confront your husband for not giving you an orgasm."

Will places a hand over hers and says in that dry way, "Publicly."

"Yeah. Truly. How could she?"

"Let's hope he makes it through this without slipping her a cyanide pill or something."

"He didn't really seem upset."

"Logan has a low libido."

Cass drops his arm. "You know this because . . .?"

"A wild guess."

An image of Susan surfaces, and she feels a pinch sympathy for her friend.

"For starters, most guys will make comments about women, especially when you know them as well as we do Logan. He never says a word."

She skates a frown his way. "Tell me you're not passing any juicy tidbits from our bedroom."

"Don't be absurd, Babe." He stops and draws her into a hard hug. "Let's go home."

The rest of the way, they banter about Logan's puppet show, his Buster Brown, and Tige, and the laughter carries them up the stairs, into the sleeping house and their own private bedroom.

Tuesday of a New Year and a no-work day for Susan in her newish-three-day-a-week job, she invites Cass to join her for shopping. There's word of a new shipment of rice at the supermarche. Cass drives them down Mimosa Road, in silence with an edge Cass feels and maybe Susan does not. Cass rides the edge until they reach Avenue de la Justice, near the super-marche. She locks the car and hires one of several young men vying to guard it before she presses her basket to her hip and sends Susan a soft tease about the motive behind her invitation to shop together. "Let me guess. You gave Logan the car as an olive branch."

"It was already arranged. I need it tomorrow." She paused, frowning. "Olive branch?"

"Come on, Susan, don't play dumb. For New Year's Eve. The Group Therapy revelation."

"Oh, that." She shrugs, turning her bright smile across the walkway.

"I mean, how is he? I have to say, that puppet show was brilliant."

"I didn't know he had it in him."

"Pretty funny. He's got amazing shoulders."

"And a low libido."

"Really? That's . . ." The words *That's what Will said* slide into a skid, just in time to prevent their spilling out between them.

"That's what?"

"Interesting. I mean, it must be hard."

"To be me?" Susan lifts up a single hard laugh.

"You kidding? Hard to be you, looking like Kim Novak?"

Susan laughs again, softer this time.

They enter the supermarche, already at full occupancy with Zairois of-means and North Americans and Europeans. At once, shouts erupt at the far end of the long aisle between 40-kilo bags of rice and shelves bearing canned marmalade, canned peaches, and toilet paper. Large numbers of Zairois are knotted in a circle around a center figure hunched on the cement floor, inside a whirlwind of fists and elbows launched at him. A word rises above the knot, "Moyibi moyibi."

Neither Cass nor Susan knows much Lingala. Cass turns to a tall young Zairois in an open-necked shirt and a light sports coat. He takes in the scene with an aloof air. Nothing he hasn't seen many times.

"Moyibi? *Qu'est-ce que c'est?*" Cass says.

"C'est un voleur. Il a vole des legumes." He's a thief. He stole some vegetables. It is so with thieves in my country. It is ever so. He must know this thievery is not permitted.

"Not permitted, eh?" Susan says as they move on through the aisles of mix-matched offerings, on to the freezer cases. They stand over a case containing a small perfectly-formed vervet monkey, lying in frozen splendor on its back.

"But frozen monkeys are permitted," Cass says with a shiver.

"Bushmeat," Susan says. "Flown in from some tropical forest, I imagine."

"Too weird. I guess we have to walk a while in their moccasins," Cass says. For now, she feels in sync only with the vervet's icy grave.

The newness of 1975 ages into habit and heat rising. Bouts of rain pummel the streets of Mimosa and thicken the lawns that will never go dry again. If looks were true. Of course, as any thinking person knows, looks give a brief sketch of what our eyes can see. But there is more, so much more.

On a Wednesday Cass will never forget, Leon steps into the kitchen as always. He stands immobile at the edge until Cass says, "Bonjour, Leon. Tout va bien?" Everything okay?

He stares at the linoleum, at this hands lifted as if in prayer, finally at Cass. "Je dois vous laisser." I must leave you.

"Pour aujourdui?" For today?

"Pour tourjours." For forever.

"Mais pourquoi?" Why

"Ma soeur, elle est morte." My sister is dead.

"Oh no. No. Mais je suis desole." I'm sorry.

"Oui. C'est triste. Les enfants …" He leaves his sorrow and the children wordless on his breath.

Now Cass drives to Mama Yemo in the Mazda Will has left for her use today. She parks and steps under a covered walkway toward the hospital entrance. She steps inside with her satchel. She hasn't yet mapped out a plan for her visits here among the paralyzed. So far, she's focused on Ilinga, mostly talking and, selfishly, working on her French with him. He's keen to learn some English, and today she has a picture dictionary to help with this goal. Cass isn't crafty, but she knows simple macramé techniques and she's gathered twines of various thicknesses in her satchel, thinking she must move on to others, those with working hands, and show them now to make simple items, such as plant holders or belts. Someone more adept than she—and there will be those—will discover ways to make wall hanging and such art pieces.

She pauses in the alcove inside the door, to gather her courage for the coming conversations. A man's voice catches her, muffled and close. English. No, American. Familiar. A laugh, stifled and low. Will, she thinks. It can't be, he's in surgery.

She steps toward the enclosure that appears to house the sound. A shade is drawn. She sees no one.

Now, a higher voice, a woman's, slightly nasal, also American, also familiar, but less so. Susan? But it can't be, she's working. Inside the small enclosure? Yes, it must be an administrative office. Cass steps up to the door, tries the knob that does not turn. She sees nothing. The voices continue, muffled, low, and intimate.

She tugs the satchel onto her shoulder, steps back through the alcove, casting a painful glance at the Pavilion she meant to enter, and opens the door to the covered walkway and the world away from the muffled voices, low and intimate, and oh-so familiar. Each known by the other, biblically, as they say.

No, she thinks. The No-no-no surges through her throat and skids full-on to her belly and her heart, where it will lodge in perpetuity. All doubt about the voices and the truth they hold, the world of deceit and duplicity they front, all doubt is gone. Gone to graveyards, every one, as she and her SDS-mates sang during the Vietnam War, that time lived so far from Will and yet closer than ever in her life, that time when he was hers, and hers alone.

The golden hour before sunset comes, as ever, and the irony is not lost on Cass that this moment of most excruciating beauty, of light spinning gold and red streams over the grounds she must walk, this is the moment she tells Will she knows and the world as she knows it ends.

She feeds the boys early. She herself can't bear the thought of a single bite touching the gut already stuffed with the unpalatable. She bathes the boys and reads them a tale from Kipling's *Just So Stories* from her own childhood. She tells them to play quietly in their room while she and Daddy have a talk.

"What talk, Mommy?" Corey swivels his round face from his Lincoln logs to his mother standing far above.

"Big people talk," she says.

"It means an argument," Matheo says with all the heft of his five years.

"Not necessarily."

"It does so, Mommy.'

"Well, we'll see. Daddy's just driven up."

She pours herself a glass of Portuguese red wine and descends the steps to meet him on the sidewalk, at the house end, where the coleus cease and the marigolds set in. "Hey, Babe." He sends the greeting that always precedes his hug.

She sips her wine and watches him, unsmiling.

"You're starting before me?"

"So it seems. Wine's on the counter. I'll meet you by the banana tree. Out back."

"Oh? Are the boys in the house?"

"They can wait. Out back."

"It's like that, is it?" He goes inside.

She takes herself along the north side of the house out to the big lawn, so lush now she can hardly believe it's the same plot they first saw in July before the big rains hit and a friend betrays her and her life upends. She couldn't know all that awaited her from another season. She sits flat on the lawn, marking with disinterest how the morning's rain seeps through her pants, caring only for the words she gathers to her tongue.

At last he appears. Bermuda shorts have replaced trousers. He wears an open-necked shirt and holds a Primus beer, a towel, and a light frown as he joins her on the grass. Inside the fierce heat of her face, red and streaked with hours of tears, she wonders if he's reading his future there.

He sits cross-legged on the towel, tilts his Primus for a long swallow. "What's going on?"

She breathes through flaring nostrils, stares.

"What's happened? Are you all right?"

"How was surgery this morning?"

"Surgery? Fine. Oh, the usual. Kwanza fell asleep again." It's the second time he's mentioned the anesthetist slipping into sleep under the operating table. "It's no wonder," he adds, "poor guy has two jobs and four kids. When's he supposed to sleep?" The first time he told it, they'd both chuckled over the discrepant image.

This time she plucks a blade of grass and tears it, unsmiling. "Kwanza. I know he has two jobs. Do you suppose he has a deuxieme bureau?" Zairois for a second wife.

"No idea. Why?"

"Seems to be going around. Even among expats."

He frowns, exhales and squints hard. "All right, Cassie. What's this about?"

"Let's see. I went to the hospital this morning."

"Yeah."

"Thought I'd branch out from Ilinga. Talk to some of the others. I got distracted. Two people talking. A couple. Intimate. I couldn't keep from listening. I couldn't turn away. No mistaking their intimacy."

"So?" A boisterous, bullying so that in a different light or life would get her laughing.

"Do you not imagine that I know your voice at its most intimate after all our years? Will?"

He tilts his head back as if star gazing, in darkness. He rights his head and nods once, his blue gaze unblinking on her face. Gazing back, she wishes he could lie with feeling and let the shock and sadness vanish but there's no mistaking the admission. Whatever else he is, he's not a liar. Not a liar of commission, but of omission oh, yes, he can withhold the truth, as he has for weeks, months, however long, peeling away her innocence, leaving her naked, cozened before the world.

He stands and reaches down, to pull her up. "Don't. Don't touch me. Don't even try." She bats away his arm and stands on her own steam. "So my husband is fucking my so-called friend. Ducky, isn't it. Just ducky."

"Cass Cass, it's not what you think."

"What I think. What do I think? I think I'm a schmuck. And you're a bastard." She brushes her butt, wet from the grass, and lands both fists to his chest as she pummels and pummels.

He hard grips her arms between them. She stomps hard on his foot. He drops her arms, cursing, and she spins away from the grass, for the stairs, dark now. The Golden Hour has ended.

Later in the night when neither sleeps, she lies in the guest-room bed. This will be her room now. There will be no guests going forward. What would be the good of inviting anyone into this nest of treachery and shame? Forget it. Judas lives here. Also, a twit, a patsy. Save yourself the pain.

Through the hours of lying down, she streams a ration of plans going forward. He'll be at work when she pockets the stash of zaires tucked in the volume of World Poetry next to Yeats' "Second Coming." And won't that be true poetic justice. After all, things do fall apart. The center does not hold. Perfect. Then she'll pack up the boys and purchase three plane tickets out of this hole of heat and horror.

Of course, she'll go home, though the sad part is she doesn't hate Kinshasa, not really. She's coming round to the life here. They've talked of taking the boys on a safari vacation to Kenya. And what do you know? Susan and Logan have been having the same talk. We could combine forces, Will said just recently. He did, the bastard.

No point in her staying on now. She isn't the one who signed the contract. And she can imagine the shock of discovery coating his face. See him reading the note she's left on the mountain of orthopaedic journals on his desk. He won't miss her. Oh, maybe he'll miss the services she performs, but not her body, and not her true self, he's made that clear. He'll have his Susan. They'll be free to let loose their passion, wherever the mood strikes. Logan won't care. That's obvious, he of the low libido. Maybe he'll perform his nightly puppet show for the couple.

In the dark room, she catches a flicker of his expression when he realizes she's taken the boys. My boys, he calls them. They are the first question he asks each evening after work, the first laugh he lifts up is theirs. It's from them and for them. A shadow of longing falls on her face, her neck, her breasts, for the father-son moments that will leave her life. Gone. They are so gone.

Her brain leaves off the plan of vacating Kinshasa for now, and picks up the stream of moments before now when she's seen and heard Will and Susan together, when she might have known. Should have known. Anyone with a brain would have known. That day at Susan's, before Christmas and the strange phone call she intercepted, the man speaking French with an American accent and sounding curiously like Will. But it was so curious she chucked it into the bin of the absurd. And what about those dinner parties with Tommy and Lindy and Vernoy where Will and Susan always manage to sit together. Vernoy. She wonders if he suspects them. Or, maybe he knows, for he seems to have a bigger picture of what's true, what's real, what's important than the rest of them. He seems to have a direct line to another realm. And there they all were walking together that night after Christmas dinner, out on the dark street, and Will and Susan were walking side by side laughing at some joke known only to the two of them. She'd known then, had she not? but would not allow herself to hold that knowing. The ridiculous game Susan inflicted on them should have been a clue, her unveiling her prized hotness before God and everybody. Most telling of all, was the phrase used by the two of them, "He has a low libido." Not a guy thing at all, as Will claimed, but a thing shared between lovers. The bastard, she thinks again.

She squeezes her eyes and her fists to stem the stream and hears the shuffle of Will poring over journals and notes in his study next door. So, he prepares, as ever, for the Board exam that lies ahead, and inhabits the deep discipline that, even now, keeps him true to the path begun in childhood when he was asked what he wanted to do when he grew up, and it was always, "I'm going to be a doctor."

And what of me? she thinks, and this unleashes another stream, the fula fula ride to town, and the two Zairois men asking, 'What is she for?'

Yes, she thinks, *what am I for? What am I to become now?*

PART THREE

Nineteen

Sofia waits through the long days into the new week. She waits with Kamina and Fimi in her hut and carries on the work of living with the fear of learning the worst. She waits for Bwana Tommy to return, for he is the one who will drive them to the prison. When she sees him she will ask Madame Cassandra to call Alicia, for she alone among Sofia's family has a telephone. And they will go again together. This is her plan. She believes Madame will do this, though it is a strange time at that house now. Inside that grand hotel/house, she has no smile for Sofia, as always before. Madame's is the look of a jackal who knows he is hunted. Sofia believes Madame is angry at Doctor Will. He has taken another Madame to his bed. This is a thing known in the village, where secrets pass quickly. The knowing came from the hospital where the two were seen and heard. Sofia feels sad for Madame Cassandra, but she cannot speak of this to Madame.

The new week arrives at last. It is early in the day, and Kamina and Fimi are already gone to school when Bwana Tommy steps up to her doorway and calls her name.

She lifts the door cover and invites him to enter, laughing for the way his presence causes the room to grow smaller. She offers him tea and a biscuit.

He tells her no thanks. This No from fat bwana darkens the news that will come.

She says can they please stop at Madame Cassandra's for a fast phone call, so Alicia can meet us there.

He tells her there is no need. That can wait. He asks if he can sit a moment. He promises not to break the chair. His smile goes quickly. She sits facing this bwana who has news she does not want to know. Still he tells her what is what.

He went already to the Prison Centrale de Kinshasa. He went alone because he felt he could bring more freedom as one alone to do what he needed in that sorry place. He had thought to call a man he knew with a long gun and bring it, but instead brought a knife from Madame, which he kept hidden under his shirt. Sofia smiles at such a picture as this. Moon Face was there and also another guard who was fat like Bwana Tommy.

He asked that they take him into the second hall, where they last saw Daniel. He speaks slowly. Sofia's dread begins to rise. He tells of spiders scurrying across the concrete floor and one dangling from a bar and turning a circle in the air. He tells of the smell like an animal carcass left too long in the sun.

"Daniel?' Sofia's voice is a scratching sound, like a mole wanting to get out.

"No people. The cells were empty. There was no one."

When he came, at last, to the empty cell, he stepped up close and squeezed the bar and turned at last to the fat guard and said, Where is Daniel?

This guard said to Bwana Tommy, Who is this Daniel? He did not know this man.

Bwana Tommy drew close to this guard, so close he could smell the pilchard taste from his meal. This guard stepped back and lifted his long gun from his shoulder and Bwana Tommy was not afraid. He does not know why. But Moon Face had much fear in his boy-face and he walked fast away. Tommy stayed with the fat guard and the two fat men faced one another in that sour place. You must know Daniel, Tommy said. Tell me where he is. I must know.

The fat guard looked at his boots on the concrete and the crawling spiders and told him, Ezali kufa. He is dead.

This is true? Tommy said in a hard voice that told him he must not lie or he will have more to fear.

It is so, the fat guard told him. He took no pleasure in this tired telling.

When? Tommy said.

He was a strong man. He lived longer than the other two. But there was that last time the visitors came, then he died before night.

Sofia asks about the food they left for his dinner. Did that Moon Face give it to Daniel?

It is a useless question to wonder about those guards who care only for their own bellies. Tommy takes a white handkerchief from the pocket of his shirt and wipes it over his face and neck and closes his eyes for a long time and he cannot speak and there is no need.

There will be now the keening she cannot help, but not here for all the village to know she grieves so for the man who is not hers, but Alicia's. It must wait until she can go to the river and take the cover of the river's voice for her own. She and Bwana Tommy sit for more minutes until he opens his eyes and nods and takes a slow walk to the village faucet and Mimosa Road outside where his Mazda car sits.

She takes her own slow walk to the place of the bridge on the river, where the current is fast and the rapids sing loudly, and she lets loose one hundred days and nights of sorrow for the man who was not her own. She does not care. She will not cease from sorrowing, but she keens enough for now.

She mounts the steps at Madame Cassandra's. She enters as always, first her own knock, then her opening the door freely, as if the house is her own. It is no more her own than Daniel, but such is the way of her coming each day. It is early, but not so early that she sees Dr. Will at home, for now things are different in this house, and he leaves earlier than before. Someone has made coffee, mostly gone now. She empties the pot and starts a new one, making noise with a spoon to the glass pot to let Madame know she's come.

It's the children who come to find her, not Madame. Corey dances up to her, jumping and hugging her waist. Always for this boy, she has been gone too long and he cannot believe his luck to see her at last. Matheo stands at the edge of the kitchen waiting for her to stop laughing with Corey, as she always does. Matheo frowns and says, "Mommy is still sleeping." He says it in a blaming voice, for everyone knows it's not right for her to sleep now when he must get ready for school.

Sofia steps toward Matheo, folding her arms and frowning, and so lets him know she listens, she understands him. This boy does not make her laugh like the little one, but her heart warms for him, too. "Is no problem. You are big boy, yes? You can find school clothes for yourself. Then eat breakfast."

Matheo frowns more deeply, but also nods and returns to his room and shuts the door loudly. Sofia guesses he's trying to punish his mother for sleeping too long. She fills a bowl with the Cornflake cereal Madame found somewhere at the marche. Once she tasted the dry chips Corey loves and finds them more like bon bons. She readies the dining table for Madame and the children. She herself eats in the kitchen. In the beginning Madame urged her to eat with the family, but Sofia could not. Finally, Madame stopped asking.

She fixes herself a cup of tea as she opens a can of pilchards and prepares the rice for her own breakfast to eat after she walks Matheo down to the gate where he catches his bus.

Matheo steps now into the kitchen, looking like a school boy from a rich country. He wears shorts and a shirt with buttons. She smiles a little to see the buttons a bit askew. She tugs him close and re-buttons the shirt and, to herself, admires the fine tie-shoes they make in a rich country. Sofia remembers when Daniel took them to the Bata store and bought rubber sandals for Kamina and Fimi. She cannot forget how happy they were that day, for there are many in the River Village whose feet go bare.

After their small breakfast and some other readiness, Sofia walks Matheo down the wide street to the gate where the school bus will meet him. Corey dances along beside her, always stretching the reach of her hand, which holds his. There's no wait this day, and when the bus pulls in, Matheo steps toward it just as a bigger boy, a Zairois, trips a small boy hard to his knees. Matheo moves in close and pulls the little one to his feet and, together, they take the steps inside. The pushing boy wears the same fine tie-shoes as Matheo, and he holds a fine ball in his right hand. He believes he is the boss of everyone. The others must believe it, too, for they look away.

Sofia's anger cannot permit such meanness by this tall son of a rich Zairois. Still, holding Corey's hand, she pushes herself forward and grips the rim of his shirt. He jerks himself around to see who dares to touch him so. Sofia answers with her own question in the Lingala the boy speaks at home. "Nkombo nay yo nani?" What is your name?

The boy looks down at her, the boss inside him shrinking from her fierceness, and says nothing.

Sofia says, "Yebisa ngai nkombo na yo tata." Tell me the name of your father.

The boy frowns and his low grumble tells her, "Doctor Moyo."

She tells him, Your father is doctor. I know your house. It is not far from Madame's. I shall speak to him. He will want to know the way of his son with a small boy.

He makes a face of one who cares not what is what, but she sees the fear in him, and she will not forget.

There is such a face on Madame Cassandra when Sofia tells her about Bwana Tommy and his news of Daniel. Madame lets out a cry that sounds like laughter but cannot be, before her anger pours out into the kitchen, and sends Corey twirling and crying, 'What, Mommy, what's wrong?"

"Just big people problems."

He stretches and climbs onto a kitchen chair. "I'm big. See how big."

"Yes, you are a big boy. Go find your Lincoln logs, ok?"

He jumps down and away, and Sofia watches Madame with a cold eye and makes herself ask in her limited French, "Madame, vous rirez?" You laugh?

"Non non," she tells Sofia. She only weeps for Daniel. But that man, the President. She laughs because of him. She could not believe he would truly do this thing to a man like Daniel. But this proves he is not a man at all but a beast like the leopard image he wears on his head.

Sofia tells her, "Nayebi," I know, "Nayebi." She means I have known before you. I have known of this man when you were still in your rich country. I have always known this thing I cannot bear, but I must.

Twenty

Cass has no contact with Susan for several days after the moment she's calling her marital apocalypse. During the interlude, she assumes Will has told Susan, mostly from the length of silence between them. In their friendship days, they were constantly back and forth. But when Susan calls Cass for the first time, Cass realizes he has not. An odd lapse, she finds. Perhaps he's embarrassed or assessing his next move. Yes, that would be more like him.

"Hey, kiddo, I need to do an errand. Wondered if you could take the girls for a couple hours after nursery school."

Cass has waited for this first face-off with her now-former friend. Her plan is to start calm and reveal her knowing without yelling but with a slow chill. "An errand?" Cass breathes calmness into the question.

"Oh, you know, I told Logan I'd mail a package for him. While I'm at it, I'll pick up a few things at the market."

"Unh huh. Taking the girls would be . . . in-con-ven-ient? You guess." She feels a kind of pleasure in the excruciating slowness with which she draws the line between them.

Silence, then, until Susan says, inflection rising, "Cass?"

"Susan?" Bitch, she thinks.

"What's . . . is something . . . what's wrong?" The faltering inquiry tells Cass where they are, that Will has, indeed, said nothing, or she wouldn't have called, but that Susan knows. She gets the gist of what Cass somehow has learned from Cass' own side of the conversation.

"Is something wrong? Interesting question. You tell me."

More silence. The static of her throat clearing. Her voice lowering into a range that could be seductive under the right conditions. If they were still friends, she'd call Susan on her tone. *You've got to know you are your mother's daughter.* she'd say. "Cass. If you're thinking there's something really going on here, you're nuts."

"I'll give you that I may be nuts. I'm definitely a patsy. But that doesn't explain why you're lying to me." Saying the words has a soothing effect on Cass. Not that she's proud of making anyone squirm, her betrayer, but she feels, for this single moment, a sense of control.

"We didn't . . . I didn't mean for it to happen . . . it just . . ."

"Oh, I know. Isn't it a bitch when things get out of hand. Never mind, Susan, no problem. He's all yours. Enjoy your . . . errands." She slams the receiver down harder than she intends. She plops herself hard onto the living room couch, slowing her racing pulse. When a level of calm has overtaken the rage, she covers her face in her hands and weeps.

"Mommy?" Corey crawls in beside her and lays his head in her lap. "Was somebody mean to you on the phone? Who was mean, Mommy? Cause I want to kick his butt."

"No, Sweetie," she says, smoothing a curl from his forehead. "It was nobody."

For days after the revelation, Cass stays clear of the hospital. She feels badly, mostly for Ilinga whom she promised to come see regularly. She hates to imagine him waiting in vain for her; he has so little to distract him from all he has lost. There's also her segue into enlisting Ilinga in Xavier's plan, though she's left off all those imaginings in the wake of her personal trial. She can barely recall what she had in mind for him. He was close to Mobutu, that was it. When he told her, her mind clutched the relationship between those two, as some kind of lifeline. But was it really? Given his physical limitations, what specifically could he do? Serve as a decoy, perhaps. The idea of using a man of his innate dignity in such a cheesy way makes her shiver.

Well, Ilinga and her project will have to wait. She can't bring herself to go near the place of her undoing. She knows how foolish she's being, how absurdly she's letting her emotions drive her days. Even when Will leaves her the Mazda and rides with Logan or Tommy, in that ardently regardful way he takes with her now, she stays away from the place that is his domain, after all, not hers. She's an add-on, a helpmate, a position she's full-on rejecting. Now and then, she considers seeking real employment in Kinshasa, since apparently she's staying. She has a university degree, after all. Maybe she could hire on at that Jesuit University, the one called Lovanium, as an English teacher. Or, at Tasok, the American School, but she's met the Head of School a few times, and he tells her those hirings occur at job fairs during another season, on another continent. Besides the whole idea of assuming a full-time job feels like a messy, daunting business, given the kids. True, she has Sofia, but only part-time. When she tries a mental orchestration of all her working full-time would entail, she shuts her eyes and banishes the notion altogether.

There's another complication. That familiar subliminal nudge has returned, full bore. She's feeling it now, the pulse deep in a pocket of her heart, a voice tolling inside, 'This isn't right. You know he must be stopped.' She circles round again to that other plan still extant in the minefield of possibilities inside her, seeking a refuge from raw humiliation. She'll resurrect the plan she buried after the goat fiasco. The renewal of the plan comes from Sofia's sad news of Daniel, which highlights again all that Mobutu is capable of doing to his own people. Nothing is beneath him, it seems. He must be stopped. Here, then, is the answer, plain-spun and exceedingly clever. Here is the end of her searching, the way she can stay on in Kinshasa, right the wrongs done her, the payback for Will's betrayal. She can't be certain that Xavier will trust her again; she might have blown it for good. But if she shows him the zaires he needs, she suspects he'll take them. She'll tell Will that she and the boys will stay on. Divorce can wait till they return to the States. Meanwhile, he can do whatever his sky-high-libido requires. She'll follow her own passions. Knowing him, he'll assume it's a guy. He'll never suspect the old SDS actor who ran free while he was off in a far country watching for VC to emerge from the hills around Da Nang.

She can do all of this with no danger to Corey and Matheo. They won't be stuck out on a mud-glommed roadway, fair game for some squat soldier to muscle them with the barrel of a rifle. They'll be with Sofia or their father while she meets Xavier and becomes the Cassandra her father named, the one Will does not know.

Her first task is to create a money stash of her own, a different take on Virginia Woolf's "Room of One's Own." Not too big a stretch, since Will has never begrudged her cash enough to run the house. Nor is he a bean counter. So it is that each Monday after his car leaves the driveway, she opens the volume, *World Poetry*, to Yeats, and withdraws twenty zaires, returns the volume to the common shelf and tucks the lone bill into her copy of *Fear of Flying*, a favorite of hers she stashed into her luggage at the last minute before coming over.

Xavier sits across from her at the table at the edge of Café de la Paix, where they first met that long-ago Thanksgiving week when her world was intact. The wide smile from their first meeting is absent. He avoids eye contact, and when he does meet her gaze, his is brooding and restless, as if he can spare her only a moment. "So?" comes the opening he deigns to offer. Then, in silence, waits for her to speak.

'Thanks. Thank you . . . for coming." She inhales slowly to strain the shaking from her voice. She's thanking him, as if he's doing her a favor. But there is something of that dynamic in this meeting. At last, she says, "I want to help bring justice."

Now it comes, like a spark, different from his trademark smile. He shakes his head. "So you said two months ago."

"I know. Something's changed."

"The world turns, Madame Ramsey. Change is ever with us."

"I get why you're upset. But I'm in for real this time. For good. I won't bail on you again." She unzips the pocket inside her purse, and removes the envelope containing one hundred zaires and places it on the table between them.

He holds his stillness. But the brooding affect he brought to the table lightens.

She waits, folding and unfolding her hands in her lap. It's unwise to appear weak in this arrangement, lest he think he can abuse her good nature and squeeze out more than she's able to give. She was a fool with Will whom she's known for more than a decade. She doesn't want to be a fool with this Xavier person she knows hardly at all. She lengthens her torso and straightens her shoulders. "I have done work for justice and peace in America. I see the brutality being done here in your country. If I can help by paying rent for a room, I will. Maybe I can do even more."

He watches her with interest now, surliness gone. He feels some part she's holding back and he waits for her to continue.

"But when we must be in contact, call me in daytime, by midafternoon, not in the evening when my husband is home. Or, I call you. Ca va?" As the words leave her tongue, she realizes she should call them back. She has no more need to cache her secrets from Will. He can call her any old time he wants. This is a new day. She has nothing to fear from Will, now that the worst has happened. What can he do to her? Cut her out of their community property? Not a chance. She has the moral high ground here, although the thought crossing her consciousness gives her quiver of self-disgust. She's sounding like some kind of Anita Bryant knock-off.

Still, she has no need to worry. She'll do whatever she needs to do going forward.

He receives this last stream of information with interest, she can tell by the wide grin of their first meeting at Mobutu's reception. "Ca va," he says.

So it begins, her re-entry into Xavier's project. She's content to be a minor player. More than content, she feels a touch of healing from raw betrayal, her sense of nerves frayed and exposed for all to see and pity. Always in her thirty years, this has been her M.O. Steel herself against inciting pity. Even when Will was in Vietnam and she lived with her own parents, she resisted whenever one asked how she was doing, was everything all right. A spike of anger would precipitate an involuntary shrug and she'd answer abruptly. Of course, why do you ask?

How absurd, she'd chide herself later. They were just being parents, compassionate parents. Now she's a mom herself, and she knows how primal is that impulse.

And here she is, once more, experiencing that same spike of anger and resisting even the possibility of someone offering, God forbid, sympathy, for her fall from beloved to betrayed. Not that anyone besides the main players knows about the Will-Susan affair. Unless, of course, Lindy and Tommy know. They would be the ones, if any. She can hardly bear the thought of facing their knowing, their pity.

Vernoy would be different. He lives above the fray. *I'm with Rip,* he announced during the Group Therapy fiasco. Or, the way he talks about faith: *Faith isn't a bucket of coins somebody loses. Faith is our window on the universe.* Even if he did know, she wouldn't mind. Not at all. Marital infidelity isn't a realm of behavior he'd traffic in. She might even welcome a chance to confide in someone, now that Will and Susan have absconded with her friendship.

The next chance she gets, a Saturday with Will having morning rounds at hospital, and Sofia willing to stay on with the boys, she calls Vernoy. "A visit would be fine," he tells her.

"Now?"

"Anytime."

She leaves the boys with Sofia and heads over to Vernoy's at the far opposite corner of Mimosa. She sets out in a jog, the January heat pressing on her neck and the back of her head, sweat gathering at her temples, and soon resorts to a walking pace. His is the smallest dwelling in the compound, near the tennis courts. As she reaches the fenced-in courts, she's thrown into that moment months before when she staked her small childish claim to independence and got caught out in a downpour. How she escaped censure from Will who'd brushed off her offense. She remembers stepping into his hug, at home then in those open arms, and feels a quick stab of hunger for that innocent time.

Vernoy stands behind his push lawn mower and watches her approach down the front walk. "Sorry to interrupt a man at work," she says.

"Not at all. You saved me."

"So you don't have a gardener to save you?"

"It's one of my exercise regimens. I tend to run to fat. Not that you need telling." He grins a little, parks the mower by the sidewalk, and steps toward the wide front porch.

Her easy giggle follows him inside.

He carries a pitcher of lemonade and two glasses to his patio table under the shade of a massive blooming tree. She asks the tree's name.

"A kind of acacia, actually. One of the hundreds of varieties. In fact, it's one of our namesake trees, mimosa. A winter flowering species."

"My. Such detail. So you're an arborist as well as a lawyer and an insurance guy."

"Jack of all trades, etcetera. Did you have a specific topic in mind, Madame Ramsey?"

A quick smile at his courtly manner, then she sobers. "Let's start with the name. From here on out, I won't be answering to Madame Ramsey."

"Is that so? How, then, will you prefer to be addressed, going forward?"

"Cass will do. Or Ms. Ramsey, for now. Do you know what this is about?"

"I might hazard a guess. Perhaps you should save us from my foolishness and enlighten me." His deep voice softens.

"I don't know if the rumor mill is onto this. But I'm feeling isolated and there's no one else that I'm inclined to . . ." She stiffens and flips back a sweat-drenched tuft of hair. Her tone takes on an odd belligerence. "If you don't care to be in-the-know, speak now or . . .'

"Speak away, Cassie."

"It's about Will and Susan. They've become . . . an item. Had you heard anything?"

'No. But I'm in a bit of bubble over here. You know, this house is, appropriately, an outlier, like me. More a cottage for a single person than a quasi-mansion for a family of four like yourselves."

She gazes at him, annoyed with his little digression, and with herself for baring her private humiliations. She wonders if he heard her confession. Or if he even gets what she's talking about, and she gives her sad tale an add-on surprising them both. "They're fucking, Vernoy."

"I know, Cass. I understand. The two of them, your friend and your life-mate. Makes it a double-betrayal. I get what you're saying."

"Do you?" she says with an edge of belligerence, likely coming from her awareness of how common her complaint sounds in the words liberated from the cell inside her head. I'm a living cliché, she thinks, flooded with a sense of her own foolishness. She comes abruptly to standing. "Well, that's quite enough drama from me for one afternoon. I'd better head back. The kids . . ."

"Cass." He propels her name to her. "You haven't finished your lemonade. Besides, I do get it. Trust me. I've been where you are."

She turns and sees a deepening of the lines around the eyes that take her in. He's very tall, perhaps taller than he wishes. "Oh, not the double-barreled kind you're facing. My wife . . . Well, it's a different thing since we're on different continents, you see. Still, it hurts."

She sits again, sips her lemonade. "You're still married, then? To her."

"Yes, well, sheer laziness, if you want to know. And all that history. I do love her, still, I suppose. God knows why."

"So it's possible for a couple to survive such a thing as this?"

"'Tis. I suppose it depends. Only you know where it leaves you two."

"I can't speak for . . . him. Or, her. For myself, it's like I've been evicted from my own home, and find myself in a strange country. It's very cold in here. Nevermind the ninety-degree temp."

"Nice metaphor. Seems particularly apt."

She nods. They sit in a silence that feels restful, comforting, like the paunch he has above his belt line, and she feels her other secret stirring. She sips her lemonade, and an image from her old SDS days surfaces She's holding a sign in the quad at the U.W. She skipped a class that day to join the anti-war protest. Her new friend holds an identical one: "Whose war Is It?" Behind them, a fellow protestor says, "I have access to one. Sometimes my dad forgets to lock that closet." Cass leans in to her companion. "Hear that? They're talking guns?" Cass turns around for a look at the speaker, a skinny, wild-haired guy, who nods to Cass and tips his own sign, "Hell No, We Won't Go." She remembers thinking he was too old to be called up anyway. She feels an affinity now for her younger sign-carrying self. Holding that sign hardly made her guilty of sedition, any more than throwing money at a plot to unseat Mobutu makes her an assassin. Does it?

She realizes how full the Xavier secret feels inside her, how keen she is to find a sounding board for the plan she's joined. So minor this role is, after all. Maybe she can find a way to pass her secret to Vernoy without arousing his censure. If anyone would hold her secret as a sacred trust, it would be Vernoy. He wouldn't betray her, would he?

"Daniel. Remember him?" she says suddenly.

He looks startled, amused. "Big fellow, outgoing? Ministry of Communication, you said."

"Right. We talked about him at Thanksgiving."

"Kinshasa Prison, God help him. Is he still there?"

"He's dead."

"Dead." Vernoy takes this word in with his hunched shoulders and his wide neck, to join the other dark images behind his eyes. He sits as if bracing for a pummeling to his belly. He leans forward in the soft arm chair and makes two fists, involuntarily, it seems to her. "I shouldn't be shocked. Anymore. I knew it was no good when you told me where he was. I heard another horror story. Quite recently. From a reliable source."

"Do tell."

"A man went missing for some days. Another soft dissident, shall we say? Word came through the proverbial grapevine he'd been dropped from a helicopter into the Zaire River. Near the rapids."

Revulsion swells inside her, forcing her arms outward in a What-now? gesture. "The President's work?"

"Fundamentally. Who else?"

"Yes, well, here we are."

"Indeed." He relaxes into the chair and turns a steady gaze on her. "And where is that, Ms. Ramsey?"

"We brought in our ace-in-the-hole. Tommy. Turns out he wasn't our man, after all." He can't miss the slice of reproof in her voice. She gives up a bitter sound, more bark than laugh. "No good. He couldn't interrupt what was already in motion for Daniel. No way he could navigate . . . that cesspool." She touches the cool lemonade glass to her face, which feels hot in the air-conditioned room.

Still, he gazes at her, with some new mirth. "You remember when you asked me about Paul Carlson maybe being a spy?"

"Of course. You told me, 'This line of inquiry is fraught with peril. Terra incognita.' How could I forget? And you said I'm nothing here. No-thing. Oh, and something involving a firing squad."

"You have a splendid memory, Ms. Ramsey."

The tipping point has arrived. The moment when she opens her mouth and confesses her part in the plan. Now, she thinks. The moment for telling is now.

And the point of telling is . . .? another voice rises: *Don't involve Vernoy. Keep him out of the loop, for his own good.*

"Ever heard of Dietrich Bonhoeffer?" Vernoy breaks in.

"Don't think so."

"German theologian. Very devout. His friend Eberhard Bethge remembers him once remarking that he was willing to kill Hitler. So, he ends up joining a plot to kill the Fuhrer."

"But that isn't how Hitler died, is it?"

"It's how Bonhoeffer died. Killed sometime in April of '45. Right before the liberation."

"I think I get your point."

"Two passionate men willing to embrace suffering by standing up for truth. Perhaps clearer in Bonhoeffer's case. Okay. And how do their stories end?"

She lifts her open palms toward him, in an I-give-in. In so doing, she releases the notion of telling him at all. She'd meant to learn what would happen if authorities were to discover her role. He's lived here much longer and knows the lay of the political land, when the authorities are bluffing and when they're prepared to act out their bluffs.

But if she tells him and he threatens to out her, she'll be forced to withdraw her support from Xavier, again. She doesn't believe Vernoy would turn on her. By his own lights, he's an outlier. He lives in a bubble. More to the point, he wouldn't stoop so low. Still, she doesn't want to put him in such a position. But if his own finely-tuned sense of justice were to force his hand, what then? She'd risk losing this way of surviving her stay, her ace-in-the-hole. She'd be back to that painful question, overheard in the *fula fula* weeks before, that has become her ground-of-being, her *raison d'etre*: What am I for?

"Not to worry. I do have good recall. Well, I'd better get back."

"Remember. It is possible to come through this kind of . . . breach. Divorce isn't the only possible outcome."

"I'll keep it in mind." She moves toward the exit and opens the door.

He follows her and calls as she steps down his walk. "Cass." She turns.

He stands in the doorway holding out a card. She takes it and stops to read.

"I had these made when I activated my phone, years ago. Same number. Keep this on you, Ms. Ramsey. Let it be your ace-in-the-hole." His gaze on her sluffs his usual hang-loose manner and hardens into a plea.

"You'll be my one phone call." She grins to soften the bite of sarcasm, adding, "Don't hold your breath."

"Never presume to know what's coming down the pike in this place. I don't. Nor should you. Keep it handy "

"Got it." She waves the card.

"Never presume," he says again.

She turns from the house and sends Vernoy a hard wave with the back of her hand. And she walks home at a leisurely pace, relieved that she's escaped her own impulses and left with her secret intact.

Twenty-one

Sofia waits for the house to be free of Madame and Dr. Will when she takes the paper Alicia gave her listing her telephone number. The boys play their log game in the bedroom they share now that Madame sleeps in the room they used for playing. She feels in Madame a sorrow she must avoid. Madame is her patron, not her sister. It is a tricky business to walk on this forbidden path to her heart. Madame says nothing about the change of her sleeping, and Sofia does not ask.

She stands before the telephone sitting on the desk of Dr. Will. She lifts the receiver and moves the dial by the numbers on her paper, then listens to the strange clicking sound of the phone calling for Alicia. It feels like a machine she holds to her ear, and as the clicks go on, she holds it apart from her ear. To her, this telephone seems for the mondeles who come to her own country like the drums that play in her village giving news for all to know.

At last, Alicia speaks into the phone from her house in the fine neighborhood. The Alicia who answers is small and full of breath, like a child from running.

"Sister, it is Sofia."

The voice waits.

"You must know this thing of Daniel. That fat Bwana Tommy learned of Daniel. He told me. Now I must tell you." She halts.

A hum starts on Alicia's side. The knowing begins even before the telling is complete. "When?"

In these days of waiting while you wonder, he is already gone. "Kufa," she says. They speak Lingala, the language of the street, for such news as they must share now.

There comes a sound from Alicia's side like water running through a drain. Sofia says nothing. She waits. At last, Alicia says, "I knew. That last time in Kinshasa Prison."

"Yes, you knew," Sofia says. She carries pictures in her head from that last time with Daniel alive. Alicia's cry, "He is dead, dead, my Daniel." Bwana Tommy belly-pushed Moon Face to the cell, Mama Kundi played her healing harp, and the tall man-figure lying inside the cell came to his knees and called the name of Alicia and not Sofia. He was never hers. And now he is no one's.

"Sister, you knew. And because of Bwana Tommy, all the family knows." Even as she hears the word family, Sofia asks herself what family can there be? With this word family another picture comes. Gabriel and his wild eyes meeting his dead son, the striking arm meeting her face, and the bellow from his belly sorrow, 'Woman you are dead to me, too.' There are the children of Alicia and Daniel. The father of Daniel and Gabriel is not long with the ancestors. There is yet the mother and there are uncles she does not know.

"I must tell his mama. Each day she asks me about Daniel and each day I tell her I know nothing more."

"Where do you find her?"

"She is with me since his tata died. Now I must tell her this thing and her keening will fill the house and drown out my own. I believe I will bury her, too, before the earth dries up again."

"Angh," Yes, Sofia says and they part from the telephone until the day comes to bury Daniel.

She returns the receiver to its place and turns. Matheo watches her with a frown.

"What is it?" she says.

"You look like the phone is hot," he tells and holds the receiver many centimeters from his ear to show how she does. "See?"

She brushes his yellow hair to show that he is a fine big brother. As always, she feels a sadness for this boy's serious ways. All the world who meet Corey laugh at his easy ways. But like her own Kamina, Madame's first-born takes the world on his shoulders. The world is heavy for a boy of five who imagines he is too-soon a man.

Sofia goes to the faucet where the large mortar is kept for the time death comes to the village. She carries it to her hut and places it just so, upside down beside her doorway, and in this way tells her village of Daniel. He is not of this village, but he came here those many fortnights without fail. He is not her own, but he is more hers than Gabriel ever was and she must honor him by this sign.

And Gabriel weighs on her memory. She wonders, in dread, if he will come to bury his brother. A part of her wonder hopes he is with the ancestors, too, and another part hopes he will come for Daniel, and be a different Gabriel, too.

Twenty-two

They eat at different times now, first Cass, then Will. To avoid questions from the boys, she feeds them first. She can't bring herself to tell them what's going on, that although they're still living in the same house, Mommy and Daddy are separated. This is just a prelude to the divorce that awaits them upon their return to the States late next year. She doesn't want to frighten and upend their sense of security. And her pain is too raw to trust herself to be fair to Will, because how can you be fair to a bastard? Still, somehow they know something's amiss, she suspects. Nothing overt, just a sense of imbalance in their reactions, an uptick in their bickering.

One evening Matheo refuses to eat his supper. She reminds him that he loves pigs-in-a-blanket, the biscuit-wrapped hot dog whose ingredients Cass took an entire morning searching for in Kinshasa's odd notion of a grocery store.

"Yes but not with him," he jabs his arm in the direction of Corey, who's "a stingy rotten warthog" again. And again, Corey's face folds into infinite despair.

"I want to eat pigs in the blanket with Daddy," he pronounces over the steady engine of Corey's weeping outrage.

"But Daddy's coming home too late," she says.

"Daddy's always coming late. Do you make him come late?'

"Of course not, silly. I'm not the boss of Daddy." True enough, though she has installed their eating hours in exchange for agreeing to continue preparing his supper. Still, she tries to sound amused and relaxed, to put her hyper-serious boy at ease.

"No, Daddy's the boss of Mommy," Corey says in full command of this basic three-year-old caveat.

Out of the mouth of babes, Cass thinks, a wave of sadness crossing her solar plexus. "Well, then, shall I give your supper to Corey?" she asks Matheo, breaking her own rule about never achieving their compliance with such a ploy.

"No," Matheo says, predictably, and snatches his biscuit setup and munches noisily.

When Will arrives home a while later, he retrieves his supper from the oven and a beer from the refrigerator and calls out, "Where are my boys?" and the two adoring boys already dressed in pajamas clamber to the table with their version of the day's trials and triumphs while he eats the chicken casserole she successfully refrained from lacing with arsenic.

Inside the room she's claimed as her refuge, Cass sits with stationary and pen crafting a letter to her friend in Seattle. Dear Suzette, she writes, at first shrinking from the resemblance to Susan, then taking a note from her earlier exchange with the boys, she thinks, Susan's not the boss of me, and continues:

Greetings from the other side of the world. A strange world, after all, my friend. You never know what a day will bring. A downpour that drowns a small boy in the village across the road from us. Our nanny's three-year-old. Yes, I did something I said I'd never do, hired a nanny and a houseboy. Imagine me succumbing to the colonialist practices.

I did something else I thought I'd never do: I moved out of the bedroom I shared with Will, into the guestroom. I learned recently that he's been fucking a woman in our circle, a supposed friend.

She rereads the nearly illegible words she's scrawled across the page, shaking her head at Suzette's probable reaction of outrage and pity. She doesn't want outrage and pity from her friend. She wants her old life back. She wants hope for happiness again. She wants singular devotion from her once and future love.

"Not happening," she says aloud and scrawls across the offending letter with black ink until her pen runs dry.

She leans her head against the wall and retrieves Vernoy's send-off from that visit: *It is possible to come through this kind of . . . breach.*

Alone on her single bed, she considers his words, in particular, his use of breach. How innocent it sounds, as if it holds the possibility of compromise or, at base, dispassionate turning point. 'This is nobody's fault, my dear. Let's be sensible. And all shall be well.'

"Dream on. Not happening," she says again. Does not apply in this case.

The following week Cass stops Will on the porch as he heads to the hospital. "FYI," she says.

He turns with his look of wariness.

"I'll be in P-1 this morning. I've decided to go see Ilinga and your other paraplegics. Thought you might need a heads-up," she says, hearing the edge of acrimony in her insinuation. He'd never stand for such a voice directed at him in their old life, especially her voice. But here they are. Get over it.

A wave of disgust crosses his face, still handsome but shadowed with fatigue.

The exchange weighs on Cass even after Sofia arrives and the children dress and breakfast, and the four of them walk together down the long wide street to the gate, where Matheo will board the school bus, Sofia and Corey will walk together back to the house, and Cass will step out to Mimosa Road and wait for the fula fula or the van to stop. And Cass will be the only non-Zairois to join the press of bodies inside the van.

This morning, she's in luck. A van, not a fula fula, bolts to a stop. She steps up and slides forcefully inside, having learned how she must enter. Show more conviction than she might feel as she becomes the fourth, abreast on the middle seat. Here in a public bus she leaves her desire to dismiss Sofia for the morning and take Corey's hand in her own, she leaves Will's pique at her acrimony and the words themselves, and she sinks into what she might say to Ilinga about the reviving the plan.

In the alcove where the overheard conversation upended her life, she pauses only briefly, eschewing a glance left, and presses into the 140-bed pavilion. As before, the moment she steps inside, Ilinga meets her gaze, as if he's kept a constant watch for her. "Bonjour Madame." His greeting is merely glad, and, despite her many days of absence, untouched by undercurrents of reproof.

She smiles broadly and places her hands over his, still inert. His gaze is warm, such that she considers telling him her marital travails. But no. It would unkind to speak ill of his doctor, even one who can do nothing for him. She glances around this end of Pavilion One where the paralyzed live. The pixie-like girl lies by the window, staring stunned into the morning air. An older man sits on his bed, a blanket covering him to the waist. Above the blanket, his upper chest has fleshy rises, like a woman's breasts.

Cass skims her gaze over beds neighboring Ilinga's for the boy of twenty-four who once hunted rabbits.

Watching her, Ilinga nods. "Le petit Loti."

"Where is he?"

"He is with us no more. He is . . . with the ancestors." Ilinga doesn't hide the tears he can't swipe away. "Quite soon after your last visit."

"Oh, no. I'm so sorry."

"I know," he says simply.

Le petit Loti, dead like her marriage. *Shouldn't have waited so long to come. So much sadness and injustice in this world. All I bring to the work of healing injustice is money, Will's money to boot. What am I for?*

His gaze takes on a wild sheen, not of anger but an intensity remembered from their last visit, and his confession as she was leaving. What if there were a way to harness his wildness. In enacting Xavier's plan, for instance. She knows nothing of what the plan entails except there are five young Zairois professionals short of cash plotting something in a hotel room. And there is rent to be paid each month. She can only guess at whatever else. She doubts Xavier would reveal details to her. But if she were to enlist Ilinga with his intimate knowledge of Mobutu, maybe then Xavier might look more kindly on her and her ideas to further the plan in some way.

Her breath catches, then balloons in her chest at this prospect. On impulse, she asks if he still remembers the gardens at Mobutu's home.

His gaze shifts right. He grins a little, drawn back into that time before his world upended. "Of course. I know them by heart, from those many days during my time of walking on two legs and traveling with the President. I remember every detail of the bougainvillea that grew thick near the front gate, and the plumeria tree just inside, the Venus fly trap and the ferns of many different greens, and even the rose that was not meant for this land. He learned of the rose in Britain and like all the citoyens, the rose lived under his thumb. Of all the plants he tended, he was proudest of his orchids. So many colors of orchid." Why, he wonders, why this question?

A long silence passes between them as the question turns in her mind. She knows little of the plan, but even with that paltry knowledge, she must take care what she passes on to him. At last, she tells him how she likes the way he looks when he remembers the garden. She asks if he believes Mobutu would still be tending his garden, or would he hire a gardener.

"Bien sur. Absolument." He speaks with a force untouched by doubt. He is a devil, yet still a man of habit, he continues. He has a gardener for the great acres of grass, but he tends the favorite, small garden for himself. Each morning before the sun rises, he comes out to his garden to walk slowly amid those plants I named for you, and others I did not name. You can bet your life on this habit, this early visit to his garden. He is more tender with plants of the Earth than with citoyens of his own country. For instance, Ilinga hesitates before going on, I did not see him place a hood over any of their heads and take a scythe to a plant not already dead. The monologue ceases. No trace of mirth on his face, but still a flicker of energy and intention. A remnant.

Their eyes meet. She speaks in slow, barely audible French, taking care to shield their words from the others. I wish to dedicate my time in your country to bringing social justice. Do you wish to join these efforts?

His "Madame" is fierce, followed by a bitter plaint, As I told you our last visit, it is already too late.

Perhaps it is too late, perhaps not. I must see a Zairois who knew Mobutu in Katanga. He has talked to me of a plan.

To you, not to me.

We shall see. I'll return sooner than the last time. I promise.

He shakes his head and repeats the words, this time as a kind of elegy for his former life, It is already too late.

Xavier regards her across their usual far back table of the café. A month has not yet passed since her last rent payment, yet she fears his look of eagerness means he hopes to squeeze new money out of the white woman from a rich country. Squash that rumor, she thinks with a twist of self-disgust at her colonialist entitlement.

"I don't come with money in hand," she says with a lilt of humor. "I come with an idea."

"An idea for . . ." Curiosity, a touch fretful, laces his frown.

"Your plan," she says voicelessly, mouthing the words.

"Madame, my associates and I appreciate your . . . payments. I am authorized to meet with you and receive your cash payments. More than that, I can tell you nothing."

"I assumed so. Yet, I have an idea you might find interesting. Depending on . . ."

"Nothing," he breaks in with rising anger. He pushes his chair back as if to leave.

"Wait. I know you might have doubts about me. Maybe your trust in me has limits. You can't deny that my money is good. The rent is paid, n'est-ce pas? My commitment is real. What more can I do to show you?"

He sinks back in his chair. A wave of weariness gives his face a tragic affect as he meets her gaze. "The work we are doing may bring the desired result. Or, it may bring disaster on our heads. The goons of this man would herd us into the stadium, plant hoods on our heads, and shoot us dead. We are prepared to face what comes. But your part, while necessary, is incognito. The bills you give us are good, yes, but anonymous. You must know if ever you were found to play a role, as an outsider, you could not be guilty of high treason. That charge is reserved for Zairois alone. It is likely you would escape. You would become, as they say, an Immigrant Interdit."

"Immigrant Interdit" She feels a flicker of familiarity with the word.

"Prohibited Immigrant."

"Sent home. I see. But what if I were to say I know someone who has been inside his private quarters? Someone who knows his personal habits known only to his family. Might this not be useful to your work?"

In his silence, he fixes on some distant point beyond her, beyond the café, beyond this moment. Then he straightens and says simply, "There is ever the question of trust."

"Of me? But what if I were not anonymous?" She feels the question belaying her to the edge of safety, and with the risk, some thrill she remembers from those old days at the University of Washington, holding up her sign of protest: "Whose War Is It?" Now, as then, she finds herself looking to join some new tribe. Back then, she joined them and the work against an unjust war. Back then, the correct answer was "Not my war," This present injustice isn't a war, not in the usual sense. Instead of asking "Whose War is it?", she should ask a question she remembers from her years in Sunday School, "Am I my brother's keeper" As a citizen of the world, the clear and fitting answer would be, "I am."

Neither speaks for a moment until he says, "Trust is the issue." But he says it softly, as if to himself alone, and she feels him giving the issue less heft, moving apace from certainty, weighing her anew. He meets her gaze with a kind of borrowed arrogance. "Who would this man be? How would you know such a one?"

She resists rising to the bait of his challenge. "I saw you at the hotel. You were five. Here's a question: Do any of you five know the habits of the man in question?" By unspoken agreement, they avoid saying the name in public.

"It is not possible to know the habits of a man hidden behind a high fence. A man surrounded by an army of guards. One guard is our companion in this matter, our accomplice. He has information that is helping us devise our plan."

She stares at him between sips of tea. "I can tell you about this person and how I know him. I promise you'll find it interesting. What have you got to lose?"

He waves a hand between them. She takes the gesture for assent and launches her delineation of Ilinga and his former dealings with the man in question. So doing, she observes his changing response in his face. When the telling is complete, she says, "So, what say you?"

He shrugs and gives a half smile. "Here is what I'm prepared to do. You come to the apartment you are funding, meet the small army of companions. You can be the intermediary for this unfortunate, and first bring to them the idea of using this man's knowledge for our own," he says. "Let them decide on the matter. Then we shall know our way forward."

"D'accord," she says. Agreed.

Evenings are long inside the Mimosa home, though it hardly feels like a home to Cass. These days it feels more like a one-room schoolhouse with invisible but carefully-observed boundaries. There are three seatings for supper, first the boys, then Cass, then Will. Once all have eaten, Will takes time with his boys to interview them about their day, and to take their questions about his. Cass stations herself behind the closed door of her bedroom and tries to block Will's time with the boys. But in her thirty years, she has always eavesdropped, on restaurant diners at tables across the room, on fellow passengers in a fula fula, and on her husband and her best friend, alas, in the heat of a stolen assignation. This habit of eavesdropping is hard for her to drop, like a junky seeking to resist an offered line-of-coke. And on the evening following her daytime meeting with Xavier, she hears Matheo say, "How come you don't like Mommy anymore?"

Will's short laugh bursts forth. "Don't be silly. Of course I still like Mommy. We're all still here, aren't we?"

He appears to take in this point for consideration. "Yeah, I don't know what, but I don't like it."

"Sorry bud. It's hard to be a grown-up."

This exchange moves on into what sounds to her like a wrestling match, with shuffling and squeals of joy, and ends with Will saying he loves "my boys."

Cass waits for Will to retreat to his study for hours of studying old volumes of *Journal of Bone and Joint Surgery,* and she runs a bath for the boys. Both of them love the nightly bathing ritual with a yellow rubber duck and a brown rubber Pooh Bear, and, for her, the forty-five minutes serves as a ritual cleansing of the previous painful conversation.

After they're dried off and dressed in cotton jammies, she reads a bedtime story, the start of *The House at Pooh Corner.* She reads the title and the part where Pooh and Piglet decide to build a house for Eeyore and they use a heap of sticks they find by the woods, then Eeyore comes round and says he had a house by the woods when he left but when he came back it wasn't there. "Very natural," he said, "and it was only Eeyore's house." Like my own old life, gone without a trace, Cass thinks, tears gathering, and she wipes her eyes before regaining her poise and continuing for twenty minutes or so. She closes the book to protests and promises of more tomorrow night, and exits to her own room.

Hours are, indeed, long inside the Mimosa home that feels, as evening wears on, like an upscale prison, but a prison nonetheless. A little before 8:00, and already darkness is full. She hasn't had her run today, and she shuts her eyes and follows her imagined form down the wide paved perimeter of Mimosa, past the likely dozing sentinel, and around to the far opposite corner near the tennis courts, where the downpour pummeled her for a time, the infamous downpour that took Sofia's boy. She could absolutely head out right now, were it not for a dull ache of tiredness in both legs. Wouldn't you know. Now that she and Will are unofficially separated and she can jog in the dark with impunity, she has no will to do so. No Will and no will, she thinks with a spasm of bitter mirth.

Instead, she removes from a top dresser drawer a smallish leather waist pack, containing her travel documents: passport, Zaire visa, shot record with the myriad of injections against the strange maladies awaiting them in this heart-of-darkness: hepatitis A and B, typhoid, cholera, yellow fever. These on top of the usual smallpox, polio, measles, etcetera. No vaccine against betrayal by husband or friend. Nope. For these afflictions, you're on your own.

She sits cross-legged on the bed and holds the passport on her knees when the door pushes open and Matheo enters and sits on the end of the bed. He watches her for a moment. leading with the wariness so familiar in him, worrisome and also dear. How has he come to this state so young? "What is that, Mommy?"

"You know what this is. It's my passport."

"I know it is. But why are you looking at it? You're going on an airplane, aren't you?"

She shakes her head at his light accusatory touch and his resemblance to Pooh's Eeyore. He's not slow, her Mattie, but earnest and worried. "No, sweetie, not without my boys."

"Not even without me."

"No, silly goose. Not for a long time. Come here." She draws him into a hard squeeze, musses his hair, and tells him "Now off to bed with you," before he can think to ask if she still likes Daddy. Her own Eyeore would know if she were lying.

Alone again in the room between the boys' whispers down the hall and Will's shuffling of papers next door, she holds the document proving where she ultimately belongs. She contemplates the passport's smooth green cover, stamped with a gold seal and the words United States of America, and a spike of fealty for her home country rises. She is one of its own. In case of calamity, this is her passport to home and safety. Whatever happens here, no matter what retribution Mobutu and his ilk care to threaten, her own USA would never permit it.

She removes her day garb of culotte and blouse, one Will bought for her before moving here. She hangs them in the narrow closet she's recently claimed, and pulls on the light flannel pj's she wears for comfort even in the tropics, and mentally reviews the two renditions of her fate as she waits for sleep. There's Vernoy's assessment of the peril awaiting any defiance of the president: *You're nothing here . . . would as soon herd us blindfolded into the stadium to face a firing squad as take a piss.* And there's Xavier's: *likely you would escape . . . become a Prohibited Immigrant.*

Whose prediction can she trust? She likes Vernoy. She admires him. But Xavier speaks from a whole life lived here. Besides, she has been to parties with diplomats from the American Embassy. She must believe that, in a worst case scenario, the Embassy would speak up for her.

She's walking up a ramp. It's the stadium, and it's steep and there are deep shadows inside. Will walks ahead, Susan beside him. They laugh together at something. A scythe appears on the ramp. It gleams in the dark. She trips on the blade and lands flat beside it. There's no cut, no bleeding, she's not hurt, it can't hurt her. She stands and lifts her foot to show Will and Susan. See? They turn and shake their heads. Matheo walks toward her, frowning. 'You're going on an airplane, aren't you.'

'No,' she says, 'no.' She wakes. The house is dark and still, her pulse racing. She's the only one awake. She whispers into the dark house, '*No, not without my boys.*'

Cass gives up on taking a turn with the Mazda for her trips to town and, instead, takes public transport. To herself, she thinks of this switch as going native, since she never meets another non-Zairois passenger. Supposedly, Vernoy takes one now and again, but she's never seen him aboard. Truly, though, it's more about avoiding face-offs with Will, dodging any shot he might attempt at interviewing her about her activities, and resisting her own tendency to backslide and beg him to forget Susan and return to her arms. As the weeks bear her away from the living nightmare of discovery, she feels less and less vulnerable to relapse. More and more, she knows they're finished.

Each time she goes to town, Cass walks out the front gate and a quarter mile down Mimosa Road to wait for her transport to downtown Kinshasa, either a fula fula or, if she's in luck, a minivan. She has never divined a pattern and must take what comes. The bus stop is a wide place where a dirt path veers off and then traces the two-lane as a kind of frontage road. A small stand of tropical fruits has appeared since her first time here weeks ago now. The plump Zairoise proprietor's response to Cass' "Bonjour, Madame" grows less hostile each time they meet, now that Cass purchases mangos and avocadoes on her return.

After a few minutes, Cass watches the approach of an ancient blue bus lined with yellow trim and a white roof. *Bad luck today,* she thinks as the fula fula lurches to a stop. Someone claimed they're called fula fulas after the English word full, explaining that Lingala gleans words from the various tongues visitors bring to Zaire. She's thinking how the name does fit, as she enters the contraption, hands her bill to the driver, and squeezes between standing passengers. She finds a free spot and firmly pinches herself between two standing passengers, where she leans her butt and holds on to a bar. Experience assures that this position is as close as she'll find to safe travel on these beater-busses, always jammed with life.

A few weeks after their arrival, Will came to work to a ward full of refugees from a fula fula rollover. There wasn't enough room inside the hospital, and some lay on the concrete patio outside the orthopaedic ward, all requiring surgery. He worked for the next three days operating forty people. Lots of broken bones. Some had died before reaching the O.R. Many more than forty remained uninjured, kissed by the miracle of escape. Back then, she lived through those events with his telling, amazed, relieved, proud of what he could do. Back then, she took on his life as her own.

No more. That was so . . . yesterday. Looking hard at those dramatic moments, she can see herself with clarity and revulsion, basking in the glory of his accomplishments. My husband, the brilliant surgeon. She was a parasite, was she not? Her own stint teaching yo-yoed in memory between sweet and sallow.

Bully for him, she thinks with a flint of aggravation. After that catastrophe of the route, Will exacted a promise from her never to ride one of those contraptions, rather like his fiat to avoid night jogging. But the jewel that was once her marriage, the one she held in check from harm with those lapses in her promise, that jewel has fallen into a deep ravine of sadness and betrayal. And here she is, giving herself over to the lurch of fate, as often as she damn pleases, thank you very much. What's he going to do? Divorce her?

The bus swerves to avoid some obstacle and nearly sends her to the lap of a seated man who casts her a startled look. "Sorry," she says righting herself and holding fast to the safety bar. She shuts her eyes to squeeze out the surge of loss that mingles, nonetheless, with her anger. She gives herself up to the certain distraction of the smells surrounding her: sweat, smoke, the acrid spew of gasoline, a hint of banana turning, and the unbroken sheath of human clamor.

The fula fula heaves and pitches along the uneven streets, careening every few minutes to a stop where a stream of life exits and another enters. After several stops, a young man behind her tells someone, in French, that he so fears being late. If he loses this job, he is a true dead man. The money is not great, but he can buy his rice, his manioc, his saka saka, and his children's school tuition and even sometimes a beer, and he doesn't mind the work, watching and parking cars of the rich at the Hotel Intercontinental is better than his last job, burying the dead.

At last, the lurching ceases and the door squawks open, and Cass presses herself to the front and the exit, stepping down to pavement with the hitch of relief she always feels.

She enters the well-worn lobby of the apartment building where the young Zairois professionals meet. She knows nothing of the other players, but, at last, she's convinced Xavier to let her bring to his team the idea that Ilinga's intimate knowledge of the president's habits might be useful to their ends. His body is useless, but his mind is strong. He can tell his remembered blueprint of Mobutu's early morning habit. This meeting will be her chance to convince the other players to see this blueprint. She knows how small this offering is. And yet she places great store in it. More than it deserves, but she doesn't care. She feels on the verge of a new phase of her role and this hope lightens her steps, and she smiles at the Zairois clustered before the elevator. She pictures Xavier facing the others, priming them for her presentation. She pictures them resisting, then letting their resistance wane as he talks. She knows Xavier to be a man of sense and honor in her dealings with him. Of course, this impression may change as her understanding increases. And, more pertinent to this effort, h e has a mazing p owers o f persuasion. Besides, she believes he gets the injustice of taking her money for a room she's never allowed to see.

She crosses the lobby carpet, an unfortunate mat of medium-brown flecked with olive. She notes the photo of Mobutu Sese Seko in leopard-skin chapeau and heavy-rimmed glasses hanging behind the reception desk, as in every other public place. She mounts stairs worn in places to the pad underneath, exits to the appointed floor, and stops at the door Xavier described. She takes a moment to collect herself, wiping sweat from her forehead and neck. But her pulse keeps its own rhythm, thrumming and throbbing at a pace she can't affect. *Get a grip, or you'll never get what you want,* she tells herself. And what is that? What does she want? She wants to move the needle on her role in this project, just a hair. Is that too much to ask? She wants to do something real, something more germane to justice than holding up a sign. She's come to this strange place on the other side of the world to finally have a shot at becoming the person her father named Cassandra, which means prophet. She knocks.

Twenty-three

The man comes to Sofia's house at first light of a new day. There's no knock possible on the cloth doorway, and he steps across the bricks onto the clean dirt floor of the great room in the small hut. The smallest person in the house wakes first to lay eyes on the one who is a stranger, but, in some remembered way, a father, too. The girl sits up on the mat she shares with her sleeping sister and rubs her eyes. Each morning, Fimi's way is to bounce from bed and begin loud songs and laughter to wake her mama. She wakes hungry for food and talk of her dream. But this day she sits and regards the man in the great room with interest and without fear. If she knows him at all, and she is strong in thinking so, he is different from the one who said her mother was dead, like her brother. This one smells not like beer but the butterfly bush and he lifts a chair near the fire ring, sits. and smiles at her. He does not laugh or speak.

When Fimi says she must wake her mama to make the fire so Fimi can eat, she is the most hungry girl, the man touches his finger to his lips for quiet. He touches a finger to his chest and she knows he will build the fire.

"Iyo," she says, Yes. Now the remembered father comes stronger to her, for before the big rain and the sadness, he made the fine new roof. She likes so much to hear the tin roof play like a drum in the night. She bounces to her feet and finds the gourd that keeps their porridge dry, and lifts it before the man, who tells her, "Sima." After.

The man takes his match and some small dry wood by the kitchen keepings and sets the fire to burning that tells Mama, who wakes with a hard frown, first to see the fire already burning and next the one who builds it. She rises on her mat to stand taller than the one who squats blowing at the flames of her fire, in her hut, the one whose last words, Woman, you are dead to me, too, are in her still. She ties her pagne tight above the breasts that will never give suck to another child of his. What do you want? she says. She waits for him to speak, and he does not.

Fimi says in her small voice brushed with care, He made the fine tin roof, remember, Mama?

It takes more than a fine roof to return to this house.

Kamina rises, too, with a look of wonder and concern before she leaves the hut for the water chore.

At last, the man tells her he knows of Daniel. He was my brother.

He was better to me than any husband. He cared more for the two living girls than their drunken father.

He has no stink of beer, Mama.

Sofia comes to Fimi and takes her hand and together they carry the second bucket to fill at the tap and there find Kamina standing with hers. Is he coming back to us? Kamina says.

He said I was dead to him. You see I am not dead.

I know, Kamina looks at the ground where mud is starting from the morning fillings.

He smells like that tree, Mama. Fimi points to a butterfly bush with purple flowers not far from the water tap, and near the entrance to her village.

Daniel was his brother. So he comes.

Elombe was my brother. I don't have him anymore, Fimi says.

Don't say that, Kamina's scold rises over them and into the other huts.

We go back now. Kamina, you carry that bucket. Fimi and I will carry this one.

Will you talk mean to him, Mama? Fimi asks.

Sofia shakes all her body above her belly, causing the water to stir. The story she takes from this shaking tells Fimi she wishes the water would wash the day clean and bring a new one, from before when Daniel still walked with them, or even before Daniel, when her father made the fine roof and he sat having supper, and there was laughter from the grown-up mat in the great room.

The day can't be washed clean, but Fimi hopes the man will stay by the fire in the hut and speak her name, as before he would laugh and lift her high and let her ride his shoulders around the village and let everyone see how high she rode.

They cross from the tap to the village, still in the hour before work. But on the river fishermen paddle a pirogue and quicken a cheer into the quiet for an early catch. On the road, a pickup truck heats its engine to humming, readying the day's deliveries. In the hut Sofia and the girls re-enter the hut, a cooking fire crackles, the kettle sings, and the man is ready to feed his small daughters. Sofia can read the messages he means to take with these actions, that the daughters will plead with her to let him stay and she will not fight them. She can't yet know if this is true.

He lifts a spoonful of porridge from the pot into a bowl and holds it out to Fimi, who covers her hands over her mouth to keep her joy inside.

Soon, he fills the other bowls and all are seated in the great room. Why do you wear the clothes of the Army when you are not a soldier? Sofia says in the voice not mean and not inviting. She does wonder.

I have changed my job, he tells her, in a voice not mean, but careful. He looks down at his own front, camouflaged by the clothes of his new work. There were too many fortnights when I worked in that company and was not paid. I hear it said that company is known to grab land it does not own. The long days I toiled there, weakened me. For that I turned to drink.

She wants to beat on his chest, but she says, Angh, in her scoffing way.

It is so, I am no more a drinking man, Sofia.

She turns on him a look of astonishment, and a laugh not filled with anger. And she tells him, And you remember my name.

He jerks his head back to give her his Yes, and a small smile she has not seen since he made the fine roof. He tells her, Now I go on work parties with the Army, and sometimes they pay me ten zaires, sometimes nothing, but better than that other company that saves its money for the fat bwanas who drive Mercedes.

Sofia feels an ache of the pride she once knew for that man. She feels him wanting to sleep under the roof he made, but cannot know if the sleeping man will be the one who is no more a drunkard, this one who knows her name, or if it will be the one who beat her after the big rain. Surely he is not dead, that one. Where does he hide him?

She knows Gabriel is coming back to the daughters, who forgot him for a time. But Fimi is knowing him now, and wants him in her hut. Maybe, too, Kamina is ready to have him again. Sofia herself thinks if he comes, the money from the Army will come, too. And this will help the daughters. So, she tells Gabriel he can stay in the hut. He nods and says he will stay tonight. Her hope is that the one before her is the man she married unspoiled by drink.

Twenty-four

Cass sees her from afar on the downslope near the gate to Mimosa. A first sighting after the marital apocalypse and the meeting that marked the end of the Susan-and-Cass story. To stay and meet the school bus or to leave, Cass pauses on the question, as bits of old conversation bleed into current memory: '*Hey kiddo,*' their old greeting, '*Wondered if you could take the girls.*' Ah, yes, the errand tactic. Then: 'Cass?' And Cass' response: 'That doesn't explain why you're lying to me,' Remembering, she feels a rush of rectitude for calling out her lies. Then Susan trying to weasel out of her betrayal: '*I didn't mean for it to happen.*'

Susan stands beside the sentinel, casting a flirtatious smile at him, which he returns freely to the blonde woman from a rich a country, at her pretty best. But Susan would never leave her house in any less-than-perfect state. Of course, she's flirting with the man at the gate. It's how she gets by in the world.

Cass resumes her steps as the yellow school bus pulls up the parking strip to the gate, brakes, and swings wide the door. Children spill forth toward their waiting moms or nannies. Cass pauses on the opposite side of the wide street, and waves to Mattie. He flaps a wave back and rushes past Susan and into Cass for a swift hug before announcing that he's playing with Jessica. "Right away. We planned it." He and Susan's oldest are tight friends, from the first meeting. Since the breach, their play dates have been tricky, mostly orchestrated between nannies. Today he speaks with a hit of belligerence, as if he knows he's venturing onto forbidden territory, and he doesn't care. "We want pigs-in-a-blanket and Orange Fanta for lunch at my house." As he speaks, Jess has slipped over to Susan and taken up the matter there.

A smile takes Cass unawares. "Tell you what. You two run on ahead to our yard. See you there in a minute, okay?"

The two seize on her words as if she's handed each a shiny gold coin and bound off. Cass watches them clamber uphill, hand-in-hand. Jess is a tall earnest kid without guile, and also, she fears, not the natural athlete of her father. Quite like Mattie, she finds. Both have an abundant regard for the rule of things. Each could use a dollop of the younger sibling's playfulness. Cass is grateful they have each other, here, especially, although once they return home to the States, these two sweet kids might be fair game to more streetwise classmates. Anyhow, she won't have their bit of fun fall victim to adult indiscretion.

Susan turns toward Cass, who can't miss the hopeful lift of her bearing. "Oh, I'm so glad you've decided . . ." She leaves off the gist of her decision when she sees Cass' face.

Cass matches her pace to Susan's, and they keep a distance on the uphill walk. "Do tell. What have I decided?" It's good Mattie isn't listening in. You sound mean, Mommy, he would say, and Cass can't disagree. But she's loving the hit of power she feels.

Susan looks at the ground just ahead before turning on Cass a look of anguish. "Look, I know what we did was selfish, but we're through with all that. It was a blip, an impulse. We shouldn't have . . ." She pauses, again leaving off the end of her thought, which is apparently too painful to bear. Poor Susan.

Rather like her refusal to remove the band-aid and reveal the fungus on her big toe. She can't go there. It just wouldn't do.

"Ri-ight." There's mirth in the word, elongated for emphasis, and, she hopes, no meanness. "No need to abandon your impulse on my account. Thing is, Susan, I've discovered this amazing sense of freedom in my quasi-single state, I guess you could call it. I'm involved in a project, you see. Before all that impulse business, it was a balancing act with Will. Now I'm free to devote as much time as I want. So, no worries."

Susan turns away, her voice careful and curious. "What project?"

"You're interested in my project? That's sweet. Thing is, it's not for publication. Not yet."

"Look, I love Logan. Low libido and all. I do. I need to repair the hurt. Truth is, I don't feel . . . *that* for Will. Like I said, we went with . . . our impulses. It's over."

"Well, good luck with the repair job." Cass wonders if Susan has any idea how callous she sounds, how egoic. She squeezes her hands hard to keep herself in check, because if she lets out the rage she feels, she'll start a tsunami of rage that won't end well, and Susan will pity her. No, she'll keep her cool and Susan will be the foolish one, not her. "Thing is, we're doing okay as roommates, Will and I. What I'm trying to tell you is I'm on a different path now. It's working." She likes how her voice sounds, calm and measured, as it skims over the real truth lying beneath: She loves Will. She wants to kill him in his sleep. She can't bear the thought of Mattie and Corey without a father.

She adds with a gust of energy, "Let's make sure the kids keep having their play times. That needs to be our focus. We can agree on that, right?"

Susan throws her arms outward and, keeping her gaze straight ahead, tells her, "I miss you."

Cass almost laughs at how easy it would be to go back to their personal good-old-days. She need only say, 'I miss you, too.' And it's true she misses their old heart-to-hearts, their jaunts through the markets, all those *before*-times. But she can't go there. She cannot bring herself to go jaunting around with the woman in the Mama Yemo alcove breathing familiar whispers in Will's ear.

They step through the gate to Cass' front yard and catch the two five-year-olds crouched at the end of the sidewalk. The two moms stay their approach, in silence, watching the kids watch a bright green praying mantis alighted on the butterfly bush. The tall green insect hovers in apparent disregard of her watchers. Before coming to Zaire, Cass read up on the various creatures they might encounter here, snakes, crocodiles, insects. Her research leaned toward dangers the various beings posed, but she also learned about the benign praying mantis whose legs fold in a praying posture, thus, the name. Two details of her research called out to her. One traced mantis back to the Greeks, whose word for mantis was prophet. She remembers thinking, My *insect-double*. The other described their mating ritual, how the male mantis does a mating dance, and, afterwards during mating, the female bites off the male's head. She remembers her shock on first reading that detail. Now she feels a beat of triumph for the female.

"Can we keep it, please, Mommy?"

In another time, Cass and Susan would exchange knowing glances, in affectionate solidarity with the young naturalists. Plot a strategy for sharing the pet mantis between the two houses. Cass might relate the female's after-coitus trick. Now she says, "You can't keep an insect as a pet, Silly Goose."

Susan says, "I'm heading next door, Jess. Come find me when you're done here."

The two young naturalists appear not to hear, and hold their vigil over the bright green prophet.

Cass takes her time to mount the staircase as the two five-year-olds clamber past, Mattie bumping Cass' legs in pursuit of Jess. "Oops, careful, don't knock the cook over," Cass calls after them.

In the kitchen, Jess watches Cass make preparation for the pig-in-blanket feast. At last, frowning up at her, she says, "Can you make one for my mommy?"

"Your mommy likes them?"

"She's so sad. Pigs-in-blanket always make her laugh. Can you?"

Sure, feed my betrayer. Why ever not? Focus, Cass thinks. *This is for Mattie's friend, not for my ex-friend, the hussy.* "I can. For you, my Sweet. Because why ever not?"

Jess nods with a gravity that fathoms the weight of her plight. Because sometimes a kid knows what must be done.

Footsteps scuff behind the door to the apartment Xavier found, along with water running, soft shushing, and some complaint in Lingala-French she can't make out before the door opens. "Madame." A grave Xavier steps aside to let her enter. She's inside the room when the door clicks shut. Her old nemesis, claustrophobia, sweeps through her, then gives way to an odd remembrance, the night months before when caught out in a pounding rain she wondered if it was her moment of comeuppance for her foolish impulse. No, that was not her moment of payment-come-due. But this moment, this stepping into a roomful of would-be mutineers, assassins, really, this move inside a subterfuge whose end she can't fathom might truly be the moment common sense exacts its pound of her flesh. She stands immobile, only her breath moving the stillness in the threadbare room. *Get a grip*, she tells herself.

Xavier's nudge brings her back to the gathering. "Have a seat, please." She does so nearest the door, keeping it in sight as if she'll need an escape hatch, which she won't, of course. Don't be ridiculous. The other half dozen hardback folding chairs make a wide circle in the narrow room. She surveys the enclosure with some distress, seeing in that instant how absurd and naïve is the sense of nobility she's been nurturing for funding the sorry studio apartment. The room lives in shadow, allayed by a single bare bulb. A cheap motel on Aurora Avenue in Seattle comes to mind. The window directly across the room from her would stream natural light but for the shuttered beige blinds, the old-fashioned kind of her childhood bedroom. Beneath the window, a twin bed sports a striking gold and black African fabric, embroidered in gold thread and imprinted with images of fish swimming upstream. One of those pictures fashioned from the wings of butterflies hangs on a slim wall between the blind window and an efficiency kitchen. These butterfly creations are elegant, but looking at them, she always has a twinge of sadness, maybe because she's heard that butterflies have only one day of life. This framed image shows a hyena, lean and low-slung, looking poised to strike its prey. She finds it an odd disconnect, the hyena's ferocity and the butterfly's fragility, its suppleness. If she were making one, she'd make it a bright green praying mantis. Maybe before she leaves Zaire, she'll find an artist to create such an image out of butterfly wings. She'll call it The Prophet.

The kitchen has a chipped white sink, a small fridge, an electric hot plate, a cupboard, and a rectangular counter top. The faint smell of grease, onion and something acid lingers. A makeshift table is set up in the center, a cheap plywood door laid flat between two sawhorses. Several legal tablets and manila folders labeled Top Secret spread across the surface, presumably a workspace. On the wall to her left, a door left ajar reveals a tiny bathroom. On the same wall, there's a neighboring door, shut, a door to something she can't know. The not-knowing seems important suddenly, and the lapse weighs on her. She's in on this, for Pete's sake. Not as deep as the men in this room, five strangers capable of who-knows-what. But she's here, after all. Doesn't she deserve to know what's hidden inside?

Maybe it's her desire to declare herself as here among them, as if a declaration were needed, that moves her to stand now and state the obvious. "Bonjour, tout le monde. I am Madame Cassandra. I've come to tell you about an idea I have." She smiles and nods at each of the five men and receives from each that brooding, indifferent stare she knows from shopkeepers in the city markets. She always finds that stare unnerving as if they're doing her a favor for selling her some small thing, and has an urge to lash out at their quiet insolence, which of course, she won't do. For no particular reason, she calls up that scene nested in her forever-memory bank, herself holding her little sign in the quad at the UW, and the woman alongside nodding approval. She dates her conversion experience to that small exchange with her new almost-friend, that moment of solidarity inside the clutch of student protesters. It was the moment she knew she was most herself when she stood up for justice.

This is a different moment, she thinks, a different clutch. This clutch doesn't give a hoot when she's most or least herself. To this lot, she's simply that White Memsahib from a Rich Country. This is not her home. These are not her people.

She looks over at Xavier. He gives a quick nod, stands and breaks in to speak in a mellow voice that wants not to be heard beyond this room. He tells the others straightaway that having Cass come was his idea. He invited her. Got it? Next he'll first introduce the others to Cass, so she'll get to know them a bit. Got it? he says again, and in this way continues in French slow enough for her to catch, so she'll understand the makeup of the cadre they're calling their *jeshi dogo,* Swahili for a small army. For her benefit, he moves into English, which is quite good, as she's observed before. Of course, he's also a master of the other languages represented, Lingala, and Swahili. He begins with himself. "Going forward, I am Duma. Means cheetah in Swahili."

"So you're Duma, not Xavier?"

He nods and makes a clicking sound with his mouth, for emphasis. "Code name Duma. You must understand the necessity of code names. From here forward. As protection from the enemy, yes. But also for your protection."

"For my protection?"

"If the effort goes badly. Not that I suggest it will. But if it does, you must not know the real names of the *jeshi dogo.* If you were interrogated, if you were tortured, you would not be knowing the real names of those involved. As I said, for your good."

Thanks for the cheery thoughts, she thinks, and says with a flicker of uncertainty, "Surely that's unlikely." And Vernoy's voice pipes in. *Never presume to know what's coming down the pike in this place. I don't. Nor should you.*

"Oui, Madame. But you must know anything is possible. Can you not know this?"

"Oui, Monsieur. Point taken. And do I not need a code name?"

"Here you are a White woman in a sea of Zairoise. There would be no point." He pauses, "Or, we could name you Mondele Mama."

"Mondele Mama." A laugh bursts from her. "Yes. White mother, isn't it? I like it." She loves the name itself. But it's more than the name. She can't account for the fullness of her pleasure in his bestowal of the name on her, the outsider. But she'll take it, and rest more easily now.

"D'accord. Now you must agree to bury the first name you knew for me. And I must tell you my charge in this work is to fund the *jeshi dogo.* I am charged with, how do you say, fund raising."

"Fund raising?" Such a proper Western-sounding job, as if they represented a charitable non-profit in the U.S. Sierra Club, say, or Save the Children, instead of Kill the Dictator. She can't help but smile at the disconnect, and her own arrogant assumption that she's the sole support of this endeavor. Cass and her big 50 bucks a month. As one of many, her role loses yet more heft, and, maybe, lessens the chances she'll need Vernoy's phone number.

"Indeed. Are you surprised? You believed you were the only one, perhaps?"

She shrugs. "Guilty as charged."

"There are many expenses," he says, and, thankfully, moves on to introductions. He starts on her left with a slender, round-faced boy, who looks twelve, but surely must be at least sixteen. He must be the night bodyguard Duma mentions. "Code name: Hyene."

Hyena. Like the butterfly image on the wall. She's tempted to ask if he's related to the butterfly hyena. But the boy looks angry, immune not only to teasing, but to any shred of humor, and she resists. He's a pitiful hyena, this one, with good cause for his anger. He gets no salary, only a pittance. These who serve the mighty one, who risk their lives to protect him are beggars. Worse than beggars, they are slaves. Now that she's heard his story, his attempt to look fierce comes off as a look of startled injury, although it's clear he'd rather she not be here.

"Next we have a doctor of anesthesia. Code name: Taba."

Taba! Cass stiffens to hear the name from her recent past. The word needs no translation. Taba is the goat in the trunk of the Mazda, Army guys in camouflage approaching the mud-stuck Mazda, long rifles riding their shoulders, Corey jumping into the stubby soldier and saying he'll kick his butt, the soldier leveling the barrel of his rifle at Corey's chubby belly, Taba bleating and saving the day, her vow henceforth to forsake all thoughts of joining any fight for justice in this place.

Yet, here she is. She misses the rundown on Taba and catches only the ending comment. "He works at Mama Yemo."

"Oh, sorry, Xavier. Duma, I mean. Where in the hospital?"

"Operating theater. With the surgeons. He has knowledge of certain drugs and ways to obtain. This will prove useful to us."

Cass steals herself to stay the streak of pain in her breasts. Xaiver/Duma knows her connection to a surgeon at Mama Yemo. Surely, she's mentioned it, though he shows no sign of this awareness. If she and Will were still speaking, she'd ask him about the anesthesiologist who falls asleep under the table while he's operating. Does he have a lean face with nose slightly off-center, from a sports' injury, perhaps, or a fist fight. Taba's gaze on her holds steady as Duma recounts his story. Taba can't have a clue about her ties to any surgeon. Why would he?

Of course, if she and Will were speaking, she might not be in this room at all. The Cass whose heart beats for justice and equality would be buried deep under the part that wants to preserve the jewel of her marriage. She shivers involuntarily at the thought of Will learning of this studio apartment and her part in this mission, however small. *You're not the only one with secrets, Big Boy. I have my own.*

Duma moves next to a man in camouflage uniform, apart from his green baseball cap. He's directly across from her, a soldier in the Zairois military. Code name: Nyoka. It means snake in our tongue. He knows jujitsu and is a bit of a shapeshifter.

"A shapeshifter? No kidding."

"Not literally. But he is agile and wily. A useful skill in the present effort."

Nyoka. She looks hard at the face beneath the cap worn backward, like any American teenager trying to be cool, except he's at least a decade older than teens. Something about him strikes her as familiar. They've met, somewhere, haven't they? But for the baseball cap, there's his Army garb, and the only Army guy she's actually met are the four who extorted the Thanksgiving taba out of her on that infamous day. The Nyoka before her looks nothing like those thugs. If not for the camouflage uniform, she'd never take him for a soldier, and perhaps that's the point. He lifts his chin in spare acknowledgment of her presence, and swipes a forefinger to the side of his nose. The gesture jolts a memory into focus. *Gabriel, Sofia's husband.* They met once at Sofia's hut in the village, not long after she arrived in Kinshasa. Since then, she's heard Sofia's horror stories of him after their son drowned. She holds his gaze now, looking for a sign that he remembers her. *Shall I say that other name, Gabriel?* But there's no inkling of recognition. And Gabriel wasn't a soldier. He was a drunk who beat his wife. If this one is Sofia's husband, he's a snake and Nyoka is the perfect code name.

But it cannot be the same man. He isn't Sofia's Gabriel. There are people who resemble others the world over. It must be the same here.

His gaze on her is sullen, as if he can read her thoughts and has no use for them. He withdraws the gaze and turns back to Duma, who gestures to the fifth player, a large man a bit older than the others. Receding hairline and aviator sunglasses grayed out to reveal eyes watching her, unnerving her. He has muscular heft but not fat. She might take him for a rancher. Or bouncer. Departing from Duma's playbook, he introduces himself, and soon she sees why. "Simba here, Madame. Good to meet our benefactor." He holds her gaze. No venom here, unless he's hiding it.

The American ease of his English startles her. "Good to meet you, too. Simba? Means lion, doesn't it?"

"Does indeed. Simba is lion, in Swahili."

"And where, Simba, did you learn your English?"

"In school here, as a boy. I was always keen to know the language of the invaders." He gives a disarming grin. "On the radio. From movies. Mostly, in Winnemucca."

"In Nevada?"

"Of course. There's only one. Well done, Madame. Not every American knows Winnemucca. Though I believe many would know Butch Cassidy."

"And the Sundance Kid. Of course. A lot of Americans saw the movie."

"And did you know his gang robbed the 1st National Bank of Winnemucca. Made off with $32,000. A lot of money in 1900. Never was recovered. These days the town is quite proud of that history."

"I didn't remember that. So, does it give you hope that the money wasn't found?" She feels daring to pose the question with its implied reference to Duma's plan.

He appears not to notice and gives a quick grin. "You could say. And I also became quite proficient in profanity in Vietnam."

"Vietnam! You did a tour with our military?"

"365 days. Posted near Da Nang. Not in Da Nang. Just outside. Too many gooks there. 1st Marine division, 3rd battalion, 5th Marines."

The revelations keep coming. Will served with the 1st Marine division, 2nd battalion, 5th Marines. The 3rd battalion was his buddy Roger's division. Six degrees of separation. She's tempted to ask if he ever met a rakish battalion surgeon with a flair for music, but she does not. "Good you survived that episode in American folly."

"Blind luck," he tells her shrugging, and withholds his views on that divisive war.

"You believe in luck?" she asks.

Simba's hand cups the pendant he wears around his neck and holds it out for her viewing. "My mother. The night before I emigrated to the States for university, she gave me this amulet. A pendant of a lion head. Here in my home country, you see, lion means strength and protection." He drops the pendant to its chain and pats the lion face. "My good luck and my protection. As you Americans like to say, so far so good. Actually, I fear taking it off." Here, he sends up a deep contagious laugh. She can't tell if he accepts the superstition or if he's speaking ironically and merely pulling her chain. Not missing a trick, he says, "Are you wondering if I believe luck will be with our *jeshi dogo*? We shall see." He laughs again, in his disarming way.

"You read my mind." She abandons the irony theory and consigns him to the world that believes in the power of amulets, or maybe, like many educated Zairois, she's learned, he believes both and holds them in a tension of opposites, like a good disciple of Carl Gustav Jung.

Xavier-cum-Duma gestures to her. "Madame Cassandra comes with a proposal for us. She's here at my invitation. I'll let her speak."

She stands and moves her gaze over the men who have spoken, and feels the heightened energy, the subliminal hum inside, the familiar nudge to set something right in the world. This motley assortment of men from a world as different from her own as possible might, in fact, be her tribe. But so far as she can tell, only three out of five want her in their jeshi dogo. Two would like to boot her from the room, or from the country. Make her a Prohibited Immigrant. Or worse, in the case of Hyene, he'd have no qualms about sending her into the stadium with a hood over her head. Of course, how much power would he really wield? Do they even do that to women? He could care less. Nyoka might be worse, she can't tell. He's less transparent than the boy, Hyene. What is he hiding? At least, there's no sign he's been drinking.

She came to this apartment and this whole project hoping to bring justice to Daniel, and, perhaps lend a touch of meaning to Ilinga's life severed from his work. But she might be out of her element here, as Vernoy keeps telling her. She turns toward Duma. "This isn't going to work."

"What do you mean? What won't work?"

"I'm not blind, Duma. At least two of your players are hostile to my presence. There's no point in my pretending I've joined your tribe." She slows and lowers her voice for emphasis.

"I don't argue. Two are hostile, it's true. They are the least sophisticated among us. They believe they have the most to lose. They are, how do you say in English, the most xenophobic. They fear letting an outsider inside of our plan."

"I'm the outsider."

"Of course. Are you not? How could you be anything else? Look. You can pull your money, if you like."

"Yes, I could. Maybe I will."

"Let me talk to them." Duma holds up a hand in a Wait,-please-gesture and launches a rapid stream in Lingala, maybe with a touch of Swahili. She can't tell if his delivery is angry or merely intense. After several minutes, Hyene meets her gaze and turns his words on her. Lost, of course, with her rudimentary Lingala. Duma translates. *Why do you come here? Who are you to our jeshi dogo? Who are you anyway, a Mondele Mama from a rich country. What do you want with our kind?*

She stares at the boy face, made old by the toxic hatred highlighted there. At first glance, she associated its roundness with Corey. Now he reminds her of Bobby Crucell, the neighborhood bully on her street growing up. Once, on her way to her friend Holly's house, Bobby met her across a deep mud puddle. He grabbed her wrist and threatened to throw her in if she didn't cough up a dollar, which she didn't have. He shoved his face inches from hers. She could smell milk on his mouth gone sour. Finally, in disgust, he folded his arms across his belly and bumped her backwards, to the ground, but away from the puddle. A pinch of mercy. This Hyene looks like a cross between Bobby Crucell and a real hyena. Plus, he could pull out a gun and shoot her. As he said, she's nothing to them.

Mondele Mama, this is not about you, she reminds herself. *You can't hold your breath for an engraved invitation to change the world:*

Dear Cassandra Ramsey a.k.a. Mondele Mama:

You are cordially invited to a Congress with enlightened others, during which event the prevailing autocrat and his mignons will be relieved of their duties. The change will be bloodless, perhaps peaceful. Refreshments will be served. Each participant will receive a gold ring. A lovely time will be had by all.

Duma watches her ease the tightening in her face. She nods. "Good," he says. "Tell them. Tell them about the *paralyse* who might offer details they cannot know."

She sits again in the chair by the exit and leans forward, measuring her gaze over the motley cadre. They're either her personal hyenas who would boot her into the stadium for beheading, or they're her partners in the work of setting things right, and finding justice for Daniel. She has at least two allies here, Duma and Simba. They won't let the others attack her here. She can say her piece and see where they land. Feeling lighter and somewhat emboldened, she lays before them the story of Ilinga, a man like themselves, but more unfortunate. He has personal reasons to share their passion against the marshal. She lays out a rapid sketch of his history and condition, and concludes with a caveat. He may not have long to live. Who can know? But maybe he could die in peace knowing he helped his country in this cause. She pauses. "And what does this have to do with you and your playbook, you are wondering, am I right?" She nods to Duma, who translates, eliciting reluctant smiles from several of the men. She moves into the details of Ilinga's intimate knowledge of the enemy in the leopard skin cap. He knew he could count on Ilinga to write favorably about him, in his role as a journalist. He came to invite him into his compound, each morning. After Ilinga's accident on the road, Ilinga's job as journalist ended, along with the president's trust, the contact, the so-called-friendship. But Ilinga has reason to believe his habits remain. Cass repeats what Ilinga told her, that the president is more tender with plants of the Earth than with citoyens of his own country. She lowers her voice to add, "For instance, he did not see him place a hood over any of their green plant heads and take a scythe to a plant not already dead. He consigns their care to no one but himself." She stresses how strict he is with his habits, how he visits his garden each morning before the world presses in on him. "You can bet your life on this habit, this early visit to his garden," she tells them, as Ilinga told her.

The room is still when she ceases her telling, after a few murmurs of recognition and dismay. The sullen indifference on the faces of all but Hyene is supplanted by puzzlement, perhaps curiosity, and something other she can't discern. Hyene still breathes distrust and leeriness. Duma zeroes in on him to complete his telling. He informs him of his plan to meet with Ilinga and have him draw up a map showing where he will be and when. "*Mondele* Mama here will come, too, to introduce him to the *paralyse*. She will be the scribe. You," he says to Hyene, "you will be first to see this map. I am counting on you."

If Hyene is surprised, his face masks it. But for the first time during the meeting, the anger masquerading as a sullen affect with a side dish of injury vanishes. He gives her a brisk nod. She'll take that. She meets his gaze with a smile and goes to the table, takes up the folder labeled Top Secret, and begins to read, "Transition to Freedom for Zaire."

Nyoka removes his baseball cap and sweeps it into a semi-circle to emphasize the heft of words she can't make out, only that she should not be allowed to read it.

Duma squints at her, considering, before nodding.

The document is entitled "Appel a la Liberte Pour Le Zaire," Call to Freedom for Zaire. She reads, silently translating from the French: "A clarion call is being issued to all Zairois citizens to release their country from bondage. As concerned citizens who value truth, we come together to stake our lives and our resources on this high calling."

Duma moves in beside her and swiftly transfers the document from her hand to his own. "For today, Madame, it is sufficient. We have accepted your request. To see the studio you support. To meet the players. We agree that our means must remain anonymous to the Mondele Mama. For our protection. And yours."

"Fair enough," she says. "Call me when you're free to go to the hospital. I'll await your phone call. Mondele Mama at your service." She says this last phrase with an easy lilt to show she understands his caution. After all, her risk pales next to theirs.

Duma gives a nod and with a fervent expression, an are-we-pushing-ahead-then touch, says, "You may have questions we cannot answer. Here's what I will tell you. Our intent is we must deliver a soft changeover. The matter will be dispensed in a swift and bloodless manner." He nods to Simba for confirmation.

"If all comes off as planned, it will be a cakewalk," Simba says.

Quite, she thinks, just like my imagined Congress. All but the gold ring. She makes a quick inventory of her reaction to his cake walk and the promise of a soft changeover. And from the fear riding just below the surface, she sends a silent phrase from Vernoy's prayer into the ether, *Make us instruments of your justice.*

Another thought enters her prayer stream: Whoever listens to these prayers surely won't step in to support a coup. Not even a soft one. Not likely.

Twenty-five

There is a night when Sofia wakes on her mat and the one she married lies with her. Sofia gasps to feel the wonder of his strong flesh against her back. She waits to learn of this touch, and when she knows no anger in it, she turns on the mat to face him in the small hut. Fimi and Kamina sleep in their alcove. They sleep, and it is good, for this is a moment not for children. This is a moment when she opens her legs and he rises over her, and he enters the dark place inside her, too long empty.

Afterward, he slumps back to the mat. She waits for him to speak. But it is Fimi who speaks from her mat in the alcove. Tata is here? she says with a high wonder and she begins her dance of joy.

It is Gabriel who answers. Angh. Tata is here, little one. He laughs. And Sofia lets out the laugh she holds from their lovemaking. Kamina lifts from her mat and joins them, with a frown and a puzzle.

Tata is here. See? Fimi says.

You woke me. School is tomorrow, Kamina says.

But Tata is here. He is better than school.

This news brings long laughter, from all but Kamina. She is too sleepy to laugh. And the night is gentle on them as they lie down to rest.

In the early hours of a new day, Sofia enters the gate of Madame Cassandra's house. Doctor Will must be so soon at hospital, as the car is not in its place. Or, he sleeps in another house now. The matter brings a smile to her lips, as she recalls the change in her own hut, and all that she lived on the mat last night.

She enters to the kitchen, where Madame has her coffee and a look of fever Sofia does not know in her. Madame tells her to make herself tea. Sofia does so with a light step she tries to mask from Madame.

But Madame sees. You look well, she tells Sofia.

Angh, Oui, Madame.

Has something happened that makes you happy? she asks.

Sofia holds on to her words while she drinks her tea and places a piece of bread in the machine that turns it into toast. At last, she tells Madame, The man I married. The one called Gabriel. He comes back to us.

Really? Are you glad? You must be glad, she says.

Angh, she says. In this moment, yes. For the future, I shall wait and see.

Ah, sounds like wisdom, Madame says. And the alcohol?

No more. For the future, I shall wait and see. He takes a different job. He left that company that made those machines for farming. It was bad.

And now?

He is a soldier for the country.

There is a brightness of shock and fever on Madame's face. She opens her mouth, but no words come. At last, she says, So he wears an Army uniform now?

Most days it is the camouflage he wears. She laughs. Not always the Army beret. Sometimes he wears his baseball cap. It is a green cap. It is having a yellow circle with a fist holding up a flame. It is the flag of the President. Before now, with that other company, he felt an anger about the President. But he came to know he was nothing to that other company. It was a bad business. The Army gave him the uniform and the money comes more certain. And he is at peace to wear the cap with that image.

Sofia hears no word from Madame, but she finds a strange look on her face. First, fear is showing in her eyes, then quickly the fear is gone and anger comes. Sofia does not know why this anger, if it is against Sofia. She has done nothing to bring this anger to Madame. Now she herself has fear and asks if she should go see the children, if they are making haste for school.

Still, Madame says nothing but drinks down her coffee and lands her cup hard in the sink. The cup handle drops from the cup to the sink, and Madame breathes out like a wind and squeezes her hair in both hands, as if her hair will fall away as the cup handle fell. Go to them, yes, please, she says, and the please is a chip from her anger. Madame pushes out the kitchen door to the steps, and the door slams hard on the house of her children. And Sofia goes to them, to see if they are hearing the anger and fearing it, too.

Twenty-six

The call breaks into the silence of Will's sanctuary. He picks up and calls out from behind the closed door, "It's for you." His call bellows without her name, since he can't bring himself to use her name, these days. "For you."

Cass crosses the room, takes the receiver, and greets the one charged with fund raising for the *jeshi dogo*. It's true she feels a measure of liberation from marital strictures, as she told Susan. But this liberation is only partial. She still guards the truth of the conversation from Will as she thinks how to answer Xavier's greeting. "*Mondele* Mama. It is Duma calling. Are you free to speak of a meeting?"

"Yes, of course, Duma."

"It is time, I believe, to meet with the *paralyse*. We will see if he must alter our plans, by his telling."

"No problem. He has nowhere else to be."

"Okay. The rent comes due so soon after, you know this. Why not take care of this matter at the same meeting. It is possible?"

"Sure. The hospital, then." She catches a glimpse of Will's profile. He's studiously avoiding her direction, but she knows how to read him. He's listening, she's certain. She hesitates, knowing too well she's reached the tipping point with the project. Since Sofia disclosed, in all innocence, that Gabriel has joined the Army, she's known she must detach from any project that includes Gabriel, code name Nyoka. How can she trust a man who blamed his wife for her son's death and beat her? One who hides that they have met? Of course, he recognized her. People change, but with this brute, what are the chances? Nil to zero. She can't help wondering if he's a mole for Mobutu. Vernoy's voice is always with her: *Never presume to know what's coming down the pike in this place. Terra incognita.*

How to explain her issues with Nyoka on the phone with Will listening? She won't withdraw, not at this stage, She'll share her qualms about Nyoka, but face to face. "That could work," she says at last.

The phone line conveys the relief he feels as he details their place and time of meeting. And she holds, in the cache of secrecy inside, her concerns about Gabriel aka Nyoka. Anyway, soon, the soft coup will do its work, and her role will be complete. There will be other less trying ways to work for justice.

She returns the receiver to the cradle and strides from the room. "Cass," he calls to her in the doorway.

Startled to hear her name from the voice so long silent, her first thought: He's found her out. He's figured out what she's up to, and he's preparing to berate her for dragging her boys into danger, by association. Do what you want with your own sorry life, but leave my boys out of it. Then she meets his gaze. There's pain and maybe hope reflected there. She raises her arms with upward palms, belligerence lifting her demand. "Something you want to say?"

"Just . . . it's over. I know it was . . . selfish."

"You wanted something. You took it. Now you want absolution, is that it?"

"I want to let all that business with . . . her go. I want to
go back to how we were. Can't we just . . . ?" He throws up his
right hand in some gesture, *mia culpa,* perhaps.

"Forget it?" she says.

He swipes a dark brown lock from his high forehead and
looks down at his hands folded on his desk.

"Forget. And forgive, you mean. So easy to say. Not so easy
to find inside, you know? For me, you see, it was a double
whammy. My life partner and my best friend in Africa. I talked
to her last week. Did she tell you?"

He shakes his head.

"No? I don't know. Maybe I can get there." She gives up a
bitter laugh. "Maybe in my next life."

"Cass." Her name on his tongue has an edge, and she feels
him wanting to lash out. Instead, he says, "I'm slated to drive
tomorrow, but I can rearrange things if you want the car."

She's on the cusp of accepting, but there's that lift, that
whiff of strength, suddenly, from keeping him as suppliant.
"No thanks."

It's a **fula fula** today, not a van. Rats. But she can't wait
for the next van. She has learned the habits and rhythm of the
local transport. Never turn one down since who knew when it
would appear? Once, after declining a van, she waited more
than an hour for the fula fula. The door squeaks open. She
enters, drops in her coins, and pushes a few meters through
the aisle of the contraption that lives up to its name. Standing
room only. Since hearing the name derives from the English
for full, she's found a little green English/Lingala dictionary
that translates full as tondi. She inhales, funneling the
breath through her mouth, trying to block the ooze of
smells, and still she takes in the sweat and smoke, the
hint of leftover booze, and a strong whiff

of perfume from the woman beside her, wearing a tight orange Western-style blouse and a brown Zairois pagne.

She grips a vertical bar with one hand and with the other clasps the strap of her purse tight to her shoulder, imagining the windfall a thief would discover inside: one hundred zaires withdrawn from *Fear of Flying,* for next month's rent. He would also find a notebook of graph paper and pencils for noting his description of Mobutu's favorite haunt. Her plan is to meet Xavier, sit through the meeting with Ilinga, be the scribe for Ilinga's description, move to a more private location, hand over the rent, and, well and truly, withdraw from the program. She's done. And throughout the trip, Will's words join the lurching clamor into the town center: *'I want to go back . . . I want to forget . . . It's over-over-over.'* Words trail the contraption's progress like streamers in a sorry parade she wants no part in, yet here is her life, her own private contraption.

Xavier arrives ahead of her at the entrance to Pavilion One. He wheels his bicycle into the large room and leans it against the first wall he meets. She follows him inside and here is Ilinga, with a touch of chiding for her long absence. "Madame. Bonjour, bonjour. Ca fait longtemps." Long time, no see, softened by his quizzical smile.

"Pas si longtemps." Not such a long time. She takes his hand in both of hers. In the humid warmth, his hand is cool.

She turns to Xavier, who steps toward him with a stiff touch of his hand. "Xavier. Enchante."

"C'est-moi, Ilinga, Enchante." Xavier's apparent emotional distance glances off Ilinga and his gentle laugh.

"You know why we've come?" Xavier says.

"Madame tells me I can be of use. Is it so?" She hears the breath of hope his words hold, and their undertone of defeat.

It's Cass who answers. "We live in hope." She retrieves the graph paper and pencil from her handbag and lifts it up for his viewing. "Your scribe, Monsieur, at your service."

Xavier and Cass each bring a nearby chair to Ilinga's bedside. Cass catches a wariness in Xavier as he takes in the ruin that is Ilinga's body. He'd heard tell, but now he sees the fullness of the wreckage. Xavier leans in to Ilinga and urges, soto voco, "Careful of eavesdroppers."

Cass almost laughs at the notion of this sorry population of patients turning informant on their covert doings. They're surrounded by sleeping paralyze, except for the young beauty gazing wide-eyed at some wonder no one else can see. A single staff member leans over a patient far across the vast pavilion. Otherwise, the coast is clear. Ilinga flips his one semi-responsive hand in a dismissive gesture.

By luck, Cass found a sheet of carbon paper on her last trip to town. She's tucked it beneath the graph, on the off chance that the other version should get lost, and nods for Ilinga to begin.

His head assumes a princely pose as he considers his task. Where to begin? He shuts his eyes. He begins at a halting pace as he pictures, then describes Mobutu at first light when he takes his first cup of tea from the kitchen to the shed. His narration accelerates as he gains remembrance and stride. Yes, in the shed he keeps his garden shears, his gloves, and his watering gourd. He has no more the look of the president of a country, but a proper gardener setting into his work. These tools along with his tea he carries outside into the small close of his favorite plantings. He had a person build a structure at the end of the close, from wood and metal. It serves as his potting shed. Here he has a long bench, where in the small hours of a midweek day, you will ever find the president seated inside this humble dwelling finishing his cup of tea. Only you must station yourself to view him through the end closest to the president's house.

Cass is no artist. But she sketches what she hears and makes every effort to hew to the truth of his words. Xavier listens closely, glancing now and then at the speaker. In painstaking increments, his wariness gives way to his usual heedful attention. Each Wednesday at six o'clock? he asks sharply.

Ilinga gives a grave nod.

Cass turns her drawing for Ilinga's approval. "Like this?'

"Yes, like this," Ilinga gives his approving nod. Or, sometimes he offers a snapped corrective. "No, not like that."

And she erases her last entry and tries again.

Ilinga moves outside of the potting shed to describe groupings of plants. His favorites are orchids. He prizes these above all else. He has a sizable grove of orchids outside of the potting shed, at the end. He has many types of orchids, and all flourish by his hand. A particular hand. I remember he said he likes to mix the planting soil with cork bark and sometimes charcoal. There is a second bench outside the shed, on the perimeter of the orchid garden. After his forty-five minutes tidying and wielding his tools with his plantings, he sits on this bench just at the end of the hour. Here, Ilinga says, There is a something now of interest.

Some new tension in Ilinga's tone snags Xavier, and he gives a small gasp and narrows his gaze. Like a hunter tracking game, he has a sighting.

"Behind the orchid garden, a copse of tall bamboo exists. This could be of use for your project," Ilinga says.

A quiver of anxiety rises from Cass' solar plexus at his mention of "your project." She completes a last entry and gazes around their trio of would-be insurgents to see if they've gathered an audience. Ilinga's section of paralyzed patients appears unchanged. The pretty young woman by the far wall has closed her eyes. An aide enters the far section, leading what looks to be a family member bringing food to a patient, since the hospital provides none to patients.

As if sensing Cass' concern, Ilinga lowers his voice to near-inaudible volume and adds a startling detail: The potting shed ends just short of the copse of bamboo. Here, he says, is a point of severest interest. The section of fence nearest the bamboo copse has a gap. The bamboo trunk presses into the gap, but once in my walking life, I touched it. I know it can be moved. There is no guard in this section.

"An entry point," Xavier says, all wariness banished.

"That's it," Ilinga says with contentment and resumes the princely pose with which he began their meeting.

"Hyene," Xavier murmurs.

Hyena. The night bodyguard. Cass experiences an uptick in her pulse at this fortuitous boon to their plan. And she turns quickly to Xavier. "Yes! An entry."

"How long does he remain in his potting shed?" Xavier asks.

"Fifteen minutes."

"Precisely?"

"Yes. Precisely."

Xavier appears feverish with this newest exchange: the once fierce skeptic recast as a believer. He frames Ilinga's long-fingered hands with his own and says, "You give us a new day."

"Very brave," Cass says.

A single tear touches Ilinga's cheek bone. A light film of sweat crosses his brow. He shuts his eyes.

"Until the next time," Cass says as they gather themselves to leave.

She can't know if he hears them, for he says nothing as the two would-be subversives move lightly from his bedside to the world outside.

Cass follows Xavier onto the covered walkway, taking care to tuck the carbon copy away before he sees. Not that it would matter. He wouldn't mind. It's nothing but a child's drawing of a long-ago memory. Still, it's a back-up they might need, and she won't risk his displeasure. She won't put Ilinga through a repeat. It seems to have tired him. She's never seen him when he wouldn't acknowledge her leaving with at least *Au-revoir*.

Xavier stops and turns with a smile. Cass smiles, joining his minor triumph, and remembers to hand over the envelope with the new month's rent money. He tucks the envelope inside the man-purse he wears over his shoulder. She's glad to contribute to his encouragement and tries to think how best to tell him her concerns about Gabriel. Meet him at the Café, maybe, before heading back. Sure, let the smile go on a bit longer. Xavier's straddling the bike as she tells him, "Could you hang on a minute? I just want to go back inside and check quickly on Ilinga. He seems so tired. Be right back."

She re-enters and steps up to his bedside. He turns his head, startled to have her beside him again. "Madame."

"I was worried."

"I was overcome, Madame. For me, it was a great gift. "

Nodding, she grins, and asks, "Are you OK?"

He rests his head on the pillow and gazes a long moment at her. "Madame, that moment. It was sufficient for this life."

"What do you mean?"

"Peut-etre que Dieu aura enfin un mot pour moi." The French words slide from his mouth with pauses for breath. She can barely make them out, but she gets his drift. *Maybe God will have a word for me, at last.*

"What . . .? No. No. You're tired, that's all."

But he says no more.

She returns to the walkway, empty of Xavier. He's pedaling toward the hospital exit, his wave trailing. He's out of voice range. Maybe he knew what she was planning, and he wanted to head off her little talk.

Later, then. Let it go, for now.

She follows Xavier's path to the street and turns left a couple blocks to the patch of concrete where already a cluster of riders awaits the next fula fula's lurching presence. As always, her pres-ence draws a series of brooding stares as the only non-Zairois waiting. After all of her rides, she's acclimated to the stares, and, this morning, they don't raise a blush. She gives a quick nod and holds her place near the front to insure her shot at an actual seat for the trip home.

Within moments, the fula fula rattles to a stop, the door swings open, and the hordes press inside. Cass steps up, drops her coin into the slot, and pushes through the aisle, claiming a seat midway to the back. The scramble for a place ensues, the door squawks closed, and the bus lurches into gear for the return downriver.

Cass shuts her eyes. As the bus tumbles along the roadway, amid potholes and gravel stands, big jams of traffic, and periodic stops to stuff yet more bodies inside, recent memories vie for her attention. Ilinga's 'Maybe God will have a word for me, at last.' What does that mean? Is he going to die? She shivers and can't bear to think all that business about Mobutu's garden may have sent him to his death. Vernoy's caution: 'Never presume to know what's coming down the pike in this place.' And from last night, words she's been hoarding all morning until now when they spin up from a long shadow of anguish. 'It's over. I want to go back to how we were.' Maybe. Then the two muffled voices in intimate congress float up afterward, still placeholders of her recent past. Maybe she's not able to let him off the hook. It's too hard. Or, maybe they'll talk. She'll see.

Another stop. She opens her eyes. A shout rises, many voices joining as the front step fills with men in Army garb, three of them in line, wielding long rifles. The first one slides some words at the driver, who sweeps an arm wide into the aisle. Be my guest. And it's back again, the moment Cass wants gone above all others, the image of Corey muscled into silence by a squat soldier thug and his long rifle. She squeezes shut her eyes, then opens them to the sight of the front man, stopped midway down the aisle. He faces her way, her seat by the window. "Mwasi." Woman, he says, not Madame. "Yaka." Come.

"Come where? Venez ou?"

"Yaka na ngai." Come with me.

"Mpo nini?" Why? She dredges up from her slim store of Lingala, her face flaming, her hands bolted hard to the seat rest by the window.

The soldier gives a breathy hum of disregard. His hand grips her forearm and yanks her around the knees of the lavish woman seated on her right. Cass pleads with her. "Salisa ngai." Help me.

"Nayoki mawa." Her words are not in Cass' stash of Lingala, something about being sorry, she guesses, as the woman turns away. What can she do? She's no match for a long rifle. Cass stumbles after her Army captor, who speaks to the driver another word not in her stash.

Cass lands in the middle of the trio. Her captor has a boyish, quite handsome face. He murmurs something that might be a joke, for they all laugh as they bundle her into the back seat of an open-air jeep between two guys. Her head burns and her chest aches as she tries to catch up with her breath, which is outrunning her, outgunning her. The men gargle out their laughs. The one on her right grabs her handbag. She grips, resisting. He tugs and takes custody of the thick leather shoulder strap bag that has seen her through life since college. "Non non. Il a tout." It has everything. "C'est ma vie." It's my life.

This last statement of hers amuses them greatly, and their laughter picks up. They seem young, younger than Cass, and she's back at university in the days before meeting Will when she found herself with a horde of fraternity boys, and she felt swamped by their silliness. But these aren't fraternity boys. They have long rifles. They work for a killer. They have her handbag with the map she made. Evidence of her part with the jeshi dogo. *What do I say if they ask me? It's a sketch I made. I'm planning to build a new garden.*

Now her handsome captor lifts the flap on her handbag and digs his hand inside.

"Hey. C'est ma propriete privee."

More laughter, as if nothing could be more ridiculous than her private property. Her captor removes his hand and withdraws the carbon copy. He holds it up to see what's what. He frowns. "Qu'est ce que c'est?"

She brings to mind the response she's prepared about the *nouveau jardin.* Then she sees again the moment at the airport when Will faced the Customs' officer over a box forbidden shotgun shells, and the officer demanded, "Qu-est ce que c'est?" and Will told him, "Pour le sportif." That had done the trick.

"Pour mon plaisir," she says as airily as she can muster.

He doesn't dismiss the map but holds it out to the soldier on her left, then hands it up to the driver, who grunts out a word in Lingala that sounds like one she knows, alas, *Koboma*, Kill.

Twenty-seven

Madame does not come. It is the hour of her coming from the downtown. Sofia does not know of the business Madame has in that place, but each time she returns, she wears the crease of worry on her face. And now Sofia wears it, too.

Madame has started to ride the fula fula into the downtown. For Sofia, this is a strange business, too, since Madame is rich enough to drive a car. For Sofia, a car is a phantom of another life. But for Madame, it is a true life and she lets it go for the strangeness of riding the smelly fula fula. She can go in her friend's car, too. But the friend comes no more to the house. Sofia has some idea about this friend and Dr. Will, but it is a hard and bumpy path to speak of such matters to Madame, who has worries enough.

Now Madame does not come, and Sofia must walk with Corey and Matheo to Mama Kundi's for meeting her Fimi and Kamina. Together, they will walk back to Mimosa and wait for Madame. At first, Sofia skips along, and together they sing the butterfly song, "Papi-papi-papillon-vole-vole-volerons." As al-ways, Corey finds a way to become the flying butterfly, laughing as he goes, and Matheo finds a worry in Madame not coming. He stops at the gate and stomps his foot. "Where is Mama?"

After all these months with Matheo, Sofia has learned she must tell him what she knows. She first tried to speak untruths, to make the world softer for the boy. That path only makes it harder for her and for him.

"*Elle est en retard. Je ne sais pas pourquoi.*" She's late. I don't know why.

Matheo's face tears into bits of sorrow.

"*Tu ne dois pas t'inquieter. Ca n'aide pas.*" It helps nothing to worry.

"I know but when is she coming?"

"*Bientot, j'espere. Maintenant nous devons aller chez Sofia.*" Soon, I hope. Now we must go to the house of Sofia.

And so she takes each boy's hand and they cross Mimosa Road into her village by the place of the new water spigot, and go to the end, where, even now, there is the sound of Mama Kundi playing her harp. They race through the dirt pathway, even Matheo finds his joy in running toward the last hut. For he, too, loves Mama Kundi and her harp. When they reach the last hut, they stop for it is the worry face of Mama Kundi that meets them.

This face joins Sofia's fear about Madame, and tells her that Mama Kundi knows of some trouble come to Madame. Fimi and Kamina come out to meet her, and the four children rejoice to find themselves all together. Sofia tells them to go to her own hut while she and Mama Kundi have a big-mama talk. And the four race away, laughing while they can.

The words between them are Lingala, and a bit of Swahili. You must tell me what you know. Quickly before the children return. Is it some sorrow of Madame?

It is Madame. Not yet a sorrow, but a worry. The Army captures Madame from the fula fula. So saying, she makes the low goat sound in her throat.

Did someone see them take Madame? Or, is it only talk of loose-lipped women.

The aunt of our village neighbor sat by Madame as the Army took her off the fula fula and into that fat jeep.

Why do they take Madame? Where do they go with her? The aunt who saw her go does not know. But where does the Army of that devil Joseph Mobutu take anyone? To the prison or the stadium.

Does that devil take a woman to prison?

I have heard it so.

I went many times to that Kinshasa Prison where Daniel died. I saw no woman in that place. And I saw no **mondele**.

There is another place to take a **mondele** like Madame. It is a place not far from the airplanes of rich countries.

There is a rush of laughter from the far hut. The children jump and chase around the huts. Soon they will return to Mama Kundi and will learn what is what. She cannot tell them what Mama Kundi told her. But if she lies there will be trouble.

"Ndjili," Sofia says. If they didn't take her to the prison that starved Daniel, there is another story that might tell where Madame goes. She heard it from Alicia in the day before her sadness, about a woman from the country of the Belge. She was a careless woman who drank much wine and sat in a public place and talked in a voice for all to hear some bad words about that devil Joseph Mobutu. After a fortnight, a man in an Army coat found the woman as she left her car. He took her to Ndjili and sent her on a plane to her own country.

"Immigrant Interdit." Prohibited Immigrant, Mama Kundi says in a voice like ash.

"Angh." It must not be so, Sofia thinks, but she watches Mama Kundi's face and sees what does not lie.

That day Sofia stays at Madame's until the red ball of the sun comes like a fat chief to rule over his tribe. She waits with the four children until Dr. Will comes in his white car. She makes rice and some kind of cow meat and goofy cake that Matheo and Corey love. When her Fimi and Kamina are there to play, Mattie forgets about his mama. Not for long. Soon he will remember. And she must know what to tell that boy. She sits with the children and they eat together. She saves a big plate for Dr. Will who eats much for a man who is not fat. As the red ball drops down in the sky, she places the supper of Dr. Will in the cold box where food is safe from bugs. Matheo stands in the center of the kitchen, watching her with eyes going dark like the sky.

At that moment, Dr. Will steps inside. Matheo runs into his belly and cries, "Daddy. Daddy."

Will lifts him high up, laughing as he says, "Hey hey hey, Matts. What is it?" He looks at Sofia. "*Et Madame? Ou est-elle?*" Where is she?

Sofia must speak alone to Dr. Will. "*Un moment. D'abord, les enfants.*" First the children.

She opens wide her arms and sings again, as if all life is a song. "Papi-papi-papillon. Come. Yaka awa. *Venez avec moi.*" She herds them like small goats on to the patio where they will dance and romp while the big people talk. She shuts the sliding door and goes to Dr. Will. He waits with a glass of wine. There is a small table in the kitchen. There they sit, hidden from the children.

"Madame?" he says again.

She knows little English and his French is small. But she must make him understand what she knows from Mama Kundi. Her heart is running like a beast after prey. "Madame est pris du bus."

"Pris du bus? What are you saying?"

Sofia pulls an arm away from Dr. Will to show the taking. "Comme ca." Like this. He watches the motion close, like his patients. She pulls her arm again.

A worry shadow covers his face. "You mean they took her away?"

"Away. Oui. Madame away." Again, she pulls her arm.

"Yes yes. Away." Dr. Will does not like that way she moves her arm. She does not often see him angry, but now the worry shadow turns red. "Wapi?" Where?

"En prison."

"Prison?!" The word is a roar from his throat. It comes at her many times, like a question, and makes circles in the kitchen before and around her.

"Docteur, is possible . . ."

"Possible. What?" He stops his circles.

"Is possible elle est en jele."

"Jele? Qu'est-ce que c'est jele?" What is jele?

"Hmn. Petit prison." Her hands make a picture of a big prison, "Comme ca," and a small one, a jele. "Comme ca."

"So jele is not Kinshasa Prison. It's a jail."

"Oui, Docteur." Sofia lowers her head.

Dr. Will leaves the kitchen and moves quickly to his room with many books and the telephone. His hands move through many papers and books, and, at last, lift the telephone and dials. She watches Dr. Will and also watches the children dancing on the deck, like small hyenas for their supper. She wants to smile, but she must not, for Dr. Will might send his anger to her. Now he talks on the telephone, in a running voice. She hears his first words, First "Tommy" then "Vernoy." She knows these names, but after the names, she knows nothing that he says. After some minutes, his words stop their running. He listens, says, "Okay." He sets the phone into its place and sees her watching. He nods and his voice is the one she knows, low and easy, and not afraid. "My friend will help me. Le Matin." In the morning.

"Tommy?" she says.

"No. Tommy n'est pas ici. In America. No. Vernoy."

She nods, too, and her heart slows, and, like him, her voice is low. It is a sorrow that the fat Tommy cannot come. He is one who knows the language of the guards. But she tells Dr. Will, "Bon, Docteur. Ca ira." It will be okay. She wanted to believe so of Daniel, but wanting did not make it so, and it is a lie now, since she cannot know such things. But it is what she will say to Matheo when he asks.

Docteur is like a child now. She cannot know what is what with Doctor Will and the pretty friend of Madame. But he wants very much that Madame will be okay.

Twenty-eight

Cass keeps watch on where they take her, though much of what they pass has no distinctive marks she can commit to memory. They're leaving Gombe, the section the Zairois call Kinshasa's business district. She's met non-medical expats who have apartments here. To her it's simply a quasi-industrial clot she's used to. She watches as they move away from Gombe, back onto Boulevard 30 Juin, and head south, she believes. Maybe toward Ndjili Airport.

Airport. They're shipping me home, she thinks. I'm an Immigrant Interdite. Vernoy. It's what he said. *He gave me that card with his number.* She leans forward. "Mon sac. J'en ai besoin." My purse. I need it.

The driver bobs his head back a notch and says something that sounds like, "Okolobaloba." No clue what it means, only that it's flush with disdain and gets the other two laughing again. What a comedian.

She leans her head back on the seat and strains her air through conscious breaths to slow her heart rate. Vernoy told her, '*Never presume to know what's coming down the pike in this place.*' She presumed she'd be immune from the claws of the devil. And here she is. What an idiot. And Vernoy said that prayer at Thanksgiving. She shuts her eyes and sends what remains in her of the prayer to "the Mother and Father of us all."

Wherever She or He might be: "Help us step forth in light and in shadow. And make us instruments of your justice and peace. And help me. Please help me." Who else can she ask? Not Will. Not after he offered to talk about . . . getting back together, and what did she say? 'Don't hold your breath.'

So, here she is. Petitioning a Being she left long ago even before life released her from childhood, and look at her now.

The ride is longer inside her than in kilometers spent. At last she is freed from the jeep prison of derisive laughter and led into a large half-brick building. The swelter of a sun long overhead follows her inside to the ever-present tang of spilled petrol, and now her own sweat, the tickle on her neck, her lip. She told Will not to hold his breath, and now she's holding hers, literally. *Breathe. Cass, breathe.*

The handsome soldier-thug deposits her inside with a young woman in a green pagne with a brown square over her lavish breast framing a photo of Mobutu. Her head is bare, but her hair is an array of short spikes: a fashion statement emphasizing power and Mobutu's signature push, authenticite. The woman leads Cass into a large low-ceilinged cell, and shoves her inside with some dozen other women, glommed together, all Zairoise, save herself. A wave of sound rises, words she doesn't know encircling her and her old reserve. She elbows through the glom, hyperventilating like her twelve-year-old self that day at the YWCA pool when she feared drowning at the shallow end. Only now there's no one to jump in and lift her to safety.

She takes herself to a far back corner, not on the bench, which is already claimed. She leans against the wall and slides down to the concrete floor. She finds room enough in a line of women to sit upright, leaning, and welcomes the cooling effect of concrete. Some do garbled moans of fury, and intermittent stomping. One lies in a C-curl. Cass decides that dead one is the cause of the ululation howls weaving and waving through the cell. She has heard it before, and understands this is the way women grieve for their dead. But why is a dead woman lying in a jail cell? And for how long?

Cass keeps her hands clutched over her own belly. Emptier than she ever remembers. She hasn't eaten a bite since her boiled egg and toast some nine hours ago. So this is hunger, not a pleasurable sensation that awaits certain filling, but a hollow growing inside her as if by some flesh-eating insect.

Someone's words about prisoners and food here surfaces. Vernoy, probably. No, Tommy. They don't feed them. The families have to bring food. Of course, that's why Alicia brought food to Daniel. *Daniel.* The name deepens the hole inside her. His family brought food and he never got to eat it. A throbbing now in her gut. Her family can't know where she is, they'll never find her, she'll be like the woman in the C-curl. But no one will ululate for her.

She wants to tell someone in this cell that her family doesn't know she's here but who will get her words? The women, most women, don't speak French and her Lingala is pathetic, *pasi wapi?* where's the pain, and *boni?* how much? She turns to the woman leaning beside her, middle-aged, plump, dark skin slick in the fading light. "Ma famille ne sait pas que je suis ici. Comprenez?'

The woman shrugs and flicks her head backwards. "Un peu." A little.

Cass tries a reduced version of her plea: She points to herself. "Moi, wapi?" and she says, "Ma famille," while opening her arms in the universal helpless gesture.

The woman gives a quick smile. "Okay."

Such a small gesture, a smile, but a comfort nonetheless. She believes her okay means she gets it. The throbbing lessens inside.

She closes her eyes and moves not into sleep but away from hunger and the sounds of bodies heaving fear, anger, grief, and into a state bearing dreams, memories, and images of Corey and Mattie. They're beyond worried, especially Mattie. Corey minds her absence, but he can play off his upset, while Mattie binds himself with his five-year-old worries. Too much so. She has to work on helping him learn self-comfort. If she can ever be with him again. *My poor babies.*

A sound of keys against metal jars her into the cell, front and center. The same guard wearing spikes and Mobutu's mug opens the metal bars and pushes a cart bearing plates of food inside. She stops before Cass' *okay* neighbor. "Nkombo?" Name?

"Marie Banza."

The guard hands her a plate and serves up a helping of a white, dough-like mound, and a dark green glob that looks like spinach. Cass recognizes the mother food of Zaire, fufu and saka saka. She has watched the women outside their huts in the River Village pound manioc root into flour with mortar and pestle. The dough is always served dark green saka saka, cassava leaves ground and blended with palm oil and onions. Cass' one-time taste from Sofia's plate nearly made her ill, so tasteless it was.

"Lisusu," more, Marie Banza says.

The guard bends down and adds one more spoonful to her plate.

Marie turns to Cass. "Ma famille."

"Oui. Bon," Cass tells her.

"Pour vous aussi." For you also.

"Moi?" Me? Cass is close to tears from this kindness she never invited or anticipated. "Merci," she says. Following Marie's lead, she takes pinches of the mother food with her bare, filthy hands into her mouth, swallows, and feels the hunger inside growing thin and still and the thrum of anxiety easing a bit. But there is her thirst, present for a while since the Army thug grabbed her handbag with her water bottle in tow, and she's greedy for a small drink. Marie must read minds, for she produces a gourd and offers Cass swallows of what must be tap water. She knows the line on tap water among expats here. Never touch the stuff until you boil it twenty minutes, to save yourself from elephantiasis or God-knows-what. And Sofia boils water each day for the family. Yet, she drinks several long swallows, and nods her thanks to Marie Banza, a stranger from a different world.

"Natondi yo. Merci," Thank you, she says again, nearly overcome with relief, a relief like that day she was belayed down a cliff in the Cascades with a boy she dated before Will. There was slack in the rope and her terror at falling one hundred feet, then the rope tightened, slack gone, and she felt held again and safe and could slow-step down the cliff. But there was still all that air, one hundred feet of air beneath her. Don't look, she told herself. *Don't think about Giardia or Cholera,* she tells herself now.

The sliver of light from the high-up window above her recedes to a circle in the center of the cell and descends into night. She's blind and suddenly aware of having to pee. She touches Marie Banza's arm. She jerks, already asleep. "Je m'excuse. Toilette?"

Marie groans her distaste, takes Cass' arm and points to the opposite corner. "La bas," Over there.

Cass stands, steadying herself by the wall, and works her steps as lightly as manageable through the black cell. Still, she bumps a belly, steps on a hand, and rouses a string of grunts and moans from darkness. She comes at last to the single toilet in the corner, epicenter of the raw smells of urine and feces that pummel her nearly to vomiting. She pees a long time, grateful for her runner's legs that make it possible to do so without touching the toilet seat. She pushes the flush handle to no avail. "C'est casse´, someone says. The water to the toilet must be cut off. The toilet is nothing but a slop bucket.

She lies on the concrete and covers her head with her cardigan sweatshirt. The sleep that comes in the night is no friend to her, for it releases in rest a string of nightmares: Corey splashing around the Okapi swimming pool. He wears the inflated floater, but soon the floater begins to lose air until it goes flat and useless for keeping him afloat. He's sinking under the surface. She can't reach him. She's too late to save him. Will and Susan appear in a line waiting to see Mobutu. Their gazes meet. They move with the line until they reach Mobutu, and, facing him, call to Cass across the room. She turns toward them in time to see them kissing. They call to her again, laughing, and again they kiss. A black bunny bounds into Mobutu. He grabs it by its head, squeezing, and flings it, wiggling, to the marble floor, then stomps on the black bunny. It stops wiggling. Will and Susan shake their heads and move on. The tiny heart pops from the squished bunny and beats on outside the body.

She wakes on the concrete floor. A sour stain coats her mouth. Bereft of sense and memory for a moment, she bolts upright and receives the foul stream of yesterday. So this is what hell is. Early day lights the cell to a soft gray and reveals some few others stirring awake and, still, the woman lies dead in a C-curl among the so-called living. Cass' new friend lies supine, legs splayed, and snores lightly. Cass takes a dollop of comfort from the sound.

She reaches for the gourd and downs a good swallow of tap water, tamping down the guilt for consuming the stuff, and pours a dab onto the hem of her blouse. She wipes the moistened hem over her face and hands and returns the gourd to Marie's side.

A low hum sets into the silence of the cell, and sharpens into a scree of pain, issued from the women framing the dead woman. The sounds of mourning ream out any trace of sleep from the cell, and Marie pulls herself to sitting, nods to Cass, and sips from her gourd.

"Qui va nous aider?" Who will help us? Cass says.

"Je ne comprends pas." I don't understand.

"Salisa. Ngai. Yo. Nani?" Help. Me. You. Who? Cass touches a hand to her chest, hating the pigeon quality of her speech. In nine months, she's learned about nine words of the language the women here speak. One word a month. And you're supposed to be such a verbal whiz. Great job, Cass.

Marie shakes her head, slowly to show solidarity with her sorrow. No idea.

Cass shuts her eyes and longs again for sleep. But moments before sinking into oblivion, a new slur of Lingala floods the cell, broken by barked commands. A female guard, a new one, stands before the bars and behind them: two men. Seeing them, Cass rises without effort to standing. Her eyes fill. She steps over and around the assembly of the living and the dead to the iron gate, and meets the guard face-on. Her arms and neck are muscled, and she wears kahki safari skirt and jacket like a Zairois Jane Goodall.

"You came." She looks into the face of Will and the world lost to her. She blinks, willing gratitude to her betrayer to vanish.

Traces remain, and she tries for a neutral affect. Still, the creases of concern evident in the handsome face bring her remnants of that other life. "We brought food," he says in a breathy tenor, "and a couple bottles of boiled water." He hands them to the guard, who unlocks and opens the gate and delivers them to her outstretched hands.

"Thank you." She keeps her voice even. "Would there be enough for my friend here? She shared her dinner last night. And her water. This is Marie."

Marie looks up at him with a dazed half-grin.

He nods and eyes the gourd. "If you like. There's four big half-sandwiches, rice, an apple, some goofy cake. The water?" He shakes his head, frowning, but says nothing about not-boiling. Nothing to be done now. That's the Will she's always known, the realist who likes that Omar Khayyam quote: "The moving finger writes, and, having writ, moves on."

"Un moment na Madame?" Vernoy urges the guard. He holds out his palm closed around a bill, she's betting. The guard touches her palm to the proffered one. The matabisi does its work, and she retreats into the shadows of the hallway.

"Do you know what this is about?" Will's voice is subdued and pointed.

Cass feels the force of her truth clawing for release. She nods, hesitates, and opens her mouth to begin the telling. "It started at the Ali-Foreman Fight . . ."

"Not here." Vernoy's caution derails her confession. "Later."

Will shuts his eyes and steals himself against saying more. She knows how he hates being told what to do.

"Anyway, thank you both for the food." Tears welling again, she fixes on Will. "And the boys. How are the boys doing? Do they know?"

"They know you're not home. Can't finesse that. But this? No. They think you're staying out-of-town with a friend. But you know Mattie. I couldn't think what else to say, so they're sleeping at Sofia's. For now."

"Sofia's. Oh, that's good They like her girls. They'll distract them until all this is, as the Brits say, sorted." She turns to Vernoy. "Do you think I'll be evicted from the country?"

"Better pray that it's so. It's your best hope."

"Praying, you mean?"

"Being evicted. Persona non-grata, immigrant interdit. Remember there's still the Paul Carlson option,"

"Don't remind me."

"Keep your head down."

A backdrop of moans surrounds their long silence. Her breathing quickens. Her voice softens. "Speaking of prayers, I still remember yours. From Thanksgiving. 'Keep our eyes and our hearts open for the ways we should step forth in light and in shadow. Look upon us with kindness in this terra incognita, and use us as instruments of your justice, truth, and healing."

"I said all that? Sounds pretty good. Didn't know I had it in me."

"It was so cool. Not the kind of prayer I grew up with. Oh, and there was a thank you to the Mother and Father of us all. I'll save that part for when I get out of this hell-hole." She sweeps out an arm.

"You might try a more targeted prayer: Say, help help."

"I might have to. So, if I were being evicted, wouldn't they take me straight to Ndjili?"

"A person given the boot isn't necessarily taken straight to Ndjili. Not normally. Whatever normal means. Typically, such cases would be taken to the nearest convenient place of custody. Pending completion of arrangement for removal."

"'Convenient place of custody.' Such a clean-sounding sounding name for a room with a toilet full of shit."

Once-upon-a-time Will would have laughed at her rare trespass into profanity. In the gray light of this morning, he looks stricken, agitated as he asks, "Are you okay?"

"I'm man-a-g-ing," She stretches the word to smooth her bitter edge. Can't let herself turn into her mother, who played the poor soul, jilted by life. "Thanks, guys, for saving my bacon."

Will nods and heads in the direction of the guard. After a moment, he turns back. "I'll call the Embassy. I've met Ambassador Hinton, more than once. Remember? Tomorrow, then."

This time, she looks at Will full-on. "I'll be here." She gives a hiccupped giggle to forestall a sob, until they leave. "And give my babies big hugs."

The moment the guard escorts them from sight, a name slips in, not in code, but in life: Gabriel. Was he the one who betrayed her? If not Gabriel, then who?

Twenty-nine

Another sun, another moon, and still Madame does not come. The world for Dr. Will is broken into pieces of sorrow and fear. He cannot bear her absence. He must go to hospital, but after, when his boys see him, they ask about Mama, and he cannot say what he fears.

Late on the third day when she goes to the door of the kitchen and will go to her own Fimi and Kamina, his voice stops her. "Sofia. Corey and Matheo, kenda na yo? Une nuit. Is possible." He gives out a strange pudding of Lingala, French, and English. But she knows his ask and his hope. Will she take his boys to her own hut for one night of sleeping?

She wonders if Gabriel will be angry if they come. But he will be more angry if he comes and Sofia is not home. Like Madame, he, too, does not come. Two nights he stays away. Is it the same reason as Madame? She cannot know. But in his years with her, he has many reasons to not come, and so she gives her answer. "Iyo, Docteur. Ekoki." Yes, Doctor. Is possible.

"Great. Thank you, Sofia. Melesi."

So, Sofia walks again with the Matheo and Corey, singing and dancing quickly across Mimosa Road to meet Fimi and Kamina, who are like a pill to soften their rememberings and fears about Mama. The children meet and laugh and she takes them together into the hut to set in place their sleeping mats.

She prepares the supper of rice and dried fish, and they eat all of it. And when the dark comes, they lie on their sleeping mats and she tells them a story about Lion Cub who finds himself alone in the forest. She tells in her tongue, for the boys learn many Lingala words with her. The words seep in like rain drenching their brains. She tells how Cub leaves his cave and wanders into the forest. He meets animal friends as he walks about looking for his mama. There is Jackal he tries to hide from. He is bigger than Cub, but he makes a big roar and Jackal comes to rest at Cub's feet, and together they move on through the woods. Next they meet Elephant. He tells Cub to climb on his trunk and so he rides and stays away from Snake and sees all from his high swinging place. He comes at last to the river, where Mama Lion is caught in a trap and cannot move. Cub sees Crocodile in the river. He knows Crocodile has strong jaws, and he calls to him. "Please, help free Mama." Crocodile pulls to the river edge. He takes the steel trap in his giant mouth and closes over it. Mama Lion walks free. Crocodile pushes back under the water and is seen no more. Elephant bends down and Mama Lion climbs on his back with Cub. Jackal goes before them to frighten any enemies they might meet, and Elephant carries them home.

They say no words for a time as the story settles inside them. Corey is the first to speak. Do you think my Mama is caught in a trap by the river?

""No no no, Sofia says.

"Where is she?" Matheo asks.

"It is why you sleep at the house of Sofia. Do not fear of Mama. Your papa will find her." Sofia's voice is stronger than her heart, but it must be so. Corey and Matheo must sleep. Tomorrow brings new wonders and new hope.

In the way of things since her brave boy left the hut to find death, Kamina and Fimi sleep in the small alcove she made for them, away from the door. Tonight Corey and Matheo sleep on the mat beside her. Matheo is a boy who knows what is what and he will tell her if Corey seeks danger in the night. For this reason, she does not fear of the boys.

It is Corey who is last of the children to stop telling his story. Only then she lies beside him and his brother. Rain comes, not the big rain of her nightmare, but a rain to soothe her and her worries to sleep.

She cannot know how long sleep takes her away. Only that it is too long, and she wakes to Matheo's moan telling of Corey not on the mat. Gone. He went out. Help.

Sofia cannot bear that night of horror. Not again. But she must. She pulls on her pagne and her go-aheads, and takes Ma-theo's hand into the night. There is only a moon in the night as they circle around the hut and the butterfly bushes, and move out and around every hut in the village, even to Mama Kundi's at the far end. Because he knows that one. He likes her harp.

"No," Mama Kundi wakes easily to tell them. She comes out to walk with them and carries her kundi, too.

Sofia wonders if he goes across Mimosa Road to his own house, and she tells this thought aloud. "Is possible," Matheo says.

"No," Mama Kundi says. "It is too far."

Matheo frowns and goes quiet. There are no more words while insects crawl in the dirt under their feet and a tree limb crackles overhead, and a hyena sets a howl in the far woods for the others to join. At last Mama Kundi stops. "Ebale," River, she says.

Sofia stares at him. "Yes, Mama Lion," he says.

"Mama Lion. your story. The river. They found her there."

They turn away from the thick rows of huts toward the river. They move in stealth away from huts, around trees, toward the voice of the river egging them forward and they run run. Mama Kundi, hinged downward at her belly, runs too. Sofia's heart beats like a drum with a new story, the one she told last night. What if Corey took his idea from her story, and the river takes him? She could not bear another small grave.

"There he is," Matheo cries. They come to the river's edge and the bridge they cannot cross, for it has no sides. Yet Corey stands strong in the middle under the bright moon. She thinks how brave is this boy, like her own too-brave Elombe.

"Nye," Quiet, Mama Kundi says. "Yo," You.

"Yaka awa," Come here, Sofia says, but softly.

Thirty

Lying on concrete just before the new daybreak, Cass imagines this hellhole transformed. The C-curl woman comes back to life, a lively plucking sound transmutes the moans into a song of celebration, the toilet repairs and empties itself, and Will and Vernoy appear at the bars of the cell, key in hand, and open the door. She meets Will's gaze and there's a joining of intentions to melt all memory of her blame and bitterness. After all, he's had his secret, but she's had hers. In fact, her secret prophetic side, her SDS days with forays into dissidence there and here, these are more global, more primal, more damaging than his straying. Are they not?

No question. The verdict is in: She's the bigger malefactor.

But when she opens her eyes to the gray stain of morning, the C-curl woman, young and beginning to decompose, lies center stage, in the place of honor. She gives off the smell of rot and cheap perfume, joined by the stench of old feces. Cass pulls herself to sitting against the concrete wall and tries to skim the queasy film from her gut with words from of Vernoy's remembered prayer. *Look upon us with kindness in this terra incognita, and use us as instruments of your justice, truth, and healing.* Taking Vernoy's suggestion into the moment, she says audibly, but hushed, "Help me, please, get me out of this hole."

For a moment, the prayer gives her a fillip of solace before it dissipates and the morning clamps tightly around her.

She reaches for the water they brought her. Was it only last night? Tomorrow, Will said. That means today. Will they come today, or will they never return? She drinks long swallows of the water she knows is good, hoping to dilute Marie's tap water to a safe level, which makes no sense, as the microbes are in her, already doing their deadly work. It was a kindness. Don't be ungrateful, Cass chides herself and turns to her benefactor, stirring now beside her. "Mbote, Marie," Good morning.

"Mbote." She scoots herself to sitting and takes a cloth from the waist of her pagne, moistens it with the gourd water and rubs her face and underarms, displaying a fastidious nature that moves Cass to wonder about her.

"Yo. Awa. Nini?"

Marie explodes with a laugh, responding, Cass assumes, to her own pigeon version of Why are you here? "Ngai vole miliki."

"Vous avez vole du lait?" You stole some milk? Cass presses and adds, "Zoba, Zabulu," Idiots, devils, and aims her thumb at the bars.

Marie gives a weak nod and shrugs.

This new information propels a fresh gust of indignation about the C-Curl woman, and, yelling, Cass broadcasts her fury at the idiots and devils beyond the bars. "There's a dead woman here. Someone needs to take her away. Give her a decent burial."

Marie watches her with a slow headshake. Another woman across the room frowns at her. Another lifts her head from the dead girl and smiles and then lies down again with the girl. Apart from these, the room is still, as if unawakened by her outburst. Marie glances vaguely her way. "Malamu te." It's no good.

A sudden craving to be heard fills her, and she bounds to the cell door, the place of their day-old words, Will's and Vern's, still echoing. *Do you know what this is about? Not now. The Paul Carlson option. Tomorrow, then.* She draws from her small store of Lingala to send another bellow. "Mwazi ezali kufa kufa kufa. Yaka awa." Woman is dead dead dead. Come.

On the third morning, her thoughts go deeply into wondering about the others. First, Xavier, that devil, her betrayer. Or not. Will she ever know the truth? And what of the others? Are they alive? She recalls Vernoy telling her, months ago, about four of Mobutu's men being herded blindfolded into the stadium and shot.

What if it's her fault? If she hadn't paid the rent, they'd have nowhere to meet in secret. If she hadn't urged Ilinga to describe Mobutu's garden, the others wouldn't have dared sneak inside and attack him. Did they actually get inside the compound, only to meet their own assasins? And what of Ilinga? Is he dead, too? She can't bear to think he could have died because she roped him into this ill-fated scheme.

Please, no. Let all these thoughts be inert in her. Go back to dark unknowing.

She pushes herself to sit leaning against the concrete, eyes half-open. A new rankness assaults her. Not the C-Curl corpse, for daylight is open enough to show the space she once held. She's nowhere in the cell. She's gone. Someone must have entered and taken her in the night. Nor is there the stink of feces across the room. They must have scooped out the toilet, though a film of urine remains.

But the dominant smell is her own foul self. She hasn't showered in three days. She hasn't changed her underwear, for Pete's sake. Once-upon-a-time, before Will, she had a few dates with a boy who rock-climbed in Yosemite Valley. One of his ascents took a number of days. He told her that after ten days you get used to living with your own stink. Lovely. Three days down, seven to go. God help her.

Maybe it's the same for hunger. But she's far from numb to her hunger, and worried besides. Since starting college, she's been a notch above skinny. Now she's there. Turned into Twiggy, a wraith, a living, breathing twig. An image of Susan's lavish roundness surfaces, along with her own ridiculous assumption that Susan was not Will's type. What a fool I was, she thinks. She stretches out her leg and confirms her fears. It is a twig, a bit of tubing. Of course he went for the voluptuous Susan.

"Mbote," the voice lifts beside her.

"Mbote, Marie."

"Sango nini?" How are you?

"Tres mal. Mabe," Cass says. "I feel ugly."

"Ugly?"

"Ebe."

Marie sends up a laugh that is round and loud and irritating, at first, then proves contagious, even this morning, "Yo. Pourquoi awa?" It's Marie's turn to wonder about her new friend/cellmate.

"Pourquoi suis-je ici?" Why am I here?

Cass holds her gaze and considers what to reveal. Should she play like Susan and keep her ugly toe hidden from view? How has that worked out, keeping secrets? 'Not here,' Vernoy said. 'Keep your voice down.' But who's listening? They're off looking for other victims to lock up. "Moi. J'ai essaye de tuer Mobutu." Me. I tried to kill Mobutu. There. She's done it. She's laid out her crime for Marie's review. Maybe her friend will hate her and call the guards. More likely, she won't understand the French.

But Marie's dark eyes widen with awe of her revelation. "Boma?" she says.

"Boma," Kill, Cass says, releasing herself to the flip side of caution, as the night of the Fight slips back to her, and the crowd cries once more, "Ali, boma ye."

Marie lifts a fist between them and gives in to a grin she can barely contain. At last, she says, "Mwasi malamu." Good woman.

The day wears into a thickness rank with anxiety, swollen ankles, and a painful gut. Marie has taken to sleeping through long hours of daylight. Cass wonders if she knows her people won't bring food until evening. Once, she lifts Marie's arm and checks her wrist for a pulse, fearful that death has claimed her as it claimed the C-Curl girl. Maybe this holding cell is like the town in "The Lottery," the Shirley Jackson short story, wherein each year the townspeople selected, by chance, one person to stone to death. The annual rite of sacrifice apparently released the town's shadow side and so insured its continued wellbeing.

But Marie's pulse is strong, and Cass takes heart that her friend's heart beats on.

Another woman, barefoot, and wearing the remnants of a flour sack cinched and tied as a pagne, goes to the bars and racks her voice into a tremolo of words Cass can't decipher. When no one comes, she tears the fabric from her neck, baring pendulous breasts and begins circling the room. The movement wakes Marie, who sits up. "C'est une fou," She's crazy, she tells Cass.

Heat rises in the over-stuffed cell. The commotion grows, loud upon loud, as other women stand and follow the track of the fou.

The spike-haired guard in green pagne rushes to the cell. "Zoba" and "Sala nye." Idiot. Shut up. Her voice barrels over them. The fou covers her ears and keeps circling the cell while the others fall back to their places on the bench and the concrete.

Cass shuts her eyes and tries to dive inside herself, seeking oblivion from the chaos, a practice that gave her solace in childhood when her ancient dentist manhandled her teeth, once even drilling the wrong tooth.

The day wears on until the red sun arrives in its roundness and rids itself of the eternal afternoon with still no trace of Will or Vernoy, food or safe water. So far, she's had no sign of abdominal cramping from bad water, and she weighs the choice of drinking from Marie's gourd. She reaches to take up the gourd from Marie's sleeping torso when a key turns in the bars. A squat man in Army camouflage steps inside and signals her to come.

This is it. I'm done for, she thinks. She taps Marie's shoulder, arousing her, and crosses her arms in a gesture of friendship. "Bolamu, Natondi yo." Good luck. Thank you.

Marie nods and raises her fist.

Cass follows the army man from the cell into the dark hallway. His English is scant. She can't know the way ahead where her executioner stands to take her from the one in khaki. At the end near the front entrance at a counter, where, days before, she was received into *the convenient place of custody,* she pauses and braces for a muscled arm, a pummeled fist, a plastic bag over her head to seal her fate.

One attendant at the receiving counter sleeps with tight braids hugging her head resting on the plywood top. The guard with spiked Afro and khaki stands hyper-ready near the entrance. Cass braces herself for a move to block their exit. The Army man thrusts his palm forward and closes it around the guard's smaller palm. *Matabisi, of course,* Cass thinks, as the guard opens the metal door to the walkway out front. Cass catches herself holding her breath. She exhales and breathes in, hardly daring to believe the deep pleasure of cool air.

"Awa," Here. A flashlight illuminates the way ahead. A sprout of hope rises as she sees the Army man leading her away from the place of custody. Phrases from Vernoy's caution play on in her head, *Your best hope, Being evicted; persona nongrata, immigrant interdit.* At the end of the walk, she makes out a black Mercedes, of all things, parked where the road ahead meets the walk. The Army man opens the back door. "Kota." He means enter, she gathers.

Who but Mobutu and his henchmen drive Mercedes? she thinks, hope wilting, *but what choice do I have?* Shuddering, she slips into the unknown darkness inside.

Thirty-one

Now is night at the river. The boy Corey dances freely on the bridge without walls and laughs as the watching others weep and bleed their fear into the darkness. It is the way of this small boy. He is like her own lost Elombe, who played with darkness until it took him for its own.

Mama Kundi plays her harp in her strong way, as memories of her own big boy riding a bicycle uphill, breathing in and out the thickness of the air around him, and never stopping to rest. Mama Kundi plays to forget how the darkness took her boy from her, and she plays loud above the roar of the waters to hold this new boy with her loud notes and will not let him go.

Sofia remembers how she herself tried to force Nzambe to find Elombe, and yet he escaped her searching, and now she fears she has nothing in herself to meet this boy. For he, too, can dance himself straight from the bridge into the rapids of the river that will take him away. And so she holds herself close on the bank and says a prayer to Nzambe and to the ancestors, "Bikisa ye," Save him.

Matheo, the boy, has no such remembrance and no such fear. He has only his own heart beating strong for his brother, and he sets to running along the bank to the place where the dirt meets the bridge. No no no, she calls to him.

He cannot hear Sofia over the voice of the river and the beating of his heart. Or, he will not hear. He keeps his feet on the dirt and his watch forward to his dancing brother. He calls across to Corey in some words she knows from his language, words about play and home and brother and die.

And Corey says some words about "ndeke nene," big bird, and Matheo calls to him, No no no. Sofia sees her story of Cub sending Corey into the darkness. She knows if her story causes him to die, she must die too.

There comes much calling and much crying from Matheo. At last, Corey stops and looks toward him, and he turns his dance into a sturdy walk on the narrow wood bridge to the dirt where Matheo waits. He reaches Matheo, who holds him hard, and his big brother fear and soft pleading turn to tears and loud anger. But Corey only laughs and soon Matheo laughs, too.

Sofia and Mama Kundi step barefoot, following their night walk, and always the name of the one he seeks rides the night air before him, "Mama." At the hut where Kamina and Fimi sleep, Corey stops and turns his face up to Sofia. The moon shines on his round face, and he asks, "Mama ezali awa?" Where is Mama?

Thirty-two

She shuts her eyes, squeezes her fists, and forces her breaths against the withering of air, the tightening in her chest. *What does a heart attack feel like?* she wonders.

"Madame Ramsey, I presume."

She dissolves in a spate of coughing and leans forward. Her right hand feels its way up front toward the massive shape in the passenger seat and the sweat soaked through to his shirt. "Tommy!"

"C'est moi, Madame, personne d'autre." It's myself, Madame, none other.

"You're back. Can I hug you?"

"I'll take a raincheck."

She joins his laughter. Tears bathe the hands covering her face, her own hands, none other, from a life reclaimed, for now.

"Can we go . . .?" She pauses. She cannot bring herself to name the place of her dearest hope, as the car rolls

He hesitates with a prolonged breath, then says, "To Mimosa? No way. Too risky."

"Okay. But where are you taking me?"

"You met my pilot, Captain Alongi. He doesn't speak English. He has basic French. You will come to know him."

"You're not coming?"

"Can't. The plane would complain. About my 340 pounds. No worries. You two can manage."

"You still haven't told me where he's taking me." She feels the childish pout weighting her words.

"Ndolo. The airport for General Aviation. It's not far. Then he'll get you out of Zaire and into Angola. From Angola, you'll get a plane to Lisbon, then home."

"Isn't Angola risky? Mobutu may know somebody there. And aren't there uprisings or something going on?"

"In Africa, there's always something. Don't worry. Captain Alongi is used to dodging danger."

His words meant to comfort bring a shiver inside the heat non-yet dissipated, and she collapses against the leather seat back. She frowns at that other shape in the darkness surrounding her, summoning her to somewhere unknown. A furious exchange of Lingala flies between Army guy and Tommy. Both men laugh. Tommy turns to Cass. "He says flying you will be like a flying an empty plane."

"Because I'm skinny?"

"Better mileage. Fewer stops to refill. Maybe more nimble."

Silence, as she mentally resists their jovial exchange and gathers the nerve to tell Tommy she's not flying anywhere until she's had a shower. "Newsflash: I'm-not-flying-anywhere-smelling-like-shit." She keeps her words low, slow, and discrete.

Another flurry of Lingala and laughter up front. "I figured you'd say that. Captain here says you got eleven hours. After that, he's bailing. It's 7:00 now. You have until 6:00 in the A.M."

"Do you honestly think it's all that urgent? They want me out of Zaire, not dead."

Captain pipes in, his voice sounding throaty and gruff. Tommy translates. "He says those guys with the President, they don't have their own brains anymore. They have only

Mobutu's. Their own brains are shot by fear. And Mobutu will remember that you wanted to kill him before he remembers you were leaving his country. Remember, they are still small boys with big guns."

The shock of his words spirals through her and raises a fever of fear, fatigue, and nausea. The Mercedes slows and makes a wide swing into a parking lot before a block of modest apartments. Who lives here? she wonders. Where are they taking me now? Tommy opens his door and steps out.

She covers her face, then turns her face toward him. "Wait. Give me a sec. I haven't eaten. I'm nauseated."

"We'll fix that." He waves a fist clutching a key and steps toward a dark door.

Thirty-three

At the first lighting of the candles, Dr. Will comes to Sofia's hut. To have him here and his head nearly touching the fine tin roof gives her own head an ache and a sorrow, as before when Gabriel called her Woman and made marks on her belly. Came his time away and then his return when she remembered the man she first knew. But he's gone again, and Madame Cassandra is gone, too. If Sofia believes the story the drums tell, she must worry that Madame and Gabriel are in bad trouble.

"Docteur! Fanda yo. Asseyez-vous," Sit down. "Quoi de neuf?" What news? She must ask, though the fear in her is strong to learn what sadness he brings.

But his worry face is gone and she sees there the face she knew when she first came to their house, the one showing kindness and calm, like her own remembered father's face. He sits, and she sits, too, as he tells of Madame now free of jail. She claps her hands at this news and so brings the children through the doorway from the early darkness. Corey and Matheo bury their faces in their father's shoulders. After some minutes, he tells them a miracle. They will make a drive to see Mama to-night. They leave his shoulders to stand, and they laugh and laugh, and, of course, Corey dances and dances.

Dr. Will tells them to wait for him outside, but stay close. He must have a grown-up talk with Sofia. So the grown-ups use three languages and many hand motions, and she comes to learn that Madame will stay this one night before she must go away on a plane. He and his boys see her later, but cannot fly away. For now.

He asks if she can move to their Mimosa house with her girls after Madame leaves on the plane. She must only sit a long time in silence with a question so far from her belief in what can be. He tells his reasons, which she already knows. What she does not know is what Gabriel will do if he returns and finds her and Fimi and Kamina gone. But there is Mama Kundi. She can move with her harp to Sofia's hut and keep it safe from snakes.

"Iyo. Nakoki," Yes. I can, she tells him.

Dr. Will rests his hands on her shoulders. Thank you, he tells her in her tongue before he goes out to meet his boys waiting by the butterfly bush. "You'll see Mama very soon."

"Now!" Corrie says with his lion voice.

"Tonight. Not long."

"Not long takes a long time," Corey says.

"I know. We have to go get ready. No worries, bud. Mommy is safe."

Thirty-four

Captain Alongi stays unmoving in the car until Tommy opens the door to the apartment and waves him off. She feels the void of the Mercedes that delivered her to freedom. For a time. Who knows for how long? She has no choice but to follow the bulky shape inside. He flicks the light switch and calls out, "Hello?" A diffuse illumination reveals the miracle she dared not believe.

Will answers from the hallway. "Right here." Tommy spells out the details of events following this night. An early flight from Zaire. He extracts their agreement to stay inside with shades drawn until then, don't show yourself to anybody, got it? This is no joke. "Six A.M., got it?" He departs.

Her departure feels like a nightmare waiting in the depths of some other night. Far from this waking time, maybe not even real. What's real is Will standing in the hallway, eyeing her with a grave expression. Tears flood her face. "I can't believe it. I can't believe I'm seeing you, I've never been so thirsty. Is there water?" She goes to a small fridge on the counter top and pulls out a plastic bottle of water. "Is this . . . ?"

"Is it good? Our man Tommy brought them. So, yeah."

She downs the cold liquid, swallowing until relief turns to cold paining her throat, and she ceases drinking. The comfort of the quenching relays to her the fatigue she's carrying, and she pulls out a chair, sits, and turns again to Will, still taking her measure as he once did on his approach across the quad early on a Spring morning. Cherry blossoms inching into bloom, he would meet her. Who would she be? He did not know. Who would she be with him? She did not know. Now she feels caught at being someone unknown to him until now, someone he preferred not to know, certainly not to marry and make children and bring to a place far from home. And if he had known all the intricacies of desire that came with her hidden gift, and her willingness to cross lines he would not cross in a thousand lifetimes, well, he would have given her his half-grin and saved that brilliant smile for someone in a different section of the quad.

Now that her secret has spilled out into their world in so inelegant a way, he'll let loose the anger that comes rarely, but at a speed and volume she can't bear. If he thought running after dark was bad, just think what he must make of this trespass of prudence and normality. Please, God. Not tonight, after having her sanity shaved to a thin barrier from terra incognita. And she's absolutely certain she won't talk to him covered with the stench of the prison. 'Give me a few minutes? I need to shower. I assume there's water."

"It's even hot. I checked."

He sounds calm. A promising sign. That and the delicious spray of water razing the filth of recent days are wonders, maybe even a forecast of better times to come. She lingers, taking maybe the longest shower in memory. A hum starts up in her throat. "Where have all the flowers gone, long time passing . . ." until she turns the shower nozzle and the song turns silent, and she must face a truth she can no longer avoid.

She dries herself and unzips a bag someone has packed and pulls on jeans and a light sweatshirt over her skinnier–than–ever-torso.

"Mommy. Mommy." Screeches of delight and relief pummel and nearly knock her off her pins. She wrestles them to either side of the couch. "Where were you? We slept in Kamina and Fimi's hut. You can hear drums over there. Mama Kundi says the drums talk." Corey takes a breath. "I don't know how they do that. Do you?"

She laughs and shakes her head. "Sounds very interesting."

Mattie frowns and protrudes his jaw, taking a cue from her lifelong habit. "I thought you flew to Seattle without us."

"Remember what I said before? I'd never do that without telling you." Even as she stakes her hopes on his innocence, a blip of guilt rises in her chest, and she can't think how to balance her truth with her fears of unleashing a flood of tears.

Will stations himself in an armchair across the room, keeping to the background of their reunion. But they haven't had supper either, and he steps to a basket prepared beforehand, again, by their man Tommy. Or Lindy, Cass thinks.

The makings of pigs-in-a-blanket are on hand, and, with orange Kool-Aid, this becomes their supper. Cass and Will have cold friend chicken and potato salad and a glass of drinkable Portuguese wine.

Supper is a normal-feeling event, with Corey half-standing, half-dancing at the table, and Mattie gulping his Kool-aid until he coughs, and both boys relaying their nightmare tales about Corey on the bridge. Soon they bound from the table and leap into playing with their stash of toys they carted from home. Corey alternates Lincoln Logs and telling his sock puppets about how drums in the village can talk. He sings, "I want to learn how to talk to the drums." Mattie alternates between arranging his Lincoln Logs and singing The Wheels of the Bus song from kindergarten.

Then they launch into a rain dance. Barefoot and stomping in the small living room, they mimic their child-notions of noble savages urging the rain gods to come through. During a pause in the dancing, Corey darts to the edge of the wood-work nearest the kitchen and squats down to commune with two cockroaches, each the size of an American nickel, as they emerge from behind the refrigerator. Before Sofia can intervene, he cups his chubby hands, captures both, and carries them to the table for her inspection. "I want to name them Cocky and Lucky. Let's take them home to Mimosa. Okay, Mommy?"

Her breath catches on his phrase home to Mimosa. She swipes tears the boys must not see. Will stands and lifts Corey into his arms and carries him to the front door. "OK, bud. I think Cocky and Lucky want to be free. Let's watch them walk down the sidewalk. Deal?" Will opens the front door and Corey bends down and releases the giant bugs to the world.

In the quiet of the kitchen, Will and Cass munch cold chicken thighs and trade hyper-vigilant gazes. Cass takes a napkin to the nape of her neck. Even after sunset, without air conditioning, the hours have congealed the atmosphere into a stew of sweat. She knows what this means. Rain is coming, make no mistake. How often she has seen such humidity pre-cede a downpour that Mattie's kindergarten teacher describes as "not your Seattle drizzle." She can't believe Captain Alongi could fly an Aero-Commander plane through such skies. The only wildcard is timing. If only it rains early tomorrow, Captain Alongi won't take off. A downpour will save her.

She sips her rose' and reviews her thought-stream. She's six-year-old Cassie absorbing the preacher's tale of Jesus put-ting mud and saliva on the blind man's eyes and giving him his sight. Still looking for a miracle. Still believing anything's possible. She puts down the chicken thigh and tells Will her theory about a possible delay due to a strong rain.

"Okay." He meets her gaze with a distracted air. "By the way, I stopped in to P-One."

"To see Ilinga? Tell me."

He pauses, makes that sub-vocal whistle while he collects his words. "There's somebody else in that bed. He's . . ."

"He died." Her voice sinks into a hollow of regret. "I killed him."

"I can't wait to hear this. He was a quad. He never left his bed. You were in detention. How does that work?" His voice has that edge it gets when he hears a fool's logic, an edge lightly muted by his half-grin.

"I recruited him. You know?" Her voice rises, quivering and shrill. "He knew Mobutu. He knew his habits. Let's say he passed on what he knew. Through me."

"Did you hold a gun to his head? He may have been a quad, but he was still his own man."

"I think the stress pushed him over. I pushed him. I thought if he could feel he made a difference, it would give him a lift."

"Look. I asked one of the nurses about him. She said he was failing. He got tired, Cass. He was ready. I'm sure it did give him a lift. A lift before lift-off. Okay?"

Eyes filling, she nods.

After the boys wear themselves out, she reads them a fable: "Why Anansi has Eight Thin Legs." They ask her to read it again. "Not tonight." She cracks the window, turns out the light, and hugs them for a long time.

Cass removes her jeans and shirt and slips on a short aqua nightgown somebody packed. Will sits in silence on the left side of the queen-sized bed, watching her. He leaves the bed, shuts the bedroom door, takes her hand in both of his, and tugs. "Cass."

There's a mini-explosion inside her, like that time in her teens when she tried inhaling a cigarette and ignited tiny bursts in her head, and so ended her brief smoking experiment. Now she feels herself yielding to his tug, stepping toward the bed and all that awaits there. She lacks the strength and the will to resist him, though the moment is not about any lack. There's desire for this body so entangled with her own. Like the coming departure, his dalliance with Susan feels distant and unreal. Her capture, her detention, the smells of feces and death, all that she's endured have made that fissure a nothing, a cipher. Wrapped only in her undone robe, she closes the distance between them and gives in to the stirrings of arousal. Having him inside her again after these weeks apart is a return to a pre-rational time, a vestigial version of herself and Will swimming in a pool created for themselves alone.

Afterward, he sits cross-legged beside her, flushed, boyish, and grave. She scoots herself to sitting against the headboard. Neither speaks for a time until she says, "I couldn't believe it when I saw you here. It was like magic."

"I couldn't NOT come. You must know that."

"Was it your first?"

"My first?"

"First time you've made it with an assassin." She gives a tentative grin.

A frown startles his face, and he hunches his shoulders as if ducking a fast-ball. "Well, there is that." He tousles her hair, still moist, and pulls her to his chest.

"I'm glad for this. Just not for . . . all the rest of it," she adds, tears welling. "So, the boys will be asleep when I leave in the morning?"

"I think it's best, don't you? They'll be . . ." The ending of his thought slips into the lament that follows, "Cass Cass, what will become of us?"

Sleep eludes her for the longest time, which makes no sense. She's never felt so bone tired, but wired, too, anxiety lacing her body fed by spectacles of planes shot down over Africa. Dag Hammarskjold's plane shot down over the Congo before it was Zaire; an Air Egypt flight, a Lufthansa plane crashing after takeoff in Nairobi. These were giant planes, but no match for the impact. A tiny plane would be a snap for the Zaire Army if Mobutu decided to go after her. What are the chances she'll see Seattle again, never mind Angola? What if she dies and her boys go back to Seattle and she never makes it there? The questions circle inside her, spoiling the rest she craves.

Sleep receives her into its mysterious bubble, at last. And morning lands her half-awake on the tail of some face-off with the spike-haired guard holding a white rabbit by its tail and swinging it around the cell. She lets go and the rabbit lands on Matheo. She rises with a moan of dissent, and remembers what day this is: flight day. Will's side is empty. There's a pouring sound. He's in the kitchen. He's at the bedside setting coffee on the side table.

"Heaven," she says. "Thank you."

She emerges from another quick shower, as if she can bank cleanliness for days to come. She shepherds her movements with care to avoid waking the boys. Still Mattie meets her coming out of the shower. She has a twist of annoyance at her watchful boy for foiling their plan and intruding on their morning. But seeing the backpack riding his small frame, ready for his plane ride, his adventure, she can't help smiling. "What are you doing?"

"I'm coming with you."

"Sweetie." She rises and tries to enfold him to her.

He backs away. "You can't tell me no. Because I am so."

She removes to her bedroom to dress, then to the kitchen, where Will has breakfast going, her fortification for the strange journey she faces. Her pack rests beside the door. "You know that I'm going to Angola? Who flies deliberately into that chaos?" She levels her voice in sub-vocal range.

"It's close. You get why close is good, right?" Will's voice turns terse.

"Of course I get why close is good. What must you think of me?" She hears the spike of pity and annoyance in her voice and catches a stray image of herself at nine, trying to catch her Britanny spaniel and, instead, chases her into a speeding car. "Sorry." She angles her head toward the hallway where Mattie stands, watchful and unmoving. "We have a problem," she says.

"Hey, bud. Going somewhere?" Will says over his shoulder.

"Mommy lied to me," he says, frowning, arms folded in a stance of belligerence.

Will meets Cass' shrug with his own. Cass swallows her coffee hoping to soothe the pain of Mattie's telling, but it cannot.

"I had a bad dream and I woke up and I saw her put her bag there. I looked in it. I saw her passport. I know she's going on a plane, and she promised she would tell me if she went on a plane. She didn't. She lied. Now she has to take me."

"Mommy should've told you, bud. You're right about that. But she didn't want to worry you."

"But she's still going and she promised."

"Sometimes it's real hard to be a grown-up person." He pauses, and continues with more energy. "You know sometimes grown-up people have two promises and they can't keep both. One cancels the other."

"I don't ever want to be a grown-up person." He makes his pronouncement with supreme five-year-old grit.

Will meets Mattie's gravity with his own. "Well, we'll see about that. But Mommy has to go home before us. She has to talk to her own mommy."

"I thought she was mad at Grandma Mable."

"She used to be. But grown-ups can get over their mad." Will delivers his explanation with a pointed glance at Cass, who nods slowly, closing her eyes. "We'll fly, too, you and Corey and me . . ." He frowns, pausing, "when we can."

Over the breakfast delivered by their man Tommy, and cobbled together by Will, talk feels artificial and constrained by the knowledge of what lies ahead. Mattie tucks into eggs, bacon, and toast, and, despite his vow to never become a grown-up person, he makes an uber-adult pronouncement. "I get over my mad at Corey because if I didn't we'd never ever play. And that would be unfortunate."

Just then, in his spot-on timing, Corey bounds to the table, bright-eyed and jammy-clad, dispelling gravity with his presence. She reflects on her two boys. Still babies, really, and yet their paths seemed set, as if pre-determined in a separate universe. And what will each do if her flight goes the way of Dag Hammarskjold's? Don't go there.

Corey forks through his bacon and eggs, carefully trimming away the egg whites he disdains. Before biting his papaya slice, he exclaims, "My papaya! Remember, Daddy? I climbed on the railing and picked that papaya from our tree. I want Mommy to have the biggest piece."

Tears well at this burst of bigheartedness from her three-year-old, and she leaves her chair and moves to embrace each boy, in turn, and tell them, "You know you're my own best boys and I love you so much." She prolongs the hug until each boy squiggles away. And they race to find their backpack of toys, and leave the grown-up people alone in the silence she breaks. "When you can? You're not saying or you don't know?"

His words are measured. He avoids her gaze. "Haven't had a lot of time to uh work this out, this week. You do know it's been a week since all this came up? Less than. I'll tell you what I know. You have to be who are you. This apocalypse has shown me a side of you I didn't know. It's not like you've been forthcoming about it. Now I know. It's who you are. I get that. But it works both ways. I have to be who I am. And at this moment who I am is the only Orthopaedist in the hospital. Hell, in the whole country, since Eric David went back to Manila. I need to train somebody in Ortho for when I leave. There is a Nigerian General Surgeon who's shown an interest. I could have him assist me and see how it goes."

"So how long are we talking? Months or years?"

"I have no idea."

Silence again. She looks at her watch: 5:54. Six minutes till lift-off. She leaves him at the table and does a last pee, a sweep of the sleeping room, and a long gaze through the cracked door where her boys spill their attention over a family of finger puppets, giving themselves to this singular moment, free and clear of the past and the future. They sit sideways, apparently oblivious of her, and she tears herself away before they catch her in the doorway. She returns to Will and her anguish about future moments she can't release. "What about the boys?"

"What about them?" His words are freighted with annoy-ance.

"They could come sooner. I mean, couldn't they?"

"They're not even four and six yet. You're suggesting I send them alone across the ocean?"

"OF COURSE NOT. With somebody."

"Who? Who'd you have in mind, Cassandra?"

Her given name comes for her like a shot. They're beyond annoyance now, having entered the realm of anger, pure, righteous, rising. Before everything in her life turned into a freefall from reason and balance, she shielded herself from his anger. It was impressive but rare, and she'd shrink from its outpouring. Let her voice soften, as if fearing, she realizes now, some midair combustion. This fear was the likely etiology of her fondness of secrecy.

Now that her world is shot-to-smithereens anyway, she sharpens her response. "Don't tell me there's no one. You don't know that." Somewhere outside, a slow gonging bell marks the hour. Before her, Will slow-shakes his head. So it's true what she's read, that time is limber and elastic. The present moment stretches. If it's so flexible why can't it stop entirely and leave her here and now, and never release her to the terror awaiting her in the next moment.

The moment shifts and releases time to its normal pace. And beneath the heat of their words, her truest fear surfaces: It matters not when the boys come, since she has no idea what dragons she will meet before then, and if she'll be at home to meet the boys at all.

The Mercedes pulls into the parking slot, insuring that their last moment together is cast in anger. Tommy approaches the apartment door. Will opens it, shakes Tommy's hand. "Coffee?"

"I'll take it to go."

Will pours the cup Tommy takes in his left hand and slings her pack over his right shoulder. She watches Will move away, big-stepping into the boys' bedroom, doing their favorite gorilla impersonation to keep them from watching her leave.

Thirty-five

In the house at Mimosa Village, Sofia takes Corey in a hug to her belly. For he's seeing Fimi and Kamina through eyes still red. But Corey pulls away and runs up to give his news to the girls. "My mommy went away. She will fly on a plane for a long time."

"My mama is here. I'll let you have her for a while," Kamina tells him with so brave a face, like her small brother before the darkness took him.

But her words make Mattie angry. "That's stupid. You have to have your own mother, and I have to have mine." He marches away to his bedroom and shuts the door, made of hard wood, not cloth, and the sound startles like a firecracker.

Kamina looks up at Sofia, who tells her it is no worry. Mattie has a sad heart for now, but it will mend. Kamina walks out to the big deck where she looks across the wide green grass and over the iron fence and across the smooth wide road to the other houses, which are exactly like this very one. She can see Mimosa Road that runs between Mimosa and her village. But the River Village is hidden behind the bushes and trees growing wild during the time of the big rains.

Sofia watches her first born watching over the strangeness of the village that is not a real village, but a village made-up by mondeles from a far country. Maybe from the place where Madame goes. She understands Mattie's anger, for it's like her own anger about Gabriel, who is gone, too, for now. Or when? She cannot know. She feels a part of herself waiting for him to return and be the man she first knew, but another knowing tells her he will never return, and she is nothing but a fool from another time. Just as she was a fool after the burial of Elombe when she told herself Daniel could be her own man, and he could not. She's a bigger fool than this small boy, who, at least, knows what is what.

Sofia s hows t he g irls t he r oom w ith t he b ig b ed w here they will sleep with her. They place their cloth satchel wrapped around some few clothes and the toothbrushes Aunt Alicia gave them and the **cahiers** and pencils for school next week.

Sofia gives the children time to play in the rich house of the mondeles while she prepares soup with chicken and rice. Before long, the girls move through the house on feet of those who know these rooms. She begins to set the long table with all the foods that will be lunch. A voice she knows calls from the top step outside the door. "Mbote ndeko." Hello sister.

"Mama Kundi!" Sofia laughs and opens the door for her friend.

The Ancient One looks small in the house of many rooms. The four children come close around her, laughing and telling all they're finding. Mama Kundi laughs her half-goat-half-coughing laugh. Corey leads the others through the door and downstairs to the wide grass.

Mama Kundi brings stories from the drums that Sofia has not heard. The news came through the drums telling of Gabriel and the others. Sofia takes Mama Kundi's hand and shows her the big soft chair where Sofia will hear what she must hear.

The first story is about some men who would make a coup against the president. This is the lie that sent Daniel to his death, but of these men, it is true. And not only men, Mama

Kundi says, but also Madame, the one whose children I saw playing on the grass outside.

"Madame Cassandra?!" Sofia's surprise is from the day Dr. Will asked her to stay in his house, but still she wonders how this can be so.

Mama Kundi lifts her bony shoulders to show she has no belief in Sofia's surprise. A mondele woman can do such things when her husband takes a deuxieme bureau.

"Yes. It must be so. The deuxieme bureau was her friend. Madame became a fou, for a time. She gave money for the room. But she knew nothing of guns."

"Angh. So you say. The drums tell a different story."
"It makes no difference. Madame is flying far from here. The President cannot find her."

"Angh. There is news of your sometime-husband."

Sofia touches her hand to her throat, where her heart beats strong. She wants Gabriel to be safe. She wants him to come and live under the fine tin roof. But there is much of him that moves outside of her wanting. She shuts her eyes and waits for news of her future.

"Gabriel lives. He takes a pirogue across the river to Brazzaville."

"Brazzaville. What has he to do with Brazzaville?"

"He was with the ones who made the coup." So saying, she coughs.

Mama Kundi's words come to Sofia in slow motion, so she might find a way to receive them. "You say Gabriel was one of the men who made a coup?"

"He was with them. But here is a curious business. He was with them and not. For the drums tell how he tricked the others.

It was that devil Gabriel who accused Madame to the President. He told his guards how to find her after she visits the paralyse."

Sofia frowns, as the meaning comes naked to her. "He accused Madame to the one who sent Daniel to die."

"Angh. So it is in this life of sorrow." A stream of tears joins the lines on the old face. "He crosses the river, for he knows the President has his own trickster ways, and can send him to the stadium, too."

"Brazzaville. He crossed the river to Brazzaville." She repeats his passage to another country and another life. And another woman to trouble with his mean ways. How can it be, that this snake goes free when his brother knew only kindness and nothing of a coup, and he died in prison?

Sofia lets out the shrill ululation sound of old grief, her breath hot and fast. And there is anger, too, from some new place inside her. Words fly out of her. "What nonsense. What rubbish. What a devil snake that man is. And do you remember at the time Elombe drowned how he said I was dead to him. Well, I am not dead. I am alive. He is nothing to me anymore. He is dead to me."

Mama Kundi sends her a toothless smile. She lifts her harp to her lap, and begins to pluck a song. Sofia takes the song for a celebration. Mama Kundi sees she has come to herself, at last. And this is a moment to behold.

Thirty-six

Captain Alongi taxis the Aero-Commander twin engine toward the take-off runway at Ndolo Airport as images of the life she's leaving drift past. Promises sealed and broken, plots raised and squashed, hopes fielded and rescinded: morsels of a life forged and upended in the far country turned into her own Heart-of-Darkness.

Cass sits up front, passenger right, but avoids looking at Alongi. He reminds her too much of the Army thug who strong-armed Corey that long-ago day of Taba-in-the-trunk. Alongi is a bit taller and not given to thuggery. Not at all. He's been nothing but kind to her. It's just that he's tough-looking, like that other soldier, like a boxer, and he hardly speaks. She's heard him laugh with Tommy, but with her, he only frowns or grunts. The Taba memory he evokes nips at the edges of her trust. And if she doesn't trust her pilot, she'll be a wreck by the time they reach the airport in Luanda.

She turns her gaze to her side of the runway, empty of other small planes, at this early hour. So far, no one's chasing them with an M-16. That's good. A strip of dirt parallels the paved runway. Beyond the dirt strip, bush grows thick.

A deafening roar fills the cabin, like an infernal fan in range of a baritone with congestion. Alongi points to headphones. She dons them and the sound recedes to a muted baritone hum of dubious quality. Vagrant images emerge of life in the Mimosa she'll never see again. The small mouse-bump in the throat of the python muscling his prey to death; her boys and Susan's girls dancing like small pagans in the pummeling rain; Vernoy's sad smile as he hears her dismiss his counsel; herself handing Xavier an envelope-filled with zaires for the failed plot. She shivers, as if to shed the pain of revisiting her mistakes. Is this her life flashing before her eyes in the hour of her death?

The twin-engine turbo-prop taxis forward and turns right into the take-off lane, and takes its slow acceleration forward, upward, into a graceful lift-off. Soon she's watching the vast network of stalls at the Grand Marche, those she and her former-best-friend navigated with such intention and hope. From high up, the stalls turn twisted and small, looking for all the world like an exotic board game to amuse an expat community with too much time on its hands. Now the Zaire River twists below, narrow and dark, hiding dangers she prefers not to know.

Captain Alongi's piloting lifts them higher over the river, over the stand of huts and storefronts, and over the dark forest jungle that borders these habitations. The rain Cass hoped for has stayed away, and the sky remains free of all but streaks of Cirrus clouds, allowing her to see the terrain far below. Somehow, she feels safer by keeping her gaze on the ground. Alongi assures her that there's no radar and no way to track the Aero Commander twin engine. Still, she worries. Mobutu and his guards might find a way to come for her. And keeping watch on the ground somehow gives her a reprieve from worry about a cadre of soldiers arresting her. Of course, it makes no sense at all. But when has that stopped her?

Alongi has hardly spoken to her this morning. Rather than upset her, his silence is freedom from making small talk, from the work of exchanging clear ideas in French or, God-forbid, in

Lingala. Once they're at cruising altitude, around 7000 feet, the flight to Luanda, Angola, passes in a timeless blur, a dreamscape of images of Corey and Mattie as she last saw them, of Will doing his gorilla act, of her friend, Suzette in Seattle, reading the letter she sent detailing her trials, of a frozen monkey she saw last week in the grocery store.

Captain Alongi breaks into her ruminations by producing a paper bag and handing it across. "Le dejeuner." Lunch, he says.

Oddly, given that she's done nothing but sit, she's hungry. She nods and gives a grateful look inside at slices of Gouda cheese, a red banana, what appear to be slices of home-made bread, and an Orange Fanta. "Tres gentille. Very kind. Malamu mingi." She pours out her thanks in three languages.

He growls his acknowledgment.

"Vous ne mangez pas?" You don't eat?

"Trop gros," Too fat. He pats his belly beneath the controls, and releases a deep, round laugh that surprises and eases her anxiety a touch.

She joins her laughter to his and wonders, again, why he's going to such lengths to help her. "Pourquoi?" Why? She sweeps her arms wide to suggest the airplane, then points to herself.

He reads her gestures. "Bwana Tommy. Il a sauve ma mere." He saved my mother.

She smiles, trying to picture this husky, wrestler specimen with a mother. She recalls Mama Kundi's words about Mobutu's mother, her influence on him, and how he changed after she died. This sighting of a child inside the gruff exterior moves her to ask the question she carries inside her anxiety. "Avez-vous peur?" Are you afraid?

He gives her a startled look. "Peur? Ngai?"

"Of Mobutu. S'il va nous trouver." That he will find us. "Moi, surtout." Me, especially.

He shrugs, tilts his head from side to side, weighing what to say. "C'est encore possible. Toujours."

Toujours, of course. Silly question. She leans back on the head rest and looks out her side to see what can be seen from 7000 feet. Not much suddenly. She's stone-blind inside a giant cloud. But not a problem for Captain Alongi, who, surely can keep them aloft. He's got this.

In the next moment, a sudden jolt and the plane veers cock-eyed. They're in freefall. Her headphones pipe in an ear-splitting whine. Her seat belt squeezes her belly. Her breathing turns audible. She shuts her eyes. A story from Will's mom surfaces in memory of a flight over Mali, when the plane entered rapid descent, and their tour guide leaned into her and said, "This is it, Maddie." Cass shuts her eyes. 'This is it, Cass.' And through the endless fall toward whatever lies below, Vernoy's prayer rises to meet her panic: *Look upon us with kindness in this terra incognita.* His prayer adapts to the moment, with cogent rep-etitions: *With kindness, God. Yes, please be kind, be kind.* Over and over. The terra incognita of Vernoy's prayer unhinges her imaginings. But there's no terra, it's only air. This is how the world ends. *Please, no. Be kind.*

She opens her eyes. Alongi's large hands move with pre-cision amid the myriad knobs of control. His low murmur of breath, the plane righting itself, they exit the cloud and find a level seam of air. They regain forward motion, and the savannah below achieves a respectable distance. Cass releases a long breath. Alongi glances at her and looses another big laugh.

Terra firma now on the runway at Aeroporto Craveiro Lopes, where the world does not end. Alongi locks them into a solid stop in the General Aviation section next to a smaller, single engine plane. He takes a moment to simply sit, nodding, eyes closed. Is he praying?

Well, whyever not? Here she offers the rest of the prayer: *We give you thanks, Mother and Father of us all.*

He opens his door and steps down to lovely pavement and comes round to liberate her from the air.

She slips a strap around her neck holding her leather purse with a wad of US dollars Will pressed into her hands, along with her passport, and a credit card in his name. She steps down and dons her small backpack. Far across the tarmac, men move around a large TAP jet, bound for Lisbon, she assumes, and wheel a baggage cart toward the silver belly of the plane she hopes to be on soon. She steps toward the terminal entrance with the name Aeroport Craveiro Lopes over the double doors, a Portuguese name, she assumes. She enters the vintage terminal feeling the fullness of gratitude to her bearish wrestler-pilot, and wishing she'd given him a farewell hug. But he's stayed back with the Aero-Commander, out of reach.

The vintage terminal is relatively empty. The few passengers visible are mostly White, wearing appropriate travel attire, summer suits and high heeled pumps or fine leather oxfords. Some stroll at leisure while several vent manic annoyance at bland-faced clerks. No military types waiting to seize and arrest her for terrorism. So far.

She waits at a counter with an overhead reader-board listing a TAP Air flight to Geneva and to Lisbon. She half-hears Alongi's growled warning, *C'est encore possible,* and feels a whiff of capture at her back. "Bom dia, Madame," the voice says.

She turns to face the watchful gaze of a dark-eyed matron with a long braid tucked forward at her olive-skinned neck. Pretty, in a ravaged kind of way. Maybe how Susan will look in another two decades. Cass inhales sharply. "English?"

"Yes. Of course. What may I help for you?"

"I'd like a flight to Lisbon. As soon as possible, por favor."

"Lisboa? Si. Is possible. There is flight in three hours' time."

Cass nods and makes the exchange, Will's credit card for a paper ticket and boarding pass, in hand, in short order. "Thank you. Merci, Madame."

"Of course."

She finds a seat beside a post in the lee of the massive room that gives the sensation of listing inward, seeking to be unseen. She pulls out a paperback from her backpack, *Fear of Flying*, Erica Jong's in-your-face polemic on being the new independent woman.

Frowning, she opens to the beginning and rereads the anonymous epigraph: "Bigamy is having one husband too many. Monogamy is the same." That bit brings a smile. She reads on down the page: "What about all those other longings which after a while a marriage did nothing to appease?"

There is that. Still. Those words could apply equally to men, could they not? Is that what was going on inside Will? All those other longings vying for embrace or expression.

A female voice broadcasting her name throughout the massive terminal breaks the thread of reflection. Anxiety peppers her pulse as she gathers her backpack and bolts toward the ravaged woman at the ticket counter, who eyes her with a sardonic gaze. "Si, Madame?"

"You called Madame Ramsey."

"I call? No." She points to a desk at the far end of the terminal. "Down there."

Cass half-sprints along the counter, nearly tripping over an African boy of Corey's age. "Excusez. So sorry." A woman standing beside him gives her a scolding glance.

At the desk, she gives her name to a young, dark-haired woman, who might be Portuguese but tells her in British-clipped English that she has a telephone call from Zaire and hands her the receiver. "Hello? This is Madame Ramsey." Her voice is raspy, tentative, as if pleading for mercy.

"You are there. Thank God."

"Will?" Relief sets her to coughing and she nearly drops the receiver.

"You get a flight out okay?"

"Lisbon. In a couple hours.

"Cass? Are you okay?" She feels the press of the familiar tenor nearer than is possible.

"Yes, yes. Are the boys with you?"

"They're doing fine with Sofia. I'm at Tommy's. He gets a special long-distance rate. I'd expect nothing less, would you?"

"Tell him Captain Alongi is a peach."

Will receives this request with his trademark mirth and passes her his news. "Akobundu, the Nigerian surgeon? He assisted me on a case this morning. He's proving a quick study. I think we might be moving up the timeline."

"Oh. That's . . . good to know."

"Good to know? Your enthusiasm is underwhelming."

"No. It's just . . ." She can't think how to express the stir of inchoate emotions inside. "Hey, if you see Vernoy, tell him . . ." She pauses on a tearful hiccup, "That prayer of his, it's-still-with me-tell him."

"I'll tell him."

"Call me again in Lisbon?"

"I'll do it. Love you, Cassie."

"I love you, too," she murmurs. She does, and will, no matter what. Still, in the silence afterward, the question threading through her days here surfaces again: And me? What am I for, after all? She can't help wondering about the shelf-life of those other longings their marriage does not appease.

A pair of Army boots enters her visual arc. She breaks from her reverie. Half-standing, she prepares to run from the Army boots. "Madame?" a male voice says.

She sweeps her gaze over the beige tile to the boots, the only sign of Army. His attire is Levi-casual, for an unmilitary, young professional. He has lean runner's legs. He wears a navy-blue bill cap. He meets her gaze from a meter away. "Xavier, it's you," she says.

"Duma, to you, Madame." He gives her a hint of a smile.

Seated side-by-side, her pulse holding a good canter, she hardly knows where to begin. Finally, she tells him how relieved she is, asks how he made his way here.

"A bus brought me, "he says. "It was long."

"And the others. Did they make it out alive? "

"All but one, Hyene."

"The young one. Just a boy. The night bodyguard."

"That young one. He was too angry. When another guard heard the noise from inside, the others slipped through the hole in the fence Simba made ready in the night. Hyene would not leave the garden until he took a *coupe coupe* to Mobutu's neck. He nearly achieved it, too, but that other guard caught his arm and used it on Hyene."

She blanches at this news and tries to evict glimpses of the head lopped and rolling away from the round-faced boy. She asks where the others went.

"They escaped by boat to Brazzaville." He hesitates, frowning. "You remember Nyoka? That one most angry at you. He was the one who tricked you. He told Mobutu's guard where to find you."

Cass flinches and covers her mouth to still the trembling. Then she lets out a yelp of anger. "I knew it. That snake." *Poor Sofia,* she thinks.

"Still he made his escape across the river. Like the others, he will not return home. Simba will try to return to your country. If it is possible, I cannot say."

"You don't like Brazzaville?" she asks.

He shrugs. "I desire a place with fewer deaths for seeking freedom. That is not the life in Brazzaville."

"Then in what place is that possible? Which country has fewer deaths for seeking freedom?"

He straightens, gaining inches and a posture of resolve. "I have a cousin, you know, the son of my mother's brother. He is a farmer in Botswana. I must go there."

"Botswana. I don't know anything about Botswana, except I hear good things about their game reserves."

"They have real leopards in that country. They are not the fake kind Mobutu wears on his head. Do you know of their president? Seretse Khama."

She shakes her head.

"My cousin says he is like Patrice Lumumba, the one I knew in Katanga. Before Mobutu and your CIA helped assassinate him."

"It was . . . a terrible thing." She hears in her ebbing voice, her lame response to terror.

He doesn't appear to notice. "That man Seretse Khama, he is a good man, a leader of quality. He does not make the public purse his own, you know? It is a place where freedom will live and it is possible I also can do a fine thing."

Her thoughts pivot to the River Village and the fine tin roof Sofia loved, the one Gabriel made. Was that before he was a snake? Or was the snake always lying-in-wait for the perfect moment to strike? "When?" she says. "When do you hope to leave for Botswana?"

A shadow crosses his face. "Not yet. I must find work to earn my ticket to that place."

"But if they come looking for you here . . . You know what they'll do if they find you."

He smiles rarely, but, oddly, does so now, and tells her he is prepared to risk more for that new place. What else can he do?

"Disappear. Go into the shadows of Luanda. Can you take a bus?"

"To hide is difficult on a bus. And the journey is long, 1600 kilometers. Plane is better, but much money."

She tries to think how much cash she has in her handbag. Will thrust some at her in the scuffle of leaving. She turns from Xavier, opens her purse, and squeezes a bit of the wad into her fist. Why not? She won't need cash. And she has the credit card. She turns in the act of handing it over when a figure catches her eye, lumbering in from the tarmac. "Captain Alongi," she says.

He approaches like a bear emerging from his cave.

Xavier bounds into a darting blur around the post and toward the exit, like the cheetah of his code name.

"Duma, wait. He's my friend, she says. And your friend. You must meet him."

"He is Zaire Army," Xavier shouts.

"He's my pilot. He's good. Stop."

He pauses and, from a distance, regards the approaching figure. Several White waiting travelers glance at him with mild interest, then turn back to their books. For a moment, she sees Alongi through Xavier's eyes: a man about her height, but robust, with a round chest and a belly pressing against the seams of his camouflage shirt. He has a forceful, even brutish physique. She can see Xavier's point.

"Pas de problem, mon ami," Alongi calls to his countryman. "Ou veux-tu aller?" Where do you want to go?

Xavier tilts his head and shoots him a sharp retort. "A quoi tu tiens?" What do you care?

Alongi shoots him a big laugh, startling Xavier as it did her. "Okolobaloba." You're talking nonsense. "Je peux te voler." I can fly you.

"Botswana. Trop loin." Too far.

"Bosoto! Yaka awa," Rubbish. Come.

Xavier recasts his movements from cheetah to velvet pan-ther, easing toward the uniformed pilot. "Attendez." She hurries to catch them and thrusts a portion of her US dollars at Alongi, who receives it with a shrug and cocks his round head toward Xavier. "Nous partageons." We share. Another chuckle, and he waves Cass off before she can besmirch him with more leakages of gratitude, which is not the point. Not at all.

The two men sync their steps toward the side door onto the section of tarmac reserved for General Aviation. She watches them move away from her, one of lithe panther gait, the other of loping bear, and toward the Aero Commander twin engine. She waits there on solid ground, as Captain Alongi gets the engine roaring and taxiing onto the runway. They'll soon be aloft and heading for whatever new lane of justice awaits them.

Cass stands watch and feels the question that follows her like a phantom: What am I for? What of Cassandra and her prophetic gift? Her subliminal nudge to make the world better has had its coming-out to the world. She can't tuck it back into hiding as if it's something shameful and dark. It's her signature offering. She must nurture it with the care she has for Mattie and Corey, not in a distant country but on her small patch of the world, in light and in shadow, where she will make her way.

Acknowledgements

This book would not exist without the grace and support of others. I extend my heartfelt thanks to the following: Nancy Kilgore for her insightful feedback; Milt Lum, for his astute suggestions on an early draft; Joseph M. Borre- manns, ATP, CFI-A, for his professional input on fly ing a small plane in and around Zaire; Zairian neighbors, colleagues, and strangers who showed us immense kindness during our lengthy stay; son Mark, son Troy and his life partner Shataia, and their two sons Caleb and Joshua, for their sturdy love and their belief in my writing. And I'm grateful to David, soulmate and first reader, for bringing this wary introvert to a distant country 9000 miles from home.

About the Author

Ruth Linnea Whitney is the author of SLIM (Southern Methodist Univ. Press, 2003), informed by two years of living in sub-Saharan Africa and other lengthy working sojourns in Africa with surgeon-husband David. The novel received the First Book Award from the Writer's Guild of PCUSA. Her short stories and personal essays appear in *The Threepenny Review, Kaleidoscope, Natural Bridge, Assisi,* and elsewhere. Her journalistic pieces appear in *Seattle P.I., Chicago Tribune, Town & Country,* and elsewhere. She has ESL teaching stints in Vietnam, Zaire, (now DRC), Uganda, and at Peninsula College in Port Townsend, Washington, where she makes her home. She serves on the Social Justice team of the PCUSA church she attends.